Winter's Rose

The Winter Murders, Book 4

E.L. Johnson

ARE YOU SIGNED UP FOR DRAGONBLADE'S BLOG?

You'll get the latest news and information on exclusive giveaways, exclusive excerpts, coming releases, sales, free books, cover reveals and more.

Check out our complete list of authors, too!

No spam, no junk. That's a promise!

Sign Up Here

www.dragonbladepublishing.com

Dearest Reader;

Thank you for your support of a small press. At Dragonblade Publishing, we strive to bring you the highest quality Historical Romance from some of the best authors in the business. Without your support, there is no 'us', so we sincerely hope you adore these stories and find some new favorite authors along the way.

Happy Reading!

CEO, Dragonblade Publishing

Additional Dragonblade books by Author E.L. Johnson

The Perfect Poison Murders
Winter's Poison (Book 1)
Winter's Crown (Book 2)
Winter's Prison (Book 3)
Winter's Rose (Book 4)

The Perfect Poison Murders
The Strangled Servant (Book 1)
The Poisoned Clergyman (Book 2)
The Mistress Murders (Book 3)
The Deadly Debutante (Book 4)
The Betrayed Bride (Book 5)

The Lyon's Den Series
The Lyon and the Bluestocking
A Lyon to Die For
In Service to a Lyon
Love, Lies, and the Lyon

Prologue

On the road to Pewsey, not far from Devizes

THE SUN HAD begun to set an hour ago. Its golden-orange rays filtered through the trees, making them seem black. A lone wind whistled overhead, its unearthly echo sending an icy shiver down Matilda's royal spine. The October sky had darkened so early that afternoon, her entourage seemed to ride into the depths of night.

Matilda of Boulogne drew her cloak's hood closer for warmth, disliking the cool wind against her cheek. The early autumn darkness chilled her and she much preferred the summer months. She would much rather have been safe and warm in a castle with her husband nearby. But that was the life of an ordinary wife, not a queen.

The world was at war, and she had a role to play. She gripped the horse's reins in her gloved hands and shot a grateful look at her loyal lady-in-waiting, Lady Muriel, and the band of armed supporters around them. She and her eleven-year-old son, Eustace, would be safe, even if it meant days in the saddle and nights huddled under a cloak beneath the stars. She would see Stephen again, and that was all that mattered.

Riding on a small mare beside her, Eustace shivered in his cloak. "I'm hungry," he said.

"I know. It's not much farther."

Matilda knew her son was aware of their mission as well as anyone in their party, but he was still a child in her eyes. Never mind that he was already promised to marry Constance, the daughter of the French king, Louis VI. She glanced at her son, taking in his youthful form. He had the long legs of his father and had already gained the skittish uncertainty and jerky movements of a colt as he grew so fast and was still outgrowing his clothes. His blond, boyish curls and cheerful smile reminded her of his father, Stephen, whom she missed with a sharp ache in her heart.

Matilda looked fondly on the approaching figure of Rupert Bothwell, the attractive, young, blond squire to Sir Baldwin of Clare. The cheerful squire was a man whom she suspected had captured more young women's hearts than he realized. He was a friendly youth who had cheered up Eustace to no end on this journey, joking and playing chess games with him, almost like they were brothers. She smiled at his approach, conscious that when he entered her presence, he would not dare to speak until she had addressed him. "Hello, Rupert."

"Your Grace." He nodded and bowed his head. His eyes flicked to her son. "Your Grace," he said.

Eustace beckoned him over, and soon the young men were chatting happily.

Matilda let out a happy sigh. At least the squire would give her son something to focus on, aside from the dull ride. She idly wondered about Stephen. What would he think of her raising armies and leading the charge on Winchester? He was a good, kind, and honorable man—and popular with the men. But she knew the attitudes of the day meant that some men would overlook a woman's contributions to the battle and would prefer to take credit for her actions. She would need to watch the men carefully and inform Stephen later in secret just who was truthful and who was not. War tried men's souls, and she wouldn't necessarily dismiss a liar, but she would want her husband to know who was claiming more than his due. Matilda had never thought of herself as a great judge of character.

Except when it came to bakers, she thought. The young baker, Mistress Bronwyn Blakenhale, a baker's daughter from Lincoln, had surprised her. When the young woman's father had been imprisoned for an attempted poisoning of herself and Stephen some months ago, Matilda had doubted her guilt and so had sent the girl to work in the castle kitchens and find the real culprit herself. Not that anyone believed the young baker would do it.

But to Matilda's surprise, the young woman had done that very thing, just as Maud's armies had swept through Lincoln. Matilda was glad that young Bronwyn had survived, for she was an interesting person. The girl had a brain between her shoulders and was not easily swayed by a pretty face. Yet Matilda did not doubt that many men would soon wish to court her. She snorted and hoped the young woman still lived, when—

An arrow flew past her head. She felt its goose feather fletching brush against her cheek.

A gasp escaped her. Matilda clapped a hand to her cheek. She pulled her horse up short. "Eustace," she cried.

"Mama," he called, riding toward her.

The light was fading. The silence became punctuated with men's shouts and cries as arrows whipped through the air, striking down armed men. Cries for help and calls to arms sounded in a horrid cacophony of noise as Queen Matilda fretted and pulled her reins tightly, urging her mare closer to her son. She reached for him and he shivered next to her, holding on to her.

The young squire, Rupert, brandished a sword and stuck close by them, alarm sketched on his face.

"What is this?" Matilda asked, crouching in her saddle.

"Bandits. Stay close."

"The queen! The queen!" a man cried. "Protect the queen!"

In the fading afternoon light, the setting sun blinded her, and she held a hand up to her eyes. Horses whinnied, and swords and shields clanged and tinged as fights rode through the woody glen, wielding short swords whilst archers fired from behind trees. Lady Muriel shrieked from nearby and her horse struck the ground with its hooves. Men crowded around Queen Matilda on all sides, the smell of rusting chainmail, the scents of sweat and horseflesh, and blood filling the air.

She called to her son, "We will be safe."

The knights around her fought against foes; it all happened so fast. Matilda urged her son to stay close, but it was frightening. The horses huddled and bunched against each other, neighing and pawing the ground as riders came at them.

Who is doing this? she wondered.

But then the knights around her, men who had sworn to protect her, fell like fallen trees and were struck down one by one. A chill passed through her.

"Mama!" Eustace shouted.

"Hush," she said.

Her horse reared and struck out with its powerful front legs, hooves striking nothing as it rose up on its hind legs. Matilda clapped her knees around the mare and held on tightly, but the terrified animal threw her off. She sailed through the air, flying, and landed on the ground—hard.

"Mama!" Eustace cried.

Matilda lay dazed on the ground. A sharp pain sent a shock through her left arm, making her gasp.

"You will not take her!" Rupert growled.

A harsh laugh, more clangs of weapons against armor and shields, and grunts as men fell.

"Mama," Eustace called from nearby.

Matilda groaned and hunched inward, fearful of the horses' hooves. She did not want to be trampled, and opened her eyes.

A dagger was pointed at her throat. She tensed immediately and froze. She blinked in the growing darkness. The burly attacker shifted his weight and took a confident stance. But something about him, his posture, perhaps, looked oddly familiar. "Who are you?"

The man laughed and came closer.

"Leave her alone," Rupert snarled. A second later, he froze, his eyes rolling back in his head. A loud groan sounded as he fell from his horse, a lone figure on the ground. The horses danced around his body as Eustace cried, and men laughed.

Matilda looked into the eyes of her captor. She reached for the small dagger in her boot but was manhandled, a warrior gripping her wrist painfully. She dropped the small blade into the grass. The warrior laughed.

"You're coming with us," a man said.

In the fading dusk, she peered at the leader of the group. He looked familiar.

The boorish man grinned, and when he spoke, he smelled like sour wine and garlic. He had food in his teeth, and his breath smelled. "I know who you are."

Matilda gave him a level look. It took some effort to speak through the pain. "Then you have the advantage, good sir, for I do not recognize you."

A muscle in his forehead quivered, and he bit the inside of his cheek. His bushy eyebrows knit together as he growled. "You should. But you will."

Then she blinked and said, "Sir—"

A fist came toward her face, and then the world went black.

Chapter One

In the Year of Our Lord, Eleven Hundred and Forty-One, the Month of October
On the road to Gloucester, near Pewsey, not far from Devizes

B RONWYN BLAKENHALE'S FEET were sore. They had covered miles without stopping. The party's horses trod on, the cart carrying foodstuffs rolled, and up ahead, a knight whistled an off-key tune. He had no sense of musicality, but he had spirit, she decided. But she didn't mind the noise. It helped pass the time as they marched west from Winchester.

Their party was of a decent size, made up of knights, squires, men-at-arms, one goodly prisoner, and servants. They had traveled now for a few days, and she'd helped make up some of the party. They kept a regular pace, not too slow but not too fast, to avoid attracting attention, and not so grueling as to tire the horses. There was no need to rush, but there was a tension that could be seen in every man-at-arms's clenched jaw, the stiffness of their postures, an alert glance here and there over their shoulders as they rode.

It was on every rider's mind and was the chief subject of conversation each night over the campfire. They needed to move, to ride, and to avoid any other people on the road. They avoided markets and towns altogether, preferring back roads and heavily wooded forests. At their approach into the shaded woody glens, Bronwyn noticed that the birds stopped singing and animals hid. Almost as if the creatures of the earth knew that here rode trouble, and death followed any who dare disturbed this party.

Bronwyn hoisted her sack over her shoulder and kept walking, carefully picking her way through rough paths of mud where the cart had rolled and the horses had walked. The air smelled of trees, wood and pine, mixed with the smell of horse and dung.

Bronwyn hadn't expected the party to be so small—or nervous. But it was clear. No one laughed or joked, and whilst she hadn't expected the group to be jovial, she hadn't known it was going to be so tense, either.

At night, the women stayed together, and the men slept in a circle around them, with members taking watch for safety. At times like that, Bronwyn wondered about the fate of Sir Robert of Gloucester and his squire, Theobold Durville.

The righthand man of Empress Maud, Sir Robert was leader of her armies, and after the empress's hasty exit from Winchester, he and his men had covered her rear flank. Empress Maud had successfully escaped from Queen Matilda's clutches, but Sir Robert had been captured by Stockbridge at the River Test. He had suffered a leg wound in battle and might have died if Bronwyn hadn't saved him.

Mere days ago, he had been brought to the infirmary, but a sly squire and traitor within the empress's camp, Tristan Langforde, had tried to kill him, along with other prisoners of Empress Maud's court. Bronwyn had caught him and saved Sir Robert's life, so now a prisoner exchange was to go ahead.

Now that Tristan and his accomplice, the Lady Susanna, had been caught and imprisoned by Queen Matilda for their crimes, Bronwyn and the other prisoners belonging to Empress Maud's court were to be exchanged for King Stephen and his men, who were being held at Bristol Prison. Except she wasn't a prisoner, not really. She had chosen to go, despite being offered a place at the queen's kitchen.

As if hearing her thoughts, her friend, Lady Alice Duncombe, a lady-in-waiting of Empress Maud, rode up to her. "I cannot believe you turned down Matilda of Boulogne's offer to work in her kitchen."

Bronwyn looked up at her. "No?"

"No. You came from nothing. You had your family's bakery in Lincoln, once upon a time, but that's gone now. You have nothing. Literally just yourself and the clothes on your back. I suppose the empress should feel flattered that she's inspired such loyalty in a mere cook, but *honestly*. It was the best option for you. Why did you turn it down?"

Lady Alice didn't know. The cooks at Winchester's Wolvesey Castle were unfriendly, and led by a bully, Master Christopher.

He had disliked Bronwyn from the start. He had bullied her, belittled her, accused her of making crude sexual advances toward her betters, and had slapped and spit at her, not to mention dumping a gravy boat over her head. She had defended herself and he'd been kicked out of the kitchen eventually, but she could still hear his sneering remarks in her ears and could practically *feel* the sludgy blobs of cold gravy as they'd slid down her hair.

Bronwyn tensed at the memory, her upper lip twitching in distaste. Whilst she appreciated the queen's offer of a place in her kitchen at Winchester, she had no desire to stay there. The men were unfriendly, and she was learning that wherever she worked, she could use a friend. But she didn't expect Lady Alice to understand that, and so she hadn't told her.

Bronwyn peered up at the noblewoman. "I'm surprised, Lady Alice. I would've thought you'd enjoy my company on the road."

"Pah. As if that were any consolation. Conversing with servants is not something I would choose to do, if there were any other option." Lady Alice tossed her head, her jet-black hair rippling over her shoulder. "But… on this journey, we must make do. Even if we don't converse with those we should like to."

Bronwyn thought of her friend, the man she'd thought of far too often, Rupert Bothwell. A handsome squire, of a stocky build with light eyes and golden, shoulder-length hair that shone in the sun, he had a friendly smile for everyone and kindness toward all.

He had befriended her back in her home city of Lincoln and was currently romancing Lady Alice, who was smitten with him. But their love was tempestuous at times, and the pair was at that moment on the outs.

Now Bronwyn made up part of the party on the way to the empress. In addition to Lady Alice, the group included Sir Robert of Gloucester's squire, Theobold Durville, with whom Bronwyn had a bit of a flirtation, and some other fighters. Bronwyn was one of the few servants and cooks who were looking after the food and would help set up camp during the journey. She didn't know the other guards, but she believed that no one would dare come near them. So far, there had been no trouble.

BRONWYN WALKED AND considered her sometimes-friend, sometimes-enemy, Lady Alice. Having walked for so long, she was relieved to see an end in sight to their traveling. Days on the road meant long hours of walking on all sorts of different terrain and it was not something she particularly enjoyed. She missed the routine and daily patterns of her former time as the daughter of a baker in the city of Lincoln.

But that had been almost a year ago now, before the famous Battle of Lincoln, and to her, it might as well have been a lifetime ago. Life and the very days had been simpler then, when all she'd had to worry about had been making sure the bread she'd baked had been up to her family's standards and selling enough at the local market. She'd dreamed of adventure, of making long journeys and riding horses. In just a few short months, she'd gotten her fill of such things.

Now that she had gotten the adventure she had once craved, she knew firsthand how dangerous the world she lived in really was. Bronwyn had managed to get mixed up in royal business time and time again and was often shuffled like a game piece between the courts of Empress Maud and her opponents, King Stephen and Queen Matilda, who feuded against the empress for the Crown of England.

Most recently, Bronwyn had been present when the city of Winchester had fallen. The empress and Queen Matilda had fought while Stephen had been imprisoned and Matilda had won. In Maud's hurry to escape the city, Matilda had captured her righthand man and military commander, Sir Robert of Gloucester.

During the battle that had commenced, Bronwyn had fled for her life and had gotten mixed up in investigating a series of plots meant to disturb the empress. She had solved them with help and had even been offered a place at Queen Matilda's court, but she had refused.

So now she was on the road to Devizes, thankfully.

The one good thing about being on the road was it had given her lots of time to think about her feelings toward two men: Rupert Bothwell and Theobold Durville.

They were like day and night, the sun and the moon. Both had earned her friendship and goodwill, but both young men also claimed a part of her heart, and she could not make up her mind on whom she cared for more. Not that she could ever say such a thing out loud. For the men to know what she really thought, how she felt about them, made her cheeks warm. Better that she stay in obscurity and in the relative safety of a kitchen, admiring from afar.

Rupert had made his preference for Lady Alice known, and they were close. And yet Bronwyn wondered sometimes. Rupert had a look in his eye when he was with her that almost felt like a longing. Waiting for something. He sometimes held her gaze a moment too long and she felt her heart skip a beat. But then he would tease her, and they would be back to being friends again. It would have driven her mad, except that she respected Lady Alice too much to act on her feelings for him. And what with her feelings for Theobold, she did not know how to act in any case.

But as they pulled into the town of Devizes and marched into the main fortress with its wooden gates, Bronwyn quickly became occupied with looking after the food carts and helping get things unpacked and sorted.

After such a long journey, everyone was tired. But unlike the nobles who had traveled with them, it would be hours before Bronwyn found a place to sleep that night. She soon parted ways from Lady Alice with the other cooks and servants to join the other hands in the kitchen.

The space was as large as the castle kitchens of Winchester and Oxford. Bronwyn quickly became quiet and threw herself into the world of work that lay beyond the tables of the nobility. There was always work to be done for idle hands.

Once the people in residence, including the empress and her entourage, had been fed and the cooks themselves sat down to a meal of leftover partridge and potage, one of the cooks said, "Oh, we'll need to feed the poor lad in the infirmary."

A few of the cooks exchanged looks. Judging from their wary expressions and quick avoidance of the head cook's eyes, no one wanted to help the invalid.

"Come on. *Someone*'s got to," the head cook said.

Bronwyn avoided the cook's eyes like everyone else when the cook said, "You. Girl, you do it."

Bronwyn raised her gaze. "Okay."

She set down her wooden spoon and climbed off of the crowded bench. Her feet ached and she felt bone tired, but she was also willing to try to make a good first impression. "Is there just the one?"

"Aye." The cook pointed her to where she could fill a bowl and take a hunk of crusty bread. "He's like a lost soul, the poor lad. And young, too. Shame what's happened to him."

"What do you mean?" Bronwyn asked.

"Some of the men-at-arms found him wandering in the woods, muttering nonsense. They thought he wasn't in his right mind and took him in. No one could understand him and he was wounded, so they brought him here. But we don't have much in the way of medicine, so there's not a lot anyone can do for him." The cook tutted. "Really is a shame. He'd be downright handsome if he weren't so unwell."

Bronwyn nodded and took a tray of warm broth, crusty bread, and some stale ale in a cup with her. She walked down the corridors before realizing she didn't know where to go and had to ask directions. In a while, she found the infirmary and pushed her way in against the door, bottom first.

She nodded to the nurse, a middle-aged woman with thinning, brown hair who sat by and said, "This is for the young man."

"Oh, good. You can set it down. I'll see he has some." The woman's stomach gurgled loudly.

Bronwyn gave a half-smile. "I'm happy to watch him if you want to go eat. The cooks are there right now."

"Hmm. You wouldn't mind?"

"No. It's fine. Can't imagine I'll be in much danger," Bronwyn said in a hushed voice.

The woman looked doubtful for a moment, her eyebrows knitting, then touched her stomach. "All right. I'll be back." She quit the room.

Bronwyn set the tray down on a side table. The room was largely empty but for a few pallets on the floor. Candles burned here and there around the room, offering a small dim light that stank of greasy animal fat. There was no disguising that smell.

Her stomach grumbled. She'd only gotten a few bites of potage and stale bread before the cook had asked her to go. But go she had, so if she was in luck, it would only be a few minutes before she could return to the kitchen and hope there was still some food left.

At Devizes, a city somewhat removed from the regular strongholds of activity for Empress Maud and her opponent, Stephen, there was more food available, which was nice. The cooks there ate well, and she could tell they had full bellies.

The sick man moaned and muttered something incoherent. Bronwyn let out a small sigh and went over to him, then froze in her tracks.

"Rupert?"

The youth's eyes fluttered open. "Bronwyn?" he croaked. Then he fainted dead away.

Bronwyn's mouth dropped open. "Rupert? Oh, my God."

Her hand darted to her mouth. He was here. Rupert was here.

She wanted to run and tell everyone. What was he doing here? How had he gotten here? Why wasn't he still with the queen and her traveling party? She had so many questions, but all she could do now was sit by his side and watch him rest.

His breathing was shallow and his skin flushed. She tentatively put a hand to his forehead. Bronwyn tenderly pushed aside a sweaty strand of dark-gold hair from his forehead and touched his skin.

She snatched her hand back. His skin burned with fever.

"Rupert?"

His eyelids fluttered and he coughed, then groaned.

She clasped and unclasped her hands, then clasped them again. What if he died here? What if he passed away without ever knowing how she truly felt about him? She could tell him how she felt. But there was so much to say. How did she share her feelings for him when he was as good as engaged to her only friend in the whole world?

She looked at him intently. He lay there on a raised pallet, not quite on the floor. His golden locks, normally outshining the sun and finest gold to be found on a church altar, now lay in sweaty, dark, tangled burnished curls around his head, and his chin had a few weeks' growth on it. The facial hair made him look older, rougher. A part of her liked it.

Then she gave herself a mental shake. Rupert wasn't hers. He was a friend, if young men could be considered friends. The last time she'd thought she'd had a friend, Alfred, a fellow journeyman baker from Lincoln, he'd kissed her and taken her by surprise. But his sudden rush of affection had been contrary to how she'd known him, even if her stepmother had encouraged a match with him. She hadn't felt any romantic feeling for him then and didn't now. Rupert was different.

He was like the sun, with a warm smile and a joke for everyone. He had a way of cheering up the slightest frown, and he managed to charm people with his friendliness and good nature. It came as no surprise to her that he was a popular squire in King Stephen's court.

But if he were the sun, then Theobold was the moon. Theobold, a fellow squire, walked proudly in Empress Maud's court, and everyone knew it. He came from a good family, had superior connections, and was the squire to Sir Robert of Gloucester, the empress's relation and righthand man. Theobold was tall, slim, and muscular, with dark hair and eyes that flashed in the night, as well as fair skin and an arrogant curl to his mouth and eyes. He was proud, and he flirted with all the women, but for some reason had pursued Bronwyn more than most.

Together they had solved a crime or two and exchanged a few kisses in private. Their moments were wild, dark, romantic, and sent chills through her body. She dreamed of him during cold nights when she thought she should not and sometimes awoke to find a blanket over her body, courtesy of Theobold, the other servants told her.

"I don't know what hold she's got over him," one woman servant said within earshot of Bronwyn. "Don't see why he's giving her such things."

"It's not for you to know, is it? Theobold's his own man; he'll do what he wants. If he fancies her, she's a lucky girl. As long as it lasts."

Bronwyn had pretended not to hear them talking, but the words had weighed in her mind. She didn't know if she necessarily had any kind of hold over Theobold's heart, and at first, he had annoyed her extremely, often getting in her way. But she had gradually warmed to him and now, she looked forward to his company. Until now.

Bronwyn bit her lip. Would he survive the night? His skin was hot to the touch, and she felt silly for even thinking about romance when he lay there being ill. She was stuck between two paths and didn't know which way to go. Did she confess her feelings to Rupert, or keep them hidden, never to be spoken aloud? He had protected her and Lady Alice when the battle of Lincoln had happened and had looked after her again, protecting her from bullying cooks. It had made clear to her that while he didn't find her attractive, he did care for her as a friend.

She remembered his words clearly as he'd boldly convinced a bullying head cook to leave her alone and had told him that no, she had not been sleeping around and throwing herself at the men. But his sharp, dismissive words to convince the bully that she had no sexual appeal had cut her emotionally, deeply, and convinced her that any affection they had between them was completely one-sided.

She pulled up a stool and sat by him. She needed to tell people. To tell Lady Alice immediately. Never mind that the last time they had seen him, Lady Alice and Rupert had had a falling out.

That didn't matter, for Bronwyn knew that deep down in her heart, her fair-weather friend loved him. That knowledge, more than anything else, made her pause and stilled her lips from speaking. She mustn't breathe a word of her true feelings to anyone. It would only complicate things and lose her both their friendship. She was sure of it.

She looked him over. He smelled like sweat and the outdoors, but that was no surprise. But as she glanced up and down his body, she could detect no open cut or wound on him. Why did he have a fever?

And yet from the way he shuddered and sweated on the pallet, casting off the thin blanket that had covered him, she knew he was ill.

She rose from her stool. She had to get someone. To do

something. It was imperative that Lady Alice was told at the very least. Maybe some guards, or the empress herself. Would she care? Bronwyn didn't know. But if he had been found and was alone, then something was very wrong. She needed to report this.

Bronwyn fretted, pacing up and down the room. Candles burned merrily, but there was no one around. She didn't want to leave him.

He looked so pale and fragile in the candlelight. His breathing was shallow, and she leaned over and gently touched the inside of his wrist. She felt a thready pulse. As if she needed any more indication that something was wrong with him.

She went to the door where some guards were walking nearby. "Hallo there," she called out.

The men stopped and looked at her. One of them, a tall, thin one with a scatter of red acne on his chin, looked her up and down.

"Could you help me? I need to pass along a message."

"Why not go yourself?" one asked.

"I can't. I'm watching my friend. He's sick. It's important. Could you help me, please?" Bronwyn asked.

One of the guards gave her a sidelong glance. "What do you want?"

"Could you send for Lady Alice Duncombe, please? It's important. She *has* to come here."

"Me, tell a lady what to do? You're joking," the guard said.

"I'm not. Tell her it's about Rupert and she'll come. Please, hurry. It's important she come." Her voice rose.

"All right, all right. Don't see what the big rush is about, anyway. He's sick, isn't he? He's not going anywhere."

Bronwyn bit her lip. "Please, just pass the message on."

The guards looked at her. "All right." One turned to the other. "You keep patrolling. I'll speak to this Lady Alice Duncombe."

"Thank you," Bronwyn said.

It felt like an age before anyone returned, but eventually, she heard voices. Alice could be heard clearly from outside the sickroom. "What is this nonsense about—" She paused upon entering. "Bronwyn. What is this?" Her gaze fell to the young man sleeping. "Rupert."

Lady Alice strode across the room in long easy steps, for she was taller than the average woman, with long legs. Her jet-black hair glistened and she smelled clean, as if she had just bathed. Bronwyn stepped back as Lady Alice went to Rupert's side.

With tender care, the lady took the stool and sat by his side, taking his hand in hers. "You stupid fool, what have you gotten into now?"

His eyes fluttered.

"Rupert, Rupert," Lady Alice said, leaning forward. "Rupert, wake up."

"Who is he, anyway?" one of the guards Bronwyn had spoken to earlier asked.

"He's a squire," Bronwyn said.

"All this for a squire?"

Lady Alice huffed. "He's not just *any* squire. He's Rupert Bothwell, squire to Sir Baldwin of Clare."

"I don't know that name," the guard said.

"And why should you? You're just a guard." Lady Alice's voice dripped scorn. "You carried your message, so unless you plan on bringing me a drink, I have no more need of you."

The man's face turned to stone. He turned on his heel and walked out.

"You could have been nicer," Bronwyn said, coming to her.

Lady Alice snapped, "And *you* could have run and gotten me yourself, rather than sending an oaf to fetch me like a dog. How long have you known about this?"

"Not long. I sent the guard as soon as I discovered it was him."

"Well. Now we have more questions. He shouldn't be here." Lady Alice's eyebrows furrowed. "What on earth is he doing here? Why isn't he with the others?"

"I don't know."

"Fetch me a cool towel. And some food for him," Lady Alice ordered.

"I'd already brought some, just here." Bronwyn motioned to the tray that sat nearby.

"Oh. And the towel?"

Bronwyn moved to a corner of the room, where a small water basin sat on a worktable. She found a fresh linen rag and brought it over.

Lady Alice reached for it, then paused, her delicate hand hovering over the rag.

"What is it?" Bronwyn asked.

"I… I've never taken care of anyone before." She paused. "What would people think?"

"Of what? You caring for him?"

"Yes. I have my reputation to think of." Lady Alice didn't meet her eyes.

Bronwyn blinked. "Lady Alice, speaking as your friend—"

"I do not have friends. Only servants and enemies."

Bronwyn let out a noisy breath. "It's only us here. I don't care, and everyone who knows you already knows you two are together."

"We are not," Lady Alice said in a hushed voice. "We aren't. Not anymore."

"Then why are you here, caring for him?" Bronwyn asked. "Why did you come?"

That earned her a level look from Lady Alice, who met her eyes once then looked away. "I still care for him. Even if we are at odds."

"Can't you end your feud? He's hurt. Whatever you were fighting about, it doesn't matter now."

"Don't you think I know that?" Lady Alice snapped at her.

"God, it's been weeks, Lady Alice. Do you even remember what you were fighting about? Is it worth it?"

Lady Alice turned red. "Of course I do. It's plagued my mind these past few weeks, not seeing him and wondering if I'd ever see him again. But now that I have, I can see where his folly has led. And I'm not prepared to forgive him. He doesn't deserve it." She frowned at his form lying there. "I don't see what business it is of yours, anyway. Why do you care whether or not we are together?"

Because I want to see him happy, even if that means him being with another woman, Bronwyn thought. "I know he cares for you. It might help him to know you are here."

At that, Lady Alice touched his forehead. She darted her hand back with a hiss. "He's hot. Is it a fever?"

"I think so, milady," the nurse said as she came back inside the room. "Thanks for watching him," she told Bronwyn. "Who's this?"

"I am Lady Alice Duncombe," Lady Alice said, rising to her feet. "This is Rupert Bothwell. He is my friend. I want you to see to it he is well taken care of."

"Aye, he is, milady. As best we can. But we don't have a surgeon here." The nurse cocked her head, taking in Lady Alice's fine dress and haughty expression.

"Why have you no surgeon here?"

The nurse shrugged. "Many men went off to fight for Stephen. Physicians aren't common 'round here. Monks are more like to help, but there aren't many. A lot left."

"Well, care for him. See to it. Let me know the minute he wakes," Lady Alice said. "Bronwyn, come with me."

Bronwyn followed Lady Alice out of the room. "What is it?"

"We have to tell the empress at once. She needs to know about this Let us not speak a word of this until we are in an audience with the empress. She must be told."

And so despite the ever-approaching night and late hour, the pair begged an audience with the empress, who eventually received them in the throne room.

Surrounded by sconces of dimly lit flickering candles, Empress Maud sat on a small, wooden throne on a raised dais, with two large standing candelabras to either side, lighting up her side of the small room. She wore a rich burgundy brocade dress, with a long leather tooled belt hanging at waist. Her light-brown hair was freshly washed and plaited into two long braids that hung at her shoulders, and atop her head sat a simple golden circlet. But the fierce look in her narrowed eyes reminded Bronwyn that the woman was much like a bird of prey—and not to be underestimated.

Armed guards stood around the room. The empress stifled a yawn at seeing them and tapped her thin fingers on the wooden armrests of the throne. "Lady Alice, Mistress Bronwyn. I'm surprised not to find you in the kitchens, Bronwyn, but something tells me I'm not going to like this visit."

Lady Alice stared straight ahead, whilst Bronwyn lowered her eyes.

"Well, what is it? Speak up. I want to seek my bed. I am tired."

"Rupert Bothwell is here, Empress. At Devizes Castle," Lady Alice said.

"And that is worth waking me because...?" The empress's voice was haughty.

"He was a member of the q—" Lady Alice stopped. "Of the party going to Bristol Prison, for the exchange."

"So? Clearly, they are finished. What of it?"

Bronwyn spoke up. "He was found in the woods near here, some days ago. The cooks said he was wounded and talking nonsense, and he has a fever."

The empress surveyed them both. "And you suspect something is amiss?"

Bronwyn nodded. "Yes, Your Grace. Have you... received word that the exchange has taken place?"

"That is none of your concern," Empress Maud said, her tone harsh. "But no. We have not. It comes as no surprise, however, considering we are traveling, and messengers would not know where we were."

"Your Grace, should we not look into this matter?"

"I fail to comprehend you, Mistress Baker. What is there to consider?"

"Stop it, Bronwyn. Can't you leave it?" Lady Alice whispered.

"No," Bronwyn whispered back.

"Ladies, I can see you have your own matters to discuss. Perhaps you will take your conversation elsewhere. I see nothing here to concern me—or you. Do not waste my time again." The empress waved a hand, and they were dismissed. There was nothing else to do but leave.

Once they'd left the throne room, Bronwyn asked, "Why did you say nothing? Why didn't you push for—"

Lady Alice glanced at her. "For what? For her to send out a search party? It is like she said, we have no reason to suspect anything is wrong. It would take messengers time to reach us. And even then, there's no evidence to suggest something is the matter."

But Bronwyn knew something was wrong. "Then how did Rupert come by his fever? He looks thrashed. Why isn't he still with the party?"

"I don't know. Maybe he was sent on an errand and got lost. Maybe he decided to leave them or take a different route. Like the empress says, it's no concern of ours," she mused, tapping her chin. "He might have changed his mind and came back for me but fell ill on the journey." Lady Alice tossed her jet-black hair over her shoulder. "But he could have sent a messenger, a note. Something. Bah. It is nothing to me what he does. He is his own person."

"But aren't you the least bit concerned? He is your friend. Don't you care?"

"Of course I do." Lady Alice growled, jabbing an aristocratic finger into Bronwyn's left shoulder and nudging her painfully. "But I also know when to keep my mouth shut and to stop asking questions. You always do this, Bronwyn. You start sticking your nose into other people's affairs and it's going to get you in trouble someday. Leave it, I tell you."

"But—"

"I mean it. The less you stick your nose in her business, the better. Get back to the kitchens. Or take a bath. You stink." Lady Alice walked away, her shoes echoing on the polished floor.

Bronwyn frowned. There was nothing to do but check on Rupert again and find a place to sleep.

The next morning, she rose early and made her way to the infirmary. There, she found Lady Alice sitting by Rupert's bedside, talking to him. Bronwyn paused in the doorway. Lady Alice and Rupert deserved privacy. Despite what Lady Alice had said, Bronwyn knew she cared for him. Maybe all that was needed was a bit of time.

Bronwyn blinked. But she cared for him too. A little sigh escaped her.

"She came here last night, and early this morning," a feminine voice said behind her.

Bronwyn turned around. A young woman, very young, in her early teens, with her fair-brown hair plaited in a braid over her shoulder, stood there. The young woman had an oval face, light-hazel eyes, and a wide forehead, with a thin nose and pink lips. She wore an ordinary gray dress for a servant and a work apron over it. But her gaze went past Bronwyn to Rupert. "I'm Philippa. Who is he? Is he a knight? He's so handsome."

Bronwyn smiled faintly. "He's squire to a knight. And he's a friend."

"And that lady, who is she?" the young woman asked, her eyes narrowing slightly at Lady Alice.

"That is a lady-in-waiting to the empress. Lady Alice Duncombe."

At the mention of her name, Lady Alice glanced over. "Oh, you're here. Good morning." She rose from the stool and walked over. "Well. Look after him. I gather we'll leave here soon."

The young woman had no guile whatsoever, for her expression brightened at these words.

Bronwyn nodded and stood back as Lady Alice passed by

without a word.

"She's a bit high and mighty, isn't she?" the young woman asked.

"She's a lady. They all are," Bronwyn said.

"Hmph. I don't see why she's so special."

Bronwyn shrugged and walked inside the room.

"Hey, what are you doing?" The young woman followed her.

"I'm taking the tray away." She looked at the tray. The bread was gone and the bowl was mostly empty. "Did he eat?"

"Some. Not much. I had some too."

"Did he say anything?" Bronwyn asked, frowning She didn't like the idea of this servant helping herself to Rupert's food.

"Not really. He kept saying a name and shaking his head."

"What name?"

"*Yoos* something or other. I don't know."

Bronwyn went to his side. "Rupert?"

He tossed and turned. His cheeks were pink and his golden hair slick with sweat.

"He needs a physician."

"We know. But the only one who knows any physick here is Mistress Hoode, and she's busy delivering babies across the city." The young woman stood beside her, closer than Bronwyn liked. She whispered, "Is he going to die?"

"I don't know. I hope not."

"Me too. He's so handsome."

He's not for you, Bronwyn thought. "Where might I find Mistress Hoode? Or is there anyone else?"

"There're some of the monks left over from the bishop. You might try there. But they keep to themselves, mostly."

Bronwyn removed the food tray and went to the kitchens. Similar to all the other castles she'd worked at, the kitchens were run by a head cook, and whilst service for all castle meals typically ran smoothly, the way that the kitchen was run depended on that cook.

Whether they were kind or fair, a fool or a bully, the way the cooks worked relied on how they were treated by the head cook. She just hoped this head cook and kitchen would be a good place.

Bronwyn brought the tray into the kitchen, which was clean and well swept, and began to see where she could help. The head cook at Devizes Castle was a Mistress Webb, a round, middle-aged woman with gray hair beneath a kerchief and round, red cheeks and a double chin. She moved with purpose and seemed almost bearlike, but her light eyes were kind and she often had a friendly word. She nodded to Bronwyn as she walked in. "You're up early."

"I wanted to check on the man in the infirmary. I know him."

"You don't say. He a friend of yours?"

"Yes." Her worry for him must've shown on her face, for Mistress Webb said, "It's a shame that Mistress Hoode is away."

"Do you know where I could find another physician? One girl said there were monks…"

"Yeh, there are. But they're a solitary bunch and not all are happy about the empress being here. Some might help you, though." Mistress Webb raised an eyebrow. "Help me with the baking this morning and then you can go. You'll find the monks at prayer. One of the cooks can direct you."

"Thank you."

Bronwyn spent the morning working, making bread dough and baking pies, tarts, cakes, loaves of bread—anything she was told. By midday, she was hot and sweaty and her feet ached, but it did feel good to work in a kitchen again. Her fingers were sore from working stiff dough and slapping it against the hard worktables, but it was a pleasure.

Mistress Webb had surveyed her work early on and nodded, her one sign of approval. After a meal, she gave Bronwyn directions and sent her out into the city of Devizes. "If I don't hear from you by nightfall, we'll send someone out to look for you."

Bronwyn smiled at this. She knew it wasn't true. Since the battle of Lincoln, she had become a refugee, a nomad, moving with the royal courts. She had no one who cared about her, not really. But Mistress Webb's cheerful words made her want to come back and almost made her think that someone actually might care. It was a nice thought. A tempting one. But not one she could take hold of seriously. It rather felt like a piece of ribbon or sand slipping out of her hands.

She would have to forge her own way in this life, she knew that now. Bronwyn just didn't know where that would lead. But first, she needed to find the monks and see if any of them would help her.

She walked out into the city. It was different from the others she'd known briefly. Devizes was different from Oxford, Gloucester, Lincoln, even London. But her nose didn't lie, and she soon found her way to the market, where there were many people walking about. It was when she was examining the bread stalls that she got into conversation with the sellers about surgeons, and she spotted a well-dressed young man with a bandaged arm.

He had short, wavy hair, light brown, and wore a man's dark-brown tunic over trousers and boots. A long sword hung at his side, beside a small bag for coin. He moved confidently, resting his hand on his hip. He did not favor his hurt arm, and yet something about his sneering smile put her off. She hesitated.

But Rupert needed her, and she would curse herself if he got worse because she was too prideful to ask for help. She marched up to the young man. "Excuse me."

"You're excused." The right corner of his mouth jerked into a half-smile.

Her chest rose. "Where did you get your arm bandaged?" She pointed to it.

He touched the clean linen bandage. "Worried about my safety? That's kind, but I'm not interested. Clear off." He made a shooing motion.

Her eyes widened. "You think I'm…" She let out a noise of exasperation and walked away. *What a horrible man.*

"Wait. Stop."

She kept walking when a firm hand gripped her arm and stopped her in her tracks. "I said *wait*, damn you," the young man said.

She glared at him. "Let go of me." She pulled her arm free.

"Look, I didn't mean… You misunderstood."

"Did I? You thought I was offering myself to you. Well, I wasn't."

He blinked.

"My friend is hurt and needs a surgeon, and I'm looking for one. I wanted to know where you got your arm bandaged, that's all. Not for any other reason." She practically growled.

His brown eyes met hers, and he grinned. "I'll take you to him."

"No thanks. Directions will do."

"Please, in this market? You're not from around here."

"What makes you say that?" She put a hand on her hip and glared up at him.

For some reason, that made him grin wider. "Your accent, for one. I've never heard an accent like yours except from up north. And the fact that you're looking for a surgeon means you're not local. You don't know where one is; otherwise, you wouldn't have asked."

She did her best impression of Lady Alice and sniffed. "Tell me where you found a surgeon."

"Allow me to show you."

"No."

"Are all maidservants as rude as you, or are you special?" he asked.

Her mouth opened, but no nasty retort came out. She had nothing. No response. She clamped her mouth shut and turned to go.

"That's the wrong way."

She spun. "I am not a…"

"I realize that now." He proffered her a bow, but it was slightly mocking. "I apologize, good lady. Allow me to show you the way to a surgeon."

She crossed her arms beneath her chest and wished she had a weapon at her belt, that she might rest her right hand on it and show she wasn't to be trifled with.

When she did not speak, he said, "Come on, I said I was sorry. Besides, you'll waste more time wandering around getting lost, when I know of one only a few minutes away. Come."

She cocked her head at him. She wasn't in the practice of walking with strangers, but she didn't want to waste time. The young man had a point. "Fine. Take me to him."

They walked together, and Bronwyn did not speak. She wanted to fill the empty space as they walked in silence but could not bring herself to say anything. Finally, she asked, "How did you hurt your arm?"

"The normal way. An accident while jousting. Or practicing, anyway."

"You're a knight?" she asked.

"No. Training to be. I'm a squire to Sir Benedict of Almsbury. My name is Crispin Ashe. And you are?"

"Bronwyn Blakenhale."

"But you're not from here. You've got a strange accent. Where are you originally from?"

"Lincoln."

"Ah." A beat later, he asked, "Were you at the battle?"

"Yes."

"I wish I'd been." He began talking about the skirmishes he'd been in and the fights he'd had. A few minutes later, he said, "You've grown quiet."

She tossed her long, thick, blonde braid over her shoulder. "It was scary."

He spoke so eagerly of wanting to be at major battles. But he hadn't seen the town when it had burned, the people who had fled in the streets, or the crowds that had been dangerous. A mere trip could have left one with broken bones if stuck. He hadn't heard the cries of the people of Lincoln who had overcrowded the boats in the river, or their screams as they'd drowned. The memory still chilled her at night.

He hadn't seen the battlefield littered with bodies in the days after the battle or felt the ground that had squished beneath her feet, slick and damp with reddish-brown mud and blood that had looked black at night. It had sickened her.

His smile showed too much teeth. "Where's your friend? Do you work at one of the market stalls?"

"No, we're up at the castle."

"Ohhh. And are you for or against the empress?"

It was a loaded question. She wasn't prepared to answer it, especially not when asked so boldly, so loudly, in public. Anyone could have been listening. And she didn't feel safe. They stood in a busy market, people were everywhere and yet… how truthful could she be with a stranger, and an armed one at that?

"You ask a lot of questions," she said.

He laughed and rested a hand on the pommel of his sword. "It doesn't matter. He'll get what's coming to him, one way or another."

"You are allied with Maud?"

"Of course. Aren't you?" His smile widened, but his eyes were unfriendly.

"I…" She hadn't decided which way her loyalty lay, even after being a part of both rival courts for the past year. Bronwyn had always shied away from such conversations. She certainly didn't feel comfortable talking about it with a stranger. She swallowed and looked away.

"Cat got your tongue? Never mind. Lots of young women find themselves tongue-tied when they're around me. I'm used to it." He smoothed his hair. "It's this way."

Bronwyn snorted softly, but said nothing as he took her to the grounds of a monastery, where they walked through a gate and he called to speak to Brother Milton.

In a few minutes, they were directed to go through the fields and pass by a hut that served as the man's workhouse. They knocked and entered. A young monk stood nearby, mixing herbs in a stone pestle, while an older monk looked on.

"You're back. What is it?" the older man asked.

"This girl wants your help," Crispin said.

Bronwyn stepped forward. "A friend of mine is sick with fever. He's up at the castle. Can you help him?"

"All right." The older man turned to the younger monk. "Mix the rosemary carefully and don't let this burn. I'll be back in an hour or so."

The older monk packed a small, leather bag with bottles and linens and motioned for Bronwyn to lead the way. The three walked on, when Crispin touched Bronwyn's arm. "Wait a minute."

"What?" She pulled her arm free.

"What do you do at the castle? You never said you worked there."

"You never asked," she pointed out. "I work in the kitchens."

"Oh." As they reentered the market, he said, "I'll leave you here. Good luck, Bronwyn. I'll be seeing you again, I'm sure."

She did not like his smile. It seemed overly confident. "Thank you for showing me the way."

He gave a half-shrug and walked away.

She followed the monk up the hill to the castle and caught up with him.

"What's the matter with your friend?" he asked.

"He's got a fever of sorts. He was found wandering in the woods. He got sick somehow, but we don't know how he got hurt."

"What was he doing in the woods?"

"I... I couldn't say. I don't know." She couldn't or rather *shouldn't* speak of the mission he'd been on. It was important that not everyone knew.

"Very well. Take me to him."

Upon entering the infirmary, they found Lady Alice by his

side. The lady glanced over her shoulder at them. "It took you long enough. Who's this? He needs a surgeon, not last rites." Her face was pale.

"Move aside, girl." The monk set his satchel on the ground. He put a hand to Rupert's forehead. "How long has he been like this?"

Bronwyn and Lady Alice exchanged a worried look. "Days, as far as we know," Lady Alice said.

"We need to cool him down." The man stripped off the blanket covering Rupert.

An *eep* sounded behind them.

Bronwyn looked. There was the same young maid she'd met earlier. The young woman fidgeted and bit her nails. "Will he be all right?"

The monk grunted at Bronwyn. "You, help me with this. Lift off his shirt. I need to see where he's injured."

Lady Alice stepped back, crossing her arms as Bronwyn carefully pulled off Rupert's shirt. It smelled and stuck to him in places. She wrinkled her nose at the smells of sweat and body odor and dropped the shirt to the floor. She'd wash it later.

"Girl. Fetch me a new shirt for him," Lady Alice ordered Philippa, who squeaked and left. Lady Alice sniffed and gave her head a little shake.

The monk examined Rupert's body under Bronwyn's watchful gaze. Lying there on the pallet, Rupert's half-naked torso made her pause. Normally, she would have felt anxious and a wave of attraction might have made her blush, but this was... sickly.

Bruises bloomed on Rupert's body sides and arms that varied from yellow and black to purple. A gash on his left side was swollen and sore, the result of a nasty cut.

"He was in a battle, I'd say. Nasty cut there," the monk explained. "This was more than a fistfight or defense against common thieves. Help me turn him on his side."

Bronwyn gently helped turn Rupert as the monk physician

examined his head and his back. A minute later, he grunted. "All right, girls, turn your backs. I need to examine the rest of him."

Bronwyn and Lady Alice turned as the monk examined the rest of him. A few minutes later, he said, "Girl, come help me put his clothes back on."

Philippa reappeared with a clean shirt and helped Bronwyn and the monk dress Rupert once the monk had his trousers back on.

"Well?" Lady Alice started. "What's wrong with him?"

"Besides a fever, you've seen the bruises on his body, but that's no surprise. He's clearly been in a fight of some sort. Nasty cut on his side that looks infected. That and likely the time wandering in the woods has given him a chill—and a fever."

Lady Alice bit her nails. "What can be done?"

"We need to cool him down. He needs rest. And water."

Bronwyn brought over a small basin with cloths and dipped one into the water. She wrung it out, the water dripping.

"I can do that," Philippa said, taking it from her. "I'll help."

Lady Alice frowned. "Who are you?"

"Philippa, my lady." The young maidservant dipped a curtsy, better than Bronwyn could have done. "I'll look after him."

Was that a proprietary air Philippa had about her? Bronwyn couldn't be sure.

"I don't care as long as someone tends to him," the monk said. "You, Philippa. Can you spare time from your chores to watch him?"

"Yes," she said, a bit too brightly. She began dabbing at Rupert's forehead with the damp rag.

He moaned slightly and kicked at the thin blanket at his feet.

The monk moved the blanket aside. "The best thing is to let him rest. If he wakes, give him stale ale or beer and broth, blood warm. I'll come again in the evening to check on him." He nodded to Philippa. "I'll see myself out. I know the way."

Bronwyn stood by as Lady Alice surveyed Philippa with a watchful eye. She went to return to the kitchen when Lady Alice joined her in the corridor.

"I don't like her," Lady Alice said. "She's too happy to be around him. I think she fancies him."

"I think so, too."

"Hmph. Rupert. He's so foolish. He's even attracting the maids when he's ill. What is the world coming to?" Her mouth twisted, and she marched away.

Bronwyn returned to her chores in the kitchen and set about the day's work. It wasn't until the early evening that she had word from the infirmary. Philippa came into the kitchen and said, "He's awake. The young man is awake. He needs food."

Bronwyn paused, a wooden spoon at her lips. Rupert being awake sent a feeling of relief through her, but her stomach gurgled and the potage before her was steaming and tantalizing, just inches away. She'd just been about to start eating dinner. Was she never to be able to dine in peace?

Philippa wandered over to the hearth, where a cauldron bubbled. "Maybe I could…"

"Step aside, girl. You're not one of the kitchen servants. We'll make you a bowl of stew for the invalid. Bronwyn?" Mistress Webb said.

Bronwyn pushed back the stale bread trencher she'd been sharing with a kitchenhand and climbed off the crowded bench. She went to the cauldron and filled a bowl, then prepared a tray.

Philippa hovered by her elbow. "You're Bronwyn?"

"Yes. Why?"

"Oh. I didn't think 'Bronwyn' was a person. I didn't know *what* he was saying."

"He's talking?"

"Yeah. Can you come?"

"Yes." A tray prepared, Bronwyn followed Philippa to the infirmary, where an older maidservant sat by, keeping watch.

At their arrival, the older servant said, "I'm glad." She looked to Rupert. "You've got friends here to see you now." She walked over to them and said quietly, "Don't keep him up too long; he's tired and needs rest."

"I'll take good care of him," Philippa said.

Bronwyn nodded and set the tray of broth down on the nearby table. She walked to Rupert. "Are you all right?"

He was sitting up and looked at her. His eyes were bloodshot with dark hollows beneath them, and his hair was matted and oily. He smelled, even wearing a clean shirt. But his smile was genuine, and even pale, he looked happy to see her. "I'll be all right. It'll take more than a fever to take me out." He flashed her a weak grin.

"You're pale. You should eat and then lie down," Philippa said behind Bronwyn's shoulder.

"And who are you?" Rupert asked.

Philippa blushed. "I'm Philippa. Philippa Quigley. You're Rupert Bothwell."

He ducked his head in a makeshift bow. "I am."

Philippa practically gushed. "We were worried. I mean, all of us, not just me, that is…" She grinned at him. "I'm glad you're awake. I thought you might be sick for ages."

He smiled back at her. "No. But I'll have some of that soup if you're offering."

Bronwyn was almost elbowed aside in Philippa's haste to bring him the tray. She set it down on Rupert's lap and picked up the wooden spoon when he said, "I can feed myself, thanks."

Philippa stood by, just watching him.

Rupert exchanged a wary glance with Bronwyn. "Um, I could use a drink. Could you bring me one? I'm awfully thirsty."

"'Course." Philippa rose, then said to Bronwyn, "Can't you do it?"

Bronwyn shrugged. "I'm new. I don't know where to go."

Philippa tutted and let out a noise of exasperation. "Fine. I'll be back." She hurried away.

Once they were alone, Rupert let out a small sigh. He wiped sweat off his brow and asked, "How long have I been ill?"

"Days. I'm not sure how long. They found you in the woods.

And you've got a bad wound on your side."

He winced, then paused, the spoon of soup halfway to his mouth. "You found me?"

"No, others did. You've had a fever."

He dropped the spoon and pushed away the tray. "I have to speak to the king. Where am I? Where are my shoes? I have to go at once."

Bronwyn stood over him. "What are you talking about? You're not going anywhere. You just woke from a fever. You're still ill."

He shook his head. "I can't sit still. I have to warn him. You don't understand—there's trouble."

"What do you mean, 'trouble'?" Lady Alice walked into the room. "Although with you here, I have no doubt trouble will be close by."

"Alice," Rupert said. It was a loaded statement.

"Rupert."

All of a sudden, the room filled with tension. Then Rupert blinked and said, "I have to report this."

"What are you talking about? You have to rest," Lady Alice said. "We were worried sick about you. Well, I wasn't, but the others were."

"Where am I?" Rupert demanded.

"Devizes Castle. Why?"

He moved the tray back further on the pallet and swung his legs off it to touch the floor. "I have to go. We have to mount a rescue party."

"Rescue? For whom?" Bronwyn asked.

He gave her a look filled with dread. "Queen Matilda and her son, Prince Eustace."

⁌❦⁍

Chapter Two

RUPERT ROSE FROM the straw pallet, his legs shaky. He wavered and sat back down with a grunt.

Lady Alice was by his side in a moment. "You shouldn't be moving; you've just had a fever." She reached for him, but he waved her away.

"I can look after myself," he said.

She dropped her hands. "I was only trying to—"

"I have to speak with King Stephen. Where is he?" he asked.

"You can't speak with him. He's not here," Lady Alice said.

"Where is he?"

"Rupert, stop," Bronwyn said. "You're in a stronghold of Empress Maud."

Rupert froze. He cursed, making the recently returned Philippa jump. She dropped a damp rag on the floor and shot a dirty look at Bronwyn. "Look what you made me do."

Bronwyn cocked her head, wondering why Philippa was blaming her for Rupert cursing. "Rupert, what happened? You've been unwell for days."

Rupert slouched and rested his palms on his knees. He rubbed the side of his face, along the start of a bristly beard growing there. "I need to speak with the empress."

"Are you sure? Can't you tell us?" Lady Alice asked. "Tell *me?*" Her voice was quieter.

He ran a hand through his hair, his fingers getting stuck in sweaty tangles. "I need to tell Maud immediately."

Bronwyn exchanged an anxious look with Lady Alice. "I'll speak with the empress."

"Don't be foolish. You're just a kitchen maid. She'll laugh at the very idea of you begging for an audience with her. I'll do it." Lady Alice huffed. "Rupert, stay here. You, girl, look after him." She pulled Bronwyn by the arm and led her away toward the door.

Once they were outside the infirmary, Lady Alice said quietly, "We need to tell Empress Maud about this development. Rupert's appearance here is a sign of trouble."

"I agree." Bronwyn shot her a frown. "But I don't think she'd laugh at the idea of me asking for an audience. That's a bit mean."

"Oh, for heaven's sake, it wasn't meant to insult you. It was simply stating facts. Not just *anyone* can request and be granted an audience with an empress. A person needs to be someone of high standing and importance to beg an audience. You'd do well to remember that. Besides, I do not trust that girl Philippa; she likes him too much. And… there's something you should know."

"What?"

Alice led her into a castle corridor. Once she was certain they were alone, she whispered, "Since there were so many tricks pulled on her recently, the empress has decided to increase the number of ladies in her retinue."

"You say that like it's a bad thing. Is it?"

Lady Alice pursed her lips and gave a slight *hmm* noise. "Depends on who you talk to. There is myself and her taster, Mistress Agatha." Lady Alice gave a little huff. "Many people think the empress is a hard ruler, but she is merciful. She took that horrid woman back into her service when she was well within her rights to turn her away."

"The taster did admit to pulling pranks on the empress in the past. Why did Maud take her back?"

"I don't know. That's between them. But if you want my opinion, the empress needs an official taster, someone who will risk their life, and it pays well. For every bite Mistress Agatha takes and doesn't die, she earns money for herself and her family. I gather that the empress didn't have any other people lining up to take the position. Would you?"

Bronwyn shook her head. The role no doubt came with some status, but to put one's life at risk and be expected to potentially try poison at every meal? Terrifying. "No."

"Exactly. You should be grateful that you did not have to speak with her on the journey here from Winchester; I certainly had to. And we had to share a tent too. Miserable woman, that Agatha. She snores and acts like everything is fine, and like she didn't try to scare the empress out of her wits a few months ago. Anyway, our mistress has also sent word that any young women of noble birth may come to join her court. We may see quite a few young ladies flock here to vie for her attention."

"Isn't that a good thing? Maybe it will distract her from—"

"She doesn't need distraction, she needs loyalty. Especially now," Alice said. "I will speak with her. Look after yourself and I'll call for you if I need you."

Bronwyn looked at her. She felt like she and Lady Alice were friends. Often Lady Alice spoke to her like an equal and treated her like one.

But not always.

Sometimes their difference in rank was apparent, and often it felt to her like Lady Alice decided they were friends, or that they were superior and subservient in rank when it suited her.

Bronwyn had spoken to Lady Alice about this before. Were they friends or acquaintances? She couldn't be sure. But she did know one thing: they both cared about Rupert.

"I believe him," Bronwyn said. "If he says something serious has happened, we need to let the empress know."

"Yes, yes. I'll see her now. But, Bronwyn… do you really think something has happened to Matilda of Boulogne and her son?" Lady Alice asked.

"I don't know. But we have to find out. Even if it's just a

rumor. But I believe him. How else would he have gotten separated from the others in the party and why haven't we seen anyone else?"

"I'm not sure. But this is the last thing we need. Soon, young noblewomen and their families will be arriving, and I have no idea how we're going to look after them all. Apparently, the empress sent out messages inviting the noble families before we even left Winchester. Can you believe it?" She shook her head and walked away.

Bronwyn looked after her. "Lady Alice?"

"What?"

"Are you well?"

A shadow passed over the noblewoman's face. A fleeting moment, wherein Bronwyn could see that Lady Alice was not okay, not at all. She blinked hard, then gave a tight smile. "Of course. Why wouldn't I be?"

Bronwyn returned to the kitchen and went about the daily tasks, but Rupert's words played over in her mind.

A short while later, however, she was summoned to the throne room, a large room with a grand chair that had been used for the empress's main room for receiving people. But as Bronwyn followed a servant inside, the room was full of people, including many well-dressed families.

A few gave her sideways glances, and she heard whispers and mutters, along with muted talk and laughter. "Who are all these people?" Bronwyn asked the page who had brought her.

"Noble families, here to court the empress. She's been receiving them for the last hour."

The empress sat at the head of the room, wearing a long, rich-green dress of brocade, cinched with a golden belt at her waist. Her hair was tied back in a thick arrangement of intricate braids, and she wore the gold circlet on her head that shone in the light. She smiled and nodded at many, but her eyes missed nothing, alighting on Bronwyn.

Her voice cut through the noise cleanly as a knife. "Ah, Mistress Bronwyn. So good of you to join us."

Lady Alice stood at the left-hand side near the empress, with Agatha, the empress's taster. The woman's angular face simply made her appear harsh and unkind, especially as her eyes narrowed at Bronwyn. Mistress Agatha's short, brown hair peeked out from her veil, and her lips pursed in displeasure.

Now that she knew about the empress's mercy when it came to taking the mean taster back into her service, Bronwyn looked upon Mistress Agatha with a wary eye. The older woman was crafty, and it amazed her that somehow, Agatha Carre had managed to convince the empress to take her back into her court, and not just end her life for her crimes against her. Maybe Empress Maud truly was merciful.

Bronwyn and Lady Alice's eyes met, but neither spoke. Mistress Agatha was thin and middle-aged, her face tan from so many days riding in the sun from Winchester to Devizes, but there was no mistaking the hard lines of her mouth or the dark glitter of her eyes that spelled trouble.

Bronwyn curtsied.

"I hear that the squire has awakened and shared some alarming news. That apparently there was an attack on Stephen's wife and their son."

Murmurs sailed through the crowd.

"While these are merely rumors, I wish to have them investigated and disproven, one way or another. Trust someone in their court to bungle things up, like something so simple as a ride from Winchester." The empress gave a sharp laugh and leaned forward in her seat. "Who will ride out to look into this matter for me?"

Bronwyn looked around. The noble families stood there yet somehow all seemed to avoid the empress's eyes.

Then a familiar voice spoke up. "I will, Empress."

Heads turned. It was Theobold Durville, the black-haired, quiet, serious squire, servant to Sir Robert of Gloucester, the empress's military commander who was currently in Winchester, being held prisoner by King Stephen.

He was also the young man who had stolen her heart. Her chest rose and fell at the sight of him, and there was no hiding her admiration for him. He stood in a simple woolen shirt, jerkin and trousers, with a weapon hanging at his belt, but there was no hiding his aristocratic bearing or the quiet confidence of his stance. She had no doubt he would conduct himself with honor.

He took a step forward, so that others might know him. "I will do it, Your Grace."

His voice sent a shiver through Bronwyn's body, right down to her toes. They had kissed, briefly, some weeks ago, and she had often thought of that kiss in her spare moments. Did he think of her? Could he care for a young woman who spent her days covered in flour?

"Thank you, Theobold." The empress turned. "But I cannot send just one squire alone. Who will go with him?"

"I will, Your Grace," another familiar voice said.

Bronwyn looked to see. It was the young nobleman from the market, the one who had shown her the way to the monk physician.

"I do not know you," the empress said. "Name yourself."

"I am Crispin Ashe, Your Grace. My father owns a hundred acres in Wiltshire, near Oare."

Bronwyn gasped. Him? What was he doing at Empress Maud's court?

"I see. Well met, Crispin."

"I will lead this expedition, Your Grace. I can bring twenty men with me," he added.

The empress turned. "Perhaps you will. Who else?" she asked the congregation.

Bronwyn frowned at him. What was he doing courting the empress's favor and offering to lead the expedition? She planned to keep an eye on him. She didn't trust him one bit.

There were a few more volunteers, and then the empress motioned for Bronwyn to approach. "You, Mistress Baker, are always around when trouble is afoot. Do you know anything of this matter?"

"No, Your Grace."

"Very well. Learn what you can from the young man and tell the cooks I want a meal prepared for the scouting party."

"Yes, Your Grace."

"Good. Begone." The empress waved her hand and Bronwyn was dismissed.

She met Theobold's eyes briefly for a second, but he did not wink or smile. His face could have been cut from stone. She curtsied and returned to the kitchens. Bronwyn told the cooks of the empress's order, then joined them in preparing meals for the day.

A few hours later, she took a meal of potage and crusty bread to Rupert, who was awake and sitting comfortably in the infirmary. He ate a little and balanced the tray on his lap.

Philippa stood by, watching.

"Could you bring me a drink?" Rupert asked her.

She nodded and left, with an unfriendly look toward Bronwyn.

Once they were alone, Bronwyn gave a little smile. "You have an admirer."

Rupert glanced back at the doorway through which Philippa had left. "She's a nice girl."

Bronwyn looked him in the eyes. "Can you tell me what happened?"

He ran a hand through his greasy hair. "We were riding through the forest when we were attacked. Someone struck me from behind and I fell off my horse. The queen and prince were surrounded."

Rupert frowned. "It was dark. I couldn't see who they were. But one of the men sounded familiar. When I woke up, it was night, but the men had gone. The only ones still there were dead. I think the attackers must have thought I'd died too, or they didn't see me. It was so dark. I called and looked around but couldn't see or hear anyone. I woke up a few times and then I could hear your voice, and I woke up here."

"They found you wandering in the woods, a mess."

He gritted his teeth. "We need to go after them."

"The empress is organizing a search party."

"Good. When? I have to join them."

Bronwyn bit her lip.

"What? I'm fine. I feel fine now," he said. "Really."

"How will you be able to help them? You were wandering around. And like you say, it was dark. Would you be able to find the place again?"

He raised an eyebrow. "I think the sight of a bunch of dead bodies would be easy to find."

She frowned. "I don't like this."

"What is your problem? I don't need you and Alice mothering me. I can find them on my own."

A snicker came from the doorway. They looked to see Theobold standing there with his arms crossed. "Why is it whenever I look for Bronwyn, I find you?"

"Maybe she likes my company more," Rupert quipped.

"Or maybe you just love charming women. Can't help it, can you? Even on the sickbed," Theobold said, coming forward. "Bronwyn, can I have word? In private."

"Sure." She rose and followed him out, brushing by Philippa as she returned, carrying a brimming cup of ale.

Bronwyn walked a little with Theobold out of the infirmary and down the castle corridors, until he led her outside to stand a little ways against the wall of the building. They were outside of the main castle but still within its walls, and Bronwyn closed her eyes to feel the afternoon sun on her face.

She opened her eyes a moment later. "What did you want to talk with me about?"

"I don't like you being there, with him."

"He's my friend."

"I know. But he's also squire to a knight for Stephen, unless you've forgotten."

"I haven't. I was talking to him about the fight," Bronwyn said.

"Ah, yes. The so-called 'battle' he was in. Do you believe him?"

"You don't?"

Theobold leaned in toward her, his arms crossed over his body.

Her gaze drifted to admire his muscular arms, his fair skin, and his short, dark hair, which reminded her of the night sky. He was slim and handsome, and something about the way he looked at her made her shiver.

She swallowed, feeling his eyes on her. His gaze rested on her lips.

Theobold said, "It wouldn't surprise me if this were a plot to lure the empress out into the open. They already have Sir Robert. Why wouldn't they make a play for the empress too?"

"You think it is a trap?" Bronwyn asked.

"I'm not sure. But Rupert has quite willingly taken on two masters before. You remember a few months back, when he *just so happened* to be in the right place at the right time and was there to save the empress's life when she was choking at dinner?"

She nodded.

"I can't help but wonder if this is part of a greater plan to end the war as we know it. Lure her out into the open to investigate, capture her, ransom her or kill her, or refuse to let her out of prison until she relinquishes her claim to the Crown. They could do all manner of things. We need to protect her, not chase after dubious rumors from a two-faced squire."

Bronwyn lifted her chin. "But I believe him. He wasn't lying. I saw the wound on his body. He really has been sick."

"I don't doubt it. But wounds can be given, and taken. Maybe he went along with the plot willingly, or maybe he was just a pawn. Either way, I don't trust it, and neither should you."

She frowned at him. "I can't believe Rupert would willingly go along with a plan like that."

Theobold shrugged. "The country is at war, Bronwyn, and we are stuck in the middle. Believe what you want, but you can't ignore that something is going on. I just hope for your sake you trust the right person."

She put her hands on her hips. "And *you* know what is right?"

He leaned closer. "I believe in my heart that I do."

They stood so close. Her heart began to pound in her chest.

His gaze slid to her lips again.

She said, "Theobold…"

He grasped her chin and tilted her head up.

Her eyes fluttered closed as he pressed his lips to hers and kissed her. Not just a light, pleasant kiss. This was pressing. This was more. She felt his body lean against hers, pinning her to the stone wall.

Her chest rose and fell as she turned her head aside to come up for air. She looked at him through heavy-lidded eyes. Her lips tingled. "I…"

"What on earth are you doing?" a voice demanded.

Theobold and Bronwyn turned. There stood the empress, with Lady Alice and her taster, Mistress Agatha, behind her.

Bronwyn had come to know the taster from their time together back at Winchester and knew the woman to be a foul, spiteful creature, who took delight in the misfortune of others. There was no hiding the taster's knowing smile as she glanced from Bronwyn to Theobold.

The empress's face could be cut from rock. Her eyes narrowed. "Mistress Blakenhale. Return to the kitchens. Theobold, I had thought better of you." She *tsked*.

Agatha's eyes danced at the sight of Bronwyn in trouble. Lady Alice's mouth pursed. She shot Bronwyn a look of disapproval.

Theobold spoke first. He bowed his head. "I'm sorry, Your Grace. I—"

She held up a hand. "Save it. I have no wish to hear why one of my squires is dallying with a kitchen maid in plain sight, when both of you have more important things to do. Theobold, you will travel with the search party at first light."

Agatha tittered behind her hands.

Theobold turned red, bowed, and walked away, leaving Bronwyn to face the empress's ire alone.

Bronwyn curtsied and lowered her gaze.

"I am displeased with you. I had thought you had more sense than this."

Bronwyn's head snapped up. "Your Grace?"

The empress glared at her. "You should be spending your time more wisely. Look to educate yourself in the kitchens and make yourself useful. If you need more chores to fill your days, I am sure the washerwomen or scullery maids will have work for you."

Bronwyn blushed. "Yes, Your Grace."

"Go." The empress made a shooing motion. "Do not let me see you out here again, throwing yourself at young men. I had thought better of you." She shook her head.

Bronwyn hung her head, feeling a wave of shame come over her. "Yes, Empress."

She stood back as the empress walked away. Agatha grinned whilst Lady Alice shot her an even look as they passed by.

Bronwyn returned to the kitchens and spent the rest of the day working. Against her wishes, she did not go to visit Rupert again or seek out Theobold. Instead, she worked and did everything asked of her. No chore was beneath her; no task was too small. The castle was always busy and full of people, and there was always work to be done.

It wasn't until the following evening, when she was preparing the evening meal for the empress and noble families, that word came down from the servants. It started first as whispers, then murmurs, until the cooks and pages were openly chatting about it.

Bronwyn finished setting a seasoned trout fillet on a wooden platter and signaled to the pages to take it away as other platters and trenchers were sent out to the main hall. As one page approached, she asked, "What's everyone talking about?"

"You didn't hear? The search party the empress sent, it's come back." The young page, a youth of about sixteen with sandy, cropped hair that fell into his eyes, took the nearest food platter.

"Did they find anything?"

"Aye. Bodies." The page turned a shade paler.

"They're all talking about it right now. Apparently, there're rumors that it was the party of people escorting Matilda of Boulogne and her son to Bristol, to exchange for the king."

Bronwyn tensed. "Was the queen found?"

"No. They think she must've fled, or…" He shrugged. "Can't imagine the empress is that bothered. If everyone's in prison or missing but her, has she won the war?"

"I don't think it's as simple as that. It can't be."

The page's face darkened. "Well, it's no business of yours, anyway. That's why they're where they are and we're here." He shot her a dirty look and took a full platter of roast chicken and sausage away.

Bronwyn absently helped arrange the other food platters to go out. With so many noble families visiting, there were many more mouths to feed. But her mind wandered. If the rumors were true, then had the queen gone missing? Was she lying in a ditch somewhere? And what about the prince?

She was sweeping the floor when the order came through. A page arrived in the castle kitchens and went straight up to her. It was the same youth who had told her of the rumors before. But this time, he looked a trifle smug, as if he knew something she didn't. She stopped her sweeping. "Yes?"

"You're summoned. The empress wants you."

"Why?"

"Don't know. I didn't ask. But you'd better come. Now."

She put away the broom and followed the page through the castle corridors until they reached the throne room. But unlike earlier, where it had been packed to the rafters with families and hundreds of people, this time, there was just a small number.

The page and Bronwyn were let through by two armed guards, who gave them shifty looks and held their spears as if to show they knew how to use them. Bronwyn walked ahead, conscious that as the doors opened and closed behind them, many pairs of eyes were now watching.

Show no fear, she thought. But she couldn't comprehend why she would be summoned. She swallowed and raised her chin. *Be like Lady Alice*, she thought. *Show no fear.*

The page marched forward, his shoes quiet on the wooden floor, and stopped a good distance from the empress. "Your Grace." He bowed. "The baker girl you sent for."

"You may go." Empress Maud waved a hand away at him, as if he were a fly.

The page glanced at Bronwyn, then bowed and walked out. From the widening of his eyes, he'd been keen to listen in on the discussion.

Bronwyn was glad he was gone. She curtsied and rose, her gaze on the floor.

"Mistress Blakenhale," Empress Maud said.

Bronwyn raised her gaze. "Yes, Empress."

"It seems that the rumors flying about are true. It looks as though Stephen's little wife and their son have managed to go missing." She snorted.

Bronwyn tensed. A stillness came over her, and she dimly felt her heart pounding in her chest. The queen and the prince had gone missing. Rupert had been right.

The empress said, "That squire claims their party was attacked. My men have found proof of a fight and a number of the dead, but none are royal. Do you comprehend what this means?"

"No, Your Grace."

"It means that either Stephen's little wife and son are still out in the wild, possibly dead in a ditch somewhere, or they have been taken by bandits. Who would want them, I have no idea," Empress Maud joked.

When no one laughed, the empress cleared her throat. "So, we will mount a little expedition to find them. They could be a useful bargaining chip for me, and I mean to have them. Or if they are already dead, then to find proof of their demise. I don't care how, but I want proof. You understand?"

"You mean *I* will be going to find them?" Bronwyn asked.

The empress leaned forward, her hands gripping the solid, wooden armrests of her chair. Her eyes gleamed. "Smart girl. Yes, you are. In the past, you have been like a hound sniffing out trouble, and I have a mind to make use of your talents here. You will accompany some members of my court. Do not get lost along the way. I don't care if it's their clothes or the hair on Matilda's pretty, little head. Find them, or find out what happened to them. But, Mistress Blakenhale, do not return until you find something."

Bronwyn swallowed. This was a punishment, surely.

The empress beckoned her forward, so close that Bronwyn stood not but a foot away.

Empress Maud whispered, "And maybe then that will teach you to step outside your station. You belong in the kitchens, or wherever I choose to send you. I have plans for Theobold, and they do not include dallying with kitchen maids in plain sight. I will not have my court being thought of as a den of iniquity and base morals."

She bowed her head, her cheeks feeling warm with embarrassment. "Yes, Your Grace."

"Your Grace, I must protest," a voice interrupted.

Bronwyn looked to see Theobold step forward. "Your Grace, I don't see why a baker's daughter has to come. She'll only slow us down."

"You'll need someone to cook for the lot of you," the empress said.

Another voice said, "He's right, Empress. The roads aren't safe for women these days. If anything should happen and we get separated, we couldn't look after her. She'd be a distraction."

Bronwyn's cheeks flamed. They spoke as if she were not standing right there. "I can look after myself." She glanced at the empress, who looked at her evenly. Had the empress forgotten the moment when Bronwyn had saved her life from a random attacker? Perhaps... or perhaps not. It didn't matter. Bronwyn knew that when she had to, she would pick up a weapon and fight.

Theobold frowned. "It's a bad idea. She'll only slow us down, and like Crispin said, she'll distract the men. They need to be sharp if we're to find any trace of the missing folks."

"Does she even know how to fight?" Crispin asked, eyeing Bronwyn, who glared at him.

"Hmm." The empress tapped a finger against the right armrest. "You are only looking for two missing people; there shouldn't be any fighting. You will go, and she will join you. That is all. Choose twenty men and leave at dawn. Report back to me when you find something. Oh, and take that ill squire with you. I won't have a turncoat in my castle."

That was the end of it. They bowed, Bronwyn curtsied, and she left the throne room. She went to the kitchens and told the head cook, who tutted and shook her head. "Why you?"

Bronwyn gave a little shrug. "I know the squire who was found in the woods. They probably think I can help."

"Doubt it." The head cook motioned for another servant to help pack a meal for the men.

Bronwyn lost herself in the busy work but couldn't shake the feeling that this was a punishment. The empress sought to punish her for kissing Theobold—that much was clear. But what plans did she have for him? Bronwyn would dearly have liked to know.

She went out of the kitchen to use the privy when she bumped into Theobold again. Both said, "Oof," and stepped back.

"Oh. Hello," Bronwyn said.

He backed up another step. "Bronwyn."

"Excuse me." She turned.

"Wait. I was coming to see you."

"Why?"

"I wanted to talk to you." He looked around in both directions, but there was no one else in the corridor but the two of them. He stepped close, enough that she could smell the clean scent of him. He'd recently bathed. "I don't want you to come with us tomorrow."

"What?"

"I mean it. The empress isn't thinking clearly. She thinks to send you as a woman she trusts, but—"

"Theobold, you're wrong. She wants to punish me for kissing you. That's why she's sending me away. She wants me to go on this errand. You heard her yourself. I have to find out what happened to them."

He shook his head. "No. It's not right. And it's strange. A young woman like you joining a bunch of knights and squires in a search party? It doesn't make sense. We can look after ourselves."

"Well, what do you expect me to do?"

"Oversleep. Pretend you're sick. Eat something bad and *make* yourself sick. I don't care. It's not safe for you out there and I don't want you joining us."

She frowned at him. "You don't think I can protect myself."

"It doesn't matter what I think. It's what I know. As soon as a fight happens, or any kind of trouble, you'll either be a target or a distraction. I can't afford to be distracted if there's a fight." His jaw was set.

They frowned at each other. Her heart wanted him to tell her how he felt. That he would be too distracted because of her— because he cared for her safety.

But he said no such thing, and met her frown with one of his own. "It's not only that." He added. "This Crispin fellow, how much do you know of him?"

She blinked. "I only met him at the market the other day. He showed me to where the physician monk was. Why?"

"He's acting as though he's leading the expedition. He talks a lot, and I think he's trouble."

She cocked her head at him. "You don't like him."

Theobold gave a half-shrug. "I don't trust him. He's trying very hard to get close to the empress, and in her good graces."

She raised a quizzical brow. "Aren't you?"

He stared at her. "No. I serve my master, and the empress. I am not a social climber, nor do I have any wish to be."

His hard stare made her cheeks feel warm. A prickling sensation went down her spine.

"I'm sorry, I..."

"Leave it. We can't be seen together. Not anymore."

Her mouth dropped open. "What do you mean?"

His brown eyes flicked away, then back again. He ran a hand through his dark curls. "I mean to say, I... don't think we should see each other anymore."

"Why?" Her throat felt tight.

Since they had arrived at the castle, she had thought he must have known where she was, yet he'd never come to visit her. True, she hadn't been there long, but... had he been keeping a distance on purpose?

"The empress spoke with me too, about seeing us together. She was furious. And... she gave me some things to think about." He sighed. "We are too different, Bronwyn. And I think too highly of you to use you like other men would."

"What?" Her voice carried in the corridor.

Theobold's head snapped to look down the hallway, then back again. "Keep your voice down."

"Don't tell me what to do," she uttered.

He came closer, his brown eyes blazing. "Bronwyn, I swear to God, I..."

"You what?"

He stared at her then, his eyes falling to her neck—and her chest. His gaze slowly rose to her lips, then her eyes. "I have my master to think of. My empress. And my place in this world. My reputation to think of."

"What do you mean?"

"I am squire. You are a kitchen maid. I have family connec-tions and obligations, a knighthood to prepare for. The empress herself said she has plans for my future. You…"

"Have no one."

"That's not true. You have Lady Alice—and Rupert."

"Ha. They have each other," she said.

He shrugged. "They are allies, and that's more than some people have." He stepped back. "I have my future to think about. I can't spend time dallying with—"

"A kitchen maid?"

"With anyone. My master may send me all over the country, and with him in prison, the empress needs me. She needs loyal men around her." He sighed. "Try to understand. It's not anything you've done, it's me."

"I wish I could believe that." She leaned against the wall, pressing her hands against the cold stone. She wanted to feel something tangible. It wasn't fair. It wasn't right. She cared for Theobold, and he didn't want to see her anymore because he had important things to do?

She swallowed. "Is this because of the empress seeing us together?"

He looked away. "That was just the last straw. I've been feeling this way for a while."

Now that did sound like truth. It just pained her to hear it.

"Oh." Her voice was quiet. "Did I do something wrong?"

"No. This isn't about you," he said. "I care about you, Bron-wyn."

She felt utterly confused. "But you don't want to see me anymore?"

"No, it's just…" He cursed and ran a hand through his dark curls again. "We're just too different, all right?"

"You're not making sense. You care about me, and you don't want to see me. I don't understand."

He'd lost his patience, she could tell. He put his hands on either side of her shoulders against the wall. At another time, she might've felt slightly excited by the closeness, but now she felt in trouble. His mouth twisted unhappily. "You want to hear the truth? Fine. You're too common for me, all right?"

Her world came to a sudden halt. Bronwyn stared at him, stunned.

He stepped back. "I have my future to think about. My good name. I should be with ladies and highborn young women, not maids. I didn't want to hurt your feelings, but you didn't understand. All right?" His tone was curt.

"I thought you liked me."

"I do. Too much. I need to be courting ladies of high station and acting like a knight, not getting caught in corridors with you. It's not fair to either of us." He blinked and looked away. "I don't want to use you. It wouldn't be right."

Better to end it now, she realized, *rather than let me fall for him further and lose my heart to him completely.* She nodded. "I understand." A lump had arisen in her throat. She tried to swallow it, and nodded again, then felt like a fool. With a twist of her skirts, she walked away, hurrying to the privy. She didn't want him to see her cry.

But cry she did, quiet sobs that shook her frame as she used the castle toilets. She was relieved it was only herself in there. She held her apron to her mouth to keep the sound from getting out and wiped her eyes with a clean part of the cloth. She couldn't believe it. She had thought Theobold really liked her. How wrong she was. What a fool she'd been.

Once she'd finished using the privy and had wiped her eyes, she walked back to the kitchen and took up a spot at the roasting spit. It was long, heavy work that people usually disliked doing, as it was teasing and unfair. Turning a great spit and seeing the butchered carcass of a pig or boar or sheep, slowly roasting, the fat spitting, the smell of the juices running... Just a few minutes was enough to make one's mouth water. But it also meant that she would be easily ignored, which was what she wanted.

Bronwyn worked until her arms ached, her eyes streamed

from the smoky spit, and the hour had grown late. She helped the kitchenhands turn the cooking fire down so it was safe, and then, once she'd helped clean the worktables, went to find a place to sleep in the main dining hall, where the other servants often slept.

By the time she'd found a space by the wall, not far from the large, stone hearth, she was bone tired. Her feet dragged, and she moved almost drunkenly, her limbs clumsy with fatigue. She tried to move quietly, and by the time she'd lain on the floor near some of the other women servants, she fell asleep within seconds.

But what seemed like mere moments later, a hand shook her. She jolted awake, her eyes wide. What she wouldn't give for a weapon. "Huh?"

"Ssshhh." Rupert stood over her in the darkness. "The search party has already left."

Bronwyn sat up. "They did?"

He held up a finger for silence. "Yes. I mean to follow them. Will you come with me?"

A surge of appreciation filled her. Here was a person who did care and wanted her with him. She'd go with him in a heartbeat. Bronwyn nodded.

He held a hand to her, and she accepted the hand up. They moved quietly in the early hours before dawn and slipped out of the main hall and out to the stables. He quickly and quietly saddled a horse, a plain one, and together, they rode out in the early morning light.

Chapter Three

BRONWYN SAT ON the horse, a small mare, and Rupert sat behind her, his arms secured around her waist and holding on to the reins for stability. It wasn't the first time they had ridden together, but she felt a slight mixed pleasure at behind so close to him.

She couldn't help it—she fancied him, and even though a part of her heart felt cracked and heartsore at Theobold severing their romantic connection, she still relished being supported by a man.

Bronwyn wished she didn't have a crush on Rupert, but she did, ever since their first meeting, back at Lincoln. She gave herself a mental shake. It was no use to think of Rupert romantically. They were friends, and he was involved with Lady Alice. That was real. What she'd had with Theobold had been only… fleeting. Like a flame, flickered out as fast as it had lit.

She wondered if what they'd had had been real at all.

"You're too common."

"I have my reputation to think about."

"My good name."

She sniffed at his words that played in her memory. It was unfair of him to use her upbringing and place in society against her. So what if she didn't come from a rich family or didn't have thousands of acres to her family name?

"Bronwyn, are you listening?" Rupert asked.

"What? Sorry. I was miles away."

"I can tell. What's eating you?"

"What do you mean?" Riding in front of him, she couldn't very well turn around in the saddle to look at him.

"You've been in your own thoughts since we left the castle." He paused. "Is it because they left you behind? I heard from Philippa and Lady Alice that the empress wanted you to join the search party."

"No. I mean, yes, I'm mad about that. But…"

"Is it Theobold?" he asked.

She stiffened in the saddle. "I don't want to talk about him."

Rupert sniffed. "Fair enough. It's none of my business, anyway." A moment later, he added, "But if you wanted to talk about him, you can. I won't judge."

That sent a shiver of anger through her. "Why would you judge me? Am I too common for you, too?"

"What?" Rupert pulled the horse up short. "What are you talking about?"

She sat stock-still. Her emotions swirled inside of her like a whirlwind, threatening to crack her calm veneer. Bronwyn muttered, "Let's keep going. We have to catch up."

"Wait. I want to know what's wrong," Rupert said. "You can't say something like that and expect me to ignore it. Did he call you 'common'?"

Her silence was answer enough.

"He did. That rat bastard. Why? Who does he think he is? He's just a squire."

"Oh, yes, with dreams and ambitions. He has a knighthood to prepare for, and he has to look after his master, and the empress, and he can't be dallying with someone like me."

"'Like you'?"

"A kitchen maid. I'm not highborn enough for him."

"What an idiot," Rupert said flatly. He nudged the horse with his heel, and they kept riding. "I'm sorry."

"It's not your fault."

"You've done nothing wrong," he said.

"I know. He said the same thing," she said bitterly.

He tensed behind her. "Sorry."

She shrugged.

"You've got nothing to apologize for," he said. "It's his problem. If he can't see a pretty young woman in front of him and appreciate her, that's on him. You've got better things to do, Bronwyn."

She felt cheered by that. He'd called her 'pretty.' She shouldn't have felt so warmed by that, but she did. She tried to ignore the warm feeling that filled her chest at the compliment. She wanted to ask him about his words before the bullying cook, Christopher, back in Winchester some weeks ago but decided not to. This wasn't the right time. "Thanks." A moment later, she asked, "Why did you wake me? Why aren't you with the search party?"

He coughed. "I heard the men talking. They didn't want to include me. They think since I'm Stephen's man, that I'll lead them into a trap or try something. Some thought I was too ill; others thought I was faking being sick. So when I rose this morning and saw them leaving, and without you, I thought maybe something had happened. So I went to see you. Figured you'd want to come, anyway, so here we are."

She nodded. "You could have let me sleep."

"Nah. You're up early in the morning, anyway, and besides, the empress gave you a mission. You may be a woman, but you're like a lady squire. If you're given an order, you do it. That's how I see it, anyway."

She thought about it. In a way, he was right. She felt obliged to go, as it had been the empress's order. And she wanted to prove Theobold wrong. She could defend herself and even be useful. But… she wasn't entirely sure who her master or mistress was.

"I think we'll have a better chance of blending in," Rupert said.

"What do you mean?"

"A party of a bunch of knights riding around will attract attention. A man and a woman on a horse won't. We'll be overlooked. But people will talk if they see the search party."

"Were there very many that left?" she asked.

"About ten. A few knights and their squires. It *is* odd the empress wanted you to go too. Why is that?"

"I think she's punishing me." She relayed to Rupert how the empress and her ladies had caught her and Theobold kissing, and the empress's dislike of them together.

Rupert laughed. "That must've been quite a kiss to get her attention."

Bronwyn blushed, and she nudged her shoulder back playfully, then winced. She felt hurt again at Theobold severing their relationship.

"The empress must keep a tight lead on those around her. She probably has plans for Theobold and didn't want you getting in the way," Rupert said.

"So she sends me out on a fruitless search?"

"It won't be fruitless. We're going to look around," he told her.

"Do you know where to go?"

"Not exactly. But I figure if we follow the way the party went out into the woods, we'll find something."

They rode on. "Tell me what happened again," Bronwyn said.

Rupert scratched his head. "We were riding and it was twilight; the sun had just set, I think, when our party was attacked. I tried to stay by the queen and prince, but someone hit me from behind, and I fell off my horse. I think I must have tried to get up and find them, but the next thing I remember is your voice and waking up in the infirmary."

"Can you remember anything else about the attack?"

"No, not really. One of the voices sounded familiar, though. I can't say who it was, only that I've heard his voice before."

The search party wasn't hard to follow. The men might have

had an hour's head start, but there were few people on the roads at such an early hour, which made their quest easier.

Bronwyn and Rupert rode quietly through the city and out again, past some sleepy guards and onto the main road. A little ways out, Rupert motioned the horse into the woods, away from the road, and farther.

Once the pair was in the forest, the woods grew noisy. With just the two of them and the horse, birds didn't care about their presence and chirped loudly. Gray squirrels darted around trees, rabbits hid, and even a red fox froze mid-stride to stare at them, then trotted on.

As the day's light grew, Bronwyn felt a little better. Her heart was sore, but she was a morning person and felt better and more awake as the day grew brighter.

Then Rupert said, "Stop."

"What is it?"

He tugged on the lead to slow the mare, handed Bronwyn the reins, and slipped off the back of the horse. "Stay here."

She sat stock-still, looking down. The ground seemed so far away. Without the comfort and protection of his arms to steady her, she felt nervous.

The mare sensed it and shifted on her hooves, nickering softly.

"Easy, girl. Easy. I'm right here," Rupert said, patting the mare's side.

He took the reins and quietly led the mare and Bronwyn through a thicket. The ground was damp and wet in parts from the morning dew, which meant it was muddy. Small pools of standing water stood nearby, and Rupert kept clear of those. "Don't want to twist an ankle."

"Could you let me down?" Bronwyn asked.

He gave her a hand and she slowly slid off the horse's back. She wobbled a little and grasped at Rupert for support, but he wasn't prepared for it. They fell, crashing into the soft undergrowth.

Bronwyn looked into Rupert's blue eyes.

Their faces were close, near enough to make a friendship something more.

She swallowed. "I'm sorry, I—"

He grunted. "You're heavier than you look."

And that ended all thoughts of romance in her mind. She rolled off him and put her hand right into a muddy puddle. Bronwyn grimaced and stood, wiping her hands on her apron. "You think you were attacked near here?"

"Something was. Look." He rose and pointed to a tree, which had a bloodstain on it. Even dried, there was no mistaking the sight.

He led her and the horse over to an area that was littered with armor, swords, helmets, bucklers, and shields. The grass had dried and wet again, many times over from the days' rains since the fight, but it was clear that a fight had occurred.

Bronwyn left Rupert then to look around the space. There was armor and weapons but no men. "Where are the bodies?"

"They would've been buried already," he said. "Once the men found this space, they'd have buried the bodies straight away. Better that than let the animals get them."

"Oh. What are you hoping to find here?"

"Same as what the empress wants you to look for. Any sign of what happened to the queen or prince."

She looked among the shields and weapons as Rupert tied the reins to a tree and joined her. "It wasn't a large party, but there were enough of us. We shouldn't have been attacked at all."

"What do you mean?"

"I wonder if someone knew we would be traveling that way."

"How could they have?"

He gave a half-shrug. "Not sure. But it seemed so sudden. There were at least fifteen armed men, not including myself, the queen, the prince, and a lady-in-waiting, Lady Muriel. For them all to die seems wrong."

"You think someone else escaped?"

"It's possible. Or..." He scratched his chin. "Or someone led us this way, knowing we'd be ambushed."

"But who?"

"I don't know." Rupert knelt and looked beneath a torn jerkin and shield. He picked up a small chess piece. "But whoever he is, he's a filthy traitor."

Bronwyn breathed in. "I don't understand. You found a game piece?"

"Prince Eustace and I would play in the evenings. He was teaching me." He held it up. "This proves it. This was our party."

"So now what?" she asked. "What does knowing this is where they were prove?"

"They were clearly taken by the attackers."

"What are you two doing here?" a voice asked.

Bronwyn and Rupert looked. It was Crispin, and not far away stood Theobold and a handful of other riders.

Crispin nodded to them. "So, if it isn't the two unwanted servants. And here I thought any sensible person would have been sleeping in bed."

"I'm a squire," Rupert pointed out.

Bronwyn thought, *I wish I had a bed.* Instead, she said, "We're here looking, same as you."

"There's nothing to find. We've looked over the area. There's nothing but scattered weapons and shields."

"I found a chess piece," Rupert said.

"So? This isn't the time to play games," Crispin joked.

"It's the prince's."

Crispin's smile disappeared. "How do you know?"

Rupert held it up. "We were playing on the journey. The prince was teaching me."

"How do you know it's his and not another traveler's?"

"I just do." Rupert met his gaze.

Bronwyn cocked her head. She wasn't wild about the idea of basing decisions on hunches, but in the absence of real evidence, what did they have? Rumors and a green glen filled with weapons. "Who buried the bodies?" she asked.

"Huh? Oh. I did. And a few of the other men. Why?" Crispin asked.

"How many were there?"

"I don't know. About fifteen or twenty. Who cares?"

"No reason. I was just wondering."

Theobold came over, his mouth twisted. He glared at Bronwyn. "I should've known you two would be here. You're like a bad habit. What do you want?"

Bronwyn opened her mouth to speak when Rupert said, "We're looking into this, same as you."

"Well, you made a wasted trip. There's nothing to find."

Bronwyn glared back, then looked away. She didn't want to see him. The very sight of him bothered her.

The group bickered further until one of the knights bid them all to return to the castle. As they did, a guard approached and said the empress was waiting.

Their horses returned to the stables, the group, including Bronwyn and Rupert, were directed to a smaller room in the back of the castle. Unlike the stately great hall, this was a small, wood-paneled room with naught but a round table and a few stools. It was not a comfortable room, but one meant for work. The table was strewn with rolls of parchment, a wine jug and glasses, even a quill.

The empress received them, her expression sour. "Finally."

"Your Grace?" one knight said.

"I presume you found nothing in the woods?"

"Nothing worth mentioning, Your Grace. We found the sight of the fight again but nothing other than helmets and weapons."

"Well, *I* have news," the empress said. "But this jest is in poor taste. I have no time for children's games."

Bronwyn cocked her head curiously. She wanted to ask outright but knew better. When in the presence of an empress, one waited for her to lead the conversation.

Not everyone appeared to know that, though. "What do you

mean, Empress?" the knight asked.

"This." The empress pointed to a small bit of parchment that lay on the table.

The knight, an older man with a slight limp and a scarred face, approached the table and glanced at the parchment. "It's a ransom note."

"Yes. It looks like the squire was right. Someone has taken them." Her voice was clipped and curt.

Theobold spoke. "You don't think it was perhaps someone trying to fool you? Maybe someone in the great hall before, someone who overheard the order to search the woods."

Empress Maud's mouth curled in a sneer. "Who would dare? I am an empress."

"There were many families there, Empress."

The knight looked at Theobold. "You don't think one of the noble families is behind this? That would be a cruel joke."

Theobold shrugged. "If my time in the empress's court has taught me anything, Sir Martyn, it is that there are many people who would wish to get close to the empress, but not all are trustworthy."

"Hear, hear," another knight said.

"A pretty speech, Theobold, but... You make a good point. I had not considered that one of the noble families might be behind this. But why play games with me? Just to cause trouble? There's already been enough of that." She tapped the parchment. "And what of this?"

She picked up a chess piece. Bronwyn's heart sank. "I recognize that chess piece, Your Grace. It is similar to one that the squire Rupert found at the scene of the battle. Forgive me, but Squire Theobold's theory of a jest does not make sense. We now know this isn't some silly prank—it's a sign. Whoever took Matilda of Boulogne and her son are serious, and this chess piece proves it."

$$\text{\emph{Chapter Four}}$$

Chapter Four

BRONWYN LOOKED AT the piece found with the ransom note. Rupert was right. It clearly had been taken from the fight in the woods. Someone had the queen and prince, but who?

Rupert spoke, "Your Grace. That is proof." He held up the chess piece he'd found in the clearing. "When I was traveling with the quee—" He paused. "With their party, the boy and I would sometimes play chess. He was teaching me the game. We found this piece earlier today. I think it is proof that the message you received is real. Not a joke."

Theobold's face clouded.

Bronwyn nodded. The empress frowned and helped herself a goblet of wine. She wiped her mouth. "Fine. So the message is true."

"What does it say?" Bronwyn asked.

A few of the knights frowned at her, including the empress, who shot her a glare. "I did not give you leave to speak, Baker."

Bronwyn bowed her head.

"But now that you have, I will tell you. The note demands we give over a princely sum for their return. And it enclosed the chess piece. A sign they have the boy, I suppose."

Bronwyn bit her lip.

"It also says we are expected to leave it by the city gates in three days' time at midnight."

The empress pulled out a chair and sat, leaning back against the low, rounded seatback. She tapped a slim finger to her lips.

"Will you pay the ransom, Your Grace?" Theobold asked.

"Hmm? No, of course not," Empress Maud said. "It's an obvious attempt to steal from me. And what they ask if far too great. I would have to raise taxes for months and empty the treasury. No."

Bronwyn glanced at Rupert, whose jaw set. His posture stiffened, and he stared straight ahead.

"But they do not have to know that. I have had my men mint coins in my image the past few months, so we will add a few of those to the bag and fill the rest with playing chips. By the time they come for it, we will have them."

Crispin spoke. "Your Grace. I would like to lead the capture."

A knight guffawed. "You? A squire?"

A few of the knights present exchanged smiles as Crispin's face turned red. But he stayed resolute and looked at the empress.

Empress Maud surveyed him over the rim of her wine goblet. "I agree. But… squires need chances to prove themselves, do they not?"

The knight looked unconvinced, crossing his arms over his chest. His mouth turned downward, and his chin set stiffly.

"Very well. You can lead this. But do not disappoint me. I want to find out who did this."

The knight's eyes widened, but he did not protest.

Theobold frowned and rested a hand on his short sword. She knew he disliked Crispin but found that she no longer cared. She felt a fleeting sense of loyalty toward Theobold, having had him in her thoughts for months, but now… she was too hurt, too messed about. And her emotions and heart had paid the price.

"I will come, too," Rupert said.

"And I," Theobold added.

"Very well. Crispin, sort out the arrangements. I want an end to this nonsense." The empress sipped her wine. "Baker, bring me some of those white rolls I am fond of. Enough for me and my ladies."

"Yes, Your Grace." Bronwyn curtsied, then paused. "Empress?"

"What?"

"I have a question. Whoever took Matilda and her son had targeted you specifically to get the ransom note. Why not send a message to Stephen instead? Why you?"

The others looked at her. Rupert with a slight smile and respect, Theobold with a frown, and Crispin with curiosity. A few of the knights echoed Theobold's frown.

One knight, a tall fellow with cropped, blond hair, said, "A girl shouldn't speak to the empress. You should return to the servants' hall."

"Hold. She has served me well in the past. She is loyal, despite her faults." The empress examined Bronwyn with a hawk-eyed gaze. "You think someone is trying to cause trouble?"

"We know that for certain, Empress. But I wonder why would they ask you for money, when it's Stephen's wife and son they've captured." She shifted her weight from foot to foot. It felt awkward, almost like she were advising the empress, when she wasn't completely sure to which court she was allied.

"Maybe she's closer? The fight happened just outside the city," Theobold said.

"Perhaps. But what if this was meant to disrupt both sides?" Bronwyn asked. "Think about it. If I'd stolen away Stephen's wife and child, then the hostage negotiations cannot continue. They're stopped. That's put a stopper in everyone's plans."

Everyone was silent.

"I'm sorry, but who are you? Empress, is this wise to speak of such matters before a mere baker?" an older knight who bore more than one battle scar on his face asked.

"No, but I have worked with her before. She has proven her loyalty, whereas others more senior than her have been a disappointment. If the conversation is not to your taste, you may leave us."

The knight stayed but crossed his arms over his chest and

gave Bronwyn a hard stare.

Bronwyn blushed at being the center of attention. "I mean—"

Lady Alice spoke up. "Your Grace, I could help."

The empress uttered a low giggle. She hid her mouth behind her hand. "Lady Alice, I'm sure you have many talents, but this is not a conversation for ladies-in-waiting."

Lady Alice turned red, glared at Bronwyn, lifted her chin, curtsied, and walked out.

The empress shook her head. "She means well, but she has all the deception of a spoon. Now, then."

The knights all began talking at once with the empress, and Bronwyn felt overlooked. Perhaps she'd said enough. She curtsied and left.

But as she quit the room and was walking back to the kitchens, a voice called, "Girl. Wait there."

She turned to see a knight walking toward her. She waited.

The man stood before her. He had the girth and confident stance of a knight. He was her senior by about ten years or so, maybe more. He had a strong chin, dusted with a few days' growth of facial hair and a cloth shirt beneath a leather jerkin, but there was no mistaking the sword and leather scabbard at his side—or his serious expression.

"I am Alwin Hughes, of Wiltshire. Who are you, whom she calls 'Baker'?"

Bronwyn curtsied. "Bronwyn Blakenhale."

"Your accent is different. Where are you from?"

"Lincoln."

"Were you at the battle?"

She gave a brief nod.

"You must have had quite a time. Did the empress rescue you?"

"I fell in with her camp."

"I see. But she trusts you. Why?"

What could she say? That she'd saved the empress's life before? No. That would be bragging, and not something she should talk about. "We came to know each other. She likes to talk to the people."

He surveyed her with interest. "It's odd she would call in a baker to her private study."

"She did order some rolls."

"Ah, yes. But I was out in the woods this morning and saw you with the squire. You were the girl she ordered yesterday to find the missing people, aren't you?"

Bronwyn inclined her head.

Sir Hughes scratched his chin. "You're an interesting one, I'll give you that."

She looked at him. "You recently joined her court."

"I did. But I hope to make something of myself in serving her. It is my honor to serve. So it is with us all." He gave her a cheerful wink.

Bronwyn smiled and ducked her head in a small nod. "I'd best get back to the kitchens. Excuse me."

He called, "Well met, Mistress Blakenhale. Till we meet again."

Bronwyn held up a hand in a wave and hurried away. She had little interest in getting entangled with knights, especially when she wasn't sure whom she could trust.

Back in the kitchens, she was met by the head cook, Mistress Webb. "You didn't find anything in the woods this morning?"

"Nothing," Bronwyn replied, conscious that many servants were listening.

"Ha. That's what they get for sending a cook out to do a knight's job. At least they were well fed. Come have a bite to eat."

Bronwyn had a bowl of potage and then set to work. As she rolled out the dough and added honey to make them sweet, she thought about what she'd seen.

She wanted to help but didn't know how. But she couldn't shake the idea that someone close by had the queen and the prince under lock and key somewhere and wanted to disturb the hostage negotiations between the two rulers.

She added honey and rolled out the dough again, shaping them into soft rolls, thinking. By making it so that the queen and the prince didn't reach their destination, that meant that whoever was expecting their arrival would still be waiting, and within a few days of their arrival not happening, they would likely write to the king or send out a search party of their own.

In the meantime, King Stephen would be expecting the safe arrival of his wife and son. Back at Winchester, he would be waiting the news. Bronwyn would have expected the thieves to demand a ransom from him, or of the people at the prison. But they hadn't. Whoever had stolen the queen and prince had demanded that the empress pay. Why?

She thought on this as she laid the rolls on a hot platter to bake. By demanding the empress pay, whoever was behind this either wanted to weaken the empress or make it look like she had done it herself. That would make the relationship worse between Maud and Stephen, and it might escalate the war, as it would look to all parties like the empress had gone against her word and taken his family as hostages.

So the question was: who had known that the queen and prince had been traveling and where, and who also had known that the empress would be nearby at Devizes? Maybe they hadn't and had just been lucky. But more importantly, who would have the most to gain by all of this?

A short while later, she had a platter of warm sweet bread rolls and enlisted the help of a page to show her the way to the empress's chambers. But as she climbed the stone steps to the empress's solar, she couldn't shake the feeling that this capture of the queen and prince was actually an attack against Empress Maud, even if no one else viewed it that way.

So it was that as the page knocked on the empress's door and the guards let them enter, Bronwyn walked inside with a serious face. She bobbed her head for practicality, as she wasn't able to curtsy very well whilst holding a tray of warm bread rolls, and stood by, awaiting the empress's attention.

"Ah, Mistress Baker. Very good. And you brought enough for us, even better. I do so like her sweet rolls with honey." The empress beckoned Bronwyn forward and took one, nibbling at it delicately. "Delicious."

"Ahem." Mistress Agatha cleared her throat, none too subtly. "Surely, you wish for me to taste it first, Your Grace. To avoid any deadly mistakes. We wouldn't want you to die because a cook was careless." She looked evenly at Bronwyn.

"No, you are quite right, Mistress Agatha." Empress Maud nodded. "However, in this instance, I count myself lucky. One, that I have a cook here whom I trust, and second, that you endeavored to warn me, however late it was. Do have a care and be faster next time. Or who else will we have to blame but yourself?" The empress smiled sweetly.

Mistress Agatha turned red and murmured something but was quiet.

Bronwyn moved to the ladies in the room. They were Lady Alice, Mistress Agatha, and the empress herself, along with two young women Bronwyn didn't recognize, both of a young age, perhaps in their early twenties, and well dressed.

One had rich, blonde hair that hung in rippling waves, and her face bore the golden kiss of the sun, having a slight warm tan and freckles dotted on her nose. She didn't acknowledge Bronwyn at all, simply helping herself to a roll.

The second had warm, auburn hair, pinned back in a braid. Her face had a pinker tone and was a touch paler. She wore dark green but had acne on her chin. She gave Bronwyn a sour expression and took a roll, fiddling with it.

"You haven't met my new ladies. This is Lady Edith and Lady Isobel."

Bronwyn inclined her head, whilst the ladies didn't. They simply looked at Bronwyn, then away, making small talk with each other.

Bronwyn tried to hide her smile. It didn't surprise her at all that they would ignore her. Despite the empress's attempts to raise her up, she was, and always would be, a servant. It didn't matter if it was a lady, or a squire like Theobold. A servant she was and there was no changing that.

She served the rolls and left the platter.

"Such a shame about the Lady Morwenna," Lady Isobel said. "I never did hear what happened to her."

"She had to return home, I think," the empress said, nibbling at her bread roll. "A dear girl. And so pretty."

"Yes, she'd told me about a few of the knights and squires who had caught her eye. Wasn't Theobold one?"

"He's here at the castle. You'll have to meet him. A very charming young man. Just the right sort of gentleman I would choose for you, Lady Isobel. I'm sure your mother would agree." The empress's smile didn't reach her eyes as she glanced at Bronwyn.

"If you'll excuse me, Empress, I'll be going."

"Yes, yes. Of course. Now, Lady Isobel, you must tell me more about—"

Bronwyn curtsied again and left. Once the door had shut, she let out a breath and walked down the stone steps, only to hear the door creak open again and a whisper.

"*Bronwyn.*"

She turned around. Lady Alice stood at the top of the stone spiral stairwell. She walked down the steps, her blue dress swirling around her ankles.

"What is it?" Bronwyn asked.

"Is it true? That you and Theobold are no longer together?"

Bronwyn looked away. "Yes."

Lady Alice's breath came out in a quiet huff, almost a sigh. "Oh. I'd hoped I was mistaken. What did you do?"

"What do you mean? Why are you assuming *I* did something wrong?"

"Well, we did all see you two kissing out in the courtyard. It was a bit brazen."

Bronwyn felt anger bubble up inside her. Where was the solidarity amongst women? Was there no loyalty to be had between friends? But then as usual, had she fallen into the delusion of thinking they were allies? Perhaps she'd been wrong this entire time—and naive.

"I won't deny my part in that. But… he decided I…" No. She wouldn't repeat his words.

"You're too common."

Lady Alice didn't deserve to know, and for all Bronwyn knew, she might agree with him. Had their romance been doomed from the start? She didn't know.

"I can see you're hurt. Well, I shall step on his foot the next time I see him and tell him he is an oaf who is clearly oblivious to what is right in front of his face," Lady Alice said simply.

Bronwyn looked up.

"I won't deny that the empress is trying to play matchmaker a bit. I think it amuses her to play at courtship and arrange matches with her ladies. He's just a fool to play along." Lady Alice cocked her head. "I say, are you all right?"

"I'm fine. I just… need to go." Bronwyn curtsied to her and walked away.

"Bronwyn, wait. What in the world was that?" Lady Alice followed her and touched her shoulder.

"What?"

"You curtsied to me just now. You've never done that before. What is wrong with you?"

Bronwyn thought, *You're a lady. I'm a servant. It's only right I should curtsy to my betters.* She swallowed. "Nothing. I'm fine."

Lady Alice let out a very unladylike curse. "I don't believe it. He's gotten inside your head, hasn't he?"

"What do you mean?"

"He's made you feel lesser, to make himself feel better about cutting you loose. That's it, isn't it?"

Bronwyn hung her head.

"Good God. What did he say to you? I'll put a frog in his bed, I swear."

Bronwyn gave her head a little shake. "Just that I'm common. Too common for him." She said the words in a rush of breath and blinked back tears. "He needs to spend his time serving the empress and his master, not dallying with a servant girl like me."

A tear escaped and coursed down her cheek. Bronwyn brushed it away angrily.

"I cannot believe this. And he thinks he will actually have a chance at becoming a knight. Ha. Not if I have anything to say about it. He's a rake, and a cad, and blackhearted, and—"

"Leave it. He's made his choice. He has his life and I have mine. He will serve the empress, and I will go back to the kitchens."

Lady Alice stared at her. "God, you're so dramatic sometimes. I swear, you belong with a bunch of jonglers or jesters. People deserve to know how poorly he treated you. His master should know how he threw you over. It's not right. I want to tell everyone—"

"It's not your place to tell, Lady Alice," Bronwyn said.

Lady Alice's dark eyes flashed. "I could ruin him. The right word in the wrong ear, and he could be a laughingstock. I don't care if his master is sitting in prison, rumors fly twice as fast as messengers do, and he could know soon enough."

"I don't want to hurt him."

"You don't understand. Part of becoming a knight is obeying the code of chivalry, and part of that is the kind treatment of women. For Theobold to do that to you, it's just wrong."

Bronwyn shook her head. "No. Leave him be. I don't want to hear anymore. What's done is done." She bobbed her head. "Excuse me, I have to go."

"But, Bronwyn, wait."

Bronwyn hurried down the rest of the stone steps and back to the kitchens. She was happy to have the work, and there was always work to be done. That day, she helped turn the spit for the evening meal of roast pig, and then after the evening meal, she helped scrub pots with the potboys.

These were children and youths who were old enough to be useful around the castle and needed a bit of minding. But they would also learn how to work inside a castle, which was useful, and they got food to eat. Not everyone would be so lucky.

QUEEN MATILDA HELD her son close. The blindfold around her eyes was tied tightly, and it had pained her at first. But she had to be strong for Eustace.

They were both scared. After the attack, she had woken up in darkness, blindfolded. She'd called out for her son, who woke up crying. They'd found each other in the dark and held each other close. He'd wet himself, the poor thing. She didn't care. "It will be all right," she'd murmured. "Someone will come and rescue us."

Eustace had wept, in that stage between when a youth is shedding his childhood and starting to become a man.

Voices above them said, "Shut your mouths, if you know what's good for you."

She called out, "Who are you? Why have you blindfolded us?"

Then it hit her. Because they didn't want to be seen, in case she recognized them. Did she know them?

"No one's coming for you."

"Do you know who I am? I am the Queen of England."

A man laughed, an arrogant sound. "And now you're the Queen of Muck. How do you like your new kingdom, Your Grace?"

So they were in a prison of some sort. That explained the smell. She could hear the slight scents of damp, and of the air being underground, that dark, earthy smell where ground and stone met. The rustling of mice came from nearby.

A thought chilled her. Had they been stolen away and dropped inside an oubliette? Her blood ran cold. Had she and her son been dropped in a dungeon and left to die?

She hastily scrabbled and tugged at the stiff blindfold, which had become matted with blood at the back of her head and plastered to her face from rain and tears. After a few minutes, she pulled it off.

Something dropped nearby. She let go of Eustace to reach for it and scrabbled around on her hands and knees. It was a piece of old fruit. An apple.

It was soft and mushy, but holding the small fruit in her hand made her stomach growl. She handed it to Eustace. He had to eat. He had to survive. "Eat this," she told him.

He ate gladly, and only after he'd eaten all but the core did he say, "But what about you?"

"I'll be fine. I'm not hungry." She hoped he could hear the confidence in her voice and not the lie.

BRONWYN DID NOT see or hear from anyone in the next few days that followed aside from the other cooks. She kept to herself but wondered how the plans were going. Then she had an expected visitor, shortly before dinner.

She was preparing platters of food with the other servants, when Crispin entered the kitchen. He looked around, appearing a bit lost amidst the bustle of activity around him.

She wiped her hands clean and came up to him. "Crispin?"

"Ah. Just the woman I was looking for." He dipped and dodged as servants carried platters of fish and bread out past him. "Is there somewhere we can talk?"

"Sure." She motioned him over to the pantry, where it was less busy, even if they were facing a large, walk-in area full of bags of flour, bread loaves, cured fish, and birds hanging to be plucked. "What is it?"

"Tonight is when we have to leave the ransom outside for the attackers. I wondered if you wanted to join us." He spoke quietly, almost shyly, as if he were a boy asking her to dance.

She looked at him. "I'm surprised. Why me?"

"You've been involved with this from the beginning. I thought you'd want to come along."

She had been wondering how it would go. "What would you need me to do?"

"I'm not sure. I haven't thought that part out. But look, tonight a few of us are going to be watching at the castle gates. You'll come?"

She hesitated.

Crispin said, "Theobold will be there too."

Her cheeks turned pink. Did *everyone* in the castle know about their broken romance?

"I don't know about your relationship, and frankly, I don't really care. But he didn't want you to come, and I think that's a mistake. The empress trusts you, even if you are a kitchen maid. As I'm organizing this mission, I'd like to you come. If you're not too tired."

"Where will you be?"

"Outside the city gates on either side of the main road. It'll be dark. If you want to come, join us before midnight. Tell the guards I sent you, and they'll let you through." Crispin shot her a look. "I won't blame you if you don't want to come. It's dirty work, not for young women. I wouldn't ask, but…"

"I'll be there."

THAT NIGHT, AFTER the other servants had sought out places to sleep, Bronwyn slipped outside of the castle and into the city of Devizes. She didn't know the area very well and so lost her way a bit, but eventually, she made it out to the city gates, where the two guards on watch let her out.

Even in the darkness, she felt it was overly quiet. There were people walking around inside the city, and the normal sounds of people living on top of each other, arguments, laughter, singing, drinking, talking. Dogs howling and cats fighting. But as the gates shut behind her, she felt a bit vulnerable.

Bronwyn stuck to the shadows and quickly walked off the main road, off into the wooded green, where the ground was rather less even. She soon met a party of armed men.

"Bronwyn?" Theobold asked, his voice instantly annoyed. "What are you doing here? Go home."

"I was invited," she whispered.

"Who is she?" a man asked, eyeing her. "Oh. This is the girl with the empress earlier. You're a kitchen maid, yeh?"

"Yes," Bronwyn whispered back.

"So where's our food?"

"I-I didn't bring any. Was I supposed to?" Bronwyn asked.

The man let out a noise of frustration. "What's the point of bringing along a kitchen servant if she doesn't bring any food? I'm hungry."

"That's not why she's here," Crispin said. "And you should've eaten more at dinner. It's not her job to look after you."

The man grunted. To Bronwyn, he said, "Just don't get in the way."

She moved a few feet away and lay down on the ground, flat. She could easily see over the grass and watch the main road, with an excellent view of the castle gate.

"What are you doing?" a man asked.

"Blending in. What are *you* doing?" she whispered back.

The man made a noise, and then a bunch of the men knelt in the bushes and watched.

Bronwyn asked, "Where is the ransom?"

"By the right gate, off to the side," Crispin said.

She noted movement on the other side of the road. There must have been more knights there.

"And now, we wait," Theobold said.

Bronwyn was quite content to lie there on her stomach and watch. Minutes passed. One or two stragglers approached the gates but were ignored.

Then a drunken man stumbled up to the gates and banged loudly. "Lemme in, I tell you, I've got a house and a wife and…"

"God, he's going to ruin everything. Whoever's behind this isn't going to come if he's there," Theobold said. "I'm going to talk to him."

"No, leave him be. You'll alert whoever is coming that we're here," Crispin said.

Bronwyn privately agreed with Crispin but stayed silent. Their voices were loud enough and cut through the silence.

The drunken man lurched to one side and began to urinate against the wooden gate. The sound of urine hitting the wall made Bronwyn smile. If that was the most exciting thing that happened that evening, she'd be relieved.

He banged on the gates again. "Here now, lemme in. I live here, I swear on Almighty God. I just… wish I could remember."

Theobold was up and walking toward the man in a flash. He had a hand on the pommel of his weapon by his side and began talking to the drunk.

"Christ, is he always like this?" Crispin demanded. "How in God's name did he manage to become squire to Sir Robert of Gloucester with an attitude like that?"

Bronwyn held up a finger for silence, but it was too late.

Now the gates opened, and Lady Alice came out. "I don't know who you are, but you're not getting any money," she boldly said.

"Oh, good God," Bronwyn muttered. "I can't believe it."

Next to her, Crispin cursed. "What is she doing here?"

"Trying to help, I imagine."

He let out another rude curse and shot to his feet, making a run for the noblewoman. At the sight, Lady Alice's mouth dropped open and gave a squawk before she began shouting.

Now two other men from the other side of the road had

joined them, and the drunk man had gotten belligerent. He pushed one man, and a fight broke out.

"Gods. What a mess," Crispin said.

Bronwyn said, "Wait, look." She pointed, but Crispin was already gone. All of the men now were pushing and arguing in front of the gates, creating a loud ruckus.

Bronwyn shook her head and leaned forward in the grass. She peered into the darkness, but with the men all arguing, it wasn't easy to see past them. She raised her head, ever so slightly.

There. A small person, subtly moving toward the gate in the shadows.

"Look at that," Bronwyn breathed, but of course, no one was there to hear her. She leaned closer, beginning to rise from her place in the grass. Bronwyn slowly, silently, rose to her knees and felt pins and needles in her limbs from lying on her stomach for so long. Her hands were wet and cold from the grass and she wiped her hands on her dress.

Then the person went to the gate, amidst the fighting.

"They're taking the bag," Bronwyn whispered aloud. She got to her feet and ran toward the gates.

The person fled into the shadows.

Bronwyn sprinted after them. She ran past the group of armed men, barely spotting where the person was heading. "Stop!" she called out.

The person must have looked behind them because there was a sound of a *thud* and the *clink* of coins.

Bronwyn dashed toward the sound.

The person was kneeling on their hands and knees, and Bronwyn launched herself at them, crashing into them. They fought, and she was instantly pushed and scratched at by long nails. Her attacker emitted a womanly sound and pulled at her hair. Sharp pain tingled along the top of Bronwyn's head as she gritted her teeth.

Their feet got caught in each other's skirts. Bronwyn elbowed the woman in the gut, only to receive a hard punch to the right cheek. "Oof."

Pain blossomed through her cheek. She rocked back but held on to the woman's skirts. Bronwyn got kicked in the chest and fell back, coughing, then, shaking her head, scrambled after the woman. "Stop," Bronwyn called weakly.

She ran and tumbled onto the woman, crashing into the undergrowth. The woman snarled a curse and they rolled down a slight incline, rocks and pebbles digging into their limbs, falling and tripping against thick, gnarled tree roots, until they came up fast against a tree trunk. *Thunk.*

Bronwyn paused. The world was spinning. She blinked hard and gave her head a little shake to clear her head. The world still spun, so she closed her eyes and felt around for the woman.

The mystery woman wasn't fighting back, and indeed, just lay there. *She must be out cold*, Bronwyn thought.

"Bronwyn? Bronwyn!" Theobold's voice echoed through the trees.

"I'm here!" Bronwyn called. "I'm here."

Her body hurt, and the world began to spin again. She closed her eyes and opened them again. She had to stay alert.

Her face lit by a sliver of moonlight, Bronwyn leaned forward as the other woman began to stir. She sat up and froze.

"Don't move. You're surrounded," Bronwyn said. "There're armed men all around us."

The woman let out a curse.

Bronwyn got a good look at the woman's face and her mouth dropped open. "Morwenna?"

It was the empress's former lady-in-waiting, and a treacherous one, at that. Bronwyn had never thought she'd see the young woman again after the empress's failed coronation attempt in London some months back.

Lady Morwenna glared at her and let out a noise of exasperation. "The kitchen maid. God help me." She rolled her eyes. "Follow me if you ever want to see Matilda of Boulogne and her snot-nosed brat ever again."

Chapter Five

BRONWYN FLINCHED. OF all the people, she'd never expected to meet Lady Morwenna again. She couldn't help but remember how foul the young woman's temper was, or how rude she was toward servants. "What are you doing here?"

Lady Morwenna rose quickly, despite having been in a fight. "Do you want to find them or not?"

"All right. But let's wait—"

"We can't wait," Lady Morwenna said. "Come with me now or I'll run. You'll never see me or them again."

Bronwyn bit her lip. "Fine. Let's go."

Lady Morwenna limped, and Bronwyn darted after her like a shadow. She wanted to call back and alert the men but couldn't. Not without risking losing the noblewoman. So she stayed close.

The calls of the men echoed in her ears as they retreated farther into the woods and away from the city gates. The darkness fell like a silken, black curtain around them, but Lady Morwenna picked her way around the mud and gnarled roots and fallen branches with confidence.

Bronwyn began, "What happened to you? After the empress's coronation in London—"

"Ha. A joke if I ever saw one. Would you stay around and face an angry mob? I fled, like any sensible person." Lady Morwenna huffed, as if Bronwyn had asked a foolish question.

"I heard Theobold went after you."

"He did. We're very close."

Bronwyn was silent. She shouldn't have asked that.

"What's your interest in him?" Lady Morwenna asked.

"Where are the queen and the prince? How do you know where they are?"

"You really are naive, aren't you? God. I must have offended someone. Why did it have to be *you*?" Lady Morwenna muttered.

"Keep walking. Where are they?"

"This way." Lady Morwenna limped.

Her scalp prickled. Bronwyn felt pain from her earlier tussle and fall down the incline with Lady Morwenna. Her hands were wet. She wiped them on a nearby tree and hoped someone might see and find them. If only she could leave a trail of some kind…

The young women walked through the dark woods, staying close to each other. Then up ahead, there was a little clearing and deeper into the forest, the ruins of a tower.

Lady Morwenna said, "They're here."

"Were you part of their capture?"

"What do you think?"

Bronwyn stayed near as she approached the ruins. On the edge of the tower it led down to a pit, and in the moonlight, she could barely see two figures huddled there. "Hello?" Bronwyn called out.

Immediately, voices called, "Help us! We're down here!"

Bronwyn turned to Lady Morwenna. "We need a rope, or a ladder."

"Search me. *I* don't have anything."

Bronwyn looked around. She needed help. "I—"

"I'll help you," a familiar voice said.

Bronwyn turned. "Crispin."

"At your service." He took off his cloak and began tearing it into three long strips. He knotted them together.

Bronwyn removed her apron and handed it to him. He nodded in approval and added it to the now-knotted makeshift rope. It wasn't very long, but it would do.

"You." He turned to Lady Morwenna. "Have you a cloak?"

"Do I *look* like I have a cloak?" She snorted. "No. And I wouldn't share it with you, anyway. I'm not ruining a perfectly good cloak for *them*."

He muttered something rude under his breath and turned to Bronwyn. "I'm going to lean over the side and try to pull them up. Can you hold my legs and pull me back when I need you to?"

"Yes." She looked at Lady Morwenna. "Will you help?"

Lady Morwenna shrugged. "If I must."

He lay on the ground and crawled over to the edge, reaching down. "Take my legs."

Bronwyn held his right ankle firmly. Lady Morwenna grudgingly took his left. Crispin was tall and had long arms. He said, "Reach for the sash, Your Grace. Try." He leaned over farther and said, "Pull!"

Bronwyn gripped his leg harder as he got closer to the edge. If they all fell in, they'd be in trouble.

He leaned so far over the side, Bronwyn worried and held as hard as she could, when he shouted, "Yes! You can do it." He began to shift backward. "Pull me up."

Bronwyn and Lady Morwenna tugged him back and helped pull him over the side, along with a youth, who rolled over and breathed heavily. "Thank you."

"It's all right, lad, now let's rescue your mother." Crispin leaned over again. "I… Where'd Lady Morwenna go?"

She had disappeared. In the moment when Bronwyn had helped pull Crispin back over, she must have run off. Bronwyn wondered, how did Crispin know Lady Morwenna? To her knowledge, they had never been introduced.

"Never mind. Boy, help hold my legs so we can reach your mother. Ready?" He pushed himself closer to the edge.

The youth held on to Crispin with an iron grip. He smelled like sweat and urine, and he needed a bath. He looked at Bronwyn with tired eyes. "Who are you?"

"Nobody. You're…?"

"I am Prince Eustace," the youth said gravely.

They pulled and tugged as Crispin leaned farther and farther over the edge, then cheered. "Yes, hold on. I'll pull you up."

After a few tense minutes, they pulled up the queen as well. She cried with relief and hugged Crispin. "Thank you, young man. Thank you."

Prince Eustace hugged his mother, and they held each other close. The queen said, "Bronwyn? What are you doing here?"

"She's the one who found you," Crispin said, blinking. "You know this baker?"

Bronwyn rubbed the side of her face. "Your Grace, I followed Lady Morwenna here."

"Lady Morwenna? Who is that?"

"A former lady-in-waiting to the emp—to Maud," Bronwyn finished.

"Ah. Fine. Where is she now?"

"I don't know. I think she must have run off."

"Pity. Where can we go? Anywhere but here would be preferable," the queen said.

They all looked to Bronwyn. "I…" She swallowed. "I'm not sure."

She and Crispin shared a look.

"You are on the outskirts of a city that is allegiant to the empress, Your Grace," Crispin explained. "The nearest castle is her stronghold. If she were to learn of your presence here…"

"It might make things worse. I understand," Queen Matilda said simply.

It was true. If they were found, people might try to capture them again and hold them for ransom, or give them to the empress, or kill them. Or some might be loyal to her cause and protect them. But most curiously of all, Crispin was loyal to the empress. Why would he care?

"So what are we to do?" the queen asked.

Bronwyn thought quickly. She didn't know any townspeople in the city who might help, and rumors would spread if a young noblewoman and her son were found. The empress might learn about it quickly. Where was somewhere they could hide in safety? Maybe Rupert could help.

"I could hide you both in the kitchens," Bronwyn said.

"I beg your pardon?" Queen Matilda said.

"We could hide you in plain sight. You could both work in the kitchens. There're lots of servants, so you'd be busy and no one would know any different."

"But… I am not a servant. I am a queen," Queen Matilda said. "And I don't know the first thing about cooking."

Bronwyn smiled.

"I have a better idea," Crispin said. "We go into the city and beg sanctuary from the church. They have to give sanctuary to all who request it. And with the brothers to look after you, word could be sent to your husband to provide for your safety."

"A much better idea," Queen Matilda said. "Thank you. We'll do that." She chuckled. "Me, work in the kitchens."

They walked together through the darkness, into the woods. The wind howled and moaned through the trees, and twigs snapped loudly beneath their feet. "Where are we?" Queen Matilda asked.

"Outside Devizes."

"That makes sense. We were nearing Pewsey when we were attacked, I think. But it was so dark."

Bronwyn walked behind them to offer some sense of safety. But her thoughts lingered. What would happen when they reached the other men? The knights and men looking for the thieves behind the ransom might find them, and then what?

"Stop," Bronwyn said.

The others stopped. "What is it?" Crispin asked.

"It might not be safe. There are men looking for whoever captured the queen and prince and they will be searching for Lady Morwenna, since she came for the ransom." Bronwyn addressed the queen. "If we arrive with yourselves, they might deliver you both to the empress."

The queen made a noise. In the darkness, Bronwyn could see Eustace move closer to her.

"We split up," Crispin said.

"What? No." The queen held her son close to her side. "We are not getting separated."

"You must, Your Grace. They will suspect you both but won't bat an eye if Bronwyn brings a new hand to the kitchens." He turned to Bronwyn. "Keep the boy with you. I'll hide the queen at the local church."

She drew him aside for a moment and hissed, "We both know you are loyal to the empress. Why would you help them?"

"Perhaps because like you, I am unsure of where my loyalties lie. Or maybe I just have a soft spot for a mother and her child in need. It is clear they need help. Now stop dallying. Every minute we pause increases their chances of getting caught by the wrong people."

And just who are 'the wrong people' in his mind? she wondered. While she agreed they must hurry, she also questioned his loyalty. Was he allied to the empress or the queen? This was a prime opportunity for Crispin to turn the queen and prince over to the empress and take the credit. So why was he trying to hide them? Was he really that concerned over a mother and child?

"Is there a monastery or nunnery? Someone who would take us in?" the queen asked.

Crispin returned to Queen Matilda's side. "I can't be certain, Your Grace. And at this hour, we can't go knocking on doors in the middle of the night."

"Very well. Just get us out of here. I don't want to spend another night outdoors."

"Yes, Your Grace."

The group walked toward the trees. "Stay together," Crispin warned.

The sounds of men calling hit their ears as they grew closer. Men were running, and after a short time, they came up from the small ravine, climbing.

"All right. Bronwyn, you take the prince. I will see to the queen. Go."

The queen grasped Eustace close. "Stay safe, and obey the cook. I'll see you again soon. I promise." They hugged, and she released him. She gave Bronwyn a hard look, her face sketched in shadow from the moonlight. "Do not let my son come to harm, Mistress Blakenhale, or it will be the worse for you."

"I understand," Bronwyn said. She stood back and waited for Eustace to come to her.

He looked at her. "Who are you?"

"I'm nobody. Just a cook," she replied. They continued walking. "My name is Bronwyn."

"Will I really work in the kitchens?" he asked.

"Yes. If that is acceptable to you?"

"Oh, yes. I never get to go there."

She cracked a smile. "You might not be so excited once we get there. But it will be good cover for a while."

"Will I have to be there for very long?"

"No. Just so we can keep you safe." She asked, "What do you remember about the night you were attacked? How long were you in that pit?"

"A few days. It was dark when the men attacked us, and we were held prisoner somewhere. When I woke up, we were in the pit. It was horrible." He paused. "Can I have some food? I'm hungry."

"I'm sure you can."

He rubbed his stomach.

He and Bronwyn walked through the trees, to encounter some knights talking. "Oh, it's you. Who's this?"

"A boy I found wandering in the woods. He was lost. He's cold and hungry. I'm going to bring him back to the kitchens to warm up."

The knights ignored her then and waved her on.

They walked together, Eustace sticking close by her as they reentered through the gates.

Rupert appeared before them. "Bronwyn, we were looking for you. Where did you—" He stopped in his tracks. His eyes widened and his mouth dropped open. "Pr—"

"Rupert, meet Wat. I found him lost in the woods." The name tumbled out on her tongue and she felt heartsick about it. Wat had been the name of her father's young apprentice, barely ten years old. He'd been a blond ruffian who'd loved sweet honey cakes. She wondered if he was still alive. If not, she was keeping his memory alive by passing on his name, she supposed.

Rupert swallowed and mastered himself, tugging at his collar. He nodded. "Hullo, Wat. I'm Rupert."

The young men bowed to one another, pretending they had just met.

"I'll show you the way," Rupert said. Quietly, to Eustace, he said, "I'm so glad you're all right. Are you well?"

"Well enough. We were in a pit when this girl and a knight saved us."

"Who?"

"Crispin," Bronwyn said.

"Oh." A beat later. Rupert said, "That was lucky."

"I'm hungry." Eustace's stomach growled. "And I'm cold. Where can I get something to eat?"

"I'll show you," Rupert said.

Bronwyn followed them to the kitchens, where they fed him a bit of leftover potage and a hunk of bread.

"That's it?" Eustace asked, eating at one of the worktables.

"You're going to have to get used to plain fare while you're here," Rupert said. "Just pretend it's a game. It's only for a little while."

Eustace burped and rubbed his stomach. "Done."

Sure enough, he'd polished off the hunk of bread and the leftover potage. He let out a huge yawn. "Where's my room?"

Bronwyn and Rupert exchanged a look. "Eu—"

"'Wat.' Call me 'Wat,'" Eustace said.

"Wat, there is no room for you. No bed, either," Bronwyn told him.

The prince's mouth dropped open. "What?"

"Servants tend to sleep on the floor," Rupert said.

"What, in the dirt?"

"No, but… you'll see." Rupert rubbed the back of his neck.

"But I am a prince. I am…"

"You're Wat, a boy lost in the woods, for the next few days," Bronwyn said.

Eustace looked at her in dismay. "But…"

Rupert said, "Come with me. I'll get you a spot near the fire." He grinned.

"Okay." Eustace wiped his mouth. "D'you think my mother is all right?"

"I'm sure she's fine." Rupert glanced at Bronwyn. "Good night." He pressed her hand and gave it a squeeze. "You have done an honorable thing this night. Thank you."

His hand was warm, but all too soon, it was gone. She felt a warm tingle from his touch, but it soon faded.

Bronwyn cleaned up the empty trencher and watched them go.

But as she made her way out of the kitchen, she bumped into Theobold.

She stepped back and looked at him with a familiar sense of hurt. "Sorry." She moved to walk past him when he said, "Wait. It's you I've been looking for."

"Why?" Curiosity filled her, and her chest tightened. Was he filled with regret for breaking off their romance? Did he want to get back together with her again? A part of her dared to hope.

He let out a breath. "The person who was running to collect the ransom? It was Lady Morwenna. The empress's men captured her. She's in the prison cells now."

Lady Morwenna. So she had run off, but not to safety. Had she been unlucky, or had her capture been part of her own scheming plot? Bronwyn wondered.

"She was the one I spotted trying to collect the ransom money at the start. I ran after her in the woods," she said.

"Yes, you look it," he said unkindly. "You've got a stick in your hair."

"I do?" She put a hand to her hair and pulled out a twig. "Oh."

She felt foolish for hoping. And partly angry at him for pointing out the state of her hair. She'd run after Morwenna in order to help, but now she wondered why.

"We fought in the woods and got lost. I guess she went back for the money."

"Yes, we captured her." He ran a hand through his black hair and shifted on his feet.

"At least then the empress will know of Lady Morwenna's deceit."

"'Deceit'? How can you say that?" Theobold gave her a hard stare. "There is nothing to suggest she is at fault here."

"Excuse me?" Bronwyn put her hands on her hips. "Are you that foolish that you refuse to see what is in front of you? She was caught trying to take the ransom money. She was stealing from the empress. What more proof do you need?"

Theobold shook his head. "There is more to it than that. These matters are not so one-sided, you know. And there is no proof to suggest that Lady Morwenna was anything other than a pawn in someone else's plan."

They frowned at each other, neither budging.

"Think, Bronwyn. Rupert says the queen's party were attacked by men, likely hired mercenaries. I hardly think one young noblewoman like Lady Morwenna could succeed in that alone."

He had a point. But his mention of Lady Morwenna's noble status stung her. If he thought so lowly of a lady's ability to pull off a scheme like this, how low was she herself in his estimation? Lower than dirt, she suspected. She now wondered how they had come to fancy each other at all.

He swallowed. "I am going to interrogate her in the morning, once the empress has been told."

Ah. Bronwyn recognized now why he was so uncomfortable,

and a part of her heart went out to him in sympathy.

As the descendant of a line of executioners, Theobold came from a family profession that was revered by some but reviled by more. He disliked the trade of questioning and putting people to the rack, or using whatever methods necessary to get answers. It was why he'd worked so hard to train as a squire, in the hopes of becoming a knight and bringing true nobility and respect to his family, whilst breaking away from their profession.

But that didn't mean everyone agreed with his decision, and sometimes the order came for him to interrogate prisoners. If the order came from the empress herself, he could not ignore it. And such was his loyalty to Maud, he would not.

"Is there no one else?" she asked quietly.

"No. No one." He turned a shade paler.

"Perhaps she will submit to your questions and not try to hide anything. She'll feel more comfortable around you, anyway, considering."

He looked at her, a question in his eyes.

"Your family connection, I mean. She knows you. And you'll be able to tell if she is lying."

His mouth twisted. "I wouldn't expect her to lie—ever. She is a noblewoman. Lady Morwenna has been taught better than that."

"Ha." Bronwyn laughed, and it was bitter. How little he knew her. "Have you forgotten she was behind the plot to steal the empress's crown earlier this year? And that while you were inconveniently locked in a room, she was fleeing the city?" She snorted and shook her head. "You either have a poor memory, or... you are very trusting. Good luck."

"Bronwyn." He put a hand out to stop her.

"What?" she asked rudely.

"You might be questioned too."

"What?" She stared at him as he lowered his hand.

"The men saw you run after her. I saw you. For her to return and be captured, but for me to find you back here... it doesn't seem right. Not to me."

"I ran after her. We fought and fell down an incline. I hit my head and when I woke, she was gone. By the time I got back to the gate, the men were gone."

"And so I find you in the kitchens, when you should be asleep."

"I was hungry."

He sniffed. "Fine. But if I find out you're lying to me…"

She faced him. "Are you telling me as a friend or an interrogator?"

His face turned red. "That's not what I meant."

"Isn't it? Why all the questions, then?"

He muttered something.

"What was that?"

"I said, would you believe that I was worried?"

"About losing your precious Lady Morwenna. Yes, I do believe it."

"No, you fool. I was worried about *you*." His gaze darted to her lips.

She glared at him, her chest rising and falling. Damn him. Damn his good looks, his dark eyes that haunted her, his fair skin and touch that sent shivers down her body. Damn the sneering tilt of his mouth, and his muscular body that looked good enough to touch. And damn him most of all for making her feel this way. She didn't want to think about him. She didn't want to feel—

Their eyes met. Hot fury met cold steel.

He grabbed her arm and pulled her to him, crushing his lips to hers.

Chapter Six

THEOBOLD'S LIPS WERE bruising.

Bronwyn hated and loved it at the same time. This wasn't like any of Theobold's former kisses.

This was harsh, rough, and brutal. His hands curled up in her messy hair and tangled in the blonde strands, and she pressed harder against him, relishing the muscular feel of his body beneath his shirt and trousers. The sword scabbard banged against her leg painfully, but she didn't care.

She felt him lean more into the kiss, his hands dropping to her waist as he pulled her closer. Pressed so tightly against him, the roughness of his jerkin rubbed against her chest, teasing her. Something awakened within her, and she began to feel warm between her legs with arousal.

He broke off the kiss. "Bronwyn, I—"

She shoved Theobold back, hating herself for ripping him away.

He grunted and backed into a stone wall.

"Don't ever do that again."

He glared at her, his lips rough. His eyes were dark with desire, like the moon with shooting stars, black pools of night. He was angry. But the slow smile that curled at the corners of his mouth and knew better... It made her heart flutter.

He'd tasted salty and she wanted to kiss his neck and taste more of him.

It made her angrier. Why had she fallen into his arms so quickly? She was furious with herself.

He took a step toward her.

She backed up.

He came closer.

She met his eyes for one fleeting moment, then ran.

His laughter filled her ears as she ran away, toward the main hall. As she got closer, she slowed down. Her heart pounded in her chest. She took a few deep breaths to calm herself and walked quietly into the main hall, toward the sleeping forms of servants.

The fire in the hearth was mostly quiet now, with a few glowing embers. Her eyes had adjusted enough to the darkness that she could see the sleeping servants well enough, and so she tiptoed around them and found a place to sleep against the wall.

As she lay awake and watched the others sleep, their chests rising and falling and the air punctuated with snores, she touched her lips. They felt bruised and rough. She'd never had a kiss like that before, not from Theobold—from anyone. This had been different.

And the self-satisfied smile on his face, like a cat that had gotten all the cream. The sight of his eyes as they'd raked up and down her body, how they'd tarried by her lips, and the touch of him as he'd lost his hands in her hair and pulled her close.

The rush of it, how the kiss had surprised her and teased her. How it had diffused both of their anger in a second.

How it had pained her to push him back and reject him, when her body had wanted more.

It was some time before she fell asleep.

THE NEXT MORNING, Bronwyn was shaken awake by another servant nudging her in the side with his foot. "Get up, sleepy. You can't sleep the day away."

Bronwyn yawned and winced. Her body ached from the fight and tumble in the woods with Lady Morwenna. Her arms were sore, her leg muscles ached, and her sides felt bruised. She sat up and gingerly pulled back some of her wool dress to examine her legs. Sure enough, there were small cuts on her legs.

She rose and remembered what Theobold had mentioned about her hair. Bronwyn reached to her head and shook out her hair. Little leaves, dirt, and twigs fell out. She let out a little sigh of disgust. And to think, Theobold had kissed her when she'd been like this. He'd put his hands in her hair. Good Lord.

She brushed down her skirts and stretched, yawning again. She needed a bath. But there curled up by the fire, lay Eustace and Rupert.

A moment later, Rupert stirred and rose, stretching with a loud yawn. He seemed to remember his surroundings and glanced over at the young prince. He met Bronwyn's gaze and nodded hello.

She met him across the room. "Good morning," she said quietly.

"Morning." He motioned to the sleeping form of Eustace. "What do we do about him?"

"If you can stay and watch him, I'll ask the cook if she could use another pair of hands."

"All right," he said. "We need to find him another set of clothes. He stinks, but his clothes are too fine. He'll stand out immediately."

"You're right."

They parted ways. She went to the kitchens and found the head cook, who looked her up and down. "Bronwyn, you're looking a bit rough today. What happened? Did you get into a fight?"

How right she was. "I got lost in the woods and fell down a small hill. Found a boy who was lost too."

The head cook raised an eyebrow.

"Not like that. I brought him back here until his mother could find him. Could he work in the kitchens for a few days? He's pretty dirty. I don't know how long he was out there."

"Yes, yes, of course. You should know by now, we always need more hands and I'll never turn down a mouth to feed. Bring him here."

"Um, he could use a bath first."

"All right."

A short while later, Bronwyn brought Eustace to a bath, where he could bathe in peace. While he bathed, she fetched some clothes for him and reentered the room.

He squeaked, and she heard a splash of water.

"It's only me," she said.

"You may enter," he said grandly.

Bronwyn snorted and closed the door behind her. "I brought you some clean clothes."

"But those are poor people's clothes."

She opened her eyes. He sat huddled in the tub, peering over the side.

She cocked her head. "Pr—Wat. These are what you'll wear while you're here."

"But…"

Bronwyn shook her head. "We have to keep you safe. You can't go walking around looking like… Like…"

He lowered his head glumly and kicked at the bathwater. "I hate this."

Just wait, Bronwyn thought, *it's going to get a lot worse.*

Once he'd dressed, she bundled up his old clothes and brought him down to the kitchen, where she introduced 'Wat' to the head cook.

"Well, you'll do, I suppose." Mistress Webb looked at him. "You ever wash a pot, boy? Or turn a spit?"

"No."

"Well, now's your chance. First, you eaten anything today?"

"No."

"Food first, then pot scrubbing. Come with me." She had a

kind touch about her, and she gently led Eustace to the main table and soon had a platter of bread and cheese in front of him.

Bronwyn crept back to the room where the bath was, shut the door tight, and had a bath in the remaining water. It was tepid and cool, but she didn't care. She was keen to get a moment to herself and get clean.

Once she was washed and dressed, she made ready to toss the prince's dirty clothes in the nearest fire, then paused. There may come a time when he would need to prove his identity, and his fine clothes would help do that. What if he needed them? Would it be better to hide them?

She decided to quickly wash them in the leftover bath water. They smelled and were dirty, so by the time she'd finished, so was the water. She rinsed them out and twisted them to get all the water out, then aired them as best she could in the small safety of the room. Bundling them in a small ball and looking for somewhere to put them, she decided to ask for help.

But as she walked outside, two guards marched by, followed by the empress.

Bronwyn immediately stood and knelt into a passing curtsy. She did not expect to see a pair of slippered feet stop before her. She looked up.

Empress Maud stood there in a fine, crimson dress, her silken hair pinned back into long braids, a gold circlet on her head. "Mistress Blakenhale," she said. "I believe I told you not to return to my court unless you'd found the missing royal bastards. Have you found them?"

Bronwyn hung her head, hoping her warming cheeks did not betray her. She felt an urge to wipe her sweaty palms on her dress and restrained herself from doing so. "No, Your Grace."

"Then what are you still doing here?"

"Doing washing, Your Grace."

"Haven't we laundresses for that?"

"I needed to bathe, Your Grace."

"Hmph. It sounds to me like you're dallying here when you

should be out looking for them. Do it now. I don't want to see you back here again."

"Empress," a voice said from the right.

Bronwyn and Empress Maud looked at the sight of Theobold striding toward them. He ignored Bronwyn entirely and bowed low to the empress. "Your Grace, there has been a development. We found one of the thieves who came to collect the ransom last night."

"Oh? Good. Let me see them."

"It is a person known to you, Your Grace." He spoke quietly. "It is the Lady Morwenna."

Did the empress turn pale? If so, she recovered her composure in an instant, Bronwyn thought.

"What on earth is my old lady-in-waiting doing mixed up in this foul business? Bring her to me at once."

"Your Grace. Awaiting your pleasure."

He does have a honeyed tongue. Bronwyn eyed him keenly, and for a split second, his eyes met hers, sending a blush skirting along her cheeks. She looked away.

"Very well. Bring her to me. I will receive her in the throne room."

He rubbed the side of his face. It sent a thrill through Bronwyn. She'd felt the rough scratches of his unshaven cheeks only hours ago.

"Forgive me, Your Grace, but is that wise? She sits in the prison cells."

The empress's eyes widened. "What is she doing there?"

"I thought—"

"You thought wrong. Take her out of there immediately. She is a lady and a member of my court."

"But, Your Grace…"

Bronwyn stared. It seemed the empress too, had a short memory when it came to Lady Morwenna.

"I will receive her anon. She may have made mistakes in the past, but she is a lady of my court and deserves better treatment than common criminals and miscreants. Bring her to me. And if she is harmed, I shall blame you." With that, the empress swept away in a flash of crimson skirts, her long braids snapping behind her back.

Theobold bowed as she left, then slowly raised his head.

Their eyes met. Bronwyn swallowed. "Good morning."

His pale face warmed into a smile. "Good morning. Sleep well?"

She looked away. "Excuse me. I—"

He stood in front of her. She could smell him. His warm breath, the musky scent of his skin. His eyes, brown like chestnuts, began darkening. His gaze lowered, down to her mouth.

She moved away.

"We have to talk, Bronwyn."

"We have nothing to talk about."

He reached for her wrist, but she slipped away.

As she walked down the corridor, she heard his dry chuckle. It sent a shiver down her spine.

Back in the kitchen, Bronwyn kept an eye on the prince, who was a little quiet at first but had soon made fast friends with the other children. A smart lad, he stuck to the story about being lost in the woods.

Bronwyn had safely stowed the boy's damp clothes in Lady Alice's room and found the head cook waiting for her.

"He's a bright lad, that one. Shame he's gotten so lost. We'll look after him."

Bronwyn nodded and started to help with turning the spit for a large haunch of deer. She'd only been working a few minutes when a page came for her.

"Mistress Baker?" the young page asked.

"We're all bakers here, my duck. Who are you looking for?" the head cook asked.

The youth scratched his head. "The empress said to bring the baker's daughter."

Mistress Webb glanced at Bronwyn. "I'm guessing that means you. My father was a stonemason."

"Sorry." She ducked her head in apology.

"Never mind. If the empress wants you, there's naught what we can do about that. Go on."

Bronwyn went. She followed the page to the throne room, knocked, and was received. The room was empty but for a few men-at-arms, knights, and the empress. She felt Theobold's eyes on her as she entered the room. As she followed the page, she spotted Rupert standing on the sidelines.

Meeting her eyes, he gave her a slight nod and friendly smile. She moved on.

The page led her toward the empress, who sat on the large, wooden chair. Her eyes were like daggers, her mouth pinched. She said, "Lady Morwenna, repeat what you told me just now."

Lady Morwenna stood there before the small assembly of knights and guards. Her long, brown hair hung in dirty tangles and she swayed on her feet, then fell to her knees.

"Guards, help her."

Theobold was at her side in an instant, helping her to stand.

Lady Morwenna raised her head. Her thick hair hung in dirty waves by her shoulders, and her dress was tattered and worn. "I-I'm so sorry, Empress. I should never have fallen in with such a man. It was foolish of me, and wrong."

"What happened, Lady Morwenna? Tell us," the empress said.

"The man thought it a good idea to attack the party on their way to the hostage negotiation, and take Matilda of Boulogne and her son for ransom."

The room was still. Bronwyn couldn't even hear a person breathe.

Lady Morwenna continued. "I knew it was wrong. But I was in love, and even though I knew in my heart, it wasn't right, the man I love persuaded me to go along with his plan."

"So you both were behind the attack," Bronwyn said.

Lady Morwenna shot her a glare over her shoulder. "No. It was all him. I was a pawn. He knew of my loyalty to the empress and thought he was doing her a favor. He hired the mercenaries who attacked the party and killed the men. I only looked after the hostages and fed them so they wouldn't die. I never thought he would drop them into a pit."

Empress Maud's eyes widened. "Where are they now?"

Lady Morwenna lowered her head. "I don't know, Your Grace. In the darkness, they escaped. I know not where or how. They must have escaped when I was fighting with her." She pointed at Bronwyn.

Heads turned to her. The empress's eyebrows rose. "You were fighting with Lady Morwenna?"

"Yes," Bronwyn said. "I did." Stepping forward so she stood no longer behind Morwenna, but at the same distance from the empress, just a few feet away. "I saw her collecting the ransom and wanted to catch her."

"But what were you doing there? There were knights already present."

"There was a bit of trouble with a drunk, Your Grace," Theobold said.

"Crispin, this cannot be right. One drunken man distracted your knights from catching one woman?"

Crispin colored but said nothing. He shot Theobold a dirty look.

"I see." To Bronwyn, the empress asked, "And how was it that you two began fighting?"

"I ran after her. I didn't know who it was, and we tumbled and fell."

"So you know where Matilda and her son are?" Empress Maud asked Lady Morwenna, who shook her head.

"Not anymore, Your Grace. They escaped during all the confusion."

Empress Maud banged her fist on the wooden armrest, making a few people jump. "That is it. Such incompetence. I cannot stand it. Not in my court." She seethed and stood, her pale face pinched and angry. Her hands clenched into fists, and she stalked forward like an angry cat.

Bronwyn gripped her skirts. Lady Morwenna had run away. Could it be she had done so to avoid being identified by Crispin as being involved, or because she did not want to be recognized by the queen? Either way, it was curious behavior.

The empress whirled around. "Crispin. I value your ambition to lead, but this mission was clearly above your capabilities. You have much to learn."

Crispin bowed his head.

"I cannot overlook the fact that you were leading this mission to catch the mercenaries behind the queen's disappearance, even if it was only a woman. And for none of your men to catch her at all, but a baker's daughter…" The empress tutted. "I trusted you. I put my faith in you."

"My men were dealing with an incident, and I did catch the Lady Morwenna," Crispin started.

"Yes, very convenient, that."

"Seems to me it's more like the baker girl did and you helped," one knight said, earning a dirty look from Crispin.

The empress said, "It wouldn't surprise me if she'd come of her own accord. Did she?"

Lady Morwenna gave a little shake of her head.

"Fine. Lady Morwenna, it pleases me to see you return to court after the situation in London last June. You are welcome here. I trust you have seen the error of your ways."

"Oh, yes, Your Grace." Morwenna fell to her knees in a deep curtsy. "Ever so much. I'll never trust him again."

"Good. But on that note, who was he? Your lover?" the empress asked.

"I… I daren't say."

Bronwyn stared. Lady Morwenna was hiding the man's identity? Why?

"Why is that? No doubt he abandoned you to be found, once

he saw you were unable to successfully recover the ransom. I would guess he fled. Am I right?"

"Yes, Your Grace."

"You must have loved him very much," Empress Maud said kindly.

"I did, Your Grace. I still do." Lady Morwenna inhaled noisily. "Even if he has made an error in judgment, I still love him."

"That is very noble of you, but of little use to me. Am I right in thinking you do not know where the prisoners are?"

"That is correct, Empress."

Empress Maud turned to the nearest knight. "Find them. Search the woods, and the city. Inquire if there have been any sudden mothers with children begging for aid. See if anyone took them in. I'll bet someone did. Find them."

She added, "Crispin, Theobold, join the search. I want them found immediately. And if anyone has been hiding them, I want them brought in for questioning. This is *my* city. Any conspirators will be judged guilty of treason against their empress." Her voice rang out like the cold steel.

Bronwyn stiffened and clutched the sides of her skirts. She raised her head, staring straight forward. She did not wish to attract the empress's attention, or worse, her ire.

Empress Maud turned to Theobold, her skirts swirling by her feet. Her expression brooked no argument. "You may dislike your family's profession, but if I have need of it, I will use you, Theobold. You will need to interrogate anyone who dares hide such highly prized prisoners."

Theobold stiffened and hung his head. He let go of Lady Morwenna, who then entwined her arm with his. She wasn't letting him go so easily, Bronwyn noticed.

"As for you, Mistress Baker…" The empress approached her. "You are far too mixed up in this business. Wherever I find trouble, you are not far away."

"Let us make use of her, Empress." To Bronwyn, Sir Miles Fitzwalter, one of the empress's loyal followers and most trusted advisors, stepped forward.

Bronwyn tried to hide her revulsion, but the thin man made her skin crawl. He clasped his hands as if in prayer, and he spoke so calmly, his voice slithered like oil over her. She wanted to bathe after being in his presence. His eyes were knowing and stared right through her. They both knew he had tried to have her killed. Would he try again?

Sir Miles said, "Go to Bristol Prison and bring a message to the chatelaine there, Lady Mabel. Tell her that Stephen's little wife and son are lost, and unharmed, at least by us. This was not our doing. By the Grace of God, he will find them again."

Bronwyn swallowed. "What of the hostage situation with Sir Robert of Gloucester?"

The empress tapped a long index finger against her chin. "Hmm. Say we are searching for his family, but that is only a matter of time. Have him send Sir Robert and we will return his wife and son to him."

Bronwyn wrinkled her nose. Such demanding terms would not tempt anyone with a bit of sense to agree to that.

"Why send a kitchen maid as a messenger? Surely, there are pages, messengers, and knights who could do a better job," a knight said.

The empress's face reddened. Bronwyn swallowed. She had been sent on missions by Sir Miles before, and at least once before, he had sent her to die, only to be surprised when she hadn't. Now she was barely questioning the logic at all, she simply hoped to survive.

"Your Grace," Theobold began, "perhaps that is too hasty. He is, after all, the ruler of Winchester and has Sir Robert in his prison."

Bronwyn thought grimly how easily the queen's contributions to the battle at Winchester were overlooked. It was Queen Matilda who had raised an army and routed the empress from her stronghold at Winchester while her husband had sat in prison hundreds of miles away. Yet her achievements were being overlooked. Bronwyn greatly disliked Theobold at that moment and shot him a dirty look.

"Yes, I know," the empress snapped. "And I did not ask for your opinion, Theobold. You are not a knight, but a squire. If I have want of your opinion, I will ask for it. Until then, be a good chap and stay quiet."

Theobold shut his mouth and turned a shade pink.

"Go. I shall think on the best course of action. You are all dismissed. Lady Morwenna, come. I am sure you are in need of rest. You are clearly in want of a bath."

Lady Morwenna inclined her head. "I am ever grateful, Your Grace."

"Bah." The empress shot Lady Morwenna a half-smile. "It does me good to see you again, Lady Morwenna. Be welcome."

The empress left, with Morwenna in her wake. Bronwyn stood by as Morwenna shot a triumphant smile in her direction and tried not to roll her eyes.

But the empress's words about the people hiding the queen and prince had sent a shiver down Bronwyn's spine. She hoped to God that Crispin had helped the queen hide or escape. But it was also clear they had to move soon. The longer they waited in the castle, the greater the likelihood of discovery, and Bronwyn didn't want a prince's death on her conscience.

Chapter Seven

A MINSTREL AND jongler played in the distance as Bronwyn returned to the kitchen, her thoughts askew. This was a dangerous game she had begun to play. Anyone caught hiding the queen and prince would be interrogated by Theobold and possibly killed. For what other punishment could there be for treason? She dreaded to think of it.

She kept an eye on Eustace, although he didn't need any looking after, she discovered. He had made friends with the other children and he certainly ate as fast as them, wolfing down his food at the midday meal with the others.

But as Bronwyn worked with bread dough to make rolls for the noble families and loaves for the evening meal, she heard a polite cough at her shoulder. She turned around.

There stood Crispin. He helped himself to a cooked bread roll that was cooling on a tray. He tossed it in the air and caught it deftly, then bit into the soft roll. "Did you make this?"

"No. One of the other cooks."

He nodded, chewing.

"Did you need something?" she asked.

"I wanted to talk to you. This seemed like as good a reason as any." He held up the half-eaten roll. "I see you secured your part of the deal."

Hiding Prince Eustace in plain sight, he meant. "Yes. And you?"

"Well enough." He leaned forward. "She's claimed sanctuary in a nunnery on the other side of the city. No one will notice anything different."

She kneaded the dough on the worktable before her, picking it up and slapping it on the table to knock the air out of it. "What of the empress?" she asked quietly. "They can't stay like this forever." She wondered again why was he helping the queen and prince. Was his loyalty really so fickle that he was ready to help both sides, so long as it suited him? She trusted him less because of it. But then, she realized, she was no different. And yet she just couldn't trust him. Not fully.

"Aye. I say give it a few days. Let the searches continue. Once they fail and the empress's men stop looking, then we take them out."

"Take what out?" Philippa asked behind him. "What are you two talking about?"

"Why, only that I want to order a fresh haunch of pork to be served and dinner, and capons, and hens, and I wanted to ask Mistress Bronwyn if she can take them out to the empress's dinner table on time."

"Oh. Can you?" Philippa asked.

"I'm sure we can manage." Bronwyn and Crispin looked at Philippa, who stood there patiently. "Did you need something?"

"Yes. A bowl of broth or soup for Lady Morwenna. She's feeling a bit poorly after her ordeal."

"'Her ordeal'?" Bronwyn repeated.

"Oh, yes. You must not have heard. She was attacked in the woods and threw herself at the empress's mercy. She's a lady-in-waiting, and she's hired me to look after her."

"I see." Bronwyn tried not to smirk. 'Attacked.' Was that was she was calling it?

Bronwyn quickly ladled out some broth into a bowl and handed it to Philippa on a tray with a spoon.

"Thanks." Philippa paused. "The infirmary's not the same without him."

"Without whom?" Bronwyn asked.

"Squire Rupert, of course. Have you talked to him?" Her round face was hopeful.

"No, not really."

"Oh. I thought you two were friends. Well, if you see him, could you tell him I said *hello*?"

"I'll do it," Crispin said. "Best run along now. You don't want Lady Morwenna's soup to get cold."

Philippa left, soup tray in hand.

Crispin watched her go. "There's something funny about her."

"You mean besides the crush she has on Rupert?"

He grinned. "Jealous?"

She thought of Theobold. His hands. His lips. She shook her head. "No."

"Sure? I wouldn't blame you. You could do better, of course, but there's no accounting for taste."

She laughed at him. "Go on, before I throw flour at you."

He stole another bread roll and fled with a wave.

Bronwyn snorted and returned to her work. She realized, whoever was Morwenna's lover, had also masterminded the plot to hire mercenaries and attack the queen's party, and he was still out there. Theobold's logic had been correct: there was no way Morwenna could have orchestrated it all alone. She'd have needed help.

She paused, her hands halfway through shaping a roll. Lady Morwenna and her lover couldn't have known where the queen's party would be and when without help. They would have had forewarned knowledge about the party's location and the number of men; otherwise, they wouldn't have been able to overpower them. But that meant that someone back in Winchester knew of this plot.

There was a traitor in the king's court. But who?

Bronwyn thought quickly. The person wouldn't have gone with them in the party, or they'd risk being killed, unless they had run away and abandoned the party at the first sign of trouble. But if that were the case, then surely, they would have appeared at Devizes in a manner similar to Rupert, claiming innocence.

She stiffened. Was Rupert truly innocent? Or had it been a ruse to avoid suspicion?

She rolled and shaped the bread rolls and set them aside to bake. As she washed her hands in a bucket and dried them with her apron, she thought it was more likely that whoever had hired the mercenaries had also known of the queen's plan to travel from Winchester and head over for the prisoner exchange.

The fact that there had been no message or word of the queen and her son arriving safely would have alerted the king that something was wrong. She would have to alert the king that there was a traitor in his midst.

She thought of Sir Robert of Gloucester, sitting in the cells in Winchester, having been captured at the last battle. Could he be behind this? He was loyal to the empress. But was he the mastermind behind a plot that would ultimately throw a wrench into the hostage negotiations and financially hurt his empress?

She doubted it. Of what she knew of Sir Robert, he was strong, loyal, and smart and with a fierce fighting arm and code by which he lived. But he was not a schemer. Not like others in the royal courts.

She nodded to herself. The sooner she traveled to Bristol Prison, the better.

She went to discuss this with Rupert, whom she found outside in the castle courtyard, training at arms with the other men. They held mock battles and fights with wooden training swords and practiced archery while some of the noble ladies looked on.

While Rupert fought with another young man, Crispin fired an arrow at a practice target from some distance away. He must have struck the target, for the group of ladies nearby clapped and congratulated him.

"Wishing you were one of them?" a voice asked at her shoulder.

She turned around. "Mistress Agatha." She tried to hide her chagrin at seeing one of her least-favorite people.

The empress's taster nodded in greeting. "It must be hard, being a servant like yourself. You spend your hours toiling away in the kitchen, whereas we have more important things to do."

"Like what?"

The taster puffed up her chest for a moment but also slouched, and so the effect was lost. The blonde woman pushed back a curl from her face and crossed her arms beneath her chest. "We talk, and do needlework, and flirt with the men, and play music. We gossip and learn all of each other's secrets. Especially the empress's."

"Do not speak too loudly, Mistress. The empress won't like you saying that," a familiar voice said.

It was Theobold. He stepped out from the shadows and stood beside Bronwyn, leaning against the wall.

Bronwyn tried not to show the thrill that coursed through her. "Excuse me." She moved away, back into the corridor that would lead to the kitchens. Then for a reason unbeknownst to her, she paused to listen.

"Hello, Theobold," Agatha said. "I heard about your little romance ending with the kitchen maid. It's about time you came to your senses."

"Mistress Agatha. Surely, you have better things to do than annoy the servants."

The taster made a sulking noise. "I'm not annoying. But I'd much rather spend my time with you."

He snorted. "I'm not interested. And don't believe everything you hear, Agatha. Especially the lies you concoct yourself."

"We could help each other, you know," she said.

He snorted.

"The empress doesn't trust you due to the low company you keep. It's a common joke amongst her ladies. Do you not wonder why she gave the opportunity to lead the nighttime mission to another squire, a stranger, and not you, whom she knows and is the squire of her closest ally?"

Bronwyn leaned in closer. Had their relationship not only been disapproved of by his master, but the empress as well?

"And how could you be of any use to me?" His voice was low, almost seductive.

Mistress Agatha's voice grew husky in response. "I would tell you about our conversations. Private plans of the empress, meant for our ears alone."

"I don't care about the idle talk of court ladies," he said.

"You will when it's about you. And now that Lady Morwenna is back, many more of our talks discuss you."

"What do you want?"

"You have your future to think of... and I have mine."

Bronwyn could sense his hesitation. And his curiosity.

Agatha continued. "I want to find a husband."

"Mistress Agatha, I—" he started.

"I haven't finished," she said archly. "I know I'm not so young as the rest of her ladies. But I dislike the looks I get from some of the other women at court."

"Are you not surprised? You were involved in plots to disturb the empress and your pranks hurt others. Is it any wonder they stare at you?" Theobold asked.

"They look at me with pity," she hissed. "Disdain. They have their husbands and families, but I do not."

"I do not think that is why. You pretended to be sick when you were not. Your antics threw the entire court into an uproar. All for a nasty trick. Frankly, I'm surprised the empress still tolerates you here at all."

The taster sniffed. "The empress is also a good Christian woman, and merciful. She is forgiving of those who truly repent."

He rolled his eyes. "Ah. So there we get to the heart of the matter. You threw yourself at her feet and begged her forgiveness, is that it? You said you were sorry for being blackmailed into tormenting her and promised never to do it again. By God, she must dearly need a taster to forgive someone like that."

Mistress Agatha's sniff grew louder.

"But you have the ear of the empress. She trusts you."

"Yes. And I will admit, I like the attention being her official taster brings. But I…" She muttered something.

"What was that?"

"I'm lonely," Agatha said. "Help me find a husband."

Theobold grunted. "And just how do you expect me to do that?"

"Walk with me. Pay your respects to me. Dance with me. If men see you paying attention to me, they might notice me too. Men love what they can't have. And stop skulking around corners with that little kitchen maid."

Bronwyn's head snapped up.

"You are only doing yourself a disservice being with her. Stop wasting your time. You'll only break her heart."

Bronwyn leaned against the wall. What if it was too late for that?

"You have been nothing but rude at the best of times. Why would I help you?" Theobold asked.

"Because I have the empress's ear. And I can make sure you are in her favor again. You have been a squire for years, haven't you?"

"What of it?"

"Every young man needs a leg up over the competition. You don't want to be a squire forever, do you?" She paused. "Your master sits in Stephen's prison. If he's smart, he's looking after himself. Who's to say he hasn't forgotten about you already?"

"You clearly don't know knights and their squires very well," Theobold said.

"Maybe not. But it's not escaped me that you are no longer in the empress's favor, while other squires are on the rise. Think of my offer. I won't wait forever." Her footfalls faded away.

Theobold cursed and walked after her, his boots crunching against the stones and pebbles on the dirt path.

Bronwyn waited until they both were gone, then let out a

noisy breath. Whatever plans she wanted to make to secure the safety of Eustace and the queen, she'd have trust in Crispin and Rupert.

She went back to the kitchens and did her work. The kitchens felt like a relatively safe space where she could think and work in peace. Here at least, she could do work and be appreciated, not be put down or viewed as lesser than by others.

There was still a sort of pecking order within the castle kitchens amongst the cooks, but that was always the way. Cooks wanted to climb and advance, either for the greater prestige, reputation, or money. Some just liked being in charge. From what she had seen, running a kitchen was like captaining a ship. It demanded control and the work of many hands, and if things failed, then it would be the head cook to blame.

Bronwyn wanted no part of such great responsibility and felt a pang of homesickness for her father's bakery in her hometown of Lincoln, now an empty shell, taken over by squatters.

Theobold had taken her back there once to search for her family, but they were gone. She didn't even know they were alive. She hoped they were. And in that moment, she decided she would try to look for them. Or even just find word if they lived. She had to.

Filled with new determination, she visited the infirmary and walked in on Rupert standing close with Philippa. "Oh."

They both started and stepped apart. Rupert glanced at her, a rose in his hands, whilst Philippa plucked it from him and glared at Bronwyn. "What are you doing here?"

"I came to check and see if there were any sick people who needed food."

"Well, you can see there aren't, so you can leave." Philippa's voice was nasty.

"Philippa," Rupert said.

"Sorry." Her tone wasn't sorry at all. To Bronwyn, she said, "If there's nothing else?"

"No. Sorry to interrupt." Bronwyn turned on her heel and

left, when a minute later, Rupert joined her.

"What are you doing?" she asked him.

"What do you mean? I'm walking with you." He gave her a friendly grin.

"That's not what I mean. Why were you giving her a rose?"

"I was being nice. She looked after me when I was sick and never left my side. Unlike some people."

"What's that supposed to mean? I visited you."

"I know you did."

"Lady Alice did too."

"Did she? Because I can't remember her ever doing that. All I remember is Philippa, and you. And then no one believing me."

She touched his shoulder. "Lady Alice visited. She believed you too."

"Then why is she ignoring me whenever I try to talk to her? Why does she leave whenever I draw near? It's embarrassing. I don't have to put myself up for such punishment."

"So you're giving other young women roses instead?"

He sulked. "It was just a nice gesture."

"Maybe. But you'll break hearts if you keep doing that."

He muttered, "Maybe I want to."

She shot him a look. "Rupert."

"What?"

"I'm going to pretend I didn't hear that."

"There's no harm in it," he said. "Maybe I just wanted to give her a rose to say *thank you*. You read too much into these things, Bronwyn. Just like maybe I wanted to walk with you."

She raised an eyebrow and kept walking. "We need to send Wat home soon."

"Yes. And I need to find my master."

She cocked her head at him.

He spoke in a quieter voice, looking around. "My master sits with Stephen in Bristol Prison. I've been apart from him for too long. Once he is freed, I will need to look after him and do what we can to further the king's cause. But until then, I need to distinguish myself somehow."

"You will."

"Not so far. All I've done is serve in the empress's court and gotten involved in a bungled attempt at catching a person demanding a ransom. Crispin and Theobold led greater parts than me," he said glumly, shuffling his feet.

"And yet you helped that young boy, who was lost in the woods. That's not nothing," she said for anyone who might have been listening.

He gave a half-shrug. "Aye."

"Why are you at odds with the other squires? You normally make friends so easily. I always saw you surrounded by people at court before."

"In Lincoln, you mean," he said gently, referring to the time before both their worlds had changed forever.

"Yes."

"Ever since then, I don't know. Life has become so busy, so hectic. But life as a squire, you're either looking after your master or thinking about becoming a knight."

"Is it hard, being a squire?"

"Sometimes. It's not unlike being a page, or serving as a lady's maid, I'd guess. It's just, you look after your master as best you can. If he wakes and wants food, you fetch it. You wash his shirts if you're on the road or make sure the maids don't tear them in the laundry. You have his shield and sword sharpened, polished, and ready."

"And eventually he rewards you with knighthood?" Bronwyn asked.

"There's more to it than that. A squire needs to do something, to distinguish himself. This could be in battle, or at tournaments. But it's got to be special. Men need to talk about it. I need to become worthy of being a knight, and it's more than just saying the right words at dinner and smiling at the ladies."

"Now I know why you're always practicing at swords."

He nodded. "Aye. We need to sharpen our skills, just in case.

There's always another potential fight around the corner, so you can't be soft. Speaking of which, you're looking a bit…"

"What?" She gave him a direct look.

He held back a laugh, the corners of his eyes crinkling. "Nothing. Just looks like you've been in a fight."

"Well, you know I have."

"That I do. How's the other one look?"

It was Bronwyn's turn to shrug. She muttered, "It's not fair."

"What do you mean?"

Bronwyn looked up and down the corridor. They were alone. She said quickly, "Lady Morwenna has openly caused trouble for the empress and demanded a ransom. She was part of the plot to attack the queen's party and yet nothing happens to her. No punishment. If anything, the empress is feeling sorry for her."

"Why is that?" Rupert scratched his head.

"Lady Morwenna fed her a story that she was so in love with the man behind the plot, she did whatever he asked. And she refused to give him up. So we don't even know who it was."

"What does Theobold think?"

Bronwyn's mouth turned downward. "I don't know. Maybe ask Mistress Agatha."

"Agatha? The taster? Why would I ask her?"

Her voice sounded bitter. "Because she has asked Theobold to pretend to court her, and he's considering it."

"What?" Rupert's sharp retort echoed in the corridor. He took her by the shoulder and spun her around to face him. "You mean to tell me he ends things with you, only to court an older woman? Ye Gods, she must be nearly fifty."

Bronwyn avoided his eyes. Her gaze fell to her shoes. Then she snorted. "It could be worse."

"How?"

"It could be Lady Morwenna."

He laughed. "That truly would be worse. Although honestly, whichever woman he chooses to be with, I hope he's happy. They deserve each other."

She turned. "I have to go."

"Bronwyn, wait."

She hurried on ahead, bumping into Crispin.

He said, "Oh, hello there. I was looking for you. We need to talk." He looked past her, over her shoulder at Rupert's approaching form. "Hullo there."

"Crispin."

The men nodded to each other. Crispin said, "Well, if you'll excuse us, we have some things to discuss."

Bronwyn didn't need to see Rupert's face to know his mood had changed. "You know where to find me, Bronwyn." He walked away.

They waited for him to leave, then Bronwyn said, "What did you want to talk to me about?"

"Your friend. How much does he know? About what happened that night, I mean."

"He bumped into me escorting… the young boy we found in the woods, Wat, back at the gates," Bronwyn said. She waved her hands at the sight of Crispin's alarmed face. "But it's not bad. He and Wat already knew each other. They recognized each other instantly. It's fine."

Crispin ran a hand through his brown hair. "It's not fine. It's one more thing we have to worry about. What did you say when they saw each other?"

"Not a lot. He helped sneak us back into the castle. Beyond that, he's helped Wat get used to life here. That's all." She looked into his steely-blue eyes that somehow reminded her of a winter morning. "He can be trusted. I trust him."

"If you say so." He stood back. "I wanted to let you know the empress has sent a messenger to Bristol Prison, to alert the people there."

Bronwyn tensed. "Will the messenger say—"

He shook his head. "You think like a woman. Always with your heart. It's nice, but not right in this instance. You need to think like a ruler. Empress Maud sent a messenger, all right, but she's going to use this to her advantage."

Her fingers darted to her mouth. "You don't mean… She's going to suggest that she has the queen and her son in her keeping?"

He shrugged. "I wasn't there for the particulars, so I don't know. But it's possible. I know I would."

"What will happen?"

He stood back as a pair of guards marched by, then spoke quietly. "If she's as devious as people say, then her messenger will do exactly as you imagined. The people at Bristol will believe she demands a ransom, and they'll pay it. Or risk losing the war."

"So she'll want them to believe that she can survive without Sir Robert of Gloucester, and that she has the queen and her son in her prison, here," Bronwyn said.

"Yes. She wants people to believe she holds all the game pieces. Wouldn't you?"

Bronwyn bit the inside of her cheek. "Yes. But it's not right. What are we to do with… you know?"

He nodded grimly. "I will make inquiries. The empress is displeased with you, isn't she?"

"Yes." She put her hands on her hips. "Thanks for reminding me."

"It's not that. I heard some of the ladies talking about it. The empress told you to leave and find Matilda of Boulogne and her son, and not come back without them. So I gather you'll be traveling soon, won't you? What if we were to add to your traveling party? No one would notice a few more, would they?"

"No."

He rubbed his hands together. "Excellent. I'll join the party, and then we can split off. I'll take them on to Bristol, you can continue on your way, and no one will be the wiser."

Bronwyn winced. "I don't like it. There're too many things that could go wrong."

"We don't have time to think like that. Sometimes in life you have to act, and thinking or tarrying too long will lose you that chance. In tourneys and tournaments, we have the same thing. The fight goes to the man who sees the opportunity and uses it to his advantage."

She glanced at him. "What is it you want, Crispin?"

"The same as every other squire, Bronwyn. To be a knight. And if I distinguish myself here and help bring our guests to their place of safety, then so much the better."

"Who is your master?" she asked.

His smile didn't reach his eyes. "Good old Sir Benedict of Almsbury. He's nearly eighty and needs more of a nursemaid than a squire. But he's a good man, and I look after him. I represent his interests here. Don't forget, we both serve the empress." His voice carried. "Now go back to the kitchens and act like everything is ordinary. Go about your chores. I'll come find you when I have a plan."

They parted ways, and she did as he'd instructed. But as she walked away, she couldn't help but feel a sneaking sensation along the back of her neck.

Bronwyn worked in the kitchens, until a page came by delivering a summons from the empress to bring some white rolls with honey. Without a word, she got to work. She made quick work of it and when they were ready, she called for the page to bring her to the empress.

Bronwyn was shown into a small, comfortable room, where the empress sat surrounded by her ladies.

Mistress Agatha shot her a triumphant look, while Lady Alice gave her a look of warning. The empress said, "Ah, Mistress Baker. I began to wonder if you were bringing me rolls at all." She motioned for Bronwyn to approach.

Bronwyn curtsied, which was no small feat, considering she held a platter of small round bread rolls, and brought the platter to the empress first, then the ladies. Lady Morwenna made her wait, keeping Bronwyn standing there, the platter outstretched to her, as she dithered and debated over which roll to choose.

Once each lady had taken a roll, eyes went to Agatha, who

nibbled delicately at hers. She swallowed and gave Bronwyn a level look. "They are edible. Not the finest."

Lady Morwenna snickered.

Bronwyn swallowed and stood back, the wooden platter clasped against her side.

"Now, I wanted to ask you, Mistress Baker. When are you leaving?"

She blinked. "Empress?"

"I believe I gave you an order. I told you to find the missing queen and her brat, and if I recall correctly, I told you not to return to my court until you found them."

"But—" Bronwyn held her tongue as the empress held up an imperious finger.

"No *buts*. You returned, anyway, a failure. The good Lady Morwenna has told me of your mistaking her for an attacker in the woods. I'm just glad she didn't come to any harm. We are relieved she returned to us."

Lady Morwenna smiled sweetly at the empress.

Bronwyn bit the inside of her cheek. The madness of the empress, to forgive and trust two women who had betrayed her. Was it because they were of nobler blood? She couldn't fathom it. Perhaps they truly had been contrite and had appealed to her Christian mercy. And yet… why was Lady Morwenna keeping it a secret about Bronwyn and Crispin's involvement in rescuing the queen and prince? Maybe she worried the empress wouldn't believe her, or perhaps she was biding her time for the right moment. The noblewoman was as ever, strategic, and seemed to excel in choosing the worst possible moment to cause trouble.

"As we do not know where that woman and her son are, I don't understand what you are still doing here." The empress turned the full force of her imperious gaze on Bronwyn. "So I ask again: when are you leaving?"

Bronwyn wanted to tremble and gripped the wooden platter more tightly against her side. "In the morning, Empress."

"Good." She turned to Agatha. "Tell me, did I see young

Theobold walking with you in the gardens this afternoon?"

Agatha blushed. "Yes, Your Grace. He wanted to show me the late summer blooms."

"How delightful. You are not too old, you know. He would be a good match for any woman of quality."

Bronwyn felt the empress's words as keenly as if the woman had slapped her cheeks. There it was. By the empress's insinuation, Theobold was free to court ladies of her retinue, but not Bronwyn, as a mere servant.

Her hand clenched. "By your leave, Your Grace, I will go back to the kitchens."

"Yes, yes, go." The empress waved a hand.

As Bronwyn curtsied and left, she heard a few titters and giggles behind. She left the door ajar and as she walked past the pair of guards, one woman said, "Why did you order rolls, Your Grace, when we'd just eaten?"

"I like her sweet rolls with honey. Besides, I wasn't going to bid her go before I'd had them again. That would be a waste of her talents."

More giggles.

"Do you really think she will find the queen and prince, Your Grace?" Lady Alice asked.

"What a silly question. Of course not. No one could. They're either hidden away or dead. Either way, it matters not to me. The kitchen maid is dismissed from my court, and I have no wish to see her again, unless she brings me something worthwhile. Like their heads." Her voice was chilling.

There was silence for a moment, when no one breathed.

"Now, let's have some more wine. And, Mistress Agatha, tell me all about your romance with young Theobold. He's quite handsome, you know."

The ladies tittered, and the moment had passed. So it was clear. Bronwyn was being dismissed. She felt cold somehow, and yet her face grew hot. She hurried back to the kitchens as fast as she could.

A short while later, Lady Alice paid a visit, whilst Bronwyn was scouring a greasy pot. Lady Alice walked into the kitchens like she owned them and strode over to her. The noblewoman took one look at the young potboys on either side of her, along with Wat, and narrowed her eyes. "Go."

The boys began to hurry away when she said, "Wait." She pointed at Wat. "You. I've seen you before."

Wat, a.k.a. Eustace, put on a blank expression. He shrugged.

"There are many young boys who run around the castle," Bronwyn said. "You probably saw him serving at dinner or clearing food away."

"Yes, that must be it. Go on, then." Lady Alice watched idly as the young boys disappeared. She made as if to lean against a table, then thought better of it, removing her hand in time from landing in a floury worktable. She blinked at Bronwyn. "The empress seeks to hurt you. I've never seen her this way before. She practically openly dismissed you from court. Why?"

"You were there. You saw—she caught Theobold and I kissing. She wants to punish me. I'm not a lady of quality." Bitterness crept into her tone again.

Lady Alice flicked a hand as if that were nothing. "Fine. But what do you know about this sorry business with the taster? Theobold and that woman, Agatha. She tuts and acts as if she were a lady before the new young women Maud has added to her court, but I know better."

Bronwyn knew she should hold her tongue, but she still thought of Lady Alice as a friend and liked sharing a bit of gossip as much as the next person. So she relayed what she had witnessed between Theobold and the taster.

"Ha. What fools, the pair of them," Lady Alice said. "Anyone can see he fancies you, and she is just jealous and seeks to use him."

"I rather think they plan to use each other. The empress seemed approving," Bronwyn pointed out.

"She likes a distraction. It doesn't look good for her ladies to go missing and her squires to go around kissing women in public. I rather think she wants us all to be more discreet in our liaisons." She looked Bronwyn in the eye. "Are you really going to leave?"

"I have no choice. She wants me to find the queen and prince." She hoped her tone was steady.

Lady Alice paused. "Honestly, sending you out there at this time of year, alone? It's a fool's errand. Their trail will have gone cold and there's no one to protect you. You might as well just flee her court and never come back," she said quietly. "I wish I could go with you. Where will you go?"

Toward Bristol, Bronwyn thought. "I don't know. I thought I might try to find them, and if I can't, then I'd go to Lincoln to find my family."

Lady Alice's slim black eyebrows rose. "Really? I thought they were all gone."

"I want to find out. They might have fled in the battle and come back. What if they're waiting for me?" Bronwyn dared hope.

"But what if they're all dead?" Lady Alice asked callously. "Sorry, that was harsh of me. But still. Surely, you would have had word by now as to whether they still lived."

"How? No one knows me or where I went. For all they know, I might've died."

"Or joined the empress's camp," Lady Alice said. "All right. And you'd leave me here. Honestly, it's so silly. Lady Morwenna is being insufferable, Mistress Agatha is acting like a silly lovesick girl, and the empress... is the empress. When do you go?"

"First light."

"I will tell Theobold. Maybe he will come to his senses and beg the empress not to let you go." Lady Alice smiled.

"I rather doubt that."

"Have you... talked to Rupert lately?" Lady Alice's voice was hesitant.

"Not much." Bronwyn didn't want to tell Lady Alice about the rose he'd given to Philippa.

"Oh. Well, never mind. I will ride out with you tomorrow and bid you farewell, if I wake up in time." Lady Alice nodded to her. "You… I know you are a good cook, but… you were also a good maidservant to me before. Months back. If you wanted, I could put in a good word with the empress and entreat her to let you stay. You could come back as my servant. You'd have to leave the kitchens, of course, but that's not so bad. I can't imagine you'd want to stay here, anyway…"

Bronwyn gave a slight shake of her head. To have to serve Lady Alice constantly wasn't too bad, but she would miss the kitchens. And to have to be at the beck and call with all the fine ladies present, some of whom would make it their mission to torment her, all for amusement… She would rather get lost in the woods.

"Your mind is made up, I see," Lady Alice said. "All right, then. But, Bronwyn, I would do it, you know. For you. I wouldn't do that for just anyone."

Bronwyn gave her a half-smile. "Thank you."

"Yes, well, I hope you appreciate the gesture." Lady Alice raised her head high. "Good day." She strode out.

Mistress Webb came over. "My, that one sure thinks a lot of herself, doesn't she? What did she want?"

"To say goodbye," Bronwyn said softly.

But that wasn't the last visitor she had that day. Shortly after the servants' dinner, Lady Morwenna stalked to the kitchen and found Bronwyn clearing away trenchers and serving dishes. "Ha. I thought I would find you here."

Bronwyn continued with her work. She wanted to retort back but held her tongue. Morwenna being here meant only one thing: trouble.

Morwenna stood at her side, her thick hair bound in expertly plaited braids with a ribbon that matched her green, woolen dress. "It must be hard for you, having to work day and night in the kitchens, when the man you fell for is spending his time with another woman."

Bronwyn raised her head.

"I see I've got your attention now. Good. I heard about your little dalliance with Theobold. I'm glad he's finally seen the consequences of his actions. One must never dally with the servants. Now he knows better."

Bronwyn stiffened and turned to the noblewoman, her mouth open, ready to give her a nasty comeback. But she froze at the sight of Lady Morwenna's grin.

Lady Morwenna wanted simply to get a rise out of her. She rejoiced in tormenting others.

Instead, Bronwyn nudged closer and asked quietly, just so Lady Morwenna could hear, "I wonder. You were present that night. You know the queen and prince survived their abduction, for you were there when we rescued them. Why haven't you said a word of this to the empress?"

Her answer was Lady Morwenna's slight intake of breath.

"I have my reasons. The knowledge will come out when I am ready to share it. Not that it will do you any favors. She is quite set against you, you know. She wants you out. I can't say I blame her." Lady Morwenna smirked.

"How is your eye, Lady Morwenna?"

The young woman still had some bruising from their fight around her eye, which showed an impressive array of yellow and purple. Her mouth twisted in anger and ducked her head slightly. "I am very well. But it is you whom I worry about, Mistress Bronwyn. I wonder that you even have the time to try to throw yourself at young men. Perhaps the empress is right to send you away. If you're of no use here, well…"

"That's enough," the head cook said, standing by Bronwyn's shoulder. "I don't know who you are, but no one talks to my cooks that way. Get out."

Lady Morwenna took one look at the woman, sniffed, stuck her nose in the air, and turned to go. "I am to visit the nunnery in town tomorrow, with the other ladies. I shall pray for you, Bronwyn. That you might learn a lesson and see the error of your ways."

A cloud of flour flew nearby, coating Lady Morwenna in a white cloud. She coughed and sneezed. "Don't be so clumsy," she snapped to the servants before she walked out, coughing.

Mistress Webb shook her head. "I cannot stand people like that. Don't worry, girl. Have a bath and an early night. I'll pack up a meal for your journey."

Bronwyn gave the woman a quick hug. "Thank you." She went about her chores, finishing her work, when a thought hit her. Lady Morwenna was to visit the nunnery. If she saw the queen, she would undoubtedly recognize her.

Bronwyn left the kitchen, wiping her hands on her apron as she looked for the nearest page. "Where might I find Crispin, the squire?"

The page shrugged. "Most everyone's gone to bed. There are a few men still talking in main hall. You could try there."

She hurried away, her shoes slapping the wooden floorboards. She moved to the entrance of the main hall, gazing about the room.

"Bronwyn? What is it? Have you reconsidered my offer?" Lady Alice asked, coming to her, a goblet of wine in her hand.

"No. I need to find Crispin. Have you seen him?"

"Crispin? Why? What do you want him for?"

"It's personal." Bronwyn looked past her.

Lady Alice frowned. "I don't like this. Why the urgency? It's late. Find him in the morning."

"No, I need to speak with him now."

"You don't." The noblewoman stood in her way.

"I do." Bronwyn sidestepped her.

"Bronwyn, you're making a mistake. I understand you're hurt about Theobold, but if you think throwing yourself at another squire is the answer, you're only going to hurt yourself." Lady Alice put a hand on her arm. "I mean it. Stop."

Bronwyn looked to see. There at a nearby table sat Theobold, a goblet of wine in his hand. Standing over him was Agatha. The sight made Bronwyn stop in her tracks. She hadn't thought seeing them together would hurt this much, even if it was a farce, but it did.

Mistress Agatha laughed at something he'd said and planted a kiss on his cheek. Theobold drank and looked around as people were talking. He saw Bronwyn, standing with Lady Alice, and drank more.

Bronwyn said to Lady Alice one more time, "I need to find Crispin. Where is he?"

"Over there. But if you think I'm just going to stand here and let you make a fool out of yourself, you're wrong."

Bronwyn spotted Crispin standing by the fireplace, where a warm fire was burning merrily, and approached him, Lady Alice dogging her steps.

"Bronwyn," he said, eyeing her. Seeing her expression, he said, "What is it? What's wrong?"

"I—"

"And Lady Alice. To what do I owe the pleasure?" he drawled as he gave Lady Alice an insolent wink.

Lady Alice huffed and tossed her head. "I'm here to prevent Bronwyn from making a mistake."

"And what is that?" he asked, facing her.

"Talking to you." She put her hands on her hips, frowning.

They stood but a foot apart. Lady Alice's nostrils flared, while Crispin gave her a slow smile. "And what would you suggest, rather than talk to me? Because I can think of a few things."

His gaze flicked down to her bosom, then her mouth, slowly rising to meet her eyes.

Lady Alice laughed haughtily. "Keep your thoughts to yourself, for those are all they will be."

Crispin gave her a wide smile. "Then I shall see you in my dreams, good lady."

"Ha. If you appear in mine, I shall know them to be nightmares."

He grinned. "I'll make this promise, Lady Alice. You may be the fox, but I will be the hunter. To the chase," he said, bowing.

"Bah. You are foolish in every sense of the word. Bronwyn, let me know when you are done with such jesters." Lady Alice turned on her heel and stalked away, but there was an extra movement to her step, a womanly, feminine roll to her hips, almost as if she knew Crispin was watching.

Crispin did indeed watch her leave. "A fine woman. Now, what did you want to talk to me about?"

"Lady Morwenna plans to visit the nunnery tomorrow. If she sees the… your guest, she'll—"

"I take your meaning." He swallowed. "I will need to fetch her immediately. Can you enlist Rupert to sneak out the boy?"

"Yes. But I am ordered to leave court tomorrow, on the order of the empress. You remember, she ordered me to find the queen and prince."

"I recall. But they were going to send out a messenger, weren't they? Either way, we shall have to change our plans and get them away. No one will question the boy going with you. If anyone asks, you can say he wanted to come."

"What are you two talking about?" Theobold stood there. "Bronwyn, is he bothering you?"

Crispin gave Theobold an even look. "Theobold. Why is it, whenever there's a pretty girl around, you're lurking nearby?"

Theobold frowned and ignored him. "Bronwyn?"

"I'm fine." A beat passed. "Thank you," she said primly.

Crispin glanced from her to Theobold and mimed a shiver. He grinned at her.

Theobold wavered on his feet slightly. "What could you possibly have to say to her?"

Bronwyn's head snapped toward him. "What is your problem?"

"I don't see why a woman like you should be talking to him, when—"

She rounded on him. "I will talk to whomever I please. And for your information, it's no business of yours whom I talk to." *You broke my heart, remember?* She wanted to shout.

He blinked, his eyes focusing on nothing in particular. "You shouldn't be talking with him. He's not for a woman like you."

Bronwyn bared her teeth at him. A woman like her?

"All right, I think you've had enough, mate," Crispin said, gently pushing Theobold back a step. "Any closer and you'll fall into the fire if you're not careful."

"Don't push me." Theobold pushed his arm away, more roughly than was needed. "You're not my master. You don't tell me what to do."

"And just where *is* your master? Oh, yes. In prison."

Theobold pushed Crispin, who shoved him back. Theobold wavered on his feet. Then, blinking hard, he aimed a punch at Crispin, who sidestepped. Theobold crashed to the ground. All conversation had stilled. Everyone was watching.

Crispin stepped back and dusted off his hands. "I don't fight drunks. Come to me when you want a real fight." He walked away.

Bronwyn watched as Theobold wiped his mouth. A drop of blood fell to the floor. She took a step toward him, then stopped as Agatha fell to her knees and put her arms around him. "Oh, Theobold, you don't need to fight over me," she said loudly.

Theobold looked up and met Bronwyn's eyes. He pushed Agatha away and climbed to his feet. But he lost control of himself and lurched, and then Agatha rose and caught him. She shot Bronwyn a dirty look and helped him move away.

Bronwyn quickly looked for Rupert. She didn't see him, so she headed toward the infirmary. A giggle sounded from inside the room, and Bronwyn hesitated outside the door. She decided, *this can't wait*, and walked in.

Rupert and Philippa were kissing, and a rose lay discarded on the floor. His hands were around her waist and she had her hands through his golden hair. She let out a little moan.

The sound shot an icicle through Bronwyn's heart. She meant to back away, then tripped and fell on her skirt, crashing to the floor.

"Wha?" Rupert's voice said. "Bronwyn?"

Bronwyn got up, red-faced. "Sorry, sorry. I didn't mean to—"

"You clearly did." Philippa marched over to her, her face pink. "What is your problem? Whenever I finally have a moment alone with Rupert, you're there interrupting. You're like a flea. For pity's sake, go."

"Philippa," Rupert started, coming over. He wiped his mouth. "Bronwyn? You all right? Did you need something?"

"Yes. I need to speak with you."

"Well, go on, then." Philippa crossed her arms beneath her chest. "We're waiting."

Rupert shot her a look that Bronwyn interpreted as surprise. 'We'?

He ran a hand through his hair. "Philippa, maybe you'd best give us a minute."

"Why? Why is it that when I want to spend time with you, I have to let her interrupt, but when *she* wants to speak with you, you listen?" Philippa put her hands on her hips and glared.

"It will only take a minute," Bronwyn said.

"Suit yourself. I don't care." Philippa tossed her hair over her shoulder and walked away, shooting Rupert a dirty look over her shoulder.

Rupert let out a sigh as she left. "What is it?"

"Our guests need to leave. Before tomorrow."

"Why?"

She whispered to him about Lady Morwenna's plan to visit the nunnery. "If she happens to see…"

"I understand. Have you spoken to Wat?"

"No."

"I'll tell him. We'll need to be ready."

There was a flurry of movement, footfalls that echoed. Bronwyn paused and looked at Rupert.

"Do you think someone heard us?"

"Philippa, most likely," he said.

"Can you trust her?"

"Not with this." He shook his head. "We can't speak of this anymore. I'll procure horses. Be ready to leave at dawn."

She went upstairs, to where she had bathed and hidden away the prince's dirty clothes, thinking she might need them. She planned to wash them quickly and have them ready for the morning. But as she searched in the spot and looked around the room, they were gone. A dull feeling grew in the pit of her stomach. The prince's fine clothes were gone. Where were they?

At a loss as to what to do, she entered the main hall, now deserted and empty of guests. She curled up against the wall near some other women servants and idly watched the fire burn low in the fireplace, but it was some time before she fell asleep.

$$\sim\!\!\ast\!\!\sim$$

Chapter Eight

BRONWYN ROSE EARLY. Living in the castle, her body had already become accustomed to waking early. She'd also gotten used to that sense of waking suddenly and being fully awake, needing only seconds to move.

But those seconds were precious, and she realized that for a mission like this to succeed, she needed to become faster. Quicker, more responsive. To be able to judge her safety and make her next action without freezing or watching those precious seconds ticking away.

Across the room, she locked eyes with Rupert, who was awake. At a nod from her, he gently nudged Prince Eustace, who murmured in his sleep.

She rose quietly, keeping her footfalls soft and silent against the wooden floorboards of the great hall. She smoothed down her purple dress, tightened the stained apron around her waist, and tiptoed out of the room. Servants would be waking soon. It was still dark outside, for no sunlight shone through the windows. She tiptoed down the corridor and once she was some distance away, picked up her pace, trotting down to the kitchen.

Mistress Webb, bless her, Bronwyn thought, had left her a parcel of food to take with her on the journey. It was bigger than what one person would need. As Bronwyn moved toward it, she wrapped it up securely in her apron and tied it tight.

She turned to go, when the head cook was standing there.

"You're leaving," she said.

"Yes."

"Take this with you." She offered a small flask. "Collect water from the streams, or the rain. Where will you go?"

"Back home, to Lincoln," Bronwyn said, the lie coming easily to her lips. She did plan to return to Lincoln, to see what home of hers still remained. But not yet. First, Bristol.

Mistress Webb nodded. "That's what I'll tell the others if they ask." She made to leave, then paused. "That boy, Wat. You'll be taking him with you?"

"Yes."

"He's not an ordinary kitchen lad, is he?" Seeing Bronwyn's expression, she said, "Sometimes the others would call him 'Wat,' and he wouldn't answer. Almost like he forgot that was his name. And he talks too well to be one of us. He acts different."

Bronwyn hoisted the parcel over her shoulder. "Thank you for this."

"It's almost like he was a nobleman."

Bronwyn stopped. She slowly looked up and met the head cook's eyes. The older woman was short, round, and petite, but there was a sense of honesty and no-nonsense in her expression that made Bronwyn want to tell her everything. She had a trustworthy demeanor about her, and that was dangerous. In a heartbeat, Mistress Webb could raise the alarm, call the guards, declare Bronwyn was stealing, or…

Bronwyn swallowed. "Don't know what you mean. He's just a boy missing his mama." She made to move.

"'Course he is. Bronwyn…"

Bronwyn looked at her.

"If anyone asks, I'll say he ran away. Didn't like me telling him what to do. Will you see that he gets back to his mother?"

"I'll try."

The head cook nodded. "That's a good girl. Go with God. With any luck, we'll see each other again."

Bronwyn left. Moving quickly, out into the castle courtyard, where her shoes cracked and scuffed against the pebbled ground, and over to the stables.

Inside, Rupert was moving swiftly, tying saddles and fastening reins on a pair of horses. These weren't princely horses or expensive thoroughbreds—he had been smart, Bronwyn realized. He was tying the reins onto two pack-mares, so if anyone did stop them, they could play the part of two servants going back to her home.

Eustace and Rupert stopped as she approached. "About ready?"

"Yes. You?"

"Aye." Rupert helped Eustace onto a mare and led them out of the stables. He then helped Bronwyn mount hers, but she sat unsteadily in the saddle.

At that moment, she cursed her luck. She was not a confident horse rider, and even though this was a calm and plodding mare, she still didn't trust she wouldn't fall off.

"Here, one second." Rupert mounted his mare behind Eustace.

"It'll be too heavy with both of us," Eustace said. "I can go with Bronwyn. I know how to ride."

"Are you sure?" Rupert asked.

"Yes, of course. I learned how to ride when I was four."

Bronwyn highly doubted that but didn't complain as Eustace slipped off his mare and joined her on hers. "Put your arms around me," Eustace said. "I'll hold the reins."

"Yes, Wat."

Eustace took the reins and they waited as Rupert led them slowly and quietly out of the castle courtyard. He slipped the two nodding guards at the gate two coins, which disappeared almost in seconds.

"Hold. Stop there," a familiar voice shouted.

Bronwyn turned to look. She could feel the young prince stiffen and tense in the saddle. He wanted to flee, she knew, for she felt it as well. But she also recognized the voice and knew its owner would demand an answer. Her heart began to pound and she slipped off the saddle.

"What are you doing?" Eustace asked.

"Bronwyn, let's go," Rupert said, looking over his shoulder. "Oh." He muttered a curse.

"Wait here," Bronwyn said. "If you go now, he'll get suspicious."

"All right. But don't take long. We have to go," Rupert said, motioning for Eustace to come closer.

She turned around to meet Theobold. She didn't need to see his face to know he was angry. His voice had said it all. And now, as she calmly walked toward Theobold, her heart raced in her chest. Her blood pounded in her veins. She licked her lips, feeling they were dry. She met his eyes and felt that familiar pain again, of knowing he was no longer hers.

"Theobold."

"Bronwyn." It was a loaded statement. His eyes looked at her accusingly.

"What is it?"

"What do you think you're doing? At this hour?" he demanded.

"Leaving. As the empress ordered me to."

"She told you to go days ago and you stayed. Why now?" he asked.

"She asked me again yesterday and..." Bronwyn fumbled with her hands awkwardly to make a point. "She wanted me to go. So this is me, leaving."

"Without saying goodbye?" Theobold's voice held a note of emotion in it.

Was it yearning, or was she too tired to mistake that as hope? "I have said all my goodbyes."

A flash of hurt crossed his face. "Bah. Stop being so dramatic. You have Lady Alice, and the empress, and..."

She noticed he did not include himself and shook her head. "I'm going."

Theobold stepped closer and looked over her shoulder at Rupert. His mouth withered in disgust. "And what is he doing here?"

Bronwyn disliked his proprietary tone. "He's helping me get back to Lincoln safely. The roads aren't safe for a young woman alone."

"Why him? I would have escorted you."

"When you have your master to think of, and the empress to serve? No. I wouldn't ask that of you." *Not now*, she thought. "Besides, what would Mistress Agatha think?"

Theobold's cheeks colored. "I don't know what you've heard, but it's not what you think. She made me a proposition, to improve my standing at court. I do not care what she thinks, or says, or does."

"Don't you? She seemed to be hanging off of you at dinner last night."

His eyes widened. "Are you jealous?"

"Of her? No." She looked away.

"Bronwyn, don't lie. It doesn't become you. Besides, I know you too well." He took her chin in his hand and raised it.

She tossed her head, moving away. "No. You don't get to do that. You don't get to touch me. Not anymore."

His hand fell back to his side. "Maybe I don't, you're right. But what if I wanted to? What if I wanted to kiss you right now? What would you do?"

"I'd walk away." Her pulse sped up. It suddenly felt overly warm.

His eyes darted to her eyes, her mouth, her chest. "No, you wouldn't."

"I would." She wanted to smack the self-assured smile off his face. Curse him for being so handsome.

"I don't want you to go," he murmured, closing the remaining distance between them.

"I have no reason to stay."

"Don't I count as a reason?"

Her heart pounded in her chest. A lump rose in her throat. "You made it clear. I'm too common for you."

"I'm a fool." His eyes were red and bloodshot. "I heard the horses and somehow, I knew it was you leaving. I had to see you."

Her heart lifted to hear that. She wanted to hear more. But she couldn't. "I have to go."

"Stay. Just one more day."

"No. I don't have time."

"Why not? You're only going back home. There's nothing for you there..." Theobold ran a hand through his dark hair at her expression. "That came out wrong. I meant to say that whatever is waiting for you can wait another day."

She shook her head.

"Why? Why now? And who's he?" He motioned toward the prince. One of the pack mares nickered softly and flicked its tail.

Bronwyn swallowed. "A servant boy. He was a downright mess in the kitchens. I guess he wanted to leave, so Rupert's taking him along. Maybe he'll be a junior squire."

Would Theobold believe her? Or would he question it?

"Ha. Good luck with that." Theobold turned his sharp gaze back to her. "Bronwyn, please. Don't go. I didn't mean what I said."

You didn't mean to break my heart, or just that you didn't mean to hurt my feelings? she wanted to ask. Instead, she turned her back on him.

"Wait." He took her hand.

She turned, ready to yank it back, when he squeezed it and let it fall.

Bronwyn walked away. She felt his eyes on her but didn't care. She tried to move at a steady pace and got on the horse behind Eustace. "Let's go."

The guards' eyes had been low and heavy with sleep, but they didn't miss a trick. They simply looked the other way as the gates stood open, and Rupert led, while Eustace and Bronwyn followed.

If Theobold watched, she had no idea. But a part of her hoped that he did.

But as they moved from the castle gates, screams and shouts rang out from inside the castle walls. Bronwyn and Rupert looked at each other.

"We've got to go," Rupert said. He dug his heels into the mare's sides and led them on as the guards quickly shut the doors behind them and ran to see about the commotion.

"What do you think it is?" Eustace asked, keeping pace with Rupert's horse. "Are they after us?"

"Couldn't be. No one knows who you are," Bronwyn said, willing her heart to stop hammering in her chest.

But she felt Eustace's urgency, for it matched her own. They were silent and moved quickly following Rupert's lead, along streets and down corners, through alleyways and winding around in directions.

"I don't know this way," Bronwyn complained.

"That's on purpose. In case anyone is following us, this roundabout route will lose them, or at the very least confuse them."

Bronwyn's chest tightened, and around each street they passed, her anxiety grew. She expected to see armed guards waiting for them.

They rode out into the city streets, which were different from the city of Lincoln that Bronwyn knew, but not so dissimilar. She realized that none of them knew the way, but that almost didn't matter. There was a main road that Rupert followed, being wider and more straightforward through town.

"How do you know where to go?" Eustace asked.

"Every town and city tends to have a single main road, either leading through it or past it. Doesn't matter where you are, if you can find that, you can find your way out," Rupert said.

Bronwyn nodded in agreement. That made sense. She wondered if it was true.

They left the city through the main gates, accomplished again by Rupert passing the guards some coin, and went through without a word. Not until they were well out of the city and on the main road did Bronwyn exhale a breath she hadn't realized she'd been holding.

She wasn't the only one. Eustace heaved a heavy sigh of relief, and as the light of the day grew brighter, the group's spirits lifted.

The mares were not loaded heavily, only with spare blankets and the parcel of food, so they moved fast enough. They rode a little ways down the main road, about a mile or so, until the group was well away from the road.

"Where are we going?" Eustace asked.

"This way."

"But it's off of the main road."

"That's the point."

Eustace and Bronwyn followed Rupert's lead as he rode out into the woods, to a shady glen. The walls of a stone building, clearly a church of some sort, with gardens and walled-off areas, came into view.

"What is this?"

"A nunnery," Rupert said over his shoulder. "It's where your mother's been hiding."

Bronwyn felt Eustace's renewed energy as he urged the pack horse on with a flick of the reins and a nudge of his heels, instantly sending the animal pushing forward. Bronwyn bounced uncomfortably in the saddle and gripped around his waist harder to hold on. "Oi."

"Sorry." He slowed down slightly.

They went around the outside building and grounds of the nunnery. But the grounds were quiet. They could hear a few voices in song, in praise of God's glory and the morning. Their horses' hooves were quiet on the dusty ground.

Rupert came to a stop. "I don't understand. They should be here."

"There, look." Eustace pointed.

Across a field and just at the treeline stood two horses. A tall man and a small figure, a woman, sat astride them.

"I see them. Let's go," Rupert said, leading the group on.

They moved across the field. The day was a quiet, gray, misty morning, with the grass slick with dew. The mares trotted at a good pace, but Bronwyn disliked being so out in the open. She felt a sneaking sensation between her shoulder blades and repressed the urge to look back. Was someone watching?

With every step, the tension rose in her shoulders as they crossed the green fields, picking their way around tilled grounds and patches meant for growing vegetables and fruit.

The two figures came closer into view, and Bronwyn heaved a sigh of relief as they reached the treeline. She gripped the horse's reins as Eustace slipped off the packhorse and ran to the woman on the other horse, dressed as a nun, who held him close. The woman dismounted and wrapped her arms around him.

Crispin nodded at Bronwyn and Rupert as mother and son embraced. Rupert shot Bronwyn a grin, and some of the tension left her shoulders.

Queen Matilda looked down at her son. "Are you well?"

"Yes, Mother." Prince Eustace nodded, letting his hands drop. "Can I ride with you?"

"Better not," Crispin said. "If we were to get separated, you would be more valuable together."

"But surely, if we were apart, we could be leveraged against each other," the queen said quietly. She held on to Eustace, and Bronwyn knew there was no way they would be separated. It came as no surprise to her when the queen said, "No. In this instance, I will ride with my son."

The prince joined his mother on her horse, a gray dappled mare, while the others looked on. Bronwyn felt sore from riding in the saddle but made no complaint.

"Ready?" Crispin asked. "Let's move."

The group entered the trees, quickly hidden by the leafy,

green boughs and dark trunks and branches. There was no mistaking the sounds of their horses' footfalls in the leaves and muddy paths, but now that they were five, Bronwyn felt more comfortable, more secure in the knowledge that if they were attacked, there were two squires to protect them.

But then, she thought, *the queen surely had had a team of armed fighters to look after her safety before, and they had met a grisly end.* She swallowed.

"You all right, Bronwyn?" Rupert asked. "Keep up."

She nodded and tried to focus more on riding and sitting straight in the saddle, moving with the horse.

"I do not know these woods. How do you know the way?" the queen asked Crispin.

"I grew up around here, Your Grace. My family owns lands not far from here. And I know where you'll be headed."

"How many days' ride is it to Bristol?" Eustace asked.

"Not many. We'll get there soon enough," Crispin told him.

But it wasn't long before Crispin moved his horse back to ride alongside Bronwyn. "Don't react," he said calmly, "but someone is following us."

She stiffened in the saddle and looked over her shoulder.

He cursed. "Don't do that. Didn't I just say—? God."

"Sorry." She faced front and kept riding. "Who is it?"

"I don't know. Keep riding with the others. I'll circle back around." He disappeared into the trees.

"What's happening? Where has Crispin gone?" the queen asked.

"I think to, um…"

"He needed to piss, Mother."

"Eustace, don't talk like that. You know better," the queen said, raising her chin. "Very well. On that note, I too need to… have a bit of privacy." She pulled their horse up short and dismounted.

"You shouldn't go off alone," Rupert said.

The queen let out a noise of annoyance. "I can surely look

after my own person. I'll only be a minute."

Rupert shot Bronwyn a look. "Go with her," he mouthed. He moved to take the reins of Bronwyn's horse as she slipped out of the saddle.

Her leg muscles groaned in protest as she reached the hard ground and wavered a bit. She thumped life into her sore muscles and said, "I need to as well."

"Oh, for heaven's sake." The queen gave an annoyed flick of her shoulder and started walking. "Very well, if I must have a companion, then come along. But I do not approve of this. Not at all."

Bronwyn acted like a silent shadow and followed the queen into the woods. She kept an eye on her and unlike the royal woman, who wanted a fair bit of privacy to do her business, Bronwyn simply squatted by the nearest wide tree and lifted her skirts.

Once finished, she used some leaves to wipe herself clean and rubbed her hands on the nearest patch of moss and wet grass. It wasn't as good as a bucket of water to clean her hands, but it would do. *And the outdoors always provides, one way or another,* she thought.

She rose and accompanied the queen back to the group, when Crispin rode by with another horse and rider, saying, "Look what I found."

"I tell you, give back the reins at once. This is rude treatment for a lady," a familiar feminine voice said.

Bronwyn stood by the queen, blocking her body with hers. "Lady Alice?"

Chapter Nine

CRISPIN APPROACHED, GRIPPING the reins of his horse and another, upon which sat a veiled rider. The figure, whom Bronwyn now recognized as Lady Alice, sat stiffly but competently in the saddle, and if Bronwyn hadn't known any better, she'd say the noblewoman was annoyed.

Lady Alice unwound the veil from their face. "I said, give me back the reins, you lout."

"Lady Alice? What are you doing here?" Rupert asked.

"That's what I would like to know," Queen Matilda said.

"I don't understand. Who is she?" Prince Eustace asked, scratching his head.

All eyes turned toward the young noblewoman, who tossed her head and said, "I came to join you."

"Why didn't you declare yourself? I could have hurt you," Crispin said.

"Bah. As if you would. Besides, your group was moving so fast, it was hard to keep up." Lady Alice looked toward the queen. "I..." She stopped, a hand darting to her mouth. "You found them. You found the queen and the prince." She bowed in her saddle.

Bronwyn and Rupert exchanged a look. The secret was out now.

Lady Alice turned to Prince Eustace. "I've seen you before. You work in the kitchens."

The prince gave her a big smile. "Did you think I was a real servant?"

Lady Alice's eyes widened. Her mouth hung open slightly, and she snapped it shut. To Bronwyn, she said, "Are you telling me that you had a prince in your care, and you put him to work in the kitchens *with the servants?*"

"Yes," Bronwyn said.

Prince Eustace laughed and clapped his hands. "You believed it, didn't you? You thought I was a servant."

"Yes, well. Enough of that," the queen said.

"Your Grace." Lady Alice deftly dismounted from the horse and swept a deep curtsy. "Forgive me for disturbing you, Your Grace."

"Lady Alice. Whatever are you doing here? And away from your mistress?" Queen Matilda asked.

"I..." The noblewoman walked over to Bronwyn and the queen. She said, "I would accompany you to Bristol. There has been a death at the castle and—"

"A death? Who?" the queen asked.

"Who was it?" Crispin asked.

"Are you all right?" Rupert asked her.

Crispin shot Rupert a dirty look.

Lady Alice huffed. Bronwyn knew she disliked being interrupted, even if it was by a queen. But she also did not mind being the center of attention on occasion. "Some maidservant. Lady Morwenna's new maid. You know, that snotty nursemaid who liked to coddle you like a child. Philippa, I think her name was?"

Her voice was carefree, but Bronwyn knew her expression and picked up on an emotion in her words. Bronwyn paused. The maid was dead? How? Why?

"Philippa?" Rupert repeated. "It can't be. I saw her only yesterday." He bowed his head. "She was nice."

Bronwyn nodded. She hadn't particularly liked Philippa, but the young woman was harmless. How had she died? And... Was Rupert sorry for her death because he fancied her? She shook away the thought.

"Yes, well she's dead. Someone killed her," Lady Alice said heartlessly.

Rupert's head shot up. He and Lady Alice locked gazes before the queen cleared her throat delicately.

"Well, I, for one, would like to know just what you are doing here. Why follow us? Do you mean to report back to your mistress?" the queen asked.

"No, Your Grace," Lady Alice said. "That is, not exactly. Certain events have made it so that the castle... It is no longer suitable for me there. I don't feel safe there anymore."

"Why not?" Prince Eustace asked.

"Well, aside from the fact that a maidservant was killed, I've had enough of death and murder to last a lifetime. Also... they're going to be looking for you," she told Eustace.

"Me? Why? I didn't do anything."

"Mistress Agatha, the empress's formal taster, she found some dirty clothes chucked behind some of the bathing tubs. I gather she thought she might steal them and sell them later or use them. Anyway, she had them laundered and noticed they were quite fine, but for a child. She mentioned this to Lady Morwenna and the empress. What with the maidservant dead and now a servant boy gone... It's only a matter of time before people weave these two occurrences together and think the boy's killed the maid and fled, or at the very least isn't who he said he was."

Bronwyn bit her lip. She'd unknowingly played a part in hastening their departure from Devizes. She was sorry she hadn't burnt the boy's clothes. It had never occurred to her that they might be found and laundered, or cause suspicion.

The queen and Crispin exchanged worried glances. The prince gave a small *eep* and clenched his fists.

"Yes, well," said Lady Alice. "I didn't know it was you, Your Grace. Otherwise, I'd have had the clothes burned."

"There is no reason to think that the servant boy leaving has anything to do with the dead maid," the queen said. "Tragic, yes, but, he might have just come from a wealthy family."

"And how many noble families let their children go running off and disappearing for weeks on end? I saw the boy's clothes. Gold thread. A princely thread, indeed," Lady Alice pointed out.

Crispin rubbed the side of his face. "Yes, yes, you've made your point."

"Anyway, when I heard that Bronwyn had gone, I thought, why not join her? I could use a bit of time from the empress's ladies-in-waiting. They're like harpies or geese, always gossiping. It gives me a headache." Lady Alice adjusted the veil hung around her neck.

"But surely, you needed permission from your mistress to leave court," the queen said.

Lady Alice pressed her lips together. "I... had not thought of that. I simply wanted to leave. And what with the castle up in arms over the maidservant's death, I thought it the perfect time. I don't want to be in a castle when there's a murderer running around loose." She looked at the queen. "So I came here. Will you let me join your party?"

The queen gave the young noblewoman a level look.

"Mother, she could report back to the empress," Prince Eustace said.

"Do not call her that. The woman may be an empress back in her own country, but here, she is just a woman. An interloper into my affairs," the queen said harshly. Then her gaze softened as she looked at her son.

She continued. "Very well, Lady Alice. You may stay. But I hope you brought food, for there is little to spare between us for one more."

Lady Alice's cheeks heated. "Thank you, Your Grace."

Bronwyn realized, in her haste to leave, Lady Alice hadn't brought any food with her. Just herself. She must truly have been frightened to leave in such a hurry. But why? She had been around death before.

"If we are all agreed, let us move. There's no time to waste," Crispin said.

They spent all day riding and once night had drawn on, they stayed off the main roads. The October night was chilly, and they had a small fire as they ate some of the food from Bronwyn's parcel. Over hunks of bread and cheese, Crispin announced he would take the first watch, then Rupert.

"I can keep watch too," Eustace said.

Rupert shot him an affectionate grin, like one might reserve for a younger brother. "You'll get your chance. But not tonight."

"I could…" Bronwyn started.

"Yes. I can too," Queen Matilda said.

"Forgive me, Your Grace, but I would not ask that of you. Let us keep watch. You ladies can sleep."

Bronwyn felt that her ego was a little bruised, but as the hours grew long, her eyes felt heavy, and in no time at all, she fell fast asleep.

The next morning, they rose early and after a quick meal of bread and cheese, they were on the move again.

Lady Alice made polite conversation with the queen and prince, and after a time hung back to ride beside Bronwyn. She hissed, "I cannot believe you hid them from me. How could you? How did you manage it?"

Bronwyn shrugged. "The fewer people who knew, the better."

"Even me? You can trust me."

"Yes, but Lady Alice, you are loyal to the empress," Bronwyn pointed out.

"So? What is that when there are secrets to be… All right. I see your point. But still. I wouldn't have *said* anything."

"Wouldn't you have?"

"Of course not. I…" Lady Alice paused, thinking. "Fine. I probably would have told the empress the first chance I got. But I still don't approve of you keeping secrets from me. What are friends for?"

They are for keeping a safe distance from whilst protecting a prince and a queen, Bronwyn thought, but she wisely kept silent.

"How did you hide the queen?" Lady Alice asked. "Was she at court as well? A serving wench, perhaps?" Her voice dripped sarcasm.

"No. We thought it too dangerous. Crispin hid her away at the nunnery."

"Ah, that explains why you rode out there. I wondered why your route was leading that way. That is lucky. Your timing was perfect to get them out of the city."

"It wasn't luck. It was careful planning," Crispin said, wheeling his horse around to ride on Lady Alice's right side. "We knew that the Lady Morwenna was planning to visit the nunnery the next day, so we thought it best to move them now. The event of the maidservant's death was just a coincidence."

"Hmph. You clearly don't know ladies-in-waiting very well," Lady Alice said, lifting her noise in the air.

"What do you mean?" Crispin asked.

The noblewoman's mouth upturned in a half smile. "Lady Morwenna isn't very religious. I doubt she's been in a church more than twice in her life. She certainly wouldn't be caught dead in a nunnery."

Crispin frowned. "So then why would she say she was going there?"

Lady Alice gave a half shrug. "She often says things she doesn't mean. Idle threats. Casual insults. Perhaps she only meant to toy with you."

Crispin grunted and turned his horse away, moving back up to ride beside the queen and prince. Bronwyn scratched her head. Had she overreacted to Lady Morwenna's teasing? Had they all rushed too quickly to leave the castle? But then Agatha had discovered the prince's garments she'd hidden, so perhaps they hadn't been too hasty, after all.

"What will you do now?" Lady Alice asked Bronwyn. "Now that it's clear you are not heading toward Lincoln, as I thought."

Bronwyn gave a little shake of her head. "We go to escort the queen and prince to Bristol Prison, so the hostage talks can continue."

"So you would undo what the mercenaries did." Lady Alice nodded. "I approve."

The queen looked over her shoulder. "So you agree, my husband should be out of prison?"

Lady Alice turned pink. "I... couldn't speak on politics, Your Grace. I only know that Sir Robert is a favorite of the empress, and without him, her position in warfare is weaker."

"But what of Sir Miles, her other commander? I thought he was equally up to the task," Queen Matilda said.

"I have no doubt he is, Your Grace, but he prefers to wage battles in court, not the outdoors."

"A diplomat, then."

"Quite."

They rode in silence for some time. As they stopped in the night to make camp, Lady Alice said quietly to Bronwyn, "There's another reason I left. What with Lady Morwenna always talking about her lover... It bothered me. Back in London, she was working with that lout, Sir Bors. Do you think they are still together?"

"I don't know." Bronwyn thought back to their time in London, the day of the empress's failed coronation ceremony at Westminster. Lady Morwenna had lured her down to the cells and Sir Bors had attacked her, when Lady Alice had struck him senseless and rescued her. They had fled and had not seen or heard from him again.

Bronwyn frowned. There was every reason to think that the wayward knight and Lady Morwenna might still be together—and playing for higher stakes this time.

Lady Alice said, "He might be living, or he might be dead. She may have taken on a new lover. Whoever her lover is, she pines for him. But I sometimes see her looking out a window, as if she were searching for someone. I wonder if he is nearby."

"What are you thinking?" Bronwyn asked. "That he's watching?"

"Yes. Waiting for the right moment. What if he followed your party, or me?"

"Would he leave Lady Morwenna?" Bronwyn wondered.

"Maybe. He had attacked the queen and prince before. What's to prevent him from trying again?"

Bronwyn cocked her head as they gathered fallen twigs for a fire. "Why are you really here, Lady Alice?"

"I told you. Because Lady Morwenna is intolerable, Mistress Agatha's company is worse than sour wine, the two new ladies only laugh and whisper amongst themselves and hang on to the empress's every word, without a spare thought between them, and because I feared for my life. There is a killer at the empress's court. I'm not going to stay there and act like everything is normal." She shuddered. "Are we safe here? With Crispin?"

"Yes. Why wouldn't we be? He helped me rescue the queen and prince out of the pit and hid the queen up until now."

"I don't trust him. Something about him. He makes me nervous."

"Is that because he fancies you?"

"Shut up." Lady Alice threw a twig at Bronwyn, who laughed.

The night passed without any disturbances, but even so, Bronwyn slept fitfully, tossing and turning. Her dreams were filled with images of a warrior whose face she couldn't see, Lady Morwenna laughing, and the empress, demanding when she would leave her court. By the time morning had arrived, it was almost a relief.

After a day of riding together with his mother, Eustace had been happy to ride the packhorse with Bronwyn again. She suspected he liked being in control of the horse and handling the reins, which was fine by her.

Three days later, the group was quiet, saddle-sore, and tired.

"There. Up ahead. Bristol. It's not far now," Crispin said.

"Excellent. Thank you," the queen said.

As Crispin expertly guided the mare along with the group,

they entered Bristol. It was a bustling city, with many people. Bronwyn felt a pang of warmth and pleasure at entering a city again. She was a city girl, born and bred. She didn't mind the countryside so much, once she got used to the quiet of lone bird calls, the bugs, and the vast emptiness of English fields. But there was something about the hustle and bustle of a city that reminded her of home. The range of accents, the close quarters of market stalls, the laughter and loud voices of hawkers of cherries, exotic fruits, butchers, fishmongers, even silks. She loved it.

She missed her home.

Blinking hard, she and the group joined the main road filled with carts, horses, families, travelers, musicians, men and women, and small children.

Crispin said, "If anyone asks, Your Grace is a nun. Rupert is a squire and Bronwyn and Wat, you two are servants seeking work. You're brother and sister."

"And me?" Lady Alice asked. "What about me?"

"You are… a lady on her way to her mistress. No one need know who that is."

Bronwyn blinked at the squire in surprise. Prince Eustace squirmed in the saddle, and Bronwyn suspected he was tired. They were all hot, sticky, and dusty from the journey.

"What about you?" the queen asked.

"This is where I leave you," Crispin said.

"What? Why?" the queen asked. "You deserve credit for your actions."

Did a flash of jealousy cross Rupert's face? Bronwyn couldn't be sure.

Crispin shook his head. "I dare not, Your Grace. I may have a care for any woman and her son in need, but my loyalty lies elsewhere." He paused and met her eyes. "I am the empress's man. I already take a risk leaving her castle at Devizes to lead you here. If she were to know I was helping you… it would not end well."

The queen extended her hand. "Then accept my hand in

thanks, Squire Crispin. Are you sure we cannot convince you to stay?"

And change allegiance, Bronwyn caught the unspoken question.

"No, Your Grace." He gave her hand a quick grasp.

"But that doesn't make sense," Lady Alice interrupted. "We go to another of Empress Maud's strongholds. Why would you not be welcome there?"

Crispin ran a hand through his hair. "I can't stay. I have to return to the empress and be there, court her favor. She will need all those who are loyal to her to remain and demonstrate their steadfastness." He gave Lady Alice a level look.

She was quick to take offense and faced him. "By which you mean *I* am abandoning her?"

"I said no such thing." He moved his horse closer to her.

"But you thought it. You are suggesting that. Well, I tell you now, I am not. I was fleeing for my life," she said, her black hair rippling behind her shoulders.

"Yes, you seem quite fearful. Is that why you're wearing such fine clothes but carry no weapon? What did you think? That you would fend off any attackers with a veil?" He snorted.

"Crispin…" Rupert started.

"No, I want to hear the good lady's reasoning. What was your plan, Lady Alice? Did you mean to run and flee from the empress's castle, or was it for another reason?"

Lady Alice's dark eyes flashed. "What are you saying?"

"Your timing is impeccable. A maid is dead and you just *happen* to flee at the moment when the castle is in an uproar. Why is that? Surely, your mistress would need you now, more than ever."

Her face turned red, as if he'd slapped her. Her mouth withered. "I make my own way in life."

"Yes, I suppose we all have to. I think you saw an opportunity and took it," Crispin said, narrowing the distance between them. They faced each other on their horses, barely a hand's width apart.

Lady Alice glared at Crispin, who held her gaze for a beat far longer than necessary.

The queen clapped her hands, a series of three short claps, that resounded in the air around them.

"Stop this," Queen Matilda said. "I don't have time for such petty squabbles. Stay or not, go or not. I no longer care. You have done us a service, taking us to Bristol. Those of you who wish to stay may accompany us further. Or not. The decision lies with you all." She turned to her son. "Come, Eustace. Your father is waiting."

The queen turned her horse and began to follow the trail of market traders, carts, families, horses and walkers on the main road to Bristol. The group followed, not exchanging a word between them.

Lady Alice let out an exasperated noise and kept pace with the queen. She looked over her shoulder as Crispin watched them go before disappearing off into the trees. "Well, I'm glad he's gone."

"Why do you two peck at each other so?" Bronwyn asked.

"'Peck'? What do you mean? What farmyard idiom is this?" Lady Alice asked.

Bronwyn snorted. She'd never worked on a farm before and Lady Alice knew it. But her temper was up, and so she was looking to dole out her misery all around.

"Like hens or geese. You peck at each other, finding faults. So he goes. What of it? He probably had his own reasons for leaving," Bronwyn said, watching Rupert keep pace with the queen and prince.

Lady Alice raised her veil over her head. "I do not like my motives and person being questioned. He doesn't know me. He has no right to suggest I had any mean or manipulative reason for joining you."

Bronwyn weighed the noblewoman's words carefully. Did she believe her? Was Lady Alice truly afeard for her life and so had chosen that moment to leave? But a more pressing question was on her mind.

"You heard about the death of the maid. Tell me about it?"

Lady Alice snorted. "Of course you would want to know that. Fine. I'll tell you what I know, but it's not much. When I heard that you had left at dawn, I decided it was best if I follow. Even if you were to travel to Lincoln, at least there, I could escape. I would have taken the road to Lincoln, but the guards said a party of people had gone this way instead, so I followed. I thought maybe you'd gotten lost."

Bronwyn cocked her head. Sometimes silence was all a person needed to say more.

The noblewoman sighed. "Lady Morwenna has been a torment, and Mistress Agatha too. When Mistress Agatha doesn't have Theobold all over her, paying her attentions for the men to see, Lady Morwenna longs for her lost lover, whom she refuses to name. It is most strange. Even when the empress presses her for information about him, Lady Morwenna won't speak of it. And honestly, if it weren't for the fact that Theobold was so closely tied to Lady Morwenna, I imagine he might take himself off too and find a different master."

Bronwyn raised an eyebrow. Lady Morwenna and Theobold were cousins, and closely connected through family. Her family had helped secure him the squire position with Sir Robert, and he had once told Bronwyn he had felt indebted to her family ever since. More so, since Lady Morwenna's choices meant she often fled the empress she was meant to serve, and he was usually the one sent to bring her back again. Theobold was the noblewoman's staunch defender, which riled up Bronwyn to no end. She gritted her teeth just thinking about it. The man refused to see Lady Morwenna's treachery and deceit.

"What of the dead maid?" Bronwyn asked.

"Struck in the back of the head with a bottle," Lady Alice said. "Everyone is saying there must be a killer at court, for this to happen right under the empress's nose."

"Why?"

"Well, Philippa was Lady Morwenna's new maidservant, so for her to die so soon after entering her service makes Lady Morwenna look bad. At first, she declared one could never find good servants, or trust them to properly look after themselves, but then another lady-in-waiting pointed out that the poor girl was killed, so Lady Morwenna threw a fit about how it must have been someone out to get her."

Lady Alice snorted. "As if anyone would waste their time. To the empress, it's as though Lady Morwenna can't look after her own servants. But that's not the strange thing." Lady Alice drew her horse closer to Bronwyn's and said quietly, "It was what they found with her."

Bronwyn leaned in to hear.

"They found a rose in Philippa's hands. Almost as if the killer had put it there."

Bronwyn tensed. "Surely not. I saw her with Rupert the other day, and he'd given her a rose as a thank you, for looking after him when he was ill."

Lady Alice sniffed. "And you're telling me this now?" She huffed. "That as may be, but then why was she still holding it in her hand? And anyway, what were they doing together? Why would Rupert give her a rose?" She looked down at her reins.

"I think he was just being kind."

"What man goes around giving roses out of kindness? The silly girl was besotted with him, you saw that. Any time I would enter the infirmary, she would glare at me as if I'd stepped on her mother's grave. And now look at her. Dead as dead can be."

Bronwyn frowned. "You don't think…"

"What? That Rupert killed her? No. We know him. He's a good squire, but he's not in the habit of killing young women. He'll romance them, maybe, but he's not a killer."

"Are you so sure?" Prince Eustace said over his shoulder. "When we were attacked coming here, he laid into the men. It wouldn't surprise me if he had killed someone."

Bronwyn shot the young prince a look. She'd seen the way

Rupert had looked after the youth. Like an affectionate older brother. But the prince had a point. They might know Rupert, but not his background, or whether he had killed before. The fact that Philippa had been found with a rose in her hand did not help.

"It's true, you know," Lady Alice said. "Why I left. I was so scared, I thought we might be under attack, or that someone like Lady Morwenna's lover had come to kill us all. I didn't think. I grabbed a veil and a horse and left as fast as I could."

"Will the others be looking for you?" Bronwyn asked.

"I doubt it. And if so, maybe later. The empress will be wondering about the dead maidservant, and besides, she's still on the hunt for the queen and her son." Lady Alice raised an eyebrow. "Speaking of which, how did you come to be in their company?"

Bronwyn gave her friend a half-smile.

"So it was you who rescued them."

"No. I'd never have found them without her. Crispin was the one who helped them out of the pit."

"Pit? Oh, my goodness." Lady Alice crossed herself. "I could never be in a pit. I'd rather die."

Bronwyn felt those words were a bit heartless, considering the prince and queen were in earshot. "The three of us, Crispin, Rupert, and I, got them back and hid them. But I do wonder why Lady Morwenna hasn't said anything to the empress. She was there, after all. And when I questioned her about it, she said she'd relay the knowledge when it suited her. That she had her own reasons for keeping quiet."

"Lord, what a tangled mess this is. Lady Morwenna has always kept secrets and stuck to her own counsel. I wonder what she is up to," Lady Alice said quietly, lowering her voice. "But, Bronwyn, this isn't even your fight. You don't care about them. Or the empress. Or maybe I'm wrong. Why are you helping them?"

Bronwyn looked away. She didn't have an easy answer to that question.

"It was the right thing to do."

Lady Alice huffed and tossed her head. "'The right thing.' We all think we're doing the right thing, until we find out that really we've been called in to spy and do wrong things, and until then, maybe they're not so wrong anymore, or that actually we've been wrong this entire time, and it's all we can do to fix things, but then it's too late and we're really the villain in someone else's tale." She let out a noisy breath.

Bronwyn cocked her head at her. "You all right?"

"Yes. I'm just sick of being pulled this way and that by people nobler than I, and being used. And it annoys me to see the same thing happening to you. You at least have a choice. You could walk away. Return home. Or start a new life away from all of this, and go on like none of it ever happened. It could all be a distant memory within a year. Something you tell your grand-children at home one day."

Bronwyn thought on this. "I don't know if I have a home to go back to."

"Of course you do. The bakery will still be there, even if your family isn't," Lady Alice said.

"But it wouldn't still be home without them. I don't even know if they're alive." Bronwyn's chest felt tight just saying the words. It got easier, saying them out loud. But it didn't make it any easier to think about.

"All the more reason for you to leave now, while you still can."

Bronwyn met the noblewoman's gaze.

"The longer you stay, the more you'll get wrapped up in their company. You'll be asked to do things, and be depended on. Is that what you want?" Lady Alice asked.

"I'm not sure. I like being useful." And it was true. She did like being needed. There was an excitement in helping sneak out the prince under the empress's nose and Theobold's, and she'd felt a rush of exhilaration when she'd run after Lady Morwenna in the woods. Even their fight, scary as it had been, had also been exciting. Much more so than baking a loaf of bread.

Bronwyn blinked at the realization. Did she even *want* to bake anymore? She shook that thought away. Of course she did. She loved cooking, and baking, and learning new dishes. But working in castle kitchens was often fraught with internal pecking orders and politics amongst the servants, and she more often than not came out on the wrong side of them.

"The castle is up ahead," Rupert called back. "Stay together."

The group huddled close as they rode, no one straying too far. Feeling like part of the rearguard, Bronwyn looked to see if they were being watched. But there was nothing out of the ordinary. People went about their business, farmers walking with their wives and children as leaves blew and swirled in the late autumn, while market traders called out their wares.

The tantalizing smells of roast meat and blood from the butchers' stalls hung in the air, accompanied by the drone of flies. Rupert rode up ahead to the guards and quietly announced who they were.

The guards at first were skeptical, until the queen said, "Tell your mistress, Lady Mabel, Sir Robert's wife, that we are here. She is expecting us. I am happy to wait." Queen Matilda sat on her horse quietly, her hands placed demurely in her lap.

The guards sent word ahead and stood at attention, more so than they had when the group had first approached.

In minutes, word came back, and the guards opened the tall doors of the castle gates. They entered through the forbidding stone gatehouse that was heavily armed, and a sneaking feeling made the hair stand up on the back of Bronwyn's neck.

Soldiers were posted around and archers stood on the top of the gatehouse, watching their every move. She swallowed and tugged at her thin cloak around her neck as she followed the others through medium-sized green lands dedicated to farming, with a main road passing through them.

Up ahead, they crossed a drawbridge and moat and entered the main castle area, where there was a sizeable courtyard, buildings to the right, and a plain, ordinary-looking castle at the end of the courtyard. The entire area was surrounded and fenced in by high stone walls that at once made Bronwyn feel secure and yet unsafe at the same time.

They were met by a well-dressed woman and four guards. The woman instantly curtsied and welcomed the group. "Good morrow. I am Mabel FitzRobert, the Countess of Gloucester, and Sir Robert's wife. You are all welcome here."

The woman, a tall, svelte, brawny woman with thin, black hair and a handsome face, reminded Bronwyn of a hardworking horse. Perhaps it was the woman's strong features and bony structure. Her shoulders were broad rather than curved and petite like Bronwyn was used to seeing. Her eyes missed nothing, no detail, and the firm set of her mouth hinted that she would tolerate no nonsense.

The countess motioned for groomsmen and stableboys to come forward and take the horses. The group dismounted and stood by as their small, meager possessions were unloaded and the horses led away.

Lady Mabel looked them over. "You must all be tired from your journey. I will find rooms for you. But first, I think introductions are in order." She faced them. "I am the chatelaine of this castle. And you are?"

Queen Matilda inclined her head with slight ceremony. "I am Matilda of Boulogne. My husband, Stephen, I believe you know."

"Yes. I bid thee welcome, Your Grace," Lady Mabel said, her gaze passing to the young person beside her. "And you must be Eustace."

"Yes, my lady." He gave her a solemn bow, which made her smile.

"Very good. I am glad to see you both looking well. Who are these other people?" Lady Mabel asked.

Lady Alice introduced herself, along with Rupert. When it came to Bronwyn, she curtsied and said "I'm a cook."

"Well, wonders never cease. In the space of a moment, I am met by a queen, a prince, a noblewoman, a squire, and a cook.

Pray tell, why are there no guards or men-at-arms with you? Were you in hiding?"

"Yes. It is not an easy story to tell. May we rest and refresh ourselves first, and then I will relay what happened?" the queen asked.

"Yes, of course." She led the way.

Bronwyn overheard the chatelaine ask, "We sent messengers to look for you in Devizes and on the main road, but they already returned empty-handed. Were you in great danger?"

"Yes," Queen Matilda said.

"We received conflicting messages. One that said you were lost and could not be found. And another, today, saying you were in the empress's custody and we were to charge Stephen with a hefty ransom for your return and safety. I see now that is not the case." She added, "You do realize that now that you are here, I will have to put you and your son in custody?"

The queen froze.

The noblewoman sounded apologetic. "I will prepare some rooms for your retirement, but then we will need to discuss the arrangements. Now that you are here, I am sure Stephen will wish to be on his way to Winchester. But first, I suspect you would like to visit him."

"Yes," Queen Matilda said. "I would."

"I understand. That will be arranged. May I ask, how is my husband, Sir Robert?" Lady Mabel asked.

"I..." The queen hesitated.

Bronwyn could well understand why. Not a few weeks ago, they had stood side by side in a castle infirmary, looking over his sleeping form. The queen had demanded Bronwyn's knife and debated whether she might kill him then and there, and possibly end the war for the English Crown.

But she hadn't. And now, facing Sir Robert's wife, who had safely ushered in the prisoner exchange negotiations, what could be safely said that was not a lie?

The queen turned. "Mistress Blakenhale, how fared Sir Robert when you last saw him?"

The countess looked askance at the queen but recovered quickly. She peered at Bronwyn, as if taking a moment to memorize her face.

Now with both women looking at her, Bronwyn chose her words carefully.

"Sir Robert is well. He took sick from a wound sustained in battle, but he is fine now. His squire looked after him very well."

"Thank you." Relief was evident in Lady Mabel's voice. "That Theobold, such a dear boy."

The group moved on, and Bronwyn felt a prickling between her shoulder blades. Was it that someone was watching, or that she'd had to speak to the countess herself? She wasn't sure.

Once the queen, prince, and Lady Alice had all been attended to and led to rooms to rest, the countess turned to Rupert and Bronwyn. Her eyes were hazel colored, and while her face had the hard planes and angles of a hardworking horse, her sharp gaze missed no detail.

Her voice was low. "Master Bothwell, I imagine you would like to visit your master, who resides below."

"Yes, my lady." Rupert nodded.

"Very well. I will show you to him." Lady Mabel's gaze flickered to Bronwyn. "Mistress Blakenhale, you may report to the kitchens. I trust you can find the way."

Bronwyn ducked her head in a bow. "Yes, my lady." She watched as the countess led Rupert away. No matter that she had helped bring about the escape of the prince and aided in getting the queen and him here safely. In the eyes of everyone, she was just a servant.

And now she was alone, in a castle, once again. She swallowed and asked for directions, then smiled as she entered the kitchen, a busy, bustling place.

Bronwyn looked around for the person in charge, which was easy enough to find. Usually, it was the person who had the loudest voice and was giving orders. But not always. In this kitchen, for instance, she could see it was the short, middle-aged man who was calm, friendly, offering a warm smile and who laughed with the other servants, but like the countess, his eyes missed nothing.

Their eyes met across the room. She approached and waited as he dealt with cooks who were asking him questions. She swallowed.

He had a handsome face, and he was short, stocky, and muscular. His blond hair was cut short and he stood about five-foot-six, shorter than some of the men she usually saw. But his presence and sense of command were unmistakable. This was the head cook.

"Yes?" he asked. "What brings you to my kitchen?"

"Bronwyn Blakenhale, at your service, sir. I've just come from Devizes."

His blue-eyed gaze sharpened at that, but he made no other sign of emotion. "Well met, Mistress Blakenhale. You are a cook?"

"Yes, sir."

"None of that. Call me 'Master Gregory.' Everyone else does." He nodded to her. "Why are you come from Devizes?"

"I… was traveling with a group of others who came here. Lady Mabel suggested I report here."

"And so here you are. All right. What can you cook?"

"Breads, rolls, cakes, and a few meats and fishes in sauces."

"Jolly good. Sounds like a lot, but let's see if you really can. We're preparing for luncheon. Can you do a soup?"

"Yes, si—Master Gregory."

"Go on, then. Any soup you like. It'll just be for us. You can work over there." He nodded to a worktable, where some of the other cooks were hard at work.

Bronwyn looked about. She felt comfortable being in busy kitchen again but also as if she were under scrutiny, her every move being watched.

Everywhere people worked, there were scraps. Purple carrot

peels, herb stems, bean husks, mushroom ends, and the tops of onions. She found a small bowl and began taking the bits here and there that had been left as scraps, adding them to her bowl.

"What are you doing?" one cook asked.

"Collecting the scraps. I'm making a soup."

That got her a few raised eyebrows and some amused smiles, but she carried on. Once she had the bowl full of the ends of herbs, roots, and vegetables, she took up a stray cauldron and set the cinders beneath it alight, filling it with the collection of scraps and large quantities of water. There was little seasoning to be had, but she had lots of herb ends and stalks, including rosemary, thyme, and sage, so she hoped it would be enough. In minutes, the would-be soup began boiling away.

Occasionally, she would taste it, stir, and taste it again, reducing the liquid. In an hour, it had reduced properly, and now the odds and ends had floated to the top. A lot had disintegrated into the soup, and she stirred this as well.

Master Gregory came by and tasted the mixture with a big, wooden spoon. He blinked and said, "You made this?"

"Yes."

"It's good. Better than I expected."

His words gave her a flash of pride. He'd complimented her cooking.

"But it could use something. Hmm." He left her side, returned with a handful of purple carrots, and said, "You could add these in. Also, there's some leftover peas and potage from yesterday. Add that in, too."

She chopped up the carrots, added in the peas and potage as he'd directed, and left the soup to boil away. He nodded and left her to it.

When luncheon came, the servants, about twenty of them in all, sat down around a long, wooden table and took up all the space on the benches. Bronwyn had ladled out soup enough for them all, and the bowls were passed around with hunks of bread baked that morning. The brown bread had pieces of rosemary in its soft crannies and despite the hard crust on top, it tore easily.

Spoons were passed around and after saying a quick prayer over the food led by Master Gregory, the cooks began eating. There were a few appreciative noises and *hmms* over it, with one saying, "You made this from the scraps?"

"Mm-hmm," Bronwyn said over a bite of bread.

That's the nice thing about working in a castle kitchen, she thought. *No one goes hungry.*

"It's good," was all the cook would say.

Bronwyn nodded her thanks and kept eating. Once the bowls were cleared away and every bit of soup had been either eaten or mopped up with the bread, Master Gregory leaned back in his seat at the head of the table and burped. "That was good. Well done, mistress. Why don't you introduce yourself to us?"

Heads turned. Bronwyn stood up from her seat on the bench. "Um, nice to meet you all. I'm Bronwyn Blakenhale, from Lincoln." She felt embarrassed at everyone looking at her, so she didn't say more. She felt her cheeks grow warm and sat back down.

"Well met, Bronwyn of Lincoln," Gregory said.

"Is it true what people are saying?" one woman cook asked. "That there's the queen here?"

Heads turned toward her.

"Now, Mary, don't go telling tales," Gregory said. "I'm sure Lady Mabel will tell us if we need to know."

Another cook, a thin one with perpetually ruffled blond hair, said, "But that's big news. What if she is? Then that means Stephen will go and…" He left his sentence hanging.

How much does he know about the prisoner exchange? Bronwyn wondered. How much did they all know?

"We shouldn't be talking rumors when we don't have any facts. And it just means you all need to be busier if you've got time to gossip," a servant said. It was another cook, Bronwyn could see. "Begging your pardon, Master Gregory," the man added.

He was in his mid-thirties, she thought. But there was a look, a shared glance between the man and Gregory, that caught Bronwyn's attention.

A second later, Gregory cleared his throat. "All right, let's clear this up."

And within a minute, the cooks were back at work, cleaning and wiping down the table. The table they dined at also served as a worktable, and in no time at all, it was repurposed for chopping, slicing, and dicing for the aristocrats' dinner.

Bronwyn took the now-empty soup cauldron and brought it over to where a group of small potboys and children were chattering and scouring pots and pans to be cleaned. She took a spot by them and after staying quiet for a time, using the moment as they all watched her take a small scouring rag and start cleaning the cauldron, they resumed their talking.

"Who are you?" one asked her. A boy, aged about eight, asked.

"My name is Bronwyn. What's yours?"

"Alfred. I'm like Alfred the Great, my mama says. But then she says he was a great king and I'm not, but maybe I will be someday."

She grinned at him and earned a gap-toothed smile back.

A short time later, just as the cauldron and other dishes were clean, a maid startled and dropped a wooden spoon with a clatter.

The young woman, a pretty thing with wispy hair and a coarse, brown, woolen dress and apron, blushed as Rupert entered the kitchens.

Bronwyn let out a breath. She had an inkling he was looking for her, so she straightened. They locked eyes from across the kitchen, and he approached her. "Making new friends?"

"Something like that." She stood. "What is it?"

"Lady Mabel wants you upstairs. To report. Are you free now?"

Feeling she was being watched, she nodded, when Master Gregory came to her side. He grunted and adjusted his belt around his stocky middle. "What's this? Who are you?" he asked Rupert.

Rupert gave the head cook a polite nod. "Rupert Bothwell. I'm squire to Sir Baldwin of Clare."

"I know that name," Master Gregory said thoughtfully. "Why are you here?"

"Lady Mabel wants to speak with Mistress Bronwyn. Can you spare her?"

"Aye. What Lady Mabel wants, she gets. Go along, Bronwyn, and see what she wants. But come back soon so we can get started on the prep for dinner."

Bronwyn nodded and followed Rupert out, noticing how the young maidservant sighed as she watched them leave. *He's charmed another*, Bronwyn thought.

As they walked out of the kitchens and into a small courtyard between buildings, Rupert asked, "How are you settling in?"

"It's only been a few hours." She snorted. "Well enough. How about you?"

"Same. I haven't had a chance to visit my master yet, though." He ran a hand through his hair and plucked at a stray piece of lint on his tunic. "Lady Mabel wants to hear the whole story. But I don't know if we can trust her."

Bronwyn blinked. She wasn't sure if she could trust anyone. Lady Mabel was the wife of Sir Robert, Empress Maud's righthand man, who currently sat in a prison cell in Winchester. But Lady Mabel was also chatelaine of the castle and in charge here. "What makes you say that?"

"Something about her. I don't know. I'll feel better once I'm reunited with Sir Baldwin. Come on." He kept walking and expected her to keep up.

Bronwyn decided to follow him. Her sense of direction was weak and she knew that in a new place such as Bristol Castle, she should pay attention to the twists and turns of the corridors and look to see where things were. But her mind was wandering and so she did not.

She had no idea how long she might be here and instead satisfied her mind with thinking how their party had been there no longer than a few hours before she was being pulled away from the kitchens, to report to nobility, no less.

That alone might be the stuff that tales came from, as not many servants outside the castle walls interacted with nobility, much less the queen or empress. Most people went about their lives. Bronwyn wondered if she was approaching a crossroads, where she had become a sort of puppet or game piece to be used by the ruling factions, to be traded as needed.

Bronwyn didn't mind helping the queen and empress and liked her sort-of friendship with Lady Alice. Some of the ladies-in-waiting she had encountered before hadn't been too bad. But it was often dangerous work, and ultimately, not even she knew which side she was truly loyal to. Both had their merits and disadvantages. And as she thought to herself, *I'm just a cook. A kitchen maid. What business do I have getting involved in court politics and intrigues?*

They walked down a series of stone steps and through a corridor, almost as if they were heading to a castle cellar. The air changed gradually, growing moist and cool. *It would be delicious on a hot day*, Bronwyn thought.

"You're quiet," Rupert said.

"Just thinking."

"We're here. Just report, same as you would anyone. All right? Don't be afraid."

"Why would I be afraid?" she asked.

He didn't reply, simply nodding to two armed guards who stood before a door. "She is expecting her. Lady Mabel."

The guards opened the door to a room. Rupert squeezed her shoulder and beckoned for her to go in.

Bronwyn stepped inside and instantly tensed. This was not a throne room, or a noblewoman's private solar, where she might rest and repose. She looked over her shoulder and saw Rupert nod to her as exited out through the open door behind her.

This was a large chamber, lit by torches burning in wall sconces that did not heat the air, but instead drew long shadows that flickered against the stone walls.

Inside stood the Lady Mabel, and beside her, a hooded figure. A man, dressed all in black. He wore a low hood and was burly, his shoulders set wide apart. He did not raise his head, but stood calmly, resting his hands on his thick, leather belt at his waist.

Bronwyn gulped. Iron devices stood around the room and a table stood nearby, littered with strange implements as well as an occasional candle that burned but seemed dim in the space. Even its flame was quiet.

"Where am I?" she asked.

But she already knew. This was the real Bristol Prison.

She stood inside a torture chamber.

Chapter Ten

BRONWYN STRAIGHTENED AND tried not to look around too much. But her eyes darted around, looking quickly for a weapon.

Lady Mabel stood before her, not ten feet away. She wore a thin, burgundy dress, the color of rust, and rested her hands on the pommel of a large sword that she spun idly. "Mistress Blakenhale. Mind you tell me the story of how you came here, and all of it, young lady. I do not know who you are or what your place is at court, but I wish to know." Her rough voice was quiet, but it was almost like the sounds of a blade scraping against a piece of rawhide leather. "I would advise you not to lie or omit any facts."

The guards chose at that moment to close the door behind her with a loud creak, and Bronwyn's head snapped over her shoulder. There was no escape, and no clear exit.

She breathed in and immediately wished she hadn't. The air had the lingering odors of blood, like rust, steel and iron, piss, and smoke from the animal wax of candles.

"I know from the squire Rupert Bothwell that the party accompanying the queen and prince was attacked while en route here. How did you come to be involved in this, and what is your relationship with the queen?"

Bronwyn swallowed. "I…" Words failed her. The surroundings made her uneasy, and she could feel the hairs on the back of her neck stand up.

"You dislike your surroundings?"

"Yes, Lady Mabel."

"I use this room as a space to question people whom I do not know and have reason not to trust. I find the space makes people less likely to lie, and they are often most forthcoming. Now talk. Who are you?"

"My name is Bronwyn. I'm a kitchen maid."

"How did you come to enter the queen's service?"

"I…" She fidgeted. "Back in Lincoln, my father and I sold rolls to a nobleman for the king's dinner, but a man died. Someone poisoned them. My father was accused—wrongfully—and I had to find out who did it. Or else we would have both been executed."

"You? But you're nothing but a servant. Why you?" Lady Mabel asked.

"The queen put me to work in the castle kitchens. She thought I would have an easier time finding out who was behind it."

"And did you?"

"Yes. A priest. But the battle happened, and then we got separated. My papa, he—"

Lady Mabel held up a hand. "You stayed in the queen's service after the battle?"

"No, I joined the empress's camp then. I had no home, and nowhere to go. So I joined the cooks there. Traveled with her to London for her coronation and to Winchester." She did not tell of her part in solving crimes of missing crowns, dead noblemen, or horrid pranks on the empress. She got the sense that Lady Mabel was a woman of no nonsense and simply wanted the facts.

"So how came you here? It is a long way for a kitchen maid to travel," Lady Mabel said, spinning the sword pommel in her hands. The big, heavy-looking blade twirled, its sharp point digging into the floor.

"We had word that the empress had made it on to Gloucester

and was moving to Devizes. I'd been offered a chance to stay with the queen but decided to join the empress and so joined a party moving here."

"Why did you not stay with the queen? She offered you the chance of a lifetime, to stay in her service. Not many servants would receive such an offer, or dare refuse one. Who are you to refuse a queen?" Lady Mabel cocked her head.

The woman may look like a horse, Bronwyn thought, *but her eyes are as keen as a hawk's.* "I chose to follow the empress."

"Why?"

"That is my business."

Lady Mabel stopped spinning the blade. "And just what secrets does a kitchen maid have?"

Bronwyn shrugged. "I have none. You ask and I have answered. May I go?"

"No. Not hardly. I think we've barely scratched the surface of what you know." She eyed Bronwyn keenly. "How came you to join the queen's party here?"

"I…" How much could she share? What did she say? The woman was allied to the empress, and as chatelaine, was running the prison. "I… knew they were coming here. My friend Rupert, I knew he was coming here. So I wanted to come with him."

"Why? Is he a lover of yours?"

"No," Bronwyn said vehemently. "Just a friend."

"I see. So you risked life and limb to join your friend. Did you know he was accompanying the queen and the prince here?"

Bronwyn swallowed. She strongly suspected that Rupert and the queen would have revealed that they had been in hiding, but how much of her involvement would they have said?

Sensing something interesting, Lady Mabel turned to the man beside her. "Leave us. She's of no danger to me."

The man moved away without a word, exiting the room.

"Talk. We are alone here," Lady Mabel said. "What is it? You know something, I can tell."

"I… looked after the prince in the castle kitchens, with Rupert," Bronwyn said.

"You hid him from the empress? You knowingly hid a political prisoner from her?"

"Yes."

"Why? What entitles you to make such a decision over a highly political person like the prince? You should have reported it to the empress at once."

"I worried, we both did, that the boy might come to harm if people knew about him. That a search would start for his mother. He's only a child."

"He's on the verge of manhood—and dangerous. What made you think he might be in danger in the empress's stronghold? Surely, he would be treated with the utmost care." There was an innocent tone in the chatelaine's voice that sounded false.

Now it was Bronwyn who cocked her head. "Forgive me, mistress, but I do not think so."

Lady Mabel's eyes burned into hers. "Tell me why."

There was no hiding the facts now. "A ransom demand came for the queen and prince, to the empress. A search had begun but found nothing, and so the men decided to pay the ransom, sort of. I was there the night they set it out. There was a distraction and whilst the men were fighting, I spotted a person who took the ransom and ran off with it."

"Go on."

"I followed her and we fought, and she—"

"It was a woman?"

"Yes. She said she knew where the queen and prince were being kept and took me there. Squire Crispin followed us, and together, we rescued them. We decided it was too dangerous to keep them together, and Lady Morwenna had run off—"

"Lady Morwenna? Lady Morwenna of Banbury?" Lady Mabel froze.

"You know her?"

"Keep telling the story. What happened?"

"Right. I took the prince back to the castle with me, while

Crispin took the queen with him to claim sanctuary at a nunnery outside of the city. We met Squire Rupert at the gates and he recognized the prince, so he helped us get back inside. Together, we pretended he was just a lost boy and worked in the kitchen with the other boys. It was easy enough to hide him."

"Until it wasn't. Why did you leave?"

"Lady Morwenna said she was planning to visit the nunnery. I don't know how many nunneries there are in Devizes, but I figured there would likely only be one, and it would be where the queen was hiding. I knew if she saw the queen there, she would tell the empress, and it would no longer be safe for the prince, so we decided to leave at first light."

"I see." Lady Mabel snorted. "You actually hid the prince right under the empress's nose. For how long?"

"A few days."

Lady Mabel slapped her knee, laughing. "*Days?* All this time, the empress had a prince working in her kitchens and she never knew? Saints alive, girl. You are either mad or have a death wish, I know not which. So you left with the prince, Squire Rupert, and met the queen and Squire Crispin along the way?"

"Yes. And later, Lady Alice joined us."

"Ah, yes. Why is this Squire Crispin not here?"

"He did not want to leave the empress."

"And yet he was part of this duplicitous plot. He has divided loyalties, it seems," Lady Mabel said thoughtfully. "This Lady Alice, tell me about her. Why did she leave the empress?"

Bronwyn blinked. Surely, Lady Alice would have already spoken to the chatelaine about this. "She is a loyal lady-in-waiting to the empress, Lady Mabel."

"So she says. Yet she abandons her mistress at the first sign of trouble and decides to ride with you and two political prisoners here. That speaks to something other than loyalty."

"She is loyal. There was a death at the castle, and Lady Alice didn't feel safe. She has a strong sense of survival."

"I see. But her story doesn't sit right with me. Did she know about you hiding the prince?"

"No."

"So she had some other reason for leaving. Do you think she had something to do with the dead person?"

"No. I…" Bronwyn hesitated. Rupert and Lady Alice's relationship was their business, but in this case, it might help her friend avoid suspicion. "She is in a romantic relationship with Rupert."

"Oho! What a great storyteller you are, Mistress Blakenhale. I daresay we should pull up chairs by the fire and share a pitcher of wine. I could listen to this all night. But I have no time." The countess walked around, using the large sword almost as a very dangerous walking stick.

Lady Mabel's eyes flickered to Bronwyn, quick as a snake. "So I have now in my prison a queen, a prince, a lady-in-waiting who says she's loyal but abandons the empress to join her lover escorting political prisoners, a cook who knows far more than is good for her, and one squire." Lady Mabel's face clouded. "You may go."

"Lady Mabel, what will become of us? I gather that Rupert's master is here. Sir Baldwin of Clare. And Lady Alice is still here?"

"That is none of your concern, Mistress Blakenhale." The noblewoman's hawk-like eyes slid to her. "The queen and prince will enjoy a certain amount of protection here, for their own safety. They will not be alone. One of the queen's own ladies-in-waiting, Lady Muriel, managed to come here and relayed the news about the attack."

Bronwyn's eyes widened. Lady Muriel had escaped the attack? That was news.

Seeing Bronwyn made no move to leave, the noblewoman sighed and said, "The squire will be reunited with his master and is free to join him in the cells. I have given the king and queen an hour to speak with one another, and that hour is almost up."

"And then?"

"Then Stephen will take armed guards and ride to Winchester, where he will free Sir Robert in the prisoner exchange. Once my husband goes free and presumably rides to Devizes to join the empress, the queen and her son will be free to return to Stephen in Winchester."

"Would Sir Robert not come here first, Lady Mabel?"

"Why would he do that?"

"To see you, milady. As his wife?"

Lady Mabel stared at Bronwyn, then laughed again. "You are a sweet young woman, aren't you? With a head full of romance, I can see. No. My husband's first duty is to his empress, as is mine."

"And me, milady?"

"You are welcome to stay and work in the kitchens here, or wherever you please. I do not care. But do not go far, Mistress Blakenhale. You interest me. I would suggest you stay here for a time. I like your stories. I wonder if they are true."

She waved a hand, and Bronwyn was dismissed. She curtsied, turned and without looking too much around, went out the door. Once outside it and safely back in the fresh air, she hurried up the stone steps and kept running until she found herself in the courtyard, breathing in fresh, clean air again.

Bronwyn took great deep breaths and leaned against the stone walls of the building's exterior, letting the sounds and smells of the outdoors bring her mind back to the mundane. Beside her stood empty barrels and beyond those, small sacks of grain waiting to be taken into the pantry. Workers, men mostly, walked past with hoes and rakes to carry on with the planting and harvesting. Being October, most of the harvesting was done for the year, but some plants would still bear fruit in a late harvest. The last before the first frost, she imagined.

"How did it go?" Rupert's voice came to her ears. He came out of the same entryway she'd exited. "I saw you run past. You all right?"

She nodded.

"Your face is pale. She didn't hurt you, did she?"

"No. But... I don't like it. Like *her*, I mean."

He shrugged. "Doesn't matter. We're here now, or at least I am. You don't have to be. You could return to Devizes. Or go back to Lincoln. Find your family."

"I could." She leaned her head back against the wall and closed her eyes, breathing in the ordinary scents of hay and grain. She relished the warm sunlight on her face.

"But I'd like it if you stayed," Rupert said quietly.

Bronwyn's eyes flew open. Did he really just…?

"What did you say?" she asked, just as Lady Alice came through the passageway.

"Ah, there you are. Rupert, have you seen Bronwyn—oh. You're both here," she said, eyeing them curiously. "Where were you? I've been looking for you."

"I was speaking with Lady Mabel." Bronwyn repressed a shiver. The woman's dark chamber would no doubt give her nightmares that evening.

"Ah. Well, I have news. So Matilda and Stephen had but an hour to see each other, and now he's preparing to ride to Winchester with a party of guards. He would bring his loyal knights with him, but…" She hesitated. "Rupert. Have you seen your master?"

"No. Not yet. I was trying to, but the guards wouldn't let me past without Lady Mabel's order."

Lady Alice bit her lip. "You should try again. I bet they'll let you through now. From what I heard, he's not well."

Rupert's eyes widened, and he ran, a fleeing shadow where once had stood a man.

Bronwyn turned to her friend. "What have you heard?"

"I stayed by Matilda's side as long as I could, but Lady Mabel wanted to have her own conference with her alone. As well as her son. They are to be prisoners here. I haven't seen them since."

Bronwyn nodded.

"But it seems like Sir Baldwin, Rupert's master, has taken ill from his time in the cells. He needs a physick. Whatever medicine can be found for him. But he's not so valuable as some of the other men, so nothing is being done for him." She frowned. "I only hope his health improves."

A FEW DAYS later, Bronwyn and Lady Alice met in the castle courtyard, near the stables, and took a moment to chat.

"I've been thinking." Lady Alice leaned in, her voice quiet. "If Sir Baldwin were to die, that would leave Rupert without a master."

"What would happen then?"

"He could offer his service to Stephen—or Empress Maud. Whichever he chose. If he allied himself to the empress, I'm sure she could find a knight who would take him on. And it would mean that he could stay close to me." She gave a little sigh. "I believe that in his heart, he is loyal to Stephen, just like Sir Baldwin. I'm not sure he would give up an allegiance so easily."

"Will you try to convince him?" Bronwyn asked.

"No. I would have to be subtler, more artful, than openly trying to convince him to switch sides if his master dies. But I will be watching. Truly, I want him to be happy. Could you tend to his master, if Lady Mabel will let you?"

"I could try. But I don't know anything about nursing or physick, not really."

"I'll try to find a solution. There must be a nurse, or a surgeon, a clergyman, who could use some gold to line his pockets."

"You have gold?"

"Not much, but I can pay for some small things."

"If you were my wife, you would never have to pay for anything," Crispin's slow drawl came from behind them.

Bronwyn turned. There stood Crispin, with a horse. He nodded to them both. "I've just come. I changed my mind. Didn't want there to be any confusion about the castle's new guests."

"Prisoners, you mean," Lady Alice said.

Bronwyn glanced between the two of them. There was definitely a heated moment between them.

"Why must you twist every word I say, woman?" Crispin asked.

"Why do you hide from speaking the truth? They are prisoners. You delivered them here yourself. You shouldn't shy away from calling them that." Lady Alice stalked toward him, her eyes flashing.

He stepped closer, looking down at her. "I shy away from nothing. Certainly not a woman who challenges me."

"I'll challenge you all I like." Lady Alice tossed her head, when Crispin grabbed her arm and pulled her in close. As Lady Alice stumbled, Crispin dropped the horse's reins and pulled her into a kiss.

Bronwyn stared. She blinked, then looked away.

Lady Alice squealed and shoved him away, stepping back awkwardly. "Don't you dare try that again. You lout!"

Crispin laughed. "Did you like it?"

"Your breath smells," Lady Alice said.

"You smell like flowers," he told her.

It was true. Lady Alice had clearly just taken a bath, for her damp, jet-black hair glistened in the sun. And she did indeed smell like flowers. Perhaps she'd put them in the bathwater, Bronwyn wondered.

"You take liberties, squire. Do not handle me thus again, or I will report you."

"Report me? To whom? Your empress? Oh, wait, she sits in a castle in Devizes. And Matilda has enough problems without you wasting her time about kissing squires. And the lady of this castle? She might even approve. You never know."

Lady Alice's mouth dropped open. "You think very highly of yourself."

"My family owns five hundred acres and I am due to inherit. I am prepared to fight for the right ruler of England. All I need is a title and soon a pretty wife so I can enjoy her smiles in bed." He winked at her.

Lady Alice let out a loud grunt of exasperation and turned, her long, black hair rippling behind her like a wave as she stalked away.

Crispin picked up the horse's reins and looked in the direction Lady Alice had gone. Then he looked at Bronwyn. "What?"

"I didn't say anything."

"You think it wrong of me. When she cares for the other squire."

Bronwyn shrugged one shoulder. "I think it wrong of you to steal a kiss. Perhaps a given one would be sweeter."

He shouldn't have pressed his advantage and kissed her friend that way. But she didn't think it was a bad thing for Lady Alice to have a little harmless flirtation. She wished she had someone who chased after her that way. And then at the thought of Theobold, her smile disappeared.

"I should get back."

"Bronwyn, wait." His voice was quiet. "The chatelaine here, Lady Mabel. I should introduce myself to her."

"Yes, you should. The stables are over there. I'm sure she'll want to see you."

"You've spoken to her?"

She nodded.

"Is she a goodly sort of woman?" he asked.

"You mean will she be open to your charming her?" she teased.

"You can see through me that easily?" he asked.

"A little. But I would not waste your time. She is…" *A hard woman*, she thought. Lady Mabel made her nervous. If the empress and the queen were birds of prey, then Lady Mabel was a ground scavenger, like a badger or a pine marten. They might not attack from the sky, but they were equally dangerous in their own right.

"I would speak plainly when you talk to her. She will not care for any flowery language."

"Bronwyn, how much did you tell her?"

"Everything. She wanted to know how we came to hide the queen and prince, and… I was interrogated in her chamber. It was frightening."

"What chamber?" he asked. "Did she threaten you?"

"She didn't have to. The chamber was bad enough." She raised a hand idly, and her fingers gave a solitary tremble. "I need to go. They'll be wondering in the kitchen what happened to me."

"All right. Stay safe. I'll speak to you when I can." He clapped her on the shoulder like he would a comrade.

They parted ways. Bronwyn returned to the kitchens and lost track of the hours as she joined the other cooks in preparing the evening meal. She washed and peeled purple carrots, cleaned cabbage, and stirred potage, all while taking turns rotating the spit, the juices from a fat haunch of pork sizzling in the air.

As Bronwyn let her vision unfocus in the routine of turning the spit, she realized that at that moment, she didn't care about her problems just then. She didn't care about anything.

She was nineteen, for heaven's sake. She wanted to be spending her days baking bread and collecting herbs for loaves and buying spices at the market for spiced breads. She missed the lazy days of summer, where she might nap along the river bank, dozing in the shining rays of sunshine while blue dragonflies flitted lazily around her.

Bronwyn wanted the biggest danger to be a risk of a bumble-bee sting or a wasp, not a noblewoman's threats or having to defend herself in what looked like a torture chamber. She knew she would have nightmares just thinking about it.

But now she didn't care.

Lady Mabel's questioning had chilled her, more so than any threat she had received so far in her nineteen years of life, and Bronwyn desperately wanted to go home. Back to Lincoln, to her old life, but that didn't exist anymore. And the River Witham that she had napped by many a day had seen ships sink and more than five hundred souls drown in its steps, if the stories were to be believed. For all she knew, her family had been among them, she thought grimly.

She wanted to go back home to investigate. Surely, someone, somewhere, must have heard some information about her father and stepmother, or even Wat, their young apprentice who liked honey cakes.

She marched toward the privy, but as she found the private privy and closed the door, sitting on the wooden seat and raising her skirts to urinate, Bronwyn knew that it wasn't true.

Yes, she could slip away at night or at dawn and take a route for Lincoln, but there would be dangers on the road, particularly for a young woman. But that wasn't what kept her there at Bristol. As she wiped herself dry with a dirty rag and wiped her hands on her apron, rearranging her skirts, she knew it was a lie she was telling herself.

The fact was, she did care.

Bronwyn had helped Queen Matilda and the prince because she had wanted to. She didn't expect any thanks or reward from it. She cared about her friend, Lady Alice, and Rupert and Theobold. Bronwyn wanted to know more about the death of Philippa the maid and wished she could be there to ask questions and figure out how the young woman had died.

Truth be told, she didn't care so much about the war for the English Crown. Bronwyn didn't know who was right or to which side it truly belonged, but this was the life she had fallen into.

Bronwyn returned to the castle kitchens, hearing the familiar pattern of rain outside, and thought how glad she was to be indoors and not out in the cold rain. She shivered. It was October now. Even if she left that very day for Lincoln, there was no way to say for certain that she would survive the journey, especially in the upcoming winter. Although without the knowledge as to whether her family lived, the demands for her loyalty by both royal courts, and the constant tug and pull of her friendship and love from both friends and men, Bronwyn rather felt like her days and nights were as cold as the winter sun, without a glimpse of warmth to look forward to.

"Bronwyn! Mistress Bronwyn!" a voice called.

Bronwyn turned around. Lady Muriel, a lady-in-waiting to the queen, came toward her, her narrow face briefly lit up with a tight smile.

"Bronwyn, I thought that was you." Lady Muriel clasped her arms and curtsied. "I say, it is good to see a friendly face."

Bronwyn curtsied in return. "Lady Muriel, I didn't think I'd see you again."

"I know it's been a horrible time. Walk with me a little?"

Curiosity filled her. This noblewoman had shown little interest in her before, so why now? And with the queen imprisoned, why was she wandering about the castle freely? She wanted to know. "I can spare a minute or two," Bronwyn said.

"Good. I've had such a horrible time." Lady Muriel took Bronwyn's arm in hers like they were old friends and began chattering away. "You've no doubt heard about the horrible attack on the queen's party."

Before Bronwyn could respond, Lady Muriel said, "It was terrifying. Ghastly days of riding in a wagon or on a horse in the hot sun and rain, then cold nights shivering by the fire. I swear never to go traveling anywhere ever again."

"It is a marvel you survived," Bronwyn said.

"I know. One moment we were riding in the late afternoon, early evening, and I was admiring the sunset, and then the next, we were surrounded by armed men and attacked, arrows, swords. It was so frightening. People shouting, horses rearing."

"How did you escape?" Bronwyn asked.

"My horse threw me. I fell and ran. In the darkness, it was easy to run and hide. So I did," Lady Muriel said.

"Did you see who led the attack?"

"Not really. I was so scared, and it was dark. Some men surrounded the queen and prince, and they rode away. But it had grown dark by then. But the voices, it's strange. One of the men, I'm sure I heard his voice before."

"Who was it?" Bronwyn asked.

"I'm not sure, I only heard him speak for a second or two. I hid behind a tree. There were some other men, but by that point, it was so dark, I didn't move until they left, and when I came out of hiding, the men and horses were dead. I wandered around the main road until I found a spare horse from our party and found my way here. I begged sanctuary at a church and followed some monks to get directions here."

Bronwyn wondered at this. The lady was brave, to be sure. But had she just been brave, resourceful, and lucky, or had she been some part of a larger plot? Could she be telling a made-up story?

As if sensing Bronwyn's thoughts, Lady Muriel said, "I think it was by the grace of God that I made it here. I don't know why or how I survived. Once the men had gone, I looked for the queen and prince, but they were gone, and I knew the men must have taken them. They must have been mercenaries or bad men, I don't know. All I found were bodies." The noblewoman shivered.

Bronwyn nodded.

"I knew I had to come here and tell the chatelaine what happened. They would be waiting for us. I remembered and for this exchange not to happen, this attack, it seemed too timely for me." Lady Muriel leaned in close, her eyes darting from side to side. Her voice was quiet. "I think someone must have known we were coming and where we would be. But who would want to stop us from arriving here, and why? Who would want to prevent the prisoner exchange from happening? That's what I don't know."

Bronwyn considered the noblewoman carefully. From what she knew, Lady Muriel was a loyal subject of the queen. She had undertaken a perilous journey to accompany her royal mistress to Bristol at great danger to herself, and she had made it here, surprisingly, when she could have fled and returned back home.

Her journey to reach Bristol and report what had happened spoke of strength, which made Bronwyn slightly impressed.

Lady Muriel hugged her arms to her chest. "And now the queen is here. I'm so glad she and the prince are safe. I heard that you had a part in her rescue. How did you do it?"

Bronwyn thought quickly. She liked Lady Muriel, but how much could she trust her? "In all honesty, Lady Muriel, we were chasing after a person who wanted ransom. When I followed them, they led me to a pit. To my surprise, it was a noblewoman like yourself who led me there. I think she wanted credit or help later for her part in showing us where they could be found."

Lady Muriel's narrow face clouded. "That speaks of vile treachery and treason. I'm shocked a lady would stoop to such behavior. Are you sure it was a lady and not a servant or someone like yourself, in any case, to knowingly imprison a queen and her son too?"

Bronwyn bit back a sharp retort. Just because she was of a servant class did not mean she or others in her same station would naturally be thieves or deceivers.

The noblewoman shook her head. "We do live in dangerous times." Lady Muriel patted Bronwyn on the arm. "Be well, and take care of yourself, Mistress Bronwyn."

"And you, Lady Muriel."

They curtsied to one another and parted ways.

Bronwyn returned to the kitchen, where she joined people stripping pea pods at worktables. As she worked, the young maid who had admired Rupert from earlier appeared at her side. "You're Bronwyn, right?"

"Yes," Bronwyn said.

The young woman asked, "Who was the man with you? The young man? The handsome one. Is he a knight?"

Bronwyn turned to look at her more closely. The voice belonged to a scullery maid, a mousy, young woman of average height; ruddy, red cheeks; and greasy, wispy, dark hair, but with a sweet smile and a toothy grin.

"He's no knight. He's a squire," Bronwyn said. "That's Ru-pert. He's a friend of mine."

"How good a friend?" the maid asked, her tone becoming harder.

"Who are you?"

"I'm Mary. I'm a cook here." She stood up straight and raised her chin importantly.

Bronwyn bit back a smile. The young woman couldn't have been more than eighteen or so. Still, Bronwyn wanted to shake her head. They had only been at the castle for a day or two, and already, Rupert had an admirer. She couldn't believe it.

"We're just friends," she said.

"Good." Mary gave a sharp nod and walked away.

"Wait, there's something you should—" Bronwyn paused as another cook filled her vision.

"Let one of the others do this. We need your help with the capons. Come with me."

Bronwyn stopped what she was doing and followed the young man. The tall and thin youth had short, light-brown hair, cut close to his head and ears. He spoke confidently and didn't wait or stop for her to ask any questions. He just moved with an easy, quick efficiency and seemed to expect her to follow. So she did.

He led her to a table where ten dead birds lay, including hens, ducks, and capons. "These need plucking and butchering. Can you start plucking?"

"Sure."

"Good, Master Gregory said you could do it. I'm Luke. There's to be a banquet tonight, so we need to be fast."

"A banquet for the queen?" Bronwyn asked.

Luke snorted. "Not unless you know something I don't. She's up in a tower somewhere. This meal is for the rest of the guests." He raised an eyebrow. "Didn't I hear you come in with the queen?"

"Yes."

"You don't seem like the type of cook who fusses about who they're cooking for." He crossed his arms. "And we don't here, as a rule. You better get used to that if you want to stay here."

Bronwyn nodded, most definitely not wanting to make a fuss. Instead, she got down to work and began plucking feathers. The hours passed as she helped pluck, dress, and butcher the capons, ducks, and hens for poaching in milk, then helped roast the hens and ducks in fat trimmed with rosemary and thyme.

Days later, while the noble guests were in the main dining hall at a banquet, a message came down to the kitchen. A page came and spoke to Master Gregory, whose face clouded. He raised an arm and called over Bronwyn.

At her approach, he said, "Mistress Bronwyn, it seems there is a request for you to go be present at the banquet, not to join them. Frankly, I don't know why they want you there, but you might as well go and see what they want."

Bronwyn surveyed the page, who looked about age eleven.

He shifted his weight on his feet and said, "Lady Mabel said to bring her now and to be quick about it."

"All right, best see what she wants. Go on, Bronwyn. Let's give you a fresh platter of bread to bring in case that's what they're after."

Bronwyn took a wooden trencher that soon became laden with bread and dutifully filled, then followed the page out of the kitchen and through the castle corridors into the main dining hall, but the noise and clamor surprised her, for the banquet was in an uproar.

As Bronwyn and the page entered, she stopped and stared as two men wrestled and grunted, although looking at the number of fists and punches, she realized this wasn't a friendly wrestling bout. This was a fight.

Bronwyn wondered if this was some sort of entertainment, but then she saw Rupert take an elbow to the gut, and he punched the other fighter in the back, sending him sprawling to the floor.

Bronwyn set the platter down on the table and said, "Stop!"

A few people looked at her, but no one moved.

Then a voice said, "Sir knights. Somebody move the boys apart." The chatelaine sounded bored, almost disdainful.

In seconds, two knights, burly, older men, had separated the two fighters, who cursed and stood by angrily.

Blood dripped from Rupert's nose, while Bronwyn looked closer to see... "Crispin?"

The squire looked up at the sound of his name and gave her a sharp nod. He had the makings of what looked like a puffy eye that would no doubt turn black with bruises.

A barked laugh from the countess filled the silence. "It seems you are very much desired, Lady Alice."

Bronwyn's friend blushed. Seeing Bronwyn there, Lady Alice gave her a look as if to say, *What are you doing here?*

Behind Bronwyn, Mary, the admiring kitchen maid from earlier, said, "Oh, Rupert," and hurried toward him, taking his arm, tending to him as others looked on.

A few knights and people there exchanged smiles, while others rolled eyes. They'd no doubt seen this behavior before. Lady Alice's brow knit angrily at first and then tried to affect a bored, disinterested gaze. She buffed her nails on her dress and looked away.

Crispin's upper lip curled in disgust and pulled his arms free of the knights holding him back. "I'm fine. It's over." He grunted and walked toward Bronwyn.

Lady Mabel growled, "I didn't give you permission to leave."

The squire looked at her. It was a hard, unfriendly stare.

The chatelaine said, "But I would not have you drip blood on my table. Mistress Bronwyn, attend to him and when you are done, tell the pages and cooks to bring up more food, The queen will need to be fed, I suppose."

So. That answered the question of why she had been sent for, although why the countess hadn't just requested a page, she didn't know.

"Where is the queen, Lady Mabel?" Bronwyn asked.

"In the east tower, where she belongs."

Bronwyn curtsied and walked out with Crispin. Once they were in the shadows and away from the others, she asked, "Are you all right?"

"I'm fine," came Crispin's low voice.

They walked a few minutes more before she asked, "Why were you fighting, and why did you change your mind in coming here? I thought you planned to stay with the empress."

"I did, but when I arrived, she had an errand for me, and a message for you."

Bronwyn stared at him. "What does the empress want with me?"

"She's mad that you left with the maidservant dead. She wanted you to… I don't know. She wanted your help or some such, but that's not why I'm here. Her message is that she wants you to stay here at Bristol."

"What?" Bronwyn paused, almost tripping over her shoes. "What do you mean?"

Crispin grunted. "Isn't it obvious? She wants you to spy on Matilda of Boulogne."

$$\text{Chapter Eleven}$$

B RONWYN COULDN'T BELIEVE it. Or rather, she *could*, but she didn't want to. The empress had sent her a message telling her to spy on the queen. How much more difficult could this day get?

Bronwyn blinked and said quietly, "I am not the empress's woman."

"Aren't you?" Crispin leaned in, giving her a good view of his growing black eye. "Lest you forget, we are in a prison in the empress's stronghold. Lady Mabel may be in charge here, but she answers to the empress, as do we all. If you want my advice—"

She didn't.

"—then you'll do as she asks."

"But what am I supposed to do? She sent me away from her court in disgrace. She basically told me never to return. And now she wants a favor? Why? She has everything she could want. And besides, the queen is in a tower. She's not doing anything worth reporting on," Bronwyn said.

He shook his head. "You don't understand. Until she becomes the acknowledged ruler of all England, Empress Maud will never have everything she wants. Get used to it. Now, spying should be easy for you. All you have to do is watch her and deliver her food. Tell me of any secret messages she tries to send out. The queen likes you. She trusts you. I can tell you, do this and the empress will reward you."

"Are you sure about that?" Bronwyn said.

"I have to be," Crispin said, almost cryptically. He avoided her gaze.

She wondered why. From what she knew of him, he came from a wealthy family that owned lands nearby, and he knew the area well. So why was he spending his time cozying up to an empress, trying to gain favor at her court, when, as he'd said to Alice earlier, all he needed was a pretty wife, and he was due to inherit? She wondered if there was something else behind his actions.

But maybe she would never know.

Bronwyn viewed Crispin for a moment. He was young, maybe in his early twenties, with a shock of hair that gave him a rakish look, though there were lines around his mouth and eyes. Was it fatigue, concern, or something else?

"Why were you fighting?" she asked again.

"It was dumb," he started.

Bronwyn waited.

Crispin shifted his feet. "One of the men commented that there were many fair ladies at court, but none so pretty as those in his own family and town of Wessex. I told him that he was wrong and that there are many fine ladies here at court, especially Lady Alice, who is quite the beauty. Rupert got mad and said I had no right to say such a thing, as if we were close. I said in my heart, I knew her *very well*." He rubbed the side of his face. "I probably shouldn't have said that; the people looked quite shocked. But one thing led to another." He shrugged. "Anyway, it doesn't matter. That Rupert is not short of admirers himself. I say, who was that maid running after him? She was making a right fool of herself. And he barely got a scratch on him."

Bronwyn smiled a little. Was he jealous?

"He does indeed have many admirers," she said, but she had spoken more forcefully than she'd intended.

Crispin cocked his head at her. "You like him. Rupert."

Bronwyn thought at first to deny it, but some inner sense told her he would see right through her. "I do. We're good friends," she said brightly.

"But you wish you were more," he said slowly.

"No, I..." Bronwyn paused, thinking of Theobold. "I don't know what I want anymore."

"I could help you. Help you attract him." He spoke conspiratorially. "You may work in the kitchens, but you're not ugly. You have what it takes to attract him. If you wanted to."

Crispin's voice sounded oily and annoying. It grated on her ears.

She didn't know what she wanted. She admired Rupert, yes. She fancied him fiercely, yes. But she also knew that there was an unresolved romance between him and Lady Alice, and she was not about to get in the way of that.

And frankly, Crispin's offer made her trust him less. Bronwyn stared at him, giving him a hard frown.

"All you need to do is spy on the queen, and I'll tell you what you have to do in order to have Rupert fall into your arms," he said.

A quiet gasp.

"Did you hear that?" Bronwyn asked.

"What?"

She held up a finger to her lips for silence, then waited. Hearing nothing, she said, "Never mind. But that is not what I want, and even if it were, he is... He has an understanding with my friend Lady Alice." She turned her back on him, her long, blonde braid whipping against her back. "And even if I did such a want such a thing, *which I don't*, I certainly wouldn't ask *you* for help."

Bronwyn shot Crispin a dirty look and began to walk away.

"Remember what I said," Crispin called after her. "All you have to do is so simple. It's just..." His voice grew louder. "He's probably romancing that scullery maid as we speak. Why stand by when that could be you?"

Bronwyn turned away again but spotted a slip of a blue dress turning the corner. So someone had been listening to their conversation. The question was: who?

Bronwyn walked away faster, not wanting to hear anymore.

Back in the kitchens, Bronwyn reported to Master Gregory and relayed the chatelaine's orders for more food and drink, and a tray for the royal prisoners. She set about making a tray for the queen and the prince when Master Gregory said, "Don't worry about that. One of the others will do it. Go sit and get a bite to eat."

Bronwyn took his advice, joining a few of the cooks who were lingering at the table finishing their evening meal. Bronwyn helped herself to a stale bread trencher and a potage, also filling up a spare cup with stale ale. The drink made her burp, and she didn't much like the taste, but she was thirsty, and it was safer than water. She drank thirstily, eating her pale-beige potage of beans, peas, meat juices, cabbage, and onions with a bit of fat from the meat juices that had drained from the spit earlier.

It was delicious and a little bit greasy, but she loved it. Bronwyn ate, drank, and swallowed mouthfuls and yet... did not feel satisfied. Even if by bringing them food and drink, it would give her the perfect opportunity to watch and listen, she didn't want to spy on the queen. She had no business doing so, and she didn't want or feel like she should do the empress any favors. The empress she knew was cold, plotting, calculating, and she did not doubt that the woman would have used the queen and prince as pawns to get what she wanted at great risk to their lives. Was the English Crown so great a thing that she would gladly endanger a mother and son?

But then she realized so many people had died already, maybe she was too low born to consider such things. That was the thing, Bronwyn supposed. The reason why she did not consider herself the empress's woman to call on. Some internal sense had made her decide actively not to tell the empress that she and Crispin had found the missing queen and prince, and that judgment alone had kept her from wanting to spy on them. She had no reason to, nor any incentive to want to. So why should she?

But later, as Bronwyn was with the other cooks cleaning up the kitchen and thinking about finding a place to sleep, she spotted Mary, the scullery maid, looking all rosy cheeked and starry eyed. The maid saw Bronwyn looking at her and came over grinning, almost bouncing on the balls of her feet.

"All right, Mary?" Bronwyn asked.

Mary grinned. "He's so wonderful. Rupert's the kindest, most handsome man I've ever met, and I've met knights before, you know? They're nothing to him."

The cook working beside Bronwyn laughed and rolled his eyes. "Don't go losing your heart to him, Mary. You don't know what these boys are like."

Another cook laughed and Mary blushed.

"Don't listen to them, Mary," Master Gregory said. "You just be careful whom you give your heart to. That's all."

Mary giggled and skipped away.

"That silly girl. She'll be half in love with him already by tomorrow. Mark my words," Master Gregory said.

Eyes turned to Bronwyn. "You know the squire she's talking about, Bronwyn. He a friend of yours?" the head cook asked.

Bronwyn nodded as she wiped down the work table.

A minute later, Master Gregory stood beside her. He asked quietly, "What's on your mind, Bronwyn?"

She smiled. Was it so obvious?

"Rupert has always been popular of women," she said.

"He does have a handsome face," Master Gregory agreed. "I can see why some women would like him."

"Yes, but he also befriends a lot of women, and he flirts a lot, and I just wouldn't want Mary to get her heart broken when he's not serious about anyone right now." She bit her lip and wiped the countertop harder.

"You don't think he would ruin or hurt Mary, do you?" Gregory asked.

"I think she would be wise to view him as a pretty face.

That's all."

"What are you saying about me, Bronwyn?" Rupert asked from behind her.

She whirled around, her face growing warm. "Rupert, I…"

"Telling others to stay away from me?" He shot her a dirty look. "I could tell them a few things about you too, but then that would be mean of me. I care and respect my friends. I thought you were the same."

"We are. We are friends," she started.

Rupert held up a hand. "Save it," he said. "At least now I know what you really think of me." He looked down at his shoes. "So what if I want to walk around with a pretty girl? Is that a crime?"

Bronwyn blinked and looked away. First he was romancing Philippa at Devizes, now Mary at Bristol. Was he really so fickle? What about his subtle warmth and regard for herself? Was it all just part of his natural flirtatious nature?

"No, lad, it isn't," Master Gregory said. "Don't mind us. We're just sharing gossip after a long day. Bronwyn here just didn't want young Mary to get the wrong idea about you, that's all."

Rupert shot Bronwyn a frown. "Maybe let Mary make up her own mind and stop sticking your nose in other people's business."

Bronwyn bristled, and the head cook stepped in front of her, staring Rupert in the face. "All right, mate. Was there something you wanted?"

Rupert said, "Yes, I was looking for Mary. Where might I find her?"

Tension set in Master Gregory's shoulders. He pointed. "That way."

Rupert turned on his heel and left, but not before shooting Bronwyn a dark look.

Bronwyn watched him go as master Gregory tutted under his tongue, "There goes trouble. I can just see it." He turned around. "Never mind the number of times Mary has gone and lost her heart to a young man. We've had to console her more times than I can count. But that's their business, and none of ours."

Bronwyn stifled a yawn and the head cook grinned. "You must be tired. Get thee to bed and I'll speak to you in the morning."

Bronwyn bid the other cook good night and went to the great hall to find a place to sleep by the other women servants. As soon as she'd laid her head down and had her back to the wall, she wondered, *What will Lady Alice think of Rupert's behavior, and how are the queen and prince faring in captivity?*

The next morning, Bronwyn rose and woke, her back stiff from lying curled up against a stone wall on the floor. The wooden floor had rushes on it and was relatively clean, but she had woken in different surroundings, and it took her a minute to remind herself of where she was.

She rose slowly, stretching, and after using the privy, made her way to the kitchens, where the cooks were beginning the day's work. She joined in and helped roll out dough for fresh bread, sprinkling the long worktable with a bit of flour.

As she started working steadily with the other cooks and made loaves of bread, she subtly looked around the kitchen.

"Morning, Bronwyn," Master Gregory said.

Bronwyn mumbled a greeting.

"And how do you think our Mary is today, still madly in love? Or has she seen the light and seen past Rupert's handsome face?" the head cook teased.

Bronwyn smiled. "We'll have to ask her." She glanced around the kitchen, looking this way and that. She didn't see her anywhere.

"Hmm, could be she drank too much and is sleeping it off. Although if she's actually sleeping with him, I'll give her an earful." Master Gregory bellowed, "Michael, go find Mary and wake her up. Tell her she should have been here an hour ago."

The cook left, and the head cook smiled at Bronwyn before adding, "Just you wait. We'll see what she has to say for herself."

Bronwyn got back to work, but as the minutes passed and then longer, there was no sign of the maid.

"Where has that girl gotten to?" one cook wondered aloud, and Bronwyn tensed for a second, an unhappy feeling curling down her spine. Had something happened?

Her suspicions rose when Michael returned empty-handed. "Couldn't find her. Don't know where she is."

Master Gregory frowned. "This is ridiculous. Alan, George, go find her. Bring her here straight away. I don't care if she's fast asleep or puking her guts out. I want her here now or at least to know where she is."

The two cooks left.

One cook came up to him. "You don't think something happened to her, do you? A lot of new visitors around at the castle…" He gave a not-so-subtle, unfriendly look at Bronwyn. "It wouldn't surprise me if she ran into trouble."

Bronwyn bit the inside of her cheek. If people had not been thinking that already, they would be now. Newcomers were never trusted, and it could take years for someone to finally gain someone's trust, especially in the servants' quarters.

She looked around. The cooks beside her worked, but more than one now exchanged worried looks and glances heavy with meaning, and more than a few untrustworthy glances were sent her way.

One woman cook said, "Not to worry. Master Gregory, she's probably asleep in a hay loft somewhere or stuck under a bush."

"You're probably right. Ida, go search the gardens," the head cook ordered.

"I'll look too," Bronwyn said.

"Fine. Bronwyn, go with her."

Bronwyn followed Ida, who nodded to her, wiped her hands and quit the kitchens without a word.

As they walked together, Ida said, "You're one of those people who arrived the other day with the queen. Are you her personal cook or something like that?"

"No, not really."

"Oh." The long-legged, skinny young cook kept walking, her interest in Bronwyn having waned. "I'm Ida. I've worked here for about ten years."

"That's exciting."

"Is it?" The cook didn't sound so sure.

"Well, you cook for royalty, so I'd say so."

The woman cook shrugged. "It's no big deal. It's like what Master Gregory always says: doesn't matter who's dining up at the dining hall or in the dungeons. They're just another mouth to feed."

Bronwyn made a noncommittal *hmm* noise as she followed Ida out of the castle and through the courtyard, past the stables and around the back of the castle walls, where many areas were devoted to farming.

Their search continued. Bronwyn didn't pay much attention to their surroundings; she just worked to keep pace with the cook. As she was just about to ask Ida to slow down, the maidservant came to a sudden stop.

"What the—?" Bronwyn started.

"Look at that," the maid uttered. She slowly lifted an arm and pointed. "Found 'em."

"What?" Bronwyn followed the maid's gaze. There ahead, beneath a large rosebush, lay a shape with two feet sticking out beneath its branches. The morning dew dotted the grass and caught the light, almost looking like icicles in winter. Rose petals lay scattered around her.

Relief passed over Bronwyn. "Well, at least now we know where Mary is. Mary, time to wake up."

"I'll wake her. Mary," Ida started, coming over to her. She knelt beneath the bushes and said, "Mary? Mary. Oi. Wake up. Mary... Oh!" She reared back, landing on her behind. "There's blood." She pointed.

The breath left Bronwyn's lungs as she gasped at the sight. Bronwyn's hand darted to her mouth. She quickly helped Ida to her feet.

"What do we do?" Ida asked.

Bronwyn came forward and gently touched the left ankle of the woman lying there, exposed by her dress. It was cold and icy, and the shoe, ankle, and part of the dress were damp from morning dew. The person had lain out here all night, she realized.

She swallowed. "Go get help."

"Who do I get?" Ida asked, her face pale.

"Anyone. Tell Master Gregory."

The maidservant fled, and Bronwyn sat back on her heels. She crept beneath the large rosebush, below its low-hanging branches. The body was indeed that of Mary, the kitchen maid. Mary lay on her stomach, her face down in the dirt. Black blood matted the back of Mary's head, and a bloody bottle lay nearby. The woman's arms were covered with scratches.

Bronwyn let out a sigh, crawled back out from beneath the rosebush, and waited.

The other cooks arrived. Master Gregory came at a run, with two male cooks close behind him. At his side hurried Ida, her face twisted from shock and unshed tears.

Master Gregory marched forward, his eyes seeking Bronwyn's. His eyebrows rose, in a small feat of hope, and were dashed as Bronwyn gave a quick shake of her head. Mary was dead, and there was no bringing her back.

"All right, Bronwyn. Tell us what you found," he said.

"We found her, lying there, beneath the rosebush. Could it have been an accident?" Ida asked.

"Maybe. Let's see. Lads, bring her out."

Bronwyn stood back as two of the cooks gently removed Mary's body from beneath the large bush. The moment the sunshine revealed Mary's face and the eyes that looked up at nothing, Ida burst into tears.

Bronwyn swallowed as one of the cooks held Mary in his arms. The other looked pale, almost ill.

"Matthew, go tell the chatelaine that a maid's died," Master Gregory said.

"She won't care," the cook said bitterly.

"Tell her, anyway."

Matthew grunted and hurried off. The other cook holding Mary said, "What should I do with her?"

Master Gregory gave a sigh. "It's the early morning. We don't want to create a scene or scare anyone. We'll put her downstairs. Follow me. I'll show you where to go," he said. "Ida, go to the chapel and say a prayer for Mary's soul."

"But I..." She nodded. "Yes, Master Gregory."

"Bronwyn, you come with me." The head cook turned and they made a sorry trio, she and the male cook following Gregory as he led them back the way they had come, through the garden and courtyards and back into the castle, but through a side entrance and down a set of steps, to an area that was cold and chilly and which smelled of preserved meats and cheeses.

The area wasn't well lit, so Master Gregory stepped outside and took a lit candle from its sconce. He handed it to Bronwyn and motioned for her to stay close as he began to clear space on one of the low shelves.

The area was a large pantry, with many shelves lined with cheese and racks of birds and preserved meat hanging. Once a space was clear, he motioned for the other cook to set Mary's body down.

As her corpse was lowered gently onto the shelf, the cook said, "Something's wet on my arm."

Bronwyn looked. There on his arm was a bloodstain. She met his eyes and, crossing herself, gently turned Mary's head. The back of the maidservant's head was bloody and matted, her hair dirty.

The maid smelled of cheap wine and a pale arm dangled off the side of the shelf, just as something fell from her hand onto the floor.

"What is that?" the cook asked.

Master Gregory picked it up. Holding it up by its stem, he said, "It's a rose."

Cold dread sank to the bottom of Bronwyn's stomach. She picked up the flower and set it aside Mary's body, when she noticed something.

"What now?" Master Gregory asked.

There, the palm of Mary's left hand was puckered in the center. Something dark was stuck in the skin, and the pale skin had puckered around it. Bronwyn picked it up to see. It was a thorn, but strangely enough, there was no blood around it. "That's odd."

"What?"

"There's a thorn lodged deep in her hand, but no blood. Why wouldn't she bleed from the thorn?"

"Simple. You should know that from hunting and butchering. How many times have you had to stuff things in animals for show?" the cook asked her.

"Lots. Why?"

"And why don't they bleed when we're stuffing things in them? You know as well as I do." He gave her an encouraging nod.

Bronwyn's mouth dropped open. "Because dead things don't bleed. That means that Mary was already dead when the rose and its thorn was pushed into her hand."

Chapter Twelve

IN NO TIME at all, Bronwyn, Master Gregory, and the male cook, who introduced himself to her as Colin, returned to the kitchen, where they were met by Ida, who clearly hadn't gone to say a prayer for Mary as she'd been ordered but was spreading the news far and wide to all the kitchen staff.

A young page stood wide-eyed behind the crowd of cooks surrounding her and made eye contact with Master Gregory as they reentered the kitchen.

"Master Gregory, Lady Mabel bids you come to her. Right now."

"Aye. I thought as much. You lot stay here. Get on with cooking. Especially you, Ida. You must've said a very quick prayer."

At his words, Ida blushed, for she clearly had done no such thing.

Gregory turned and followed the page out. Bronwyn got to work with the other cooks, but as soon as he'd left, Ida resumed talking, saying, "It was horrible. Blood everywhere. I don't know what she was doing."

"It's that squire who's done it. That squire of the queen's," one cook said.

"You think he was taking revenge on behalf of the queen for them putting her in prison?" another cook suggested.

Bronwyn frowned. This was getting out of hand. She knew gossip would run rife after a death, but still.

"It's that squire, for sure," said the first cook. "She told us all she was meeting him that night. And where is she now?"

Bronwyn raised her voice. "There's no reason to think he's done it."

Eyes turned to her.

"Isn't there? He was the last person to see her," the cook said.

"But how do you know? Yes, they went looking for each other, but there's no reason to think that he—" Bronwyn started.

A cook rounded on her. "Oh, so you're blaming Mary for her own death, then, are ye? It's not the squire who's to blame, eh? But Mary, because she's a servant? Is that what you're saying?"

Their looks were unfriendly.

Bronwyn felt anxious for all eyes were upon her. Her face started to warm. "That's not what I'm saying. I only mean that just because we know they were—"

"Mistress Blakenhale," Master Gregory's voice cut through the raised voices in the kitchen. He stood at the kitchen entrance, his expression stern. His stocky body had a stiff bearing, as if he were preparing to fight. He jerked his head. "Come."

Angry looks and not-so-discreet mutters followed as she walked toward the head cook. Bronwyn kept her head high and did not look at any of the cooks, as that would have been asking for trouble. But as soon as she'd finished walking by the group, one male voice said, "In my opinion, we should just shove the lot of them off the parapet."

Her blood ran cold.

Facing him, Master Gregory grit his teeth. "No one asked you your opinion, Alan." To Bronwyn, he jerked his head for her to follow.

Bronwyn was glad to be out of the kitchen, and the moment she and Gregory had left the room, the air filled with loud voices and angry words. She stuck close behind the head cook as he met with another page, who took them to meet the chatelaine.

"I only got partway there when we ran into another page demanding you come too, so I doubled back," Master Gregory said. "Just as well I did."

Bronwyn nodded. He didn't ask if she was all right; they just kept going. But she felt as if she were walking from a pit of vipers to meet a wolf. Either way, she was in trouble.

They were led to a private room, thankfully not the chatelaine's torture chamber. This was a light room that functioned as a small drawing room. It was small with plain, whitewashed stone walls, and it gave a sense of bareness and starkness, but that might have been because there was no decoration on the walls. In the room sat a chair and a fireplace, where a fire burned merrily. The morning chill had left the room, but it was drafty, and the wooden floorboards creaked beneath their feet, albeit muffled by a thin rug.

Lady Mabel sat in the chair, a glass of wine in her hand, and she surveyed them both. She waved the pages away and once satisfied, they were gone, said, "I gather a body has been found."

"Yes, Lady Mabel. A maidservant. One of the kitchen maids," Gregory said, adjusting his belt.

Lady Mabel wore a stiff, high-necked, dark-gray dress, the lacing at her bodice tied tightly. Her dark hair was pulled back severely, and in the early morning light, dark circles lurked beneath her eyes. Her mouth was pressed tightly. "How did she die?"

"We don't know, Lady," Gregory said. "We found her over in the gardens, by the rosebushes."

The chatelaine glanced at Bronwyn. "You are very quiet, Mistress Blakenhale. Perhaps you find yourself dull this morning and have nothing to say. Or are you perhaps trying to protect someone?"

"Lady Mabel?" Bronwyn cocked her head.

"Guards," the chatelaine called.

"Let go of me. I'm telling you, I'm innocent," a familiar voice said loudly as two guards and Crispin roughly pushed Rupert into the room. He tripped and fell to his knees, landing hard on the wooden floor. He glared back at the guards and looked up. "Lady

Mabel," he said. "Good morning." His tone was flippant.

"Is it? I wonder how you can be so calm at a time like this." Lady Mabel motioned with an airy wave for him to stand. "What have you to say for yourself?"

Rupert stood and glanced at Master Gregory and Bronwyn. Seeing her, he shot her a dirty look and said to the chatelaine, "I don't know what she's been telling you, but I swear, I mean no harm to the girl. She looked after me after the fight at dinner, and I met up with her afterward for a walk in the gardens. We didn't sleep together, if that's what you're asking."

Master Gregory's face could have been carved from stone. The only sign of his displeasure was the tension that made his shoulders stiffen a fraction and his hands clench by his sides. He stared straight ahead.

"Ha. I have no interest in your romantic affairs. But when you bring trouble under my roof, that is a concern. A girl is dead, and you are the last person to have seen her. Now what do you say?" Lady Mabel demanded, leaning forward in her chair.

Rupert stared at her. He blinked and his eyebrows furrowed. "Who's dead?"

"The girl. The kitchen maid."

"Mary. Mary Skellings," Master Gregory said, almost spitting out her name.

The restrained anger in his voice made Rupert look at him. His eyes opened wide and he backed up a step. "You can't believe I had anything to do with that. I didn't kill her. How did she... die?"

"You tell us. You were the last person to see her," Master Gregory said, stepping closer to him. His expression was grim.

"What? Me? No. I... I mean, we did walk together in the gardens, but only to say *thank you* and to steal a kiss or two. That was it. Nothing else happened. I swear." Rupert paled.

"And you expect us to believe that? When you've done nothing but romance sweet, innocent young women and fight over ladies-in-waiting?" Master Gregory snapped. "Aye, all the servants know. We heard about your fight with the other squire. One lady isn't enough, eh? So you had to make do with what you could get, is that it?"

"Hold, Master Gregory. Restrain yourself." The chatelaine's voice cut through the building tension like a knife. To Rupert, she said, "What the head cook says is true. You were the last person to see the girl. What have you to say for yourself?"

Rupert's Adam's apple bobbed as he swallowed. "Only that I didn't kill her. We kissed, and I gave her a rose. That was it. Honest to God."

"Don't take the Lord's name in vain," Master Gregory sputtered angrily. "He's lying, Lady Mabel. I'm sure of it."

The chatelaine tapped a thin finger against her lips and gazed at Rupert thoughtfully. "I know not what to believe. Crispin tells me that a young woman also died at Empress Maud's castle shortly before you came here. Another maid."

Rupert flinched. "I had nothing to do with that."

"No? Then why do your hands tremble so?" The chatelaine smiled, almost a friendly, easygoing look. They might have been conversing between two friends, so believable was her kindly expression.

Bronwyn knew better. This woman was dangerous, and Rupert was in trouble. She met Crispin's eyes. He shot her a look, but whether it was of warning, danger, or opportunity, she could not tell. "I believe him," Bronwyn said.

Crispin snorted, drawing the others' attention. "Of course she would say that. They—"

Bronwyn cut him off. "We know each other. We are friends. Have been since the battle at Lincoln. I know him. If he says he is innocent, then I believe him."

"So good of you to finally join the conversation, Mistress Blakenhale," the chatelaine practically purred. "It has not escaped my notice that you are often sought after as a voice of reason, or as a person to find answers where there appear to be none. Rather like a hunting dog." She simpered and sipped from her goblet of wine, a drop of red spilling down the brim.

The chatelaine set her goblet down on a side table and leaned forward, resting her hands on the armrests of her curved, wooden chair. "I have it. You will look into this matter, Bronwyn."

"Her?" Master Gregory said. "But why? She's nobody but a kitchen maid herself. And we don't know her, Lady Mabel."

"Be that as it may, Master Gregory, she comes highly recommended. And unlike some people, I do not accept some people's word as fact, just due to their station." She looked evenly at Bronwyn. "You will do this. Look into this matter and report back to me with the culprit. You have one week to either prove this squire's innocence or his guilt. I do not care either way."

"Why one week, Lady Mabel?" Crispin asked.

"Because by then, the trail will grow cold, and I imagine Stephen will have returned my husband to the empress. Our circumstances will have changed, and we will likely be forced to return Matilda of Boulogne and her brat son. So you have one week."

Bronwyn breathed in. "But, Lady Mabel, what if I do not find anything within a week? That's not a lot of time."

"If you wish to be excused from your baking duties, be my guest. I would rather have a keen hunter than a lazy cook. No, I think a week is sufficient enough. You will do this, and if you fail, then I will kill him, and you will have only yourself to blame."

"But, Countess—" Bronwyn started.

"No excuses. You are friends, after all." Lady Mabel smiled and simpered. "Guards. Take him to the cells."

Rupert's eyes widened and his mouth dropped open. "But, Lady Mabel, I'm innocent!"

He was still protesting when the guards removed him from the room, with Crispin helping.

"Well. Now that that unpleasantness is taken care of, you can return to your work." The chatelaine waved them away.

Bronwyn frowned bitterly as she silently followed Master Gregory back into the hall. She did not like this. Rupert in jail.

What would she tell Lady Alice?

As the pair walked side by side down the castle corridors, Master Gregory said, "I suppose you're proud of yourself."

Bronwyn glanced at him. "Pardon?"

"You've been here no time at all and already you're in close with the chatelaine and are working with her as her dog. Sneaking around corners and sniffing out answers. Never mind that you might dig up things people would rather stay buried."

She looked at him helplessly, at a loss for what to say. The chatelaine had given an order. She either followed it or left Rupert's fate to someone who didn't know him and wouldn't care if he lived or died. But judging by the twisted expression on Master Gregory's face, she would be wiser not to say that at the moment.

"I don't know how you've managed to worm your way into her good graces or trust so easily. Maybe you've earned it. Maybe you haven't. But as long as you're in my kitchen, I'll be watching you."

She nodded. "I don't have to be in the kitchens to look into this matter for the chatelaine. I'll go elsewhere if that is your—"

"We need all the help we can get with all the extra mouths to feed. I'll not turn away a good cook. Even if they've got another master." He frowned at her. "But I will be keeping an eye on you. If I catch you causing trouble, you'll be out. No excuses, no questions asked. Understand?"

"Yes." There was no mistaking the unfriendly look in his ice-blue eyes. It was like the calm before a storm, and she didn't want to see what would happen when Master Gregory became truly angry.

Bronwyn followed him back to the kitchen. Master Gregory approached the group of cooks standing around. "What are you doing? Get back to work."

"But, Master Gregory, what about Mary?" a woman cook asked.

"She's dead," he said flatly.

The cook flinched as if he'd struck her. Her eyes turned glassy with unshed tears.

Master Gregory said, "I'm sorry. That was mean of me." He put a gentle hand on the woman's arm as she wiped away tears. He turned and said, "Bronwyn. Go inquire about a funeral service for Mary. Then return to your work here. We can't let things stop just because…" He didn't finish speaking. He didn't need to.

It was clear to her that the cooks needed a moment, just to themselves. He was giving her an excuse to leave, and she was glad to take it. She bobbed her head and quit the room.

Once outside, she lingered a moment and overheard the cooks talking.

"Master Gregory, can we trust her?" one cook asked.

"What did the chatelaine want?" asked another.

"Is Mary really dead?" a third asked.

"Ssshhh," Master Gregory said, his voice lowering. "Yes. Bronwyn's helping the chatelaine find out who did it, so leave her be."

"Her? Why her?" a cook asked.

"She's just a servant. We can't trust her," another said.

"Trust her or not, but you'll not bother her, you understand me?" Master Gregory said.

"I don't care what you say. That squire's gone and done for Mary, and I hope he hangs for it," a cook said nastily.

"Well, the man's in prison now, so you'll likely get your wish," the head cook said, his voice hard.

Bronwyn stiffened and leaned back against the stone wall of the corridor. Rupert, hang? That couldn't happen. She needed to prevent that. She didn't dare lose the man she cared for. Not now. Not before she got a chance to tell him how she felt.

But that didn't matter right then. She needed to clear his name. But before that, she needed to tell Lady Alice he was in trouble. And what with funeral arrangements happening, Bronwyn was certain she didn't need to follow up on the matter, as she'd been asked to. Better Lady Alice learn of this first.

Bronwyn marched up to the main dining room, where the ladies sometimes were, but couldn't find her friend anywhere. She searched and eventually gave up. Instead, she wandered back to the gardens, to the spot where Mary's body had been found.

She walked around the site. The air was littered with the scents of rose, which made her breathe in happily, but… as she approached the specific rosebush with the large vines where Mary's body had been found, her smile fell.

The air might have smelled like roses, but the site was something else. Blush-pink rose petals lay scattered on the ground beneath the bush, as if someone had knocked them loose or plucked the petals and thrown them. She knelt to the ground and looked closer. Could it have been an accident? Could Mary have drunk too much, slipped on the wet grass or her skirts, struck her head on a rock, and died that way? Could it all have been completely innocent, just tragic?

The area where Mary's body had been found was shielded from the morning dew, but there were no great rocks covered in blood. Instead, a bottle of ale lay beneath the bush. She picked it up and sniffed its contents. It smelled foul, almost sickly sweet, but she didn't care for the taste of ale, so that was no surprise. But as she picked it up, a sticky residue touched the skin of her right hand.

She took the bottle in her left hand. Bits of blood and hair stuck to the bottle and dotted her pale hand with red. She dropped the bottle and stepped back, wiping her hand on her apron. A chill ran through her.

This had been no accident. Mary had been killed. Her head bashed in by the ale bottle. The sight of the blood and hair sticking to it was enough to make Bronwyn feel sick. The question was: why? Why was Mary dead? Who had felt the need to kill her, and when had this happened?

If she knew Rupert at all, she knew he wouldn't leave a young woman alone at night, when her safety might be compromised. He was honorable and was always good at looking after others. She frowned and started to tap her index finger against her mouth, then thought better of it, wiping her hands again on her apron. She wanted a bit of soap and water to clean them thoroughly. She'd dealt with butchering animals and her hands often got a bit messy when working in the kitchen, but knowing the blood had come from a person was different. It sent a small shiver through her.

She picked up the ale bottle by its neck and gingerly took it away, chucking it into the nearest midden heap. She headed for the castle laundry and after bidding good morning to the laundresses there already up and working, she washed her hands with a bit of scouring soap, rubbing the herb-filled, bristling soap against her hands and arms until her skin was pink. She soaked her apron as well and wrung it out.

Bronwyn then went in search of Lady Alice. She'd almost given up hope of finding her when she heard Lady Muriel's voice and went ahead to see. There, down the castle corridor and stepping into one of the rooms, Lady Muriel walked with Lady Alice, whose hand darted to her mouth.

Bronwyn came closer and witnessed the exchange. Lady Muriel spoke quietly, but the effect on Lady Alice was immediate. Her friend turned a shade paler, her jet-black hair standing out prettily against her fair skin. That day, she wore a thin, purple dress with long sleeves and was bound at the waist with a thin, tooled leather belt and a reticule. Being a lady, Lady Alice carried no weapon. But there in her black hair, pinned back slightly by a leather thong, was a lethal-looking hair ornament with a pretty pearl in it.

Bronwyn approached the pair. "Lady Muriel. Lady Alice." Seeing their faces, she said, "You've heard."

"A maidservant is dead. Yes," Lady Muriel said.

Lady Alice looked at her with an expressionless mask. Her eyes were narrowed, her lips pursed tightly. There was much she seemed to want to say, and yet she did not dare speak.

"A kitchen maid, last night. An unfortunate accident," Bronwyn said.

"That's not what I heard," Lady Muriel said. She leaned in conspiratorially. "I heard that the maid was killed."

Both ladies looked at Bronwyn, who tried to keep a calm expression. She gave a small nod.

Lady Alice cocked her head at an angle and peered at Bronwyn. "You're looking into this matter, aren't you?"

"I…"

"I knew it. Your face says it all." She rolled her eyes. "I don't think it's really your place to go sticking your nose into things like this, Bronwyn. It's none of your business, and—"

Bronwyn bit her lip. "The chatelaine asked me to."

Lady Alice's mouth shut like a trap.

"Did she? Why?" Lady Muriel asked.

"I'm not sure."

Lady Alice's dark eyes bored into her. "Let me guess. You just so happened to report the body and then offered your services to her, as someone who has served so-called queens and empresses before. No doubt you talked yourself up to her, as someone with a fine nose for rooting our murderers. Like a pig with mushrooms."

"Lady Alice," Lady Muriel said in a hushed voice.

Lady Alice snapped her black hair over her shoulder. She bristled like a cat. "I am so sick and tired of hearing about your accomplishments. Begone, Bronwyn. Unless you're bringing us some rolls to eat, then I don't want to see or hear from you. Go on." She made a shooing motion with her hand.

Bronwyn's mouth dropped open.

"Lady Alice, what are you…?" Lady Muriel stared at her. "I thought you two were friends."

"We are not. I am a noblewoman. I am not friends with a servant."

The words made Bronwyn's eyes well up, and she blinked back sudden tears. Once again, the noblewoman declared they were friends and demanded her loyalty, then dismissed her in public for her low station. This was getting tiresome, and it hurt. "Lady Alice, did I offend you somehow?"

"Your very nature offends me, Bronwyn. Your constant presence where it should not be, inserting yourself into other people's conversations as if you belong there. When will you see yourself for what you truly are? A servant. Now get away from me. I have better things to do."

Bronwyn's cheeks felt hot with embarrassment. She nodded, turned on her heel, and left. As she walked away, she overheard Lady Muriel say, "That was a bit mean, Lady Alice. There was no need to treat her so."

"The sooner she learns her place in this world, the better. I have no time for servants, and neither should you."

Bronwyn felt grim and hurried away faster. She'd wanted to tell Lady Alice about Rupert's involvement with the death, and to warn her, and to get her opinion. Her friend had always been a good source of information, useful to talk through her thoughts with. Now it seemed, Lady Alice had had a change of heart—again—and it made Bronwyn heartsick.

✣

Chapter Thirteen

IN THE SCANT privacy of the privy, Bronwyn let out a breath and wiped her eyes, rubbing away the tears that threatened to fall. She needed to speak with Rupert and learn what he knew about the previous evening. But Alice's words had pained her.

So often, Lady Alice seemed to choose and decide for herself when she wanted to be friends with Bronwyn.

In Bronwyn's mind, she was either friends with a person, or she wasn't. There was no in between, and she was quickly learning that she didn't care for people who changed their minds from one moment to the next. In small things, it didn't matter, but relationships, friendships—she didn't like it at all. Despite having known Lady Alice for over a year now, she wondered if they had ever truly been friends at all.

A weight of unhappiness settled in her chest, like a sore ache that wouldn't go away. She and Lady Alice had been through so much together, ever since they had been thrown together shortly before the now-famous battle of Lincoln.

They had relied on each other's friendship and had survived battles and fights together, even escaping through chutes and midden heaps to survive. But now... The noblewoman's words had acted like winter had come early and had sent an icicle through her. Lady Alice had put her down and treated her not like an equal, but like... a servant.

Which she was, that was true. But Bronwyn had always trodden that line between friend and maidservant, and as more instances had occurred, she often had been called on to look into such matters like foul pranks and deaths. She was good at it too, or so she liked to think. And if she were being honest with herself, she rather enjoyed being called upon by high-ranking members of the nobility. She liked feeling useful. It was a different sort of pleasure than having successfully made a cake. Making a well-done cake was a joyous thing, but solving thefts and murders... that made her feel good too.

But never mind. If Lady Alice did not wish to be friends, then so be it. *I have a job to do*, she thought angrily as she turned on her heel, marching out of the privy, bumping right into... "Crispin."

"Ha. Well met, Bronwyn. So you've got a mission now, and from the chatelaine herself. Anything to keep from working in the kitchens, eh?" he teased.

Her mouth flattened into a firm line. She looked away.

"You all right?" he asked.

She swallowed and met his eyes. "I don't mind working in the kitchens."

"I'm sure. I was just joking." He ran a hand through his light-brown hair. "So what will you do now that your lover is in the cells?"

"He's not my lover; he's a friend."

"Aye, well, now you have him all to yourself," Crispin said. "I heard you all talking about it as we brought him in. The chatelaine may be smart, but her voice is loud and the sound carries in these old walls." He paused. "Anyway, what will you do now?"

"I'm on my way to talk to him. See what he knows."

Crispin snorted. "So he can lie to your face? Be my guest. But he'll tell you the exact same lie he told the rest of us."

Bronwyn rolled her shoulders back. She didn't like Crispin talking about Rupert that way. "Tell me where the prison cells are."

"All right." He gave her directions and pointed the way. "But you're wasting your time. You won't learn anything useful."

Bronwyn shrugged. "I have to try."

"And when the week passes and you've got nothing? Then what?"

She didn't want to think about that, so she walked in the direction of the prison cells. Crispin's low laughter rung out behind her, echoing beyond the walls.

As Bronwyn approached the prison cells, a pair of armed guards stood from their posts and stared at her, spears held within easy reach. "What do you want?"

"To speak with a prisoner, the squire. Rupert Bothwell."

"Why? Who sent you?" one guard asked. He was tall, thin, with wispy, blond hair and acne along his right cheek.

"Lady Mabel. Ask her if you want. She wants me to sort this out." Bronwyn spoke with more confidence than she felt at that moment. Who was she to look into the matter of a maidservant's murder?

The two guards exchanged looks. The other guard, a middle-aged one with a protruding belly, scratched his chin and said, "Go on. It's not like he's going anywhere."

Bronwyn nodded and went down the set of stone steps as the old, familiar smells of a castle prison hit her nose. Moist, damp air. A sudden shift from the lightness of day to the semi-darkness of seeming night, punctuated by small torches that burned in stone wall sconces, their flames flickering. There were rats or mice among the rushes on the earthen floor. She could tell by the way the rushes trembled and shifted. The smell of urine and feces filled the air, along with the scent of unwashed body odor.

Wrinkling her nose, she went down to the cells and called out, "Rupert?"

"I'm here," a voice called back.

She headed toward the source, calling again until she found him. "Rupert."

He came up to the cell door. It was a wooden door, with only a small hold with a set of bars at the top. He stood on the other side of them and said, "Are you all right? What are you doing here?"

"I'm here to see you," she said. It made her heart glad to see him again.

He let out a sigh. "Oh, Bronwyn. It's good to see you, but you might as well go. There's not a lot you or anyone else can do for me out there. Not unless you have the ear of the chatelaine."

She frowned. It wasn't like him to give up so easily. "She's given me a week to look into this and prove your innocence." *Or guilt*, but best to stay positive.

"Don't know what good that will do," he said glumly.

"Why are your spirits so low?" she asked finally, unable to help it.

He gave her a pointed look.

"I know, you're in prison. But not for long. I'll solve this and you'll be out in no time," she said.

"It's not that." Rupert slouched against the door. His voice was quiet. "My master is with the king. They rode back to Winchester together for the prisoner exchange. He didn't even leave a message for me. Do you know how long it's been since I've seen my master?"

She shook her head.

"Months. We've never been apart for that long. And what have I done in the meantime? Served at the table of the empress, served one of her knights, likely a traitor. Lost the queen and prince to a group of bandits. And this morning, I've gotten myself accused of murder and stuck in prison. It's been a long day, and it's barely after Terce."

She wanted to reach through the iron bars to give him a reassuring pat but hesitated.

"When word reaches him of my problems, he might decide I'm too much trouble. You understand what that means?"

"No."

"He could dismiss me from his services. Master Baldwin might release me, and then I'd have nothing. I'd be a squire with no master. No better than a mercenary or a bandit. I'd have nothing. At least under his service, I have some respectability. A name worth saying. Without his name and protection, I'm nothing. Just a man."

Despondency carried through his voice. She didn't blame him as he slumped against the door, hidden from view. She heard him sit on the floor, his back to her, as he pondered his fate.

Her mind went unbidden to Theobold, and she wondered how he was doing. It had irked her, that so often, he told her she would always come fifth or sixth, after God, his empress, and his master, Sir Robert of Gloucester. He had explained that he owed his master everything, and both served and depended on him for survival. Without that service, he was without a purpose, and a master to serve. He would never have that chance to become a knight, which was his dream, rather than follow in his father's footsteps and become an executioner.

She felt she understood Theobold better now, hearing those same concerns from Rupert. But then her heart grew cold. He had made his choice and was romancing the empress's taster, Mistress Agatha. Good luck to them both. So much for his promise to stay true to her. He'd cut her loose easily enough. Was she really so low in his estimation as to be less than a royal taster?

She supposed so. And it hurt to dwell on it. Perhaps that was why she strived to keep busy.

"Tell me what happened last night."

He stood up and looked at her through the iron bars. "You don't give up, do you? Like a dog with a bone."

Bronwyn waited. She was getting annoyed with all these descriptions of her as a dog or a pig. She wasn't a farmyard animal or a beast.

"All right, I'll tell you. After the fight at dinner, Mary came and tended to me. Crispin's got a mean right punch, and I'll be honest, I'm not going to turn down attention from a pretty girl, you know?" He offered her an easy smile.

She wondered then. Was that just his way with all women? A bit of flirting here, some smiles there. How was it so easy to lose one's heart to him? Was a bit of friendliness all it took?

"Go on," she said.

"I asked her to come out with me for a walk after dinner, to thank her. I thought maybe we could walk around the gardens, I'd give her a flower, we'd share a drink, maybe a kiss, and that would be it."

"And was it?"

"Yes. That's what I keep trying to tell the chatelaine and the guards. We walked together, had a drink or two, I gave her a rose, and we sat under the stars and talked." He shifted his weight on his feet and avoided her eyes.

"And then what happened?"

"The moon was out and it was getting late, so I suggested we head back in. She wanted to stay out a little longer. I was happy to wait, but she said I should go on, so I did. The next thing I know, guards are waking me up and Crispin's saying I killed her. So now I'm here. But I didn't kill her, I swear."

"How did she die?"

"I don't know."

"Where did you get the wine from?" she asked.

"It wasn't wine; it was ale. Got it from the dining tables, as there was some left over from dinner. Why?"

There went her idea of the wine being drugged or poisoned. If it had been, it would've made it easier for the person to hit her over the head, as she would be so out of sorts, Mary wouldn't have fought back.

"So you left Mary there in the gardens at night? You didn't see her after that?"

"No. It was sometime after Compline. She seemed confident, though, and pressured me to go, so I did. It was just a friendly time together. That's all."

She cocked her head. There was something he wasn't telling her, but she couldn't put her finger on what. His voice—it sounded too calm. Too pleasant. He seemed altogether unbothered by the fact that he was in jail for murder or the young woman with whom he'd flirted—for the second time as of late—had lost her life.

"Did anyone see you?" she asked.

"Don't think so." He paused. "Does Lady Alice know? That I'm here?"

"Not yet. I was going to tell her."

He nodded. "Good luck. I don't know who would want to kill Mary, but it weren't me."

She walked back to the kitchens. She had nothing to do and nowhere to go, so she joined in the work, taking orders from Master Gregory to pluck birds for that evening's dinner.

Master Gregory came up beside her as she was busy plucking a guinea fowl. He said, "Have you learned anything about Mary?"

"Not so much. Rupert said they walked together at night and he gave her a rose, but then he left her."

His face darkened. "What sort of man leaves a woman alone in the dead of night? It's no wonder something happened to her."

She held her tongue. She couldn't defend Rupert from that, for it was true. He had left Mary. Even if the young woman had told him to go, there was still the unspoken assumption that a woman's safety depended on a man. But then, why had Mary told Rupert to leave? Why had she stayed?

"Rupert said she told him to leave. That she wanted to stay longer," Bronwyn said.

A page interrupted them. Master Gregory listened to the request, then grumbled. "Wash your hands and then get up to the east tower. Seems the queen wants her breakfast. Bring a tray."

Bronwyn wiped her hands clean and set about preparing plates of cheese, bread, potage, and a bit of meat, along with a fresh pitcher of wine. The tray heavy in her hands, she followed the page along the castle corridors and up to the tower, going carefully up the circular, stone steps.

By the time she and the page had reached the queen's chamber, Bronwyn felt winded and out of breath. The page knocked, and the pair of guards let them inside.

The smell was apparent. The queen and prince shared a chamber, which was not overly big. It had a small, poky hearth but no fire—and a lone window. The chamber pot was full. The room was drafty and held a small, round table and chairs, a bed, and little else.

Bronwyn swallowed.

At her arrival, the queen and prince looked up. "Mistress Blakenhale," the queen said.

"I've brought you some breakfast." Bronwyn set the tray down on the round, wooden table, and the prince set to it at once, stuffing his face with the bread.

The queen showed more restraint and quietly came over to Bronwyn. Her voice was quieter still. "Good morrow, Mistress Blakenhale. I did not know if I would see you again. But I am glad for it. We are starved for conversation, you see." She smiled briefly.

Bronwyn ducked her head in a part bow. "How are you?"

"Well enough. Surviving."

The prince said, "It smells in here. The chamber pot needs emptying. And the fire burned out."

"I'll tend to those, Your Grace."

Bronwyn felt pairs of eyes on her as she moved to the fireplace that was black and sooty, when a guard said, "You shouldn't be doing that."

She paused.

The guard leaned against the doorway to the room. "They're prisoners here. Not guests."

Bronwyn went up to him. "And if they die of cold, whom will the chatelaine blame? Because it won't be me."

He frowned, no doubt unused to being disagreed with, especially by a young woman. "What gives you the right? Who gave you the authority?"

"The chatelaine did. And if these prisoners die because

they're not allowed to eat or because they freeze to death, she's going to blame you for not saying anything. They're important. You know she's a queen, yes?"

The guard coughed and spat. "Don't matter to me. A prisoner's a prisoner. That's all I know."

"Right, well, I've got to be getting on." Bronwyn made up the fire, striking with flint and tinder until sparks caught. She blew on the small flame, watching as it caught, and then blew out. She gave a little sigh.

"It's all right, Mistress Blakenhale. We'll survive," the queen said.

Bronwyn wasn't so sure. The room was drafty and had a slight chill, she noted, now that she had caught her breath.

The queen moved to survey her handiwork and said quietly, "The guards are loyal to the chatelaine and Maud. They watch us day and night. They help themselves to our food. I do not doubt they report on us too."

Bronwyn pinched her nose, then realized her hands were black from soot in the fireplace and she'd probably gotten soot on her face. She wiped her nose with a sleeve and stood.

"Oh, dear. You've got soot on you." The queen smiled faintly.

Bronwyn wiped her face with her other sleeve.

"You've just made it worse."

The queen and prince shared a laugh. At first, Bronwyn frowned, then realized it was probably the first time they'd laughed in a while. The prince, she observed, was still young and coltish. He was all thin, gangly limbs, with a trace of acne on his chin. He still had a bit of baby fat on him, but she imagined he would grow into his own like a weed and become tall like his father, the king.

The queen and Bronwyn watched the prince eat. Matilda of Boulogne almost whispered, "Can I trust you?"

Bronwyn paused. "I…"

At that moment, Lady Muriel and Lady Alice pushed past the

guards. Lady Muriel said, "You cannot believe anything she says, Your Grace. That girl is a spy for the empress."

Bronwyn's mouth dropped open. Muriel frowned at her. The queen shot her a look of distaste, disappointment sketched upon her fair features.

Lady Alice smirked. "Bronwyn. I should have known I'd find you here in the soot."

Chapter Fourteen

BRONWYN GLARED AT her former friend. How she wished they were still allies, but that was not to be, it seemed.

"You cannot trust her, Your Grace," Lady Muriel repeated. "I have it on good authority that she is a spy for Maud."

"Is this true?" the queen asked. "Then why did she save me and my son from a pit if that were the case?"

Lady Alice shrugged. "Bronwyn's allegiance changes by the day. Some days she is for you; others, for the empress. I would not trust her regardless. And neither should you, Your Grace. She is, after all, a servant."

The guards looked on as Lady Alice flicked her jet-black hair over her shoulders and gave them a sweet smile.

"What a disappointment," the queen said. "Leave the tray. You can take it away later."

"I'll just be going," Bronwyn started, when the prince said, "Take the chamber pot away and fetch us a new one. That one's full."

So much for being trusted, she thought. To everyone, she was and likely always would be an ordinary servant.

Bronwyn breathed in and took the full chamber pot in her hands. The ladies gave her a wide berth as she took it away, carefully stepping around the group and out the door. Even the guards gave her space as she carried the very full chamber pot down the stone steps, trying to breathe through her mouth rather than her nose.

Once she'd disposed of its contents, Bronwyn returned to the kitchen, wiped her hands clean and sent up a servant with a fresh chamber pot and some wood for the fireplace. She felt cowardly, but she did not want to encounter Lady Alice again, unless she had to. She didn't know what she had done to offend her former friend so, but that didn't matter. She had a mystery to solve.

Discovering that the servant had brought up the chamber pot but not the wood, she tended to it herself, fetching a bundle of wood that had been chopped, and carried it up the steps over her shoulder, along with a brush and bucket to put the ashes into. She could have told a servant to do it, but something in her made her change her mind. She wanted to see the prisoners again and check that they were all right. It didn't do to be mistreated, especially when one of the people was a queen.

She was let back into the room and once again was winded and out of breath. The ladies were still there talking. Prince Eustace stood by the tall, narrow window, looking outside. The queen sat on the bed, flanked by Lady Alice and Lady Muriel in the two chairs, who were doing needlepoint.

Bronwyn set to building the fire, first scraping away the ashes into the bucket and then striking the flint and tinder until the wood caught. It wasn't much, but it would keep them warm during the night.

As she rose to leave, the queen asked, "What is it Maud wants to know?"

Bronwyn felt her cheeks warm. "I do not know, Your Grace."

"Come now. Surely, you can guess, Bronwyn." To the queen, Lady Alice said, "Bronwyn is simply trying to avoid suspicion. It doesn't suit her. I imagine the empress would want to know your plans for escape or to overthrow her."

The queen cocked her head at the noblewoman. "You seem very sure of this." She set down her needlepoint and joined her son at the window. "But I have no desire to leave this tower. Not until I know he is safe."

"I'm sure he is very well," Lady Muriel said. "He's certain to be back in Winchester by now. Besides, at least he's away from all this unpleasantness. You wouldn't want deaths to happen whilst he's here." She shook her head.

"True." The queen turned, her eyes flicking to Bronwyn. "This person who died. The servant girl. Was it an accident?"

Bronwyn thought back to Mary's bloody skull. "No, Your Grace."

"Then it was murder?"

"I think so."

"Ha," Lady Alice said. "As if you would know. Or does working in a kitchen pantry also make you an expert on murder?"

"Lady Alice, you seem to have become offended by Mistress Bronwyn," the queen said. "Pray tell, what is the reason for this? She has been useful for looking into murderous matters before. Why do you question her motives now? I thought you were both friends."

"No, Your Grace. A gross exaggeration." Lady Alice lifted her chin.

Bronwyn cocked her head. A gross what?

The queen approached Bronwyn. Her expression was calm, her eyes clear. "Are you looking into this matter of the dead girl?"

Under the full force of the ruler's gaze, she dared not lie. "Yes. The chatelaine bid me do so."

Lady Alice sniffed and stabbed her needle into the bit of cloth she was embroidering.

"I see. And have you many suspects?" the queen asked Bronwyn.

"No, Your Grace," Bronwyn replied. "Not many, but that doesn't mean there won't be some."

"Who do you have so far?"

"The squire, Your Grace. Rupert of Bothwell."

Lady Alice froze. She sputtered. "I do not think I heard you correctly. Did you say Rupert? The squire to Sir Baldwin of Clare?"

"Yes."

"But he is innocent." Lady Alice dropped her needlepoint and strode to Bronwyn. "Did you have a hand in this?"

"No. I've only been asked to look into it."

"Why don't I believe you?" Lady Alice stood in her way.

Up close, she could see a thin sheen of sweat on Lady Alice's upper brow, and there was no mistaking the daggerlike glare of her eyes. If she could have struck Bronwyn down with holy lightning, Bronwyn would have already been dead.

"Why didn't you tell me he was suspected?" Lady Alice whispered.

"I tried. You were too busy to listen," Bronwyn said hotly. *Too busy dismissing me as a servant and not your friend.*

"Bah." Lady Alice bit her lip. "So he sits in prison?"

"Yes."

"Well? What else do you know?"

Bronwyn shot Lady Alice a hard look. "I'm sorry, but I have nothing to say. Like you said, I'm only a servant. What do I know?" She stepped around Lady Alice and curtsied to the queen, then took the ash-filled bucket and empty food tray before leaving, ignoring her former friend's call of "Wait!"

Feeling bitter, Bronwyn made her way down the stone steps, ignoring the sounds of the voices that echoed.

She was so busy in her own thoughts, she bumped right into Crispin. "Oh."

"You've taken me up on my offer, then." He noted with his head toward the top of the stone stairwell.

"No. I'm not spying on the queen for the empress. I refuse."

His mouth curled into a smile. "You know… a word in the right ear could work wonders."

She huffed. "I don't know what you mean. You're speaking in riddles, and I don't have time for this." She moved around him, but he stepped in her path. "Move."

"Not until you hear me out. You may not wish to spy on the woman, fine. But there's nothing wrong with just reporting on her. What she does, what she says. It's so easy, Bronwyn. Just tell me and I'll report back to her. And the empress is generous."

She sighed. "I told you, I'm not interested." And she stepped around him again and started walking.

"Not even if it saves Rupert's life?"

She turned around.

"I thought that might get your attention." He closed the distance between them and walked with her. Other servants passed by now that they were back in the main castle courtyard, but he paid them no mind.

She walked on but did also listen and matched her pace to his. "Talk."

"What if I could save Rupert's life?"

"I'm doing that myself. I'm going to find out who the culprit is and prove him innocent."

Crispin laughed, an ugly sound. "You're joking if you think that's true. The chatelaine only said that out of amusement. She doesn't actually expect you to succeed. No one does."

She stared at him. "What?"

"Come now. A servant girl, a kitchen maid, solve a crime? You're fooling yourself. No one believes you can actually do it."

Bronwyn's shoulders drooped. "Oh."

"The best thing you can do for him is work with me. Report on the queen's words and actions. Tell me what she does. The empress will make sure he stays alive."

"How?" Bronwyn asked.

"She'll simply relay the order to Lady Mabel to keep him alive. He'll be in prison, but he'll be breathing. Isn't that better than hanging from a gibbet?"

Bronwyn shivered. She didn't want to think about such gruesome things and wished Theobold was there. He would know what to do, or at least, give her some idea. She could talk things through with him. She gritted her teeth. The last thing she wanted to do was think about Theobold when he'd ended their relationship. She mentally kicked herself.

"Lady Alice would do what she had to to save his life," Crispin pointed out.

"That she might."

"So why won't you? You could be the only thing that stands between him and certain death."

"I already am. And I'm doing all I can to save him." She turned on her heel and left. She didn't have to stick around to hear Crispin's grunt of disgust. It mirrored her own.

Bronwyn came no closer to learning who might have killed the maidservant and with each passing day, the trail grew colder. She did see Crispin and Lady Alice walking together but assumed they were only instances of flirtation on his side and rejection from hers. It wasn't until she heard a giggle that her suspicions were aroused. But when she did take the time to eavesdrop and listen, all she heard was flirtation. It made her mad. What was Lady Alice doing flirting with Crispin when Rupert sat in jail? It was unfair. He deserved someone who cared for him. Someone like… herself.

Bronwyn thought this angrily as she stood in the kitchen, kneading dough for bread rolls, when Master Gregory stood by, watching her work.

A minute later, he said loudly, "Bronwyn, go gather some fresh rosemary. If there's none in the gardens, go out in the fields; there'll be some outside the city gates."

She took a basket and glanced at him. He jerked his head toward the entrance to the kitchen and said to her quietly, "Have you learned anything more about Mary's death?"

Bronwyn shook her head.

"Ah. Well, it seems to me you should be asking yourself why you're defending a man who is so clearly at fault. I mean, the way they were fighting that night, it was enough that anyone might lose their temper."

She blinked. "They were fighting?"

"Aye. Saw it myself. We went strolling around the castle and… I, I mean. Had a bit too much to drink already." He coughed. "Found myself in the gardens. Heard them arguing but knew it was none of my business, so I didn't get involved. But never mind. It's all over now. There's nothing more to be said. Go on and get me that rosemary."

"Master Gregory, why didn't you mention this before? You were there that night she died?"

He scratched his chin. "Aye. I... wasn't sure if I could trust you. I'm still unsure. But the chatelaine has tasked you with finding out who's behind this, so I figured I should tell you. All I know is Mary was alive when I last saw her. Figured she'd had enough of that young man and she'd be back soon. If we'd known he was going to harm her—I mean if *I'd* known, I would've stayed." He looked away. "He didn't mention the fight, did he?"

"No."

The head cook frowned. "Doesn't surprise me." He bid her go and sent her on.

Bronwyn frowned to herself. She wanted time to think. She wanted to demand that Rupert explain himself, but more than that, she wanted to know why Master Gregory hadn't gone to intervene in their fight.

From what she knew of the man, he cared for Mary, like all of his cooks. Seeing a young woman fight at nighttime, Gregory likely would have intervened and separated them. So why hadn't he? And why was he only telling her this now?

She strongly suspected he was lying, and that he was in the gardens that night, but he wasn't alone. So whom was he with, and why was he protecting them?

Before leaving on her errand, she went back to speak with Rupert. What with Master Gregory insinuating that they were fighting, she wanted to speak with him about it. Because now he had a motive. And she couldn't entirely trust him.

"Bronwyn," Rupert said. His hair hung limply around his shoulders, and his face bore a few hours' growth. He needed a bath and a shave. The damp air in the cells smelled, but she was still glad to see him. "What brings you here? Have you learned anything?"

"I'd rather you tell me. What, exactly, did you and Mary do in the gardens?" she asked archly, sounding more and more like a jealous fishwife than a loyal friend.

He balked. "What business is it of yours what I do?"

She looked from him to the jail door and back again.

He ran a hand through his hair. "Fine. We walked a little, I gave her a rose, we parted ways. Is that what you wanted to hear?"

"That was all you did?" She felt her eyebrows rise.

"Well… we might've kissed. You sure you want to know?"

She shrugged. She didn't need to know. But she wanted to know. Why was he going around kissing a girl he barely knew? To thank her for tending to him?

"All right. Well, we kissed a little, but… she wasn't the woman for me."

"Why is that?" Bronwyn asked a little too eagerly, but she hoped he wouldn't notice.

"She… Mary is, *was*, a nice girl. A sweet girl. Cheeky, liked to laugh. I like that. I was just looking for a nice time, you know? Nothing serious. But she… As soon as we started walking together and exchanged a few kisses, she started talking as if we were serious, and… I had to tell her."

"What?"

"That my heart lies with another." He sighed and ran a hand through his hair. "Lady Alice and I might be on the outs, but I still care for her. She's the woman I care for. She's the one I think about."

That made Bronwyn feel both better and annoyed. If he was still having romantic feelings for Lady Alice, then what was he doing going around kissing other young women?

As if sensing her thoughts, he said, "I didn't realize how I felt until Mary started talking about wanting to meet my mother and father. She came on too serious, too fast. I had to stop and tell her I wasn't interested. She didn't like that and got angry. We argued and I started to walk away. I offered to walk her back to the castle, but she was too mad and told me to clear off, so I did. That was the last time I saw her."

She frowned. "Why didn't you tell me this before?"

He shuffled his feet. "I didn't think it was important."

She put her hands on her hips. "Try again."

He looked away.

"The fact that you two got into an argument gives you a reason to want to hurt her, Rupert. It could be said that if she pressured you to get physical with her and you turned her down, you pushed her and it was an accident, or you silenced her." She paused. "Or people might think the opposite. That you tried to force your attentions on her and she refused you, but you didn't take *no* for an answer."

He turned pale. "I would never."

"I know. But nobody else here does. We're not on safe ground, Rupert." She realized then that in that place, on what was the empress's court, she did not feel safe, either. It was not home ground. She felt more attuned to Queen Matilda than the empress. Was her allegiance leaning more in that direction? She couldn't be sure, and now wasn't the time to think about that.

"Rupert, you have to understand how this looks," she started. "First you romance Philippa, and she dies—"

"I had nothing to do with that. I have no idea how she died, or when," he said, interrupting.

"And now as soon as we arrive at Bristol, you're off walking around the gardens with a kitchen maid, and the next day she turns up dead. You have to see how it looks."

His voice was quiet. "What do you think, Bronwyn? Do you think I did it? That I had something to do with their deaths?"

"No. I think you were incredibly unlucky, or that someone is framing you."

"That's what I think, too," he said.

"But I also think you're not telling me everything. It feels like I have to *drag* bits of information out of you, when it'd be a lot easier if you'd just tell me everything."

"I have."

She cocked her head. "Tell me about the last time you saw Philippa."

He scratched his chin. "The night before we left Devizes. I gave her a rose to thank her for looking after me and nursing me while I was sick, and to tell her goodbye."

"How did she take it?"

"Um… Well… I hadn't quite gotten to that part yet when you walked in on us."

Don't remind me, Bronwyn thought darkly. Seeing him with his hands and lips on another woman was the last thing she wanted to think about.

"It was a very tender goodbye, all right? She accepted the rose, I told her I was leaving, and that was it. She was mad and angry at first, and wanted… No."

"What?"

"She wanted to know if I was running off to be with you."

Silence.

He gave a low laugh. "Crazy, right?"

His laugh hurt her inside. First he told the bullying cook at Winchester that she had no sexual appeal, and now he laughed at the very *idea* of them running off together. He truly didn't fancy her—that much was clear. She forced a laugh in return. "Completely."

He rubbed the side of his face. "So once I'd reassured her, then that was it. I kissed her hands and said I'd come back if I could, and she said she would miss me, but that it was just as well we were parting ways, since there were bound to be more men interested in her, now that she was joining Lady Morwenna as her maidservant."

Bronwyn cocked her head. Why had Lady Morwenna chosen Philippa, of all people, to be her maidservant? Had the maid hinted she knew something important? If Bronwyn knew the noblewoman at all, she did nothing without a purpose, although it was usually malicious in nature. What role had she intended poor Philippa to play? They'd never know. But she couldn't shake the feeling that it was this key relationship, or the idea that perhaps Philippa knew something she shouldn't, that had led to her untimely death.

Rupert said, "It felt like a low blow since we were just kissing, but I wished her luck, and bid her goodnight. I didn't know that was the last time I'd ever see her."

She nodded.

"Bronwyn. You believe me, don't you?"

She looked at him. "I do." She just wished the truth didn't hurt so much.

Her mind filled with more questions, Bronwyn wandered to the castle gardens, but there was no rosemary; it had all been plucked clean for cooking. She took her basket and, nodding to the castle guards, went out into the city proper. Feeling the warm sunlight on her face, she took great gulps of air, breathing in the sounds and smells of the city. It was a hilly place, with many small shops and buildings taking up spots on the inclined hills, crowding against each other.

People were everywhere, and no one paid her much notice. She went out of the west gate, and after walking along the main road for a time, she soon slipped off into the woods. It was easily done, and a part of her relished the quiet and being surrounded by the sounds of the trees, squirrels, and birdsong, even if at that moment, the only birds weren't trilling tunes, but chattering magpies.

She continued walking until she found some herbs growing and was in luck. Bushes of rosemary grew wild by some trees, so she bent and started cutting free some stems with a small blade. She hummed a little tune offkey, then became aware that the animal noises around her had grown quiet. The birds had stopped singing and chattering. Rabbits hopped nearby and disappeared behind tree roots.

She looked up. Suddenly, the day had grown darker, colder.

Clouds drifted overhead, casting her in shadow. She was not alone.

The sounds of a horse, as well as footfalls hit her ears. They were close. Too close for her liking.

Bronwyn wished she'd taken her safety seriously and had brought with her a weapon of some kind, more than the little blade she had to cut herbs. What had she been thinking, going out alone? It should be fine, but what if it wasn't?

The horse nickered softly, and a man's voice spoke gently, calming it.

Bronwyn fingered the small, dull blade in her hand for cutting herbs, her fingers going over the blade's edge. It would have to do. She whirled around. "Theobold?"

"Bronwyn." Theobold stiffened and stared at her.

Her heart jumped into her throat. Theobold was here. The man she'd dreamed of, had fallen for, had lost her heart to, he was here. In the flesh. Standing before her, looking as darkly handsome as the night sky.

His black hair was longer and unruly. She longed to run her fingers through it. His fair skin made him look otherworldly, like a knight out of legend, but dark circles hung beneath his eyes. His head hung lower with fatigue, and he moved woodenly. He wavered on his feet as if he wanted to approach her but didn't dare.

"You're here. What are you doing here?" she asked. "I'm gathering herbs."

"Oh." He reached for the gray mare beside him and rubbed its back. "That's good."

She set down the basket and the blade and walked over to him. "Are you all right? You look tired."

He avoided her. "I'm fine." He spoke brusquely. "I'm looking for someone."

She waited, the question on her lips.

"Lady Morwenna has run away," he said. "She's gone missing."

"Oh."

He came toward her then and pulled her into a hug. She stiffened and then slowly put her arms around him and closed her eyes. It felt so good to be held by him again. She breathed in his scent, which was normally clean but now smelled of sweat, dirt, and horse. She stood in his arms and just let herself breathe, feeling herself start to relax. She could feel him start to relax too, his hands curling up around her waist and up her back. Then after a beat too many, she opened her eyes and lowered her arms.

"I've been such a fool," he murmured into her hair.

"Why? What did you do?" she asked, looking up at him.

"I let you go. I should never have let you go without me." He gaze dropped to her eyes, her lips, then her eyes again.

Her heart leaped with hope. Had he come to his senses and left Mistress Agatha and their false relationship? Did he truly care for Bronwyn? Did he plan to take back his words about her common status being not good enough for him? Or was this just a brief dalliance in his mind? A distraction?

She moved to step back, but he didn't release her. She tugged, and he let her go with a sigh. She didn't want to let him go, but she'd never seen him like this before. Tired, drained of energy, exhausted. She stepped back and surveyed him. "Theobold, what happened?"

He tied his horse's reins to a tree and practically *threw* himself on the green, mossy bank as she gathered herbs. Theobold leaned against a tree as his gray mare munched on grass and relayed the news. "What with a maidservant dead, a rich boy's clothes found, and a boy gone, the empress wanted people to look into these matters and she called for you but was surprised that you had already gone—and had taken Crispin with you. Apparently, she forgot that she had ordered you to leave," he said with a small smile.

"I find that hard to believe."

"Is Lady Alice with you?" he asked.

"Yes, she joined us—she came to Bristol Castle and is there

now."

"'Us'? You and Crispin?"

"Rupert also escorted me. You remember."

"Yes, I do." His expression grew stony. "Anyway, the empress got fed up with Lady Morwenna's constant pining for her lover, whom she refused to name. And then… you won't believe it."

"What?"

"Lady Morwenna admitted to being behind the plot that disturbed the prisoner exchange."

Bronwyn's jaw dropped open. So Lady Morwenna had decided to come clean. What had she said? Had she admitted to working with another, or others? What story had she given to the empress?

"You are right to be surprised. She took credit for the entire plot. Can you believe it? She hired the mercenaries and ordered them to attack the queen and prince. And got away with it. Apparently, she hid them in a pit not far from here." He took small shreds of grass and began shredding them into tiny pieces.

Why hadn't Lady Morwenna revealed Bronwyn's part in rescuing the prince and the queen? They were not allies, so surely, she would have done her part to get Bronwyn in trouble, especially when rescuing the missing royal pair was such valuable information. She did not know *where* Bronwyn, Crispin, and Rupert had hidden them, however, so there was a limit to what the noblewoman knew, thank goodness. "What did the empress say?"

"She was stunned. She asked if Lady Morwenna had been behind the ransom attempt, and Lady Morwenna said *yes*. It was all her doing." He smirked. "She seemed proud of herself."

Bronwyn shook her head. What a fool. "What did she say?"

"The empress's knights didn't believe her. They laughed and challenged her, saying she couldn't have done all that herself. A woman like her?"

That comment raised her ire. Her blonde head snapped to him. "They didn't believe her because she is a woman?"

"Partly. But more because they know her character. She hasn't been there long, but she is well known at court. She schemes and plots, but that is her way. No one would actually believe she could mastermind a plot to disrupt a royal entourage and hold people for ransom by herself."

Bronwyn picked up her small, dull blade and returned to cutting stalks of rosemary from the bushes. "What did Lady Morwenna say?"

"She admitted to working with her lover to hire mercenaries to attack them and steal them away. She said all this over dinner. As if it were regular conversation. Can you imagine?"

Yes, Bronwyn thought. But she said, "There's no way she could have done all this herself. And for her to take the credit... Do you think she just couldn't help herself and wants credit for her actions, the attention, even if it is bad?"

"I don't know. But the empress was disgusted. She'd gotten fed up with Lady Morwenna for a while now, I gather, and this was the last of it. She could not tolerate Lady Morwenna any longer and ordered her to be put into prison."

Bronwyn stared at him.

"You can guess what happened next. Lady Morwenna screeched and all hell broke loose. The empress ordered her thrown in the cells and demanded the name of her lover. When Lady Morwenna asked why, the empress lost her temper and said, 'So that I might know who to hang in the morning.'" He shook his head. "It was a grim evening."

"So where is she now? You said she was missing?"

"I'm getting to that. The empress called me, Sir Miles Fitzwalter, and a few other trusted men to Morwenna's prison cell, where she demanded Lady Morwenna tell us everything." He turned his head and swallowed.

"What is it?"

"The empress threatened to use me and my skills. My family's profession, you know. She demanded Lady Morwenna tell her immediately, or she would be put to the rack and said I would be the one to loosen her tongue." He tugged at the collar of his green jerkin, exposing a hint of dark hair curled up from his chest.

Bronwyn breathed in through her nose. Theobold was a good, kind, young man who desperately wanted to break free from his family's tradition of being executioners. Torturing people also fell into that set of skills, which made them useful in times of war but reviled during peacetime. It was considered a low, base, dirty profession to hear Theobold talk of it, and she understood why it pained him. Not only to be associated with it in common speech, but to be at the empress's whim to be used like that, knowing he would have to comply with her orders or face her displeasure… It was a horrid situation.

"Would she have truly used you for that purpose?"

"To torture my cousin? Yes. The empress doesn't care. Blood, family…" He shrugged. "All she cares about is establishing her hold on the English Crown, and Lady Morwenna didn't just ruin her plans to get back Sir Robert. She made her look bad in front of dozens of noble families at dinner. It was an insult."

"So what happened?"

"Lady Morwenna started crying. She begged the empress for mercy and said it had been solely at the hands of her lover, that she had not been the mastermind, after all," he said.

"I thought she'd said that before, when she first returned to the empress's court at Devizes."

"Yes, she did. But this was different. She admitted then that she had been helping her lover ransom the queen and prince. At dinner, she declared herself to be the mastermind of it all, but no one believed her. Then under threat of torture, she'd said it was all her lover's fault. It had been his plan, that she had only been there because of her love for him."

Bronwyn began to feel frustrated. "And what *was* his plan? Did she reveal who he was?"

"Lady Morwenna said that it was his plan to attack the hostage exchange on the road to Bristol and hold them for ransom. Sir Miles demanded his name, and Morwenna finally said it was

Sir Bors."

"*Bors?*" So the man was still alive.

"Yes. The turncoat, who had at first been part of Empress Maud's court, and then defected to Stephen's, and back again. I thought we'd seen the last of him back in London at the empress's coronation, but apparently not. He's alive, and he's had Lady Morwenna under his thumb. She'll do anything he asks of her, or so she says."

Bronwyn's mouth curved in a slight smile. Maybe Theobold was seeing Lady Morwenna's true colors. They may have been cousins, but she was not the sweet, innocent, young woman he had previously thought her to be. That made her glad.

"The empress was furious and threw a torch at the bars. It fell and started to set the rushes alight on the floor, though the men opened the cell door and stamped it out quickly. But she declared Lady Morwenna would die at dawn. Lady Morwenna then said the empress would accomplish no such thing, for she wasn't really powerful anymore, and her true master would soon take power."

"'Her true master'?"

"Your guess is as good as mine. I would guess Sir Bors, but he's not smart or calculating enough to plan such schemes like this. He's brave, but he's brash. I'd put him in a fight, but not at a dinner with aristocrats. They'd eat him alive."

"So who do you think it is? Lady Morwenna's true master?" Bronwyn asked.

"I don't know. It could be Stephen. It could be anyone. But she seemed sure of herself. The empress called her all sorts of names and said she'd almost ruined her plans to get Sir Robert back. Lady Morwenna said she didn't care, and it was just as well, since Matilda and her son had been here under her very nose. Apparently Matilda was hidden in town, and Eustace nearby too."

Bronwyn hesitated a second, then *hmm*ed and avoided his eyes. So why hadn't Lady Morwenna revealed Bronwyn's part in rescuing them? They were not friends or allies, so why hadn't she mentioned her? Unless... she wanted to claim all credit for herself? Bronwyn wasn't sure.

"Bronwyn... you're paying a lot of attention to those herbs."

"Well, they need attention."

"You're holding a stick."

She dropped the stick and moved to another rosemary bush. Her basket was mostly full, so she wiped her hands on her apron. "I should be getting back."

"Bronwyn. Do you know something?"

Sharp as a hunting dog, he was. She mentally cursed his intelligence. "Don't know what you mean."

"Yes, you do. You're hiding something. What is it?"

"Nothing."

He rose, shedding grass all over himself. He stood in her way, his dark eyes boring into hers. "Tell me. You knew about Matilda and her son, didn't you? Is that it?"

"Umm..." She looked away.

"God's teeth, Bronwyn, you knew? You knew they were hidden away? Good God, why didn't you tell me?" He gripped her shoulders. "Tell me you didn't play a part in this plot. Do you have any idea what could have happened?"

She brushed his hands away. "Yes, I know very well. Lady Morwenna planned to leave them to die in that pit, and I couldn't let that happen. Crispin and I—"

He cursed. "Tell me everything, right now."

Bronwyn told him. How she and Crispin rescued the royal pair and parted ways, with him hiding the queen in a nunnery outside of the city and her hiding the prince in the kitchens, with Rupert's help.

Theobold stared at her. "Of all the idiotic plans... You had Eustace working in the kitchens. Like a servant. My God. And Rupert... Of course you'd enlist his aid. Why doesn't that surprise me?" Theobold spoke disgustedly and ran a hand through his dark hair. "I can't believe you didn't tell me any of this. Why didn't you?"

She felt a pang of guilt at the hurt look on his face. "You are allied with the empress."

"So are you," he pointed out. "And you did this in her castle. Whilst in her employ."

"She would have used them for her own ends. She might have killed them. It wasn't right."

"It is her right," he said, coming face to face with her. "She is an empress. It is her right to do as she pleases with whoever is in her court, including enemy prisoners."

"And you trust she would have sent them on their way to Bristol Prison, to further the release of Stephen? Or would she have ransomed them herself, or killed them?" Bronwyn said, not backing down.

"That is not for you to decide. You are a servant. She is an empress. I don't understand why we're having this conversation." His voice took on a hard, clipped tone. His accent—it sounded different to her ears. Almost... like an aristocrat.

"Well, this *servant* helped take them to Bristol and they're safe." *Sort of,* she thought.

"God Almighty, Bronwyn. You likely changed the outcome of the war with this plot of yours. She could have ransomed or exiled them, ended the war and taken the Crown. And now..." He shook his head. "I don't know whether to shake you, walk away, or kiss you."

Bronwyn gave him a slow smile. She still fancied him—that much was true. And she'd thought of him often whilst baking bread or doing her chores. She had missed him, even if they were no longer together. "Is the empress mad I refused to spy for her?"

"What? What are you talking about?"

"A few days after we arrived at Bristol, Crispin had a message for me from the empress, saying that she wanted me to spy for her. That she didn't mind my leaving court, as she wanted me to spy on the queen and report back."

"So that's why he came back and left again so quickly. I figured he had just defected. A few nobles have." He walked away, cursing, and came back. "I don't like this. Crispin is like a spider, sticking his fingers in all sorts of webs. This only happened a few days ago." He sighed. "The empress demanded that Lady Morwenna give the name of her master, but she refused, even under threat of death. So the empress decided she'd had enough. The young woman had caused her enough trouble and decreed that she would die at dawn, and so would Sir Bors, once she found him."

"So why are you here? She got away, you said? How?"

"It seems that Lady Morwenna or Sir Bors have friends at court, for Lady Morwenna did indeed escape during the night. She couldn't have gotten out on her own. Someone must have helped her. Likely more than one person. The empress was livid and sent me to hunt her down." His gaze drifted out of focus, fixed at a point over her right shoulder. "It was a task I could do, considering my master is still in prison at Winchester. So Crispin came to you at Bristol, and I've been hunting my cousin ever since."

"That's not the only thing that's happened." She told him of the dead maidservant, Mary.

"God's teeth. You do attract trouble, don't you?" Theobold pointed out. "That's the second maidservant to die in the past few days. And for Rupert to be romancing them both... He's either very unlucky, a killer, or a mark whom someone is trying to frame as a killer. Philippa's death took everyone by surprise. She was struck on the back of the head with a bottle and died, a rose in her hand. Who do you think is behind this new maidservant's death? You're sure it wasn't an accident?"

Bronwyn shook her head. "Her head was bashed in with a bottle of ale."

He nodded. "I see. You'd best be getting back. I'll escort you. I'll speak with this chatelaine and see if she knows where Lady Morwenna might've gone."

They walked together, him leading the horse and following her to the gates of the city. She was quiet for a bit of the walk, until he commented on her silence.

Bronwyn finally said the words that had been on the tip of her tongue, but she'd been too anxious to ask. She was aware the relationship between him and the taster was fake, but she still wanted to know for certain. "How is Mistress Agatha?"

The effect on Theobold was immediate, as if he'd eaten a fruit soaked in vinegar. He winced and said, "She is well. From what I understand."

Bronwyn's face grew warm. She hadn't wanted to ask, and he seemed disinclined to say more. They joined the queue of travelers entering the city, and Theobold said, "We're not together. If that's what you're wondering."

"No, I mean… Oh?" She studied her shoes.

He grinned. "I… I was foolish, Bronwyn. Utterly foolish."

Her heart rose. She wanted to hear more but… They were at the castle. The guards recognized Bronwyn and let her in but were wary about Theobold. When he gave his name and asked to see the chatelaine, he was allowed in, and his weapon was taken from him. His horse was given to a groomsman to look after, and he entered the courtyard.

"I should return to the kitchens," Bronwyn said.

"Yes, I know I kept you. I'm sure I'll see you again soon. I'll find you." He gave her a smile like those of old, and a part of her heart warmed, but also, she faltered in her steps. He had thrown her over so easily, when he'd decided that her low birth and status in society were not suitable enough for him. What had changed? Or was he like Lady Alice and fickle?

She fancied him something rotten but knew she did not want to be messed about with, either by potential friends or in romance. She hadn't the patience, or the heart for it. For once in her life, she just wanted a relationship of hers to be real. Steady— and constant. No varying or changing. Just… ordinary. Safe. Dull, even.

She returned to the kitchens with the herbs, pondering Rupert's lack of fortune with maidservants, and the news from

Theobold about Lady Morwenna. What had the noblewoman planned to do with Philippa? Had it all been completely innocent, or had she planned to use the maidservant in her schemes?

Later, Bronwyn was called to serve the nobles at dinner. She unbound her hair from her kerchief, removed her apron, and wiped her hands clean so she looked more presentable, then took a platter of bread out to the hall. But as she entered and set the platter down on the main table, she almost dropped the platter on the floor.

There, beside the chatelaine, sat Sir Bors, the turncoat.

Chapter Fifteen

B RONWYN STARED. A small bread roll threatened to fall off the wooden trencher she held out, and a nobleman said, "Have a care, girl."

She set the trencher down, removing an empty one. The gazes of the chatelaine and Sir Bors flickered to her.

The bread roll quickly disappeared, as did most of the bread, with numerous hands taking rolls and pieces. The trencher emptied quickly, and she removed it from the table almost as soon as she'd set it down.

"You. I know you," Sir Bors said, eyeing her.

She swallowed. The last time she'd seen him, they had stood in a prison cell in London, and he'd struck her and knocked her out. She was lucky she hadn't died, thanks to Lady Alice, who had hit him and helped her wake up and escape to what had become the empress's failed coronation.

But that had been months ago and seemed almost a lifetime ago now. It was hard to believe it had only been earlier this year.

She ducked her head like a good servant and tried to appear invisible. She did not speak. But she could not help notice that among the guests, Theobold was present, sat near Lady Alice. Theobold's mouth was set in a firm line, his brow furrowed, while Lady Alice pointedly ignored Bronwyn.

"You two know each other?" Lady Mabel asked Bronwyn pointedly, swirling her wine in a cup.

"I served Sir Bors in Lincoln, at the empress's camp," Bronwyn said. Would that be enough to dissuade any suspicion? She hoped so.

The man in question, a large, stocky fellow of middle age, sat back in his seat and belched, scratching his stomach. A large, gold ring caught the light and blinked on his hand. "That's the sign of a good servant. Remembers her betters. I like that." He openly eyed her chest.

Bronwyn stepped back and clasped the empty wooden trencher to her front. With any luck, he would not remember her that well. She stepped a few paces behind with the other servants and pages and moved to go, when the chatelaine said, "Bronwyn, wait a moment."

She hesitated and moved forward. "Yes, Countess?"

Lady Mabel sat at the head of the long table and said loudly, "Do you know, Sir Bors, I tasked this wench with finding out who killed a kitchen maid."

Sir Bors laughed. "A maid? You'd be better off asking a dog to do it. At least a good hound has a better chance of smelling the trail." A few noblemen nearby laughed as well, exchanging smiles.

Bronwyn wished to slap the grin off Sir Bors's face but instead schooled her features and gave a polite smile. If she was to be the butt of a joke, then so be it.

"Ah, but she came highly recommended, did you not, mistress?" Lady Mabel asked.

Bronwyn ducked her head in a bob of assent.

"And how goes your hunt, mistress?"

"Call her 'Mistress Hound,' for that is what she does." Sir Bors laughed and slapped his knee. "Mistress Hound!" He barked and a few of the others howled with him.

Bronwyn's cheeks grew warm. She glanced over and saw Lady Alice sat nearby, watching, her face serious. There was no need to warn the noblewoman about Sir Bors, for she was already sat at dinner with the man. She wondered if Sir Bors remembered

Lady Alice as well.

Seeing Bronwyn's gaze, Lady Alice quickly smirked and turned her head, speaking pleasantly to Lady Muriel beside her.

"Ah, but this hound…" Lady Mabel said. "Well. I have imprisoned a young man for the crime. If my hound does not catch me a culprit within the week, I shall have to kill him. Someone shall have to answer for the crime."

"Who is the man?" Sir Bors asked.

"A squire. Rupert Boswell? Bothwell?" The chatelaine shrugged.

"Rupert? That lad? No, he'd not do such a thing. He's a good sort. What'd he supposedly do?" Sir Bors blinked and leaned back in his seat, making the wooden bench creak.

"We think he killed a maid," the chatelaine said. "Took her in the gardens and killed her. Shame. I hate to lose a good maid."

"Rupert wouldn't do that. He's got an eye for a pretty face, but he's no killer. Not of maids, anyway." Sir Bors drank more, and he spoke so loudly and confidently, he had the attention of many of the nobles present, including the chatelaine, who watched as trickles of red wine coursed down the corners of his mouth and trailed down his round chin, dripping onto his stained, dark-gray jerkin.

He exhaled with a loud smacking of his lips, wiped his mouth, and set his goblet down on the table, motioning for a servant to refill it. "Seems to me you've got the wrong man. He was a squire of mine for a time and I can tell you, he's a lover, not a killer. Takes after me." To the chatelaine, he winked and said, "Far be it from me to tell a chatelaine what to do…"

Lady Mabel cocked her head.

"But if it were me, I'd wait before imprisoning just any squire. He's a good lad and useful too. He served me well in the empress's court. I could use him again."

"Are you asking me to release him, Sir Bors?" the chatelaine said.

"If it's not too much trouble, Lady Mabel. I could make use of the boy. Someone needs to keep an eye on him." He grinned, showing a mouth full of yellow teeth.

Lady Mabel laughed, a rich sound. "Very well. I will take you on your word, Sir Bors." Over her shoulder, she said to the page, "Tell the guards I said to release the squire from prison."

Bronwyn breathed in a small sigh of relief for a second, until the chatelaine's hawk-eyed gaze slid to her.

"But you, Mistress Hound, you'd best get a move on. I will have *someone* answer for the maid's death by the week's end. The squire may walk around free. For now."

Bronwyn did not mistake her meaning. Lady Mabel meant she could just as easily imprison him again, should she feel like it. Or someone else.

Bronwyn did not stay much longer, returning to the kitchens to prepare a dinner tray for the queen and prince. She took it up without any incident and spoke quietly with the queen, but it was only to relay the news, how Rupert had been freed, thanks to the intervention of Sir Bors.

"Sir Bors? He is here? But he is one of my husband's knights. I thought he was dead," the queen said, resting her hands on the back of a chair as she faced Bronwyn.

"He served the empress for a time and disappeared after London. We haven't seen him since. But allegedly, he was one of the men behind the attack on your entourage. One of his accomplices admitted as such."

"Then he should be punished for his crime. We could have died." Her pale, delicate hands gripped the back of the wooden chair so hard, it creaked.

"I suspect he would deny it, Your Grace. Unless you can remember him from the attack, then there is no proof. Only the word of his accomplice, and she has gone missing."

The queen's shoulders slumped ever so slightly, and she looked fondly as Eustace dug into the wooden trencher with gusto, eating potage with a hunk of fresh bread.

"I thought one of the voices sounded familiar, but I couldn't say who it was. The men who attacked us were so fast, and it was dark. To think it was a man who had once pledged his loyalty to my husband." A frown marred the queen's pretty face. "The chatelaine took the word of Sir Bors so easily. Would she not value the word of a queen? Rank my words higher than his? I am, after all, royalty."

Bronwyn bowed her head. "I cannot say, Your Grace."

Prince Eustace looked up from his potage. "Mama... Look around. We are prisoners here. Will Lady Mabel listen to *anything* we say?"

The queen's frown deepened. "You have a point. And even then, we cannot be certain it was Sir Bors." She paced the small room, with a fatigue and certainty that made Bronwyn think the queen had done this many times. "I am glad that the squire has been freed. But I would fear for him as well. No doubt Sir Bors has plans to use him. I hope the squire has a good head on his shoulders."

Bronwyn hoped so too. She took down their chamber pot and dumped it, then had a servant bring up a clean one and returned to the kitchens. She ate a bit of food with the other cooks, but there wasn't much left after the main meal, so she made do with a bit of potage from a stale bread trencher, scraping for a bit of oats, beans, peas, and meat juices from the animals cooked earlier.

Master Gregory was nowhere to be found, so she finished her meal and cleaned up, then helped the other cooks tidy up the kitchen in preparation for the next day. "Where's Master Gregory?" she asked.

"Dunno," one cook said. "He likes to take a walk around outside before turning in to bed. You could probably find him walking around."

She asked, "He seemed to look after Mary a lot. Were they close?"

The cook, a fellow in his late twenties, had a thick stature, with a round face, beady eyes, and arms as thick as hams. His apron strained against his stomach, but his red cheeks gave a sense of being jolly most of the time, or pugnacious, depending on the circumstance. He gave her a look. "We all know what you're doing, you know. Asking questions. Sticking your nose where it doesn't belong."

Bronwyn shrugged. "It's what I was asked to do. And I want to help."

The cook snorted and buffed his fingernails on his apron. "Dunno what a woman like you thinks she can do, finding a killer. You should be in the kitchen with us, not doing... whatever else. What do you really think you'll find out by asking questions?"

"All sorts of things. Were they close?"

"Master Gregory and Mary? Yeh, a bit. He knew her from when she first started, so he looked after her some. Taught her how to be a good scullery maid, then a kitchen maid. She would have risen to a cook, if she'd lasted longer. But she weren't without her troubles."

"What do you mean?" Bronwyn asked.

The large cook shuffled a bit closer to her and said, "She always did like a pretty face. She admired men of all sorts and had caused trouble for the kitchen before. Some men thought they'd try it on with her, but she's a sweet girl, so Gregory would always protect her. Think he thought that that squire friend of yers was harmless."

"You think he blames himself for Mary's death?"

"Maybe. I dunno. Could be. You'd be better off asking him yerself." He jerked his head toward the door. "Master Gregory likes to wander around the stables. See if you catch him before he takes his bed."

"Thank you." Bronwyn nodded and slipped out. Could Master Gregory be blaming himself for Mary's death because he hadn't been there to protect her? Or... had he fancied her himself and was angry she'd been romancing Rupert? What if he had made advances toward her and she had rebuffed him, so he'd been angry? Or what if she'd given him hope for the future, so he'd acted as her protector? And now it was too late. Her thoughts ran wild at the prospect.

It was strange, but while she felt comfortable being and working in the kitchens as a sort of haven or province, she also felt more and more distant from it, the more immersed she became in hunting down this crime. She felt like an outsider, not a kitchen maid or cook to be trusted, but something else.

Indeed, she observed as she walked along the castle corridors and slipped outside the castle and into the darkness of the courtyard, the nobles teased her and made fun of her, calling her 'Mistress Hound.' She hoped the name didn't stick.

Rounding the corner, she exited the courtyard and walked around toward the stables, where she heard a noise. She paused for a moment, waited, then darted around the side of the building. There in the darkness, she waited, and the noise resumed. The movement of a person. A low moan, quiet and soft. The rustle of clothes.

The clouds overhead shifted, and the moonlight revealed what Bronwyn had never expected to see.

Master Gregory stood leaned up against the walls of the stables, kissing a man.

—⟡—

Chapter Sixteen

RONWYN BLINKED AND stared. Never in her wildest dreams had she imagined Master Gregory had been romancing men. She darted back into the shadows and around the corner. It was another cook, the one she'd heard called 'Alan.' Bronwyn had heard stories about men having male lovers, but she'd never thought it might be true. She didn't know what to think about it.

But then she sneezed, and the noises stopped. She froze, then called out, "M-Master Gregory, are you around? Hello?"

There was stillness. The dark was full. She knew she was not alone, so she turned to walk away as loudly as she could, when she heard a heavy sigh and a familiar voice say, "I'm here, girl, just taking a piss."

She let out a small sigh of relief. "Oh, I'm sorry. I'll just be—"

A thick hand wrapped around her throat, squeezing tightly. She squealed and a man pinned her back against the wall of the stables. Horses nickered indoors, the sound dim. Her eyes wide, she pushed back, straining against her attacker.

"Who told you where to find us?" the mystery man demanded. In the darkness, she couldn't see his face. She kicked and the man grunted, releasing her briefly.

She gasped and shoved back, scrambling, when he pulled her hair and tugged her back. Pain rippled through her skull.

"Alan, stop that!" Gregory's voice rang out.

The man pulled her head back painfully, and she thought the

very hair might rip out of her head. She shrieked and then the man had her again, and he kicked her feet out from under her. She crashed to the ground, when a man shoved her assailant away, and threatened, "Leave her be. You'll scare the wits out of her."

"We can't trust her. She's a spy."

"Only on the queen, and you know that was put on her. The chatelaine's little joke."

"She's their hound. Mistress Hound, I heard them call her."

"You'll not hurt her again, Alan. I mean it."

Bronwyn gasped, her throat burning. "It was a joke. They were teasing me. They think I can't do it."

Two pairs of eyes looked at her. She pushed up on her hands and knees, coughing. Bronwyn raised her head, conscious of the moonlight shining on her face. "But I can."

Master Gregory groaned and put a hand over his face, whilst his companion, Alan, crossed his arms. "What do you want?"

"I was looking for Master Gregory," Bronwyn said, standing. Her scalp tingled and she gingerly touched her head. It hurt.

"You found him." The man showed no repentance whatsoever for hurting her.

She said, "I wanted to ask you about Mary. I thought maybe you fancied her—"

The man guffawed.

"—or that you blamed yourself for not protecting her." She looked at Master Gregory, who surveyed her with wide eyes. He rubbed the side of his face.

"The other cook said I could find you out here."

"Who said?" the pugnacious Alan demanded.

"I don't know his name. Big fellow, blond hair. His arms were… big." She felt at a lack for words.

"Bartholomew," both cooks said. "It figures."

"Bronwyn…" Master Gregory started, and he took a step toward her, but she backed away. "I'm not going to hurt you. And neither is Alan."

Her eyes darted from one cook to the other.

"He promises," Master Gregory said.

Alan opened his mouth, then shut it like a trap. He gave a stiff nod.

Bronwyn's shoulders relaxed a fraction. Master Gregory said, "Alan, leave us. Go back to the kitchens."

"But what if she talks? We can't trust her."

"*I* trust her. She won't say anything," Gregory said, eyeing Bronwyn.

"It's not just *your* head I'm thinking of," Alan snapped.

"I know." Gregory shot his lover a heated look. Something passed between them, some words unspoken, and Alan let out a breath and rolled his shoulders.

"Fine. But you put too much trust in her. One of these days, you're going to trust the wrong person." To Bronwyn, Alan growled, "You keep your mouth shut. Or I'll shut it for you."

Bronwyn nodded. "I won't say anything. I promise."

"You'd better." Alan walked away.

It wasn't until his tall, thin form disappeared into the night's shadows that Bronwyn exhaled a sigh of relief. She touched her throat, which hurt, and blinked hard.

"Are you all right?" Master Gregory asked.

"Yes. Why did he—"

"He attacked you because he thought you might try to report us. It's forbidden, men loving one another." Master Gregory's voice sounded tired. "Come, I'll walk you back."

Bronwyn shivered.

"You won't say anything to anyone about us, will you?" he asked.

"No. It's none of my business."

"I thought so. You have that trustworthy look about you. Even if the nobles like to joke about it and tease you, I can see now why they ask you to be their hunter." He took a breath. "Promise me you won't say anything about this, Bronwyn. Both our lives would be forfeit if anyone found out."

She nodded. "I swear."

He spat into his hand and extended it. A tradesman's promise. She spat into her hand and they grasped hands, their saliva mixing. Part of her wanted to wash her hands, and she gathered Lady Alice would squeal at the very thought of such a handshake, which made her smile. Then she remembered where she was and schooled her features into seriousness again. "I promise. I'll not say anything."

"Good girl." They shook.

Wiping his hand on his thigh, Gregory asked, "Why were you looking for me? I thought you knew everything there was to know about her death."

Bronwyn shook her head. "I didn't before, but I think I do now. The night she was killed, you were with Alan in the gardens, or nearby, weren't you?"

"Yes. Sometimes, we'll come out here. When the others have gone to bed. I thought I'd keep an eye on Mary at the same time. It was foolish, I know."

"What happened? What did you see?" Bronwyn asked.

"Not much. Like I told you before, we overheard them arguing. We came out here and then Alan went back first, and I came later. Heard them arguing, but I know Mary can hold her own in a fight, and a young man like that squire…" He shrugged. "If I'd thought Mary was in danger, I'd have come right away, but I saw him walk away. Knew Mary was all right. I went to see her, but she was crying and told me to leave her be—"

"You talked to her? After Rupert left her?"

"Yes. That's why it didn't make sense to me. But she told me to go, so I did, thinking she just wanted a bit of privacy to herself. Some women do, you know. So I left her. Never thought the squire might double back and attack her."

"Or that someone else might," Bronwyn said.

"Aye, but who would want to hurt Mary? She's just a maid."

"Did she have any other lovers? Men who might get jealous she was with Rupert?"

"No. I'd have known. There was no one," Master Gregory said.

"Had she argued with anyone earlier? Gotten in trouble?"

"Mary? No. She was a good young woman. Her only fault was she fell in love too easily."

"Hmm." Bronwyn walked on. They were almost at the courtyard.

"Oh. And she had a big mouth. Could never keep a secret," Master Gregory said, almost as an afterthought.

"What?" Bronwyn glanced at him.

"Aye, she had a bad habit of listening to other people's conversations and giggling about it later."

Bronwyn thought back to the night of the fight between Rupert and Crispin. The chatelaine had been there. Could Mary have overheard a conversation she shouldn't have?

The next day, Bronwyn reported to the kitchens for work. Alan glowered at her but gave her a wide berth. She pretended not to notice and avoided him.

Master Gregory greeted her. "All right, Mistress Hound?"
She grinned. "Woof."

He smiled back at her, and all was well, until Alan gave her a tray of food and said, "Bring this to the prisoners. They'll be hungry."

Nodding, Bronwyn took the tray, then went to the queen, who greeted her and asked, "Where are my ladies? Have you seen them?"

Bronwyn set down the tray and shook her head. "No, Your Grace."

"That is strange. Perhaps they'll come up later. They usually stay with me."

Bronwyn surveyed the queen. "You do not mind the Lady Alice being a companion?"

"You shouldn't speak to the queen unless spoken to first," Prince Eustace said around a mouthful of bread. "And servants shouldn't ask questions."

Bronwyn bit her lip. So spoke the young prince, whom she'd helped rescue not so long ago. A far cry from the quiet and eager boy she'd had working in the kitchens. But he had a point. Bronwyn bowed her head and clasped her hands.

The queen smiled, but it was bittersweet. "It's all right, Eustace. Even if the ladies warn me, *Bronwyn is not to be trusted*, I prefer to have my enemies where I can see them and make up my own mind. And truth be told, she has been a loyal servant to us both." To Bronwyn, she said, "To answer your question, I don't have much choice. Yes, she comes from that woman's court, but I am not so particular with my choice of lady companion. And she entertains me with gossip. Is it true your sweetheart, Theobold, abandoned you in favor of another servant?"

The queen spoke candidly and without any attempt at malice; she clearly thought it was old news she was repeating. But the statement of their fake relationship did still hurt, and Bronwyn took a breath.

"He did, Your Grace. But I... hope he will have a change of heart."

"Indeed." The queen took a bread roll and nibbled delicately. "You may go."

As she turned to leave, the queen said, "Bronwyn, how goes your spying? Have you found out much about me to share with your mistress?"

Bronwyn stiffened and cast a quick look over her shoulder. The queen and prince sat still, as if frozen in time. Both looked at her silently.

"I refused, Your Grace."

The queen blinked. "Why? I am sure Maud made you a good offer. I would have done."

"Because..." She didn't have much of an answer. "It didn't seem right."

The queen surveyed her, tapping the small, round, wooden table with her partially eaten bread roll. "What a curious woman you are." She waved Bronwyn away.

As the door closed behind Bronwyn, the prince said, "Why do you talk with servants, Mama?"

"Because, dearest. They know everything. And to befriend one will serve you in good stead. But don't ever forget: they are here to serve us. They are not our equals and never will be."

The queen's words echoing in her head, Bronwyn headed back down from the tower, her hand brushing the rough, curved stone as she walked down the spiral stairwell.

That early evening, Theobold found her. "Come, walk with me."

She let him lead her away, down the castle corridors and to a small alcove. The night was getting on, and the torches burned, but there was a draft. Once they were confident of being alone and in the shadows, he put his hands on her shoulders and said, "I'm leaving."

"What? But you just arrived."

He shook his head. "I tried telling Lady Mabel about Sir Bors, but she refused to listen. I reminded her that I've served her husband well these past few years, but she reprimanded me. Said if I were so good at my service, then why was he sitting in a jail cell while I ate at her table?" His shoulders slumped. "She's known me for years and yet she still trusts the word of a knight over a squire. I tell you, there's no justice in this world. She's fascinated by his charm, although what she sees in him, I can't say. But I wanted to tell you. I tried."

"What did she say?"

"Only that if this Lady Morwenna is as good at telling wild stories as she seems to be, then she should change her path and join minstrels or traveling players. At least then people would pay to hear her tales." He dropped his hands from her shoulders and glanced down. "She heard me, but she did not listen. She may not believe me and does not accept the rumors about a gossiping lady-in-waiting as proof of Sir Bors's treachery. She appreciated my coming to her, but that was all. The Lady Mabel prefers to judge things with her own eyes. Not on hearsay, especially from a squire, when she has a knight in her presence. I told her that Lady Morwenna had accused Sir Bors of being complicit in the abduction and that the empress would want him captured, if not dead, but she said without a written message from the empress, this was merely gossip, and that, she had no time for."

Bronwyn nodded. She did not like it, but one's status mattered greatly, especially when it came to being believed. A person might take the word of a nobleman over a servant every time, regardless of whether the nobleman was right or not. She rather believed the closing of ranks was partially their way of keeping the servants down at their level. But it didn't have to mean it was right, only pigheaded.

"What will you do now?"

"I have to find my cousin. Winter is coming, and Lady Morwenna is likely alone, or in unsafe company."

"And what will you do when you find her?"

His forehead wrinkled. "Honestly? I should take her back to the empress for questioning. But neither Morwenna nor I want that. I'll judge what is right when I find her. But… I think taking her back home might be the safest choice, for both of us. She'll dislike being under her family's roof, but better that than a jail cell." He looked at her. "I didn't want to go without telling you this, and goodbye."

Before Bronwyn could speak, he tilted her face up to meet his and kissed her. She felt herself relax and wanted to melt into his arms. His hands wrapped around her, pulling her close, and she reached up along his back, pressing him against her. She quite liked the feel of him, hard and muscular, smelling like horse, hay, and the outdoors, and just him. She had missed him and would miss him still while he was away. She pulled back from the kiss.

"What?" he asked, his eyes dark. He eyed her bottom lip.

"I'm going to miss you," she said.

He smiled. "Well, with any luck, I won't be gone too long. I'll find Morwenna and return her home, then come back to the empress. We won't be parted for long."

"But what about the empress's distaste for us? She disapproves of us. Ever since that day…"

"Hmm. I find that she may throw as many ladies-in-waiting and courtiers at me as she likes. What I do with my heart is my own design. *My* choice. No one else's."

"But she disapproved so much. She sent me away, as a punishment."

He stroked her cheek with his left thumb. "I know. It was horrible. We will have to be careful she doesn't find us. But, Bronwyn, I meant what I said back in the cells at Winchester. I will be true to you. I swear it."

She looked at him then. Bronwyn so wanted to believe him. But he had proven fickle—and easily influenced by others. She thought of how he'd so easily changed his opinion of their relationship and of her, judging by what others had said of their mismatched social strata. "Do you still think me common?"

His gaze, which had been lingering down at her chest, snapped up to her eyes. "I…"

"Do you?" Emotion leaked into her voice. Her throat felt tight. "Because I think I'm falling in love with you, and I can't bear it if you think me lesser."

His eyes widened. "Bronwyn." He rubbed her shoulders. "I'm the son of a man who cuts people's heads off for a living. My family is ignored and scorned for our profession. If you are common, then so am I. I was foolish to think otherwise. And I'm sorry I hurt you."

That didn't answer her question. But at that moment, she didn't care. Especially when he kissed her again and whispered, "I'm falling for you too."

Her heart opened, and her chest filled with warmth. With joy. She wanted to shout, to jump up and down. To cry and laugh and dance.

He picked her up and swirled her around in a circle, laughing, squeezing her tightly around the middle until she was out of breath and set her down, both of them giggling. Panting for breath, he leaned in close and whispered in her ear, "Do not trust Crispin." His parting words, whispers as he'd held her close, echoed in her mind. "He's full of tricks. What sort of man goes and pledges his allegiance to an empress and then leaves a few days later? She needs good, honest men around her until she has Sir Robert back. Crispin comes from a wealthy family and is respected. The other men follow where he leads, even though he is just a squire."

Bronwyn nodded. "I shall watch closely."

"Keep Lady Alice with you. She has a good head on her shoulders."

Bronwyn shook her head, her expression bitter. "We are no longer friends."

"Now that is news. Why? What did she say?"

She loved him then, partly for assuming she wasn't at fault, and for caring. "She… no longer thinks it is right for us to be friends. She doesn't want to be friends with a servant. I understand it, but it still hurts."

Theobold's expression had clouded, and his eyes turned downcast. "We all make mistakes."

She looked at him.

"Bronwyn, about what I said back at Devizes. You should know—"

She put a hand on his chest. "Don't. We both said things we didn't mean."

He met her eyes. "You are so quick to forgive. I worry I might hurt you again."

"Then try not to."

She appreciated him trying to apologize for treating her poorly and casting her off like an old coat, when he'd pledged his affection for her just weeks earlier.

"Promise you'll wait for me. Till I get back. I promise, I won't romance any other women. I swear."

She nodded. "I promise."

"Good." He kissed her again. "I'll try not to be long. But take care, Bronwyn. This place isn't safe. Not for the likes of you. I heard what the nobles called you. They tease and they joke, but it's not safe for you here. I want you to be careful."

They kissed again, and then parted ways, both casting longing looks over their shoulders at the other.

Bronwyn touched her lips, her cheeks, feeling how warm they were. She went down a spiral stairwell and upon reaching the bottom, she ran into a guard, who grunted, "Move."

A woman crying and shrieking echoed across the room. "What's happened?" Bronwyn asked.

"A lady's crying bloody murder is what. Move on." The guard hurried past her.

Bronwyn ran after him. She knew that voice. It belonged to not just any lady, but Lady Muriel. She kept pace with the guard and hurried with him down the corridor, through the passageways, their shoes thundering against the hard, wooden floors.

"Clear the way! Move aside!" the guard yelled, and more guards joined him as he led them to the source of the shouting.

Bronwyn stood in a group of guards, all crowding around the entrance to a lady's chamber. She pushed her way through and inside stood Lady Muriel, who was still shrieking. "Oh, Bronwyn, it's horrible. I can't believe it."

"What is it, Lady Muriel?"

Lady Alice stood by in a dressing gown tied tight, her long, black hair rippling past her shoulders and down her back. She rolled her eyes.

Lady Muriel's tanned face was drawn tight, and her petite hands darted to her mouth. "It's… It's… his sign."

"What sign? Whose?" a guard asked.

"Him," Lady Muriel said simply.

"Who's 'him'?" the guard asked her.

"The m-murderer. He's left me a sign, that he's coming for me next." Lady Muriel's eyes filled with tears as she pointed to a lone rose on her pillow.

Chapter Seventeen

Bronwyn stood there, staring at the innocent pink rose on Lady Muriel's pillow. It was small, but there was no denying it. Lying as sweetly as though a lover had dropped it on the good lady's pillow as a token reminder of something to come.

"What is all that noise?" came a sharp, feminine voice. "What is going on?" The chatelaine stood at the back of the group of guards and pulled some back roughly. "Lady Muriel. I demand an answer."

"It's a sign. The murderer, the one who's killed the maidservant in the gardens, he's left a message. For me." Lady Muriel pointed at her pillow with trembling fingers.

The chatelaine exhaled. "Is that all? A rose has sent you into hysterics. Good Lord." To Lady Alice, she said, "Are all of Matilda's women this silly?"

Lady Alice inclined her head. "No, Lady Mabel. But she has had a fright."

"How do you know it's a message, Lady Muriel?" Bronwyn asked. "Have you a secret admirer?"

"No. No, I do not," Lady Muriel said, her voice rising. She sat down on her bed and put her chin in her hands. "But why me? Why would he come after me?"

"Of all the nonsense. Lady Muriel, get a hold of yourself. For all we know, it could be an innocent gesture. Mistress Blakenhale may speak true; you may indeed have an admirer." To Bronwyn, she said, "I shall let you sort this. I would like to return to my morning meal without any more crying. It turns my stomach."

Lady Alice rolled her eyes.

Lady Muriel nodded forlornly, her voice quiet. "Yes, Lady Mabel. I'm sorry."

The chatelaine swept out of the room, in a swish of dark-gray skirts, the iron keys at her waist jangling as she moved. The guards, having ascertained there was no immediate threat, left, until it was just the three women in the room.

"When did you first notice it?" Bronwyn asked. "The rose, I mean."

Lady Muriel said, "Today, this morning. After I came back from the privy. I rose and went out, whilst Lady Alice was still asleep, and when I came back in, the rose was there. I screamed and called for the guards, and the rest you know."

Bronwyn turned to Lady Alice. "You didn't notice anything?"

"I take issue with you addressing me like an equal." The noblewoman narrowed her eyes.

Bronwyn's shoulders stiffened. "Lady Alice?"

"Hmph." Lady Alice patted her hair and turned her back on Bronwyn. She sat on the edge of her unmade bed and said, "I didn't see or hear anything. I was asleep. I didn't even know she'd gone to use the privy until she came back and started screaming."

Lady Muriel hugged her arms to her chest.

"Aren't you afraid as well, Lady Alice?" Bronwyn asked.

"Why should I be? He didn't come for *me*. The rose was left for *her*." Lady Alice nodded toward the lone rose on Lady Muriel's pillow.

"The idea that a strange man would come into your room when you slept isn't frightening?"

Lady Alice's eyes widened, then she huffed and drew her dressing gown tighter around her form. "The man obviously has no interest in me. I am not one to kill." She raised her chin as she spoke, as if she were too good for death.

"Are you sure it couldn't be an admirer?" Bronwyn asked

Lady Muriel.

"No. I have no one," the woman said. She looked up at Bronwyn. "I'm scared."

"I would be too."

Lady Alice sighed. "You can sleep in my bed tonight. But I'm warning you, if you snore, I'm kicking you out."

"Be sure to lock the door," Bronwyn said.

"Well, obviously." Lady Alice glanced at her. "Was there something else? You can always bring us up a tray. I wouldn't mind some fresh bread and cheese."

"Oh, yes," Lady Muriel said, brightening.

Bronwyn snorted softly and left. The ladies were remarkably calm after the incident, Lady Alice in particular. Could she be believed? There was no reason *not* to believe her story, except for the fact that they were no longer friends, and so she had to view her with the same suspicion as everyone else.

She walked down the hall and returned to the kitchens, where she asked a servant to bring up a tray and was told to bring it up herself. Gritting her teeth, she prepared a tray with bread and cheese and brought it up on a wooden trencher for the two noblewomen to share, returning to the room.

She knocked and was let inside. Lady Muriel was dressed and sat on her bed, happy to receive the tray, but Lady Alice was gone.

"Where did Lady Alice go?" Bronwyn asked.

"I don't know. To use the privy, maybe?"

The day passed without any further incident. Now that Rupert was free, she spotted him walking with Lady Muriel around the castle courtyard, in plain view. The noblewoman looked more relaxed and chatted happily, her arm linked through Rupert's.

Bronwyn smiled at the sight. At least Lady Muriel could relax a bit now that no one was going to kill her. Rupert had a way of putting people at ease. But she still was still none the wiser about who killed Mary the kitchen maid.

She walked into the castle gardens and took a minute to relax in the shade of a tree. Taking a semi-comfortable position against the tree's shady trunk, she nodded off, when she heard voices and snapped awake. Still groggy, she rolled on her hands and knees and shuffled backward behind the tree. Something made her want to hide.

A young woman walked by, her black hair shining in the afternoon sunlight. There was no mistaking Lady Alice's walk.

"My Lady Fox, you are hard to find." Crispin's voice rang out.

Lady Alice turned. "I do not seek to be caught, Master Hunter."

He laughed. "Surely, if we talk of foxes and hunters, you'd best be calling me 'a hound,' like your friend the kitchen wench."

"Bronwyn? Don't talk to me of her. She's nothing to me."

That hurt. Bronwyn's shoulders slumped, and she became conscious that she was knelt behind a tree. Her knees began to ache.

"Oho, and here I thought you were friends."

"You thought wrong."

"Good," Crispin said. "I like a woman who knows her place. You're better than consorting with servants. She's only of use to you as a servant, and the sooner she knows that, the better."

Bronwyn bit her tongue.

"Why did you call me here?" Lady Alice asked. "I did not come to talk of kitchen maids. Unless you happen to know who killed the one."

Crispin came closer, passing his hand along the dark rippling waves of her hair. She whipped around, and he snatched her wrists. He said, "You and I both know Bronwyn is a fool. She doesn't hold a candle to you. She had her chance. Now tell me, what does our prisoner do? What does she say?"

Bronwyn's mouth dropped open. That explained why Crispin had stopped bothering her to spy on the queen. Lady Alice had taken him up on his offer. "She eats, sleeps, shits, and worries about her husband in this war. She paces and reads her book of hours and prays along with her son. I am sick and tired of them both."

He trailed a finger along her chin. "It won't be long before our fortunes change. Then my master will see you for the loyal subject you are."

Bronwyn leaned in closer, straining to hear more. Who was his master, if not the empress? Why had he so easily turned on the empress and helped rescue the queen and prince, and hide them, when he could have gained a considerable amount of status in Maud's court by turning them in? Why was he here now, at Bristol, instead of Devizes, serving the empress? It all puzzled her.

"You mean *our* mistress," Lady Alice said. "The empress."

He kissed her then, and she stiffened and stepped back. "You dare—"

He kissed her again, crushing her to him, and she held her hands up against his chest. She pushed him back, but he held her close, pulling her tight, and Lady Alice just... softened against him.

Bronwyn put a hand to her mouth. Lady Alice and Crispin were kissing, and it was a romantic moment. She looked away, but then couldn't.

Lady Alice leaned into the kiss, her hands gliding up Crispin's chest and dark-gray jerkin as his hands coursed downward to squeeze her bottom. The noblewoman yelped, and he laughed and pinched her rump. Lady Alice snapped her head, liked a wild horse, and he kissed her again.

"You like that, don't you?" he said gruffly.

"You are impertinent and rude."

He laughed.

"I'm worried," Lady Alice said.

His smile fell.

"That rose in Muriel's bed. What if it really was from the killer?" Lady Alice wondered.

Aha, Bronwyn thought. *So she doesn't know who was behind the death, either.*

"I have a confession to make. That was me," he told her.

"You? Why?"

"I left it for you. I thought I'd leave it on your pillow, but then in the dark, I couldn't see and didn't want to wake anyone, so I dropped it and left. Thought maybe you were in the privy." He twirled a strand of her black hair in his fingers.

She breathed in. "I thought that it might be you. Muriel was scared."

"You have nothing to worry about," he told her. "You're too pretty to die."

"Flattery won't help you here," she said, but a small smile tugged at her lips. "Besides, I mean it. You crept into our chamber and put a flower there, while I was asleep. I was so scared when Muriel started shrieking. I thought, what if he'd come with a knife? I feel nervous just being there. This may be the empress's stronghold, but there are spies everywhere. I suspect Matilda of Boulogne has her supporters here, too, in secret. Nowhere is safe."

He wrapped his arms around her and held her close. "I won't let anything happen to you."

"You'd better not. I'm risking my neck to spy for you."

"Don't fool yourself, Lady Alice. You would have spied on the queen regardless of whether or not the empress had ordered it." He lifted her chin and kissed her again as a cheerful whistle filled the air.

Bronwyn looked toward the source and recognized the tune. As the person grew closer, she caught sight of freshly washed golden hair and a friendly countenance. *Oh, no,* she thought. *Rupert.*

Lady Alice and Crispin were too involved kissing to notice anything else around them.

Bronwyn made a noise, but Lady Alice didn't notice a thing.

Then Rupert entered the path and stopped short. "Lady Alice."

Lady Alice whirled around. Did she lean into Crispin? They

certainly seemed comfortable.

Lady Alice's face turned red. Her eyes were bright, her cheeks pink. "Rupert," she breathed.

Rupert's face could have been carved from stone. "I was in prison. I thought you would have visited me."

She stepped forward, a little unsteady on her feet. Crispin reached a hand to steady her. "I've been busy."

"So I see." He looked over her shoulder at Crispin. "Fine choice. You couldn't even wait till I was in prison before you jumped in his bed, is that it? You string me along for months, talking about our great love, and now I find you here? With him?"

Lady Alice rolled her eyes. "You take issue with my choice, when twice now, your lovers have ended up dead? And you ask why I'm with someone else? I value my head where it is, thank you very much." She huffed.

"You have something to say to me?" Crispin walked out from behind Lady Alice, putting her squarely behind him. Almost protectively, Bronwyn thought.

Crispin stood face to face with Rupert. "What do you want?"

"I came here on a stroll. But now that I'm here, I might as well tell you. You can have her," Rupert said nastily.

Lady Alice's mouth dropped open. She put a hand to her cheek.

"For too long, I've dallied with her, wasting my time. I should've known she'd leave me for someone else. She'll leave you too, at the first sign of trouble."

Crispin put a hand on Rupert's shoulder. "Mate. I understand you're unhappy, but that's a noblewoman you're talking about. Clear off."

Rupert shook his hand away. "Don't touch me."

Crispin stepped back, holding his hands up. "Fine. Just a friendly warning."

Rupert growled. "Or what? What are you going to do? Lady Alice and I were lovers, until now. I'll say whatever I want to her."

"You'll keep a civil tongue... or have me to deal with." Crispin loomed before him.

Crispin only had about an inch or two in height over Rupert, but he used those inches like he stood on a pedestal, looking down at a lesser mortal. His dark eyes narrowed. "Enjoy your stroll."

Rupert's mouth twisted as if he'd bitten into a lemon.

He stood back as Crispin took Lady Alice's hand and tugged her along, as if she were his.

Bronwyn watched them go. She felt for Rupert. She knew what it was like to have one's heart torn out and stepped on. She wanted to go and reassure him it would be okay. He wasn't alone; he had friends. But now wasn't the time.

Seeing it was just Rupert there, Bronwyn stepped out from behind the tree. She entered the main path and called his name.

He stiffened and stood with his back to her. "Leave me alone, Bronwyn."

"But..."

"Leave. Go away. Not now." His voice sounded thick, as if he had a cold or was holding back tears.

"All right." She turned and left the gardens. If he wanted privacy, she would give it to him.

THAT EVENING, BRONWYN helped serve dinner in the dining hall, and Rupert was in fine form. He was jolly, cheerful, making the lords and ladies laugh. Aside from Lady Alice, he flirted with the women. Lady Muriel giggled like a young woman, her eyes dancing as Rupert made her blush.

Bronwyn stood behind the dining guests with the other servants, watching, and observed the change in Rupert's character. Just a few hours ago, he'd seemed heartbroken, and now he was full of joy. Practically a minstrel or buffoon, he was so animated and full of energy. Perhaps it was his pleasure at being out of prison, or perhaps it was something else. Bronwyn wondered if his cheerful manner was nothing more than a farce, a happy mask that he wore to hide his broken heart.

Rupert sat near Sir Bors, who was having a grand time listening to his jokes. Bronwyn watched Sir Bors and wondered how he'd managed to make Lady Mabel believe his story over Theobold's. But then, maybe it was something as simple as solidarity among noblemen. She hoped wherever he was, Theobold was safe and would return to her soon. In the meantime, she'd need to watch her step, especially now that Sir Bors was here.

She observed the other squire, Crispin, who sat across from Lady Alice, and eyed her like a hunter watched a fox. Rupert seemed distinctly aware of Lady Alice's person, glancing at her every so often, and when she rose from her place on the bench, he moved to intercept her.

He muttered something, and Lady Alice raised her chin indignantly. Bronwyn could only guess at what they said, but Rupert played his role well, smiling as if nothing were the matter. But Bronwyn knew better, for she saw Lady Alice's dark eyes flash, and she tossed her hair over her shoulder.

Lady Alice stalked away toward the exit, and Rupert watched her go. Then he was called back by Sir Bors, and Bronwyn's attention was diverted by nobles who wanted more to drink.

The chatelaine equally seemed amused by Rupert's antics, laughing along with the rest of the noble guests. Bronwyn went to bed that night none the wiser as to who had killed Mary, and with Theobold having left to search for Lady Morwenna, there was no one she could trust or talk to about her suspicions.

But she thought of his parting words, and his warning. She must stay on her guard and trust no one. That made her feel lonely, but she knew he was right to warn her.

"Do not trust Crispin." His parting words, whispers as he'd held her close, echoed in her mind. *"He's full of tricks."*

But now he had gone, still in search of Lady Morwenna. So who could she trust?

Rupert had hidden the fact he'd been arguing with Mary the night she'd been killed. Master Gregory and Alan had been out together nearby and had seen Mary arguing with Rupert, but they hadn't intervened. And yet *someone* had struck Mary with a bottle of wine from dinner and killed her. Could it have been an accident, or was it murder?

Then the chatelaine stood and the nobles quieted. "In one day's time, it will be All Hallows' Eve. We will hold a mass and say prayers for the dead, and go souling. Anyone who wishes to visit the castle churchyard may."

Heads turned, and people began to talk amongst themselves.

"And the kitchen will, of course, prepare soul cakes and food." She grinned.

Bronwyn slipped away to relay the news to Master Gregory, who blinked. "Is it that day already? God's teeth. All right." He began to bark orders at the cooks, relaying plans for there to be dozens of soul cakes, as well as cakes, pastries, bread, and meat prepared for an All Hallows' Eve feast.

Bronwyn spent the next few hours working on baking the small, round cakes, adding dried fruit like sultanas and a hint of spice before marking each one with a cross. She and the other cooks made dozens and added them to great platters to give out the next day. Master Gregory let them all go to bed, for they'd need to rise with the dawn to attend mass before seeing to the day's baking.

She went in search of a warm place to sleep and ended up sleeping against the wall on the floor of the dining hall. The wooden floor was sticky in places but largely clean, and more than one servant slept on the floor near the fire.

She slept and woke with the sound of monks singing. Bronwyn yawned. There was no light coming through the windows, so it was early, before dawn.

That day, the cooks worked in shifts, with some attending an early mass to say prayers for the dead, whilst others went later. Bronwyn went to an afternoon mass and stood at the back. This was a busy service, for the chatelaine was there at the front, along with many of the noble guests.

The mass began and it was a solemn service, punctuated by prayers and songs led by monks. Bronwyn didn't know all the words of the prayers, for she'd never learned to read, but she would have liked to know. She mouthed the words with the rest of the commoners there and shifted her weight, waiting for the mass to end, when…

"I know who did it!" a voice cried out.

Heads turned, and whispers abounded.

The voice cried again, "I know who did it. I know who!"

"Lady Muriel, calm yourself," a voice said.

Bronwyn peered around the others, and soon, there was a bit of commotion as Lady Muriel protested and was led away by a pair of guards.

The chatelaine said, "Take her to her room. She needs rest."

Bronwyn pushed aside some of the other people there. If Lady Muriel was disturbed and declaring she knew something, Bronwyn definitely wanted to hear more. She excused herself and pushed around the people standing there, following Lady Muriel and the guards.

Bronwyn hurried quickly as the guards hustled Lady Muriel away. Bronwyn got stuck behind dozens of people and couldn't move quickly enough. By the time she'd gotten around the crowds and exited the church, Lady Muriel was gone.

Bronwyn went through the courtyard, dashing along the castle corridors, past servants and pages, trying to remember the route to the room Lady Muriel shared with Lady Alice. Eventually, she found it, but when she went inside, it was empty.

"Where could she have gone?"

At a loss, Bronwyn thought quickly. With everyone at mass or doing chores, where would the guards have taken Lady Muriel?

She hurried to the prison, and asked the guards, "Was a lady taken down here? A noblewoman?"

"You mean the harpy who's been yelling her head off? Aye. She's here."

Bronwyn could hear the calls from within. She nodded to the guards and moved to pass, when one said, "She's not coming out till nightfall. The guards said, on order from the chatelaine."

"All right." Bronwyn walked down the same corridor of cells she'd walked down to visit Rupert when he'd been imprisoned. "Lady Muriel?"

She did not have to search long, for it was the one that was locked from the outside, and a woman's muffled voice protested loudly from the other side.

Bronwyn knocked on the door. "Lady Muriel? Lady Muriel?"

"Bronwyn? Is that you? Let me out."

"I can't. I don't have the key and the guards have been ordered to keep you here until nightfall."

Inside was quiet. "Oh. But it smells in here," Lady Muriel said.

"I know. I'm sorry. It won't be long. Do you want me to bring you some food?"

Footfalls could be heard down the corridor. Someone was coming.

"Yes. Anything." Lady Muriel's small face and hands appeared around the bars. The small peephole was high up, and Lady Muriel was short, so she hopped from foot to foot to see Bronwyn, clearly standing on her tiptoes. "Bronwyn. At church..."

"Yes, what happened?"

The footfalls grew louder.

"I was standing there with the others, and then I heard his voice, and I saw him. He looked at me, and... I recognized him."

"Who?"

"The man. The one who led the attack on the queen and the prince, I recognized him. I thought he looked familiar and then when he came to the castle, I didn't think anything of it. I've seen him plenty of times before, but then it hit me that—"

The footfalls stopped.

Bronwyn asked, leaning in. "Who did you see?"

Lady Muriel's eyes widened. "Bronwyn, look ou—"

A sharp pain rang through the back of her head, sending stars through her vision and sharp shocks through her skull. Bronwyn staggered and distantly heard Lady Muriel calling out when she tumbled to the floor. The earth spun and rose to meet her in darkness.

＊＊＊

Chapter Eighteen

Pain flickered in Bronwyn's skull, sending sparks through her consciousness.

Bronwyn groaned. The back of her skull throbbed, and her eyes were closed. Something rustled by her foot and she twitched, sending it scattering away.

A woman's aristocratic voice rang out amidst other voices in clipped tones. "Do you have any idea what you're doing? She is a pet of the empress. Who will the empress and the chatelaine blame to find she's come to such poor treatment in your care?"

Bronwyn's eyelids fluttered. The voice sounded familiar.

"Bronwyn," a hushed voice said from nearby. "Are you all right?"

"You have to unlock the door this instant," the aristocratic voice demanded. "Before I have you dismissed. You'll be guarding a midden heap if you don't hurry up."

Two voices grumbled and there was a jangling of keys. Seconds later, the door opened and bodies rushed in, nudging her. Hands shook her shoulders and arms.

"Don't move her; she may be injured," a man with a familiar voice said.

"What should we do? She's clearly been attacked and left for dead," the woman said. "Wait till Theobold hears about this, he'll be furious."

"Who's that?" a second man asked.

"Her lover. Squire to Sir Robert of Gloucester, the empress's right hand and senior military commander." The woman tutted under her breath. "You had better wake up."

Bronwyn coughed and groaned.

"Oh, thank goodness," the woman said. "Bronwyn, are you all right? Wake up."

Hands felt around her face and head, and she limply waved them away, blinking. She coughed again and blinked her eyes open.

She was in darkness, on a hard, earthen floor. Rushes were beneath her, and some rodent scurried by her feet.

Three faces peered down at her.

"Uh?" Bronwyn muttered.

"Are you well?" Master Gregory asked. "Can you move?"

"My head hurts," Bronwyn said, gingerly touching her head.

Rupert knelt and slowly helped her up, while Lady Alice and Gregory stood by.

"What happened?" Bronwyn asked.

Lady Alice said, "You tell us. After Lady Muriel was dragged out of church, I saw you go after her and knew there'd be trouble. But I couldn't get away without causing a scene, so I had to wait till after mass was done. Then I met Rupert. We looked for you in the kitchens, but Master Gregory said you hadn't come back after mass, and the cooks said you'd disappeared after the noblewoman had been taken away."

Master Gregory rubbed the back of his head. "Figured you might've gotten in a bad way."

Bronwyn blinked up at him. "Thanks."

"'S'all right." He shrugged. "What happened to you?"

"I went looking for Lady Muriel but couldn't find her. She wasn't in your room. I eventually thought maybe the guards took her here, and they had, but with orders not to let her leave till nightfall. She was about to tell me something important, when everything went dark."

Lady Alice turned and glared accusingly at the guards outside the door. "You see? She's been lying here hurt for ages, and it's all your fault. What kind of guards are you? Lady Mabel will hear about this." She turned and sniffed, then looked down at Bronwyn. "Can you stand? I heard somewhere that head wounds are dangerous."

"I'll try." Bronwyn stood, with the help of Rupert and Gregory. Her head hurt, and she felt wobbly on her feet. Her vision blurred for a minute, and the world wavered, so she closed her eyes, waiting to get her sense of balance back.

"Whoa there," Master Gregory said. "Steady on. Don't push yourself."

"He's right; take it slow," Rupert said.

Lady Alice said, "We found you here, locked away, and Lady Muriel is gone." She turned to the guards. "You must have seen something. Who took away Lady Muriel?"

"It was a man. Never seen him before. He said he was there on the orders of the chatelaine to take her away for questioning. He took the keys and helped himself. The lady did shriek and cry a bit about someone being hurt, but we're used to prisoners pleading and crying. They play all sorts of tricks to try and escape. Don't pay them any mind now."

"But this wasn't just any ordinary prisoner. This was a noblewoman. You didn't wonder where my friend had gone?" Lady Alice put a hand on her hip.

The guards exchanged embarrassed looks. One was red faced, the other tugged at the collar of his shirt. "I might've left to use the privy," said one.

"And there was a lot of noise outside. I went to go see," said the other.

"So anyone might've come in," Lady Alice said in disgust.

Bronwyn's eyes widened. This was bad news, indeed. They had to find Lady Muriel. But… a part of her heart warmed to see Rupert and Lady Alice working together, and for the noblewoman to call her a friend again. She didn't feel so alone anymore.

"So what now?" Gregory asked. "Bronwyn, we need you

down in the kitchens with the others. There's lots to be done before the feast tonight."

"She can't go anywhere. She's hurt. She needs a surgeon," Lady Alice said. "Why doesn't the chatelaine have one?"

Gregory shrugged. "We call one from the city when we need it. Otherwise, people just look after themselves." He nodded at Bronwyn. "Let's see. I'll help you."

"What's that?" Bronwyn pointed.

"What's what?" Rupert asked.

"That." In the flickering torchlight, Bronwyn pointed at some scratches in the dirt. They were near where she had lain.

"I don't see anything," Gregory said.

"Look." Moving away from the men, Bronwyn pointed downward. "It almost looks like writing."

"What? Let me see." Gregory peered over her shoulder. "So it does. But it don't make sense."

"What does it say?" Bronwyn asked. "I can't read," she added with some regret.

"Oh, let me." Lady Alice moved her aside and peered down. "Why, it almost looks like… a name. Or part of one."

"What does it say?"

"Unless I'm mistaken, it's part of the name of a man here at court. I can see the 'Sir.'" Lady Alice spoke with certainty, as if highly doubting she would ever be mistaken. "But the rest is illegible. I can barely make it out."

"But why would it be here?" Gregory asked.

"Could Lady Muriel have written it in the dirt before she was taken? As a sign, in case someone came in?" Bronwyn wondered.

"Why would she have done that?" Rupert wondered.

"So that people would know." Bronwyn frowned. "She was about to tell me the name of the man who led the attack on the queen and prince, when I was hit from behind."

Lady Alice breathed through her nose. "This complicates things."

"We have to find Lady Muriel," Bronwyn said.

"Where could she have been taken?" Rupert asked.

"I don't know. Bronwyn said our room was empty. Aside from here, I can't imagine where would she be taken for questioning." Lady Alice pondered.

Bronwyn swallowed. "I think I know."

She led the group through the corridors and behind a tapestry, down a series of stone steps, eventually finding her way back to the chatelaine's dungeon, which served as a room for interrogation, questioning and at times, torture, if the weapons and implements on the tables and walls were any indication. The room smelled of sweat, damp, and worse.

Bronwyn carried a torch in her hands as she led the group into the space. Gregory crossed himself. "What manner of room is this?"

Bronwyn moved ahead and looked around, the torch's flickering light casting shadows along the walls. The flickers made it appear as though denizens of night might leap out and attack at any moment.

"I do not like this," Rupert said. "This room has a vile purpose. You should not be here, Lady Alice," Rupert said, his voice firm.

"Well, I am." The dark-haired beauty crossed her arms beneath her chest.

"Lady Muriel?" Bronwyn called into the darkness.

They waited, but there was no answer.

"We are alone here. Let us go," Gregory said. "The sooner we are out of here, the better."

"I agree," Rupert said. He led the way out, holding the tapestry for Lady Alice, who shot him a look but walked ahead and ducked her head beneath the heavy tapestry fold he held back for her.

Bronwyn followed the group out. Gregory lingered by her, and said quietly, "You'll not say anything, will you? If this all comes to light."

She looked at him quizzically. Then she realized he meant

about his relationship with the other cook, Alan.

"My only interest is in finding Lady Muriel and solving Mary's death. Nothing else."

He nodded.

They walked out back into the main corridors, which were full of people. "Who are all these people?" Lady Alice asked.

"It's All Hallows' Eve. They're here souling," Master Gregory said. "Speaking of, we should get back to the kitchens. They'll be needing more food prepared for the feast and soul cakes. Bronwyn?"

"Yes, let's go. I don't need a surgeon." She pondered, though her head was still sore. "I don't know where Lady Muriel could be."

"I will look back in our room," Lady Alice said. "I don't think I could eat at a time like this."

"I'll look back at the church, and the castle's chapel. Maybe she went there for confession," Rupert said.

"Wait a minute," Bronwyn said. "What are we going to do about the fact that Sir Bors is here? Theobold said that Lady Morwenna told the empress's court she was behind the abduction of the queen and prince and tried to take credit for it all, but that she later revealed Sir Bors to be part of the plot."

Rupert and Lady Alice stared at her.

"Are you serious?" Lady Alice asked.

"Yes. Theobold tried to tell Lady Mabel, but she refused to listen."

"Well, I'm not surprised," Lady Alice said. "The chatelaine has no proof, and she won't take the word of a squire over that of a knight. Not without some sort of evidence. And as we know, Lady Morwenna is not the most truthful of women."

Rupert stroked his chin thoughtfully. "But he is here now. He spoke for me to the chatelaine and got me released from jail. He thinks me in his debt. Maybe we can use that to our advantage."

Lady Alice shot him a brilliant smile. "You surprise me, Rupert."

He glanced at her.

"Who knew you were more than a pretty face? I'd never have guessed."

He rolled his eyes at her and tried to pinch her, when she darted away with a laugh.

The group parted ways, but no one found any sign of Lady Muriel. They agreed to go about their business as usual and keep watch for anything odd or anyone acting suspiciously. The next few hours were a blur as Bronwyn and Gregory worked, preparing platters of freshly carved haunches of pork dripping with fat that had been seasoned with salt so it had hardened into delicious crackling. That, along with freshly made bread seasoned with herbs, salt beef, mutton, and rabbit, as well as capons, pies, and fresh fruit that was late in the season, were served to the dining guests.

It was enough to make Bronwyn's mouth water as the call came for more soul cakes. She and the other cooks worked steadily, making more cakes, preparing more platters and taking others back from pages as the chatelaine's feast for the nobility went on for what felt like hours.

Finally, the rush and demand for food slowed, and the cooks were able to sit and enjoy a bite to eat themselves, taking turns to sit down at a long table and share stale bread trenchers of potage with the leftover drippings and burnt ends of the meats, along with the bits of bread that were deemed not good enough to serve to the nobles.

Bronwyn worked steadily and for longer than she would have liked, but in her mind, she had good reason why. Being away from the kitchens for so long, it didn't make her look good to the other cooks. She didn't know how long she would be there, so the more she helped out, the better. And she didn't mind the work. It felt like good, honest toil, to be working with her hands, pouring juices and meat drippings over the haunches of game, or working stiff dough between her fingers to make bread or pastry. It also gave her a chance to think. Who had attacked her in the jail? Who could have taken Lady Muriel, and why? What did she know that made her too valuable to leave there?

"Come, Bronwyn, sit," Gregory called over to her. "You've worked enough."

Bronwyn took a stale bread trencher and helped herself to some of the leftover potage from a cauldron and a hunk of rough bread. She dipped it in and sat down at the table near the other cooks, eating. She kept her head down, for she felt others were watching, when a man asked, "Who's that?"

Heads turned to see. Bronwyn looked in the direction of the others and saw Lady Alice lingering there by the entrance. She was a fair sight, as pretty as a princess in her dark-purple gown, her black hair pinned back prettily in waves down her back. She made eye contact with Bronwyn and motioned with her fingers to approach.

Bronwyn let out a sigh and pushed back her trencher. One of the potboys who cleaned dirty dishes was eyeing it, so she nudged the trencher toward him. He took it within seconds and ate its remaining contents faster than she could blink.

She swung her feet over the bench and approached Lady Alice. "My lady?"

Lady Alice's mouth quirked. "Are you feeling all right?"

"Yes, why?"

"You must've hit your head harder than I thought. Such manners from you, I never would have expected. I never would have imagined you to be so polite. I normally have to remind you to use my title." She grinned, then her smile faltered. "Um. Lady Muriel was missing from dinner. I haven't seen her. Have you or the other cook learned anything?"

"No. Did Rupert find her?"

"No. He was at the dinner too but shook his head when we locked eyes. She's still missing."

"Could she be with the queen?"

"That's a thought. I'll look now. Are you almost finished here?" Lady Alice asked.

"Yes. I was going to clean up here and the main hall."

"Ugh, I would hate being a servant. So many chores. You really do have a terrible life," Lady Alice said heartlessly.

Bronwyn snorted. "You have a funny way of speaking with servants, Lady Alice."

"I…" She paused. "We'll talk later. I'll visit Matilda, but I doubt she'll have heard anything. Meet me in the castle courtyard when you're done with your chores. I'll be waiting."

"All right. Be careful, Lady Alice."

Bronwyn reported to Master Gregory and shared the news that the lady had still not been found. His face clouded. "That's a bad omen, especially on a night like tonight. I hope to God someone finds her."

She worked with the other servants, cleaning the kitchen for the following day. They wiped down the work tables, used up the rest of the leftovers or preserved them for future use, and locked away the larder, meat, and stores for herbs and spices. Once she'd helped clear the dining room and tidy the spaces, Bronwyn felt tired and yawned, then she remembered to meet Lady Alice.

She stumbled out into the castle courtyard at night, looking around. Bronwyn was about to turn around and head back in when Lady Alice appeared out of the shadows. "There you are. I was waiting ages. What took you so long?"

Bronwyn yawned. "I was working. Chores, remember?"

"God, don't remind me. While you were doing whatever it was, I was speaking with Matilda."

And spying on her, no doubt, Bronwyn thought. "And what did you find out?"

"Not much. I found that Lady Muriel did at first go along quietly with the guards—"

"That's odd. If someone had just hit me, wouldn't she have said something? Called out to a guard, maybe?"

"We know the guards are useless," Lady Alice pointed out. "But… that's true. She might have been ordered to stay quiet or else he might have hurt her. Anyway, once she was out of the jail, she broke away and ran up to Matilda."

"Why? Surely, she could just shout and the other guards would hear. There's no reason that the queen would even hear her."

Lady Alice shrugged. "It's possible she thought at least trying to tell Matilda herself would be better. Besides, if *I'd* broken away from an attacker, I'd maybe cry out for help, but I'd want to run first and distance myself from him as fast as possible. Maybe Matilda of Boulogne was the one person Lady Muriel thought she could trust. It doesn't matter now, anyway, since she was dragged away before she could tell Matilda anything. Can you imagine Matilda's guards letting in a hysterical woman?"

"No," Bronwyn said.

"Exactly. Lady Muriel was taken away—I don't know by whom—and now she's disappeared. Matilda is worried about her and fears a plot."

"I think she has a right to be worried," Bronwyn said. "She's been here for days now. I wonder when these hostage exchanges will end."

"Soon, I hope. All this back and forth, it's enough to do my head in."

They walked together. The air was cold and a trifle chilly, but otherwise, it was a clear night. The moon shone bright and full, like a large globe of silvery white overhead. The ground crunched beneath their shoes as the pair walked over rough, pebbled ground. They did not speak as they walked first to the gardens, but the area was empty.

"Did Rupert say he'd been to the castle church again and the chapel?" Bronwyn asked.

"Yes, but he didn't find her there, either." Lady Alice shivered and pulled her shawl closer around her. "Whoever's stolen her away has hidden her well. "What about… the castle churchyard?"

Bronwyn nodded. "That's a good idea."

"Do you think it's safe? It is All Hallows' Eve," Lady Alice pointed out.

"Why wouldn't it be?"

"You know. Because."

Bronwyn smirked at the noblewoman. "You can't be believing in spirits. That's not like you."

"No, I know. But… tonight of all nights, it feels like things are different. The world is darker. I don't know." Lady Alice shuffled her feet.

A lone pigeon hooted nearby, a mournful sound. Bronwyn looked at Lady Alice. "We'll take a quick look around the churchyard and then go in."

"Fine."

They walked, their footsteps dulled by the damp grass as they walked around carved, wooden crosses and church stones. "Maybe Lady Muriel escaped from the attacker and ran away," Lady Alice said. "She escaped from the attack on Matilda's party, after all. She's good at hiding."

"It's possible." The night was growing darker, and the moon shifted behind some trees and clouds overhead.

"Let's go in. I can barely see my hand in front of my face," Lady Alice said. "And I'm cold."

"All right. At least it smells nice. I can smell the roses from the garden." Bronwyn turned and as they walked around another way, Lady Alice tripped over her feet, landing on her hands and knees.

She groaned. "For God's sake, Bronwyn, look where you're going."

"I didn't touch you."

"Then what—" She paused, looking down as the clouds flitted away overheard, revealing the shining, silvery moon above them.

The lifeless face of Lady Muriel stared up at Lady Alice, its eyes unseeing, as an insect crawled out of her mouth.

Lady Alice screamed.

Chapter Nineteen

BRONWYN GASPED AND her hands shot to her mouth to stifle a scream. Lady Muriel's body lay like an abandoned rag doll, her limbs splayed out. Bronwyn's head hurt, a sign to her that not only had she been lucky, but the sight of Lady Muriel's lifeless corpse was a warning. That could have been her, if she weren't careful. Bronwyn rubbed the back of her head, where a dull ache was starting and winced. Her fingers came back sticky with dried blood.

Lady Alice screamed and screamed, her high-pitched voice soaring into the sky, shrieking like a banshee as murders of crows cawed and flew away at the noise.

"Lady Alice, stop," Bronwyn said.

Lady Alice screamed, falling back on her hands and knees, her eyes wide. She took in a breath, her chest heaving, as two shadowy figures ran up to them.

"What's happened?"

"Aaaaaagh!" Lady Alice screamed again, pointing. "It's spirits! Bodies back from the dead!"

"Lady Alice, it's me, Rupert." He stood a few feet away, his hands up. "I'm not dead."

"Rupert?" Lady Alice's voice came out in a whisper.

The other black form said, "And I'm here too, my lady. It's me, Crispin."

"Crispin?"

Lady Alice looked from one to the other and hesitated.

Bronwyn watched as the noblewoman could not decide whom to choose, which signaled to her that despite Lady Alice walking and kissing Crispin, her heart was not completely closed to Rupert. Not yet.

Rupert moved toward her, but Crispin was faster, taking Lady Alice's hands and helping her to her feet. "Are you all right, love? I've got you."

Did Lady Alice glance at Rupert before turning to Crispin? Bronwyn couldn't be sure.

The noblewoman allowed Crispin to help her and leaned on him heavily. "Oh, Crispin, I was so scared."

"It's all right. No harm will come to you. Didn't I tell you? You're too pretty to die."

Lady Alice shivered. "Ugh, don't say that. Look."

Heads turned to where Bronwyn stood over Lady Muriel's corpse.

"Is that…" Rupert started.

"It's Lady Muriel."

"One of the Matilda's ladies-in-waiting?" Crispin said.

"Yes. Now Matilda has no one," Lady Alice said. She shivered. "Oh, God."

"What is it?" Rupert asked.

Crispin shielded Lady Alice from Rupert, turning his back to him. "What's wrong?"

"I just realized… Muriel was terrified because she thought the rose on her pillow had been a sign from the killer, meant for her. She was so scared, and I acted like it was all a joke." Lady Alice's hand darted to her mouth. "I never thought. It never occurred to me that she might be right."

Bronwyn shivered. She was right. A look at Lady Muriel's body revealed that a flower was stuffed in her mouth. Bronwyn tried to avoid the sight of the dead woman's eyes, for they terrified her. They were like glassy, black beads that stared at the sky. What would they reflect? She didn't want to know.

But as she knelt and looked closer, she saw something. "Look at that."

"What?" Rupert stood by her. "You see something?"

Crispin said. "Is that a rose in her mouth?"

"There's something there," Bronwyn said.

Crispin looked at Rupert. "I can't believe it."

"What?" Rupert turned to him with a frown, then glanced at Lady Alice.

"You're standing here like nothing's happened. When this is proof. You did it," Crispin said, pulling Lady Alice closer to him.

"Excuse me?" Rupert's mouth dropped open. "What are you on about? I didn't touch her."

"Like hell you didn't. Everyone knows you go around romancing young women and giving them flowers. Didn't you do that with Mary before she died?"

"Yes," Lady Alice said quietly. "And that maid at Devizes, Philippa."

"See. And now she's dead. And lo and behold, what do we find but tonight, you were making the good Lady Muriel laugh. I saw you flirting with her. We all did. Now she's dead too, and a flower in her mouth. What have you to say for yourself?"

Rupert stared at him. "I didn't do this. It wasn't me."

Crispin shook his head. "This is proof of your wrongdoing. They should never have let you out of prison. Once Sir Bors hears of this, he's going to cut you loose from his service, faster than you can say *guilty*."

Bronwyn was puzzled. Surely the empress would want Sir Bors dead, for his part in the abduction of the queen and prince. Unless she didn't believe Lady Morwenna, and thought this was false as well. And without Sir Bors present to defend himself... It was a puzzle indeed.

Rupert paled in the moonlight. He took a step back. "But I didn't... I swear..."

"Run, Rupert. Run," Lady Alice said, her voice getting heated.

"What are you saying? Are you seriously...?" Crispin looked at her.

"I'm not running," Rupert said.

Lady Alice pulled free of Crispin and said, "But they'll kill you. They'll hang you."

"I put my faith in God. The only one who can judge me is my master, my king, and the Lord God Almighty. He won't see me die for a crime I didn't commit." Rupert lifted his head.

Lady Alice let out an anguished cry. "Bronwyn, don't just stand there. For God's sake, talk some sense into him."

Bronwyn looked at them both. She knew Rupert wouldn't budge. He was like a donkey. Once he'd made up his mind, nothing would change it.

"Have it your way, mate," Crispin said, pulling Lady Alice along with him. "Guards!"

"No. No. Rupert..." Lady Alice said, pushing back. "Rupert, don't do this. Think with your head. Run."

Rupert was steadfast. "No. I won't."

"But—"

"Go. Take her away," he told Crispin.

Lady Alice whimpered and went with Crispin. The sound of voices and armed men could be heard in the distance. A torch, and then two could be seen, lighting up the darkness.

As they were alone, Bronwyn said, "Are you sure about this? They will surely imprison you."

"Let them. I am not afraid," he said. "And I know that I have you to look out for me."

She blinked and he crossed his arms over his chest, watching the men with the torches come closer.

"We'll always have each other's backs, yeh? Through thick and thin. Prove me innocent, Bronwyn. We both know I am. Promise me." His voice grew urgent.

"I promise."

"Good girl. Knew I could trust you." He pulled her close and kissed her on the cheek.

Bronwyn jumped. She hadn't been expecting that. He smelled like sweat, the woods, and ale. His lips had been soft against her skin, with a bit of a brush from a day's growth of facial hair.

A slow blush crept up her face and she rubbed her right cheek. "I…"

"Remember what I said," he told her before stepping forward toward the armed men.

Bronwyn watched as Rupert was surrounded by armed men and taken, thanks to Crispin's warning. She could hear Lady Alice's protesting in the distance.

One of the men with torches came up to her. "You all right, girl?"

"Yes. But there's a dead body here."

The guard crossed himself. "Jesus Almighty."

"Could you bring some guards so we can take her away?"

"Aye." He ran, taking his torch with him.

Bronwyn snorted as she now stood alone in the dark. She kneeled and sat on the back of her heels, looking at the body. There must have been some sign, some clue, as to how or why the lady-in-waiting had been killed.

She didn't have to wait long. A team of men filed out of the castle and made their way over to her with a cart, Master Gregory among them. He ran ahead of the others and said, "Bronwyn, are you all right? I heard screaming."

"It wasn't me. That was Lady Alice." She frowned. "We found Lady Muriel."

"Oh." He looked down and let out a deep breath. "That poor woman."

Bronwyn stood back as the guards brought up a trundling wooden cart that squeaked, all the more loudly in the still darkness of the night, and began to load the body of Lady Muriel on it.

But as the men moved it, something shiny fell from her corpse. "What was that?" Bronwyn asked.

"What?" a guard asked.

"Something fell from her hair."

The guard shuddered. "I don't want to know."

"I do. It could be a clue," Bronwyn said. "Lean in, give me your torch."

The guard looked at her with some revulsion.

"Give it here," said Master Gregory, who took it and then handed it to her. "What do you see?"

The torchlight flickered against the wet grass, but all she saw were bits of flowers and grass that had fallen from Lady Muriel's mouth. She couldn't see the object, whatever it was.

"Never mind. I can't see anything." She followed the group of guards that had taken Lady Muriel's body away.

It was a long time before Bronwyn got to sleep.

The next day, she met Master Gregory with a request. He stared at her, his eyes wide. "You what?"

"I want to look at her body. Can you show me where they took her?"

"Yes, but it's no place for you, or any woman. She's in the cold stores, where we keep the cheese." His brows furrowed. "You sure you want to go down there?"

Bronwyn nodded. "Come with me if you like."

"All right. But only so that you don't get into more trouble. It follows your sort around like a puppy," he said, untying his apron.

She couldn't help but agree. Bronwyn did not seek out trouble, but it seemed to find her. In any case, she was glad of the company.

Together, they headed down to the cold stores, which was a decent-sized stone room and workspace, situated below the main castle floors. The air was damp and cool, which would have been a comforting place to sit in summertime. But now, as autumn was here and winter approached, it was much cooler, even cold. That boded well for the storage of dead bodies, she realized, as surely people died during all sorts of times during the year, when the ground would often be too cold and frozen to bury them.

She followed Master Gregory down the steps and he unlocked the door. The smell hit Bronwyn's nose first. The air smelled of dairy, milk, and cheese, but also faintly of something else. She looked around the storeroom, which had shelves, and there on a low shelf, lay the body of Lady Muriel.

The noblewoman's corpse had not been wrapped in a sheet or anything. She still wore the same dress and shoes as she had worn the night before. Bronwyn stood by, her head down as Master Gregory crossed himself and said a quick prayer. Once he'd finished, she approached.

There was light in the room, due to a thin sliver of sunlight that flooded in. Master Gregory had taken a torch, anyway, from a sconce outside and handed it to her. "Go on. Let's be quick."

Bronwyn nodded and peered at Lady Muriel.

"What do you see?" Gregory asked.

"Her hands were dirty."

"So? So are mine," he said.

"Yes, but she doesn't work in the kitchens. She's a lady. She does..." She smiled. "Ladies-in-waiting just gossip and embroidery all day, don't they? It's not exactly a life of toil."

"What are you saying, Bronwyn??"

"Just that the ladies always have clean, soft-looking hands. And they're always wearing gloves when they ride."

"Been around lots of ladies, have you?"

"I suppose." She looked closer. "Look at that."

"What?"

She lifted Lady Muriel's right hand. "See her nails? They're torn and bloody. She fought back against her attacker. That explains why her hands are dirty."

He looked away, turning a shade of green.

"And..." There it was. The sign of how she'd died. There around Lady Muriel's neck were dark marks, almost the size of large fingers, that had wrapped around her throat and squeezed the life out of her. Bronwyn shuddered and breathed in.

She held the torch closer to see. "That's odd."

"What? You see something?" Master Gregory asked.

"I think so. Look, see there? There's a funny impression." She pointed.

"I don't see anything," Gregory said.

"You're standing about two feet away. This is tiny. Come closer." She beckoned and pointed. "There, you see? Right around her neck, on the left side."

A small, unique indentation could be seen, marring one of the dark-red and purple-striped bruises around the noblewoman's neck.

"What is that?" Master Gregory asked. "Could it be a mark from some sort of weapon?"

"I'm not sure. But I did see something fall from her body when they moved her last night. Let's go see."

"All right, but I've got work to do. You go yourself. Are we done here?"

"Yes, I think so." She blinked. "Wait a second. Look."

"Now what?" he asked, shifting his weight. "I don't want to be down here a second longer looking at dead bodies, Bronwyn. Let's go."

"Just a second. You know that Rupert was taken away for this crime?"

"Yes, I was there when the guards took him. Already sent down a platter for him if that's what you're wondering."

"No, look." She pointed at the body.

"What am I looking at? It's a dead body."

"Her mouth." She leaned over and was inches away from tapping at the mouth. "It's not a rose in her mouth. It's another flower."

The 'flower' stuffed in Lady Muriel's mouth was more a scatter of herbs and grass. No flowers. Certainly no roses.

"So? So the man who killed her took a different flower. Maybe he ran out of time or got confused or… I don't know. Who cares whether he put a flower in the woman's mouth or not? Why does it matter?"

"Don't you see? This breaks the cycle. This implies Rupert didn't do it," she said, the torch trembling in her hands. "Each time the body was found, there was a rose present. And it made Rupert look bad, since he always likes to walk around with women and give them a rose as a token of his affection."

"The lad should stop doing that. But it's not real proof, girl, just a theory. So what does this mean, then?"

"That Rupert most likely didn't do it. Or he could have changed the flower. But I think that whoever did kill Lady Muriel was trying to make it look like Rupert, but wasn't able to get their hands on a rose. They were sloppy." The torch wavered again in her hands.

"Whoa there. Don't go waving that thing around! You'll set the place on fire. Bronwyn, that's not proof he didn't do it."

"Maybe, but then what about the funny indentation on her neck? I'm willing to bet that's a ring."

"Aye, so what if it is?" he said, taking the torch back from her. "Lots of people wear rings."

"Rupert doesn't. He never has. Not for the year and a bit that I've known him."

The head cook's brows knit. "I'm still not sure—"

"Let's go see if we can find that ring. Come on." She dragged him out of the stores, almost hopping on the balls of her feet. She could practically taste victory. She waited impatiently as Master Gregory locked the storeroom and then followed her out.

But as they passed the kitchen, he said, "Bronwyn, I've got work to be getting back to, and so do you. They'll need our help in the kitchen. I can't go chasing murderers and things."

"But—"

"You go ahead and come back as quick as you can. Then work. You hear?"

"Yes." Slightly dejected, she parted from Master Gregory and found her way out of the courtyard, then turned around. She slipped down to the prison, where to her surprise, she found Lady Alice outside of a cell, talking quietly with the inhabitant.

"You're such a fool. I cannot believe you stood there and just—" She paused and turned, noticing Bronwyn. "Oh, it's you. Hello."

"Good morrow."

"It's not a very good morning, is it?" Lady Alice looked pointedly at the wooden door of a prison cell, from which Rupert peered out.

"Hullo, Bronwyn."

"Hullo." She revealed what she had discovered in the castle stores with Master Gregory.

Lady Alice clapped her hands. "Then does that mean—"

"Come with me and let's go searching. With any luck, we'll find that object. I bet it's a ring," Bronwyn said excitedly.

"All right, I'm coming." She turned to Rupert's cell door. "But we are not done here."

"It's not like I'm going anywhere," came his glib reply.

"See that you don't. Hmph." Lady Alice turned, raised her hand, and led the way out of the cells, as if she were the head of her own royal entourage.

Outside the cells, Lady Alice leaned in close to Bronwyn. "Do you really think you'll find something? Or were you just trying to give him hope?"

"I was being serious."

Lady Alice let out a sigh. "Well, for all our sakes, I hope you are right." She clapped a hand to her head. "Good Lord, I need to go to Matilda. She'll be wondering what's happened to all of us."

"Do you want me to—"

"Oh, no. You're not going anywhere alone. I don't want to go digging around in graveyards, but I also know that you attract trouble and mischief like sugar attracts flies. No way are you going out alone."

Bronwyn shrugged one shoulder. "All right."

They went to the graveyard, but in the daylight, it was different. "Now where were we when we found her body…" Lady Alice mused and stopped. "I can't believe I just said that. God.

Only when I'm with you, Bronwyn. Only when I'm with you."

Bronwyn looked at her. "Why did you decide to help me?"

"What?"

"Just days ago, you made it clear you hated me. You didn't want to talk to me. You treated me like I was nobody. Like a servant."

Lady Alice stopped and slowly looked up, eventually meeting her eyes.

"Only a short time ago, you were sympathetic to me, with Theobold casting me aside. Yet you've done the same thing. Before Lady Muriel and the queen, you treated me like I was nothing. Like dirt. Whenever I entered a room, it seemed like I offended you by being there. And then all of a sudden, you have a change of heart."

"I—"

Bronwyn held up a hand. "I'm not done. For over a week, I've wondered what I had done to offend you. I'd thought that we were friends." She ignored Lady Alice's wince. "That we were more than a noblewoman and a kitchen servant. But you told me I was wrong. And now, suddenly, you act as though nothing has happened and are talking to me. Almost treating me like we are friends again."

She cocked her head at Lady Alice. Her voice was small but steady, for even as her hands trembled, she was laying her truth bare, and the woman whom she had once called 'friend' deserved to know.

Lady Alice, at least, had the good grace to blush. She stood there and bit her lip. Then she extended a hand. "I am Lady Alice Duncombe, and—"

Bronwyn crossed her arms beneath her chest and gave a little shake of the head. "No. You've done that before. And I'm sick of it. We are either friends, or we are not. You cannot erase the past hurt and disagreements between us by acting as though we can start over with a handshake."

Lady Alice's chin jutted out and her eyes flashed, but she gave a short nod. Then she slowly dipped into a small curtsy and rose. "I'm sorry."

Bronwyn waited. She felt stronger, lighter for having spoken the words that were on her mind. And Lady Alice had curtsied to her. That was a first.

"I'm an idiot. I was foolish, and angry, and hurt. It burns me up that you, a mere servant, are praised by your betters for your brains and quick mind, and yet I am banished from their discussions and dismissed as being no more than a pretty face. Your rise at court proves my family was right. What if I am nothing more than that? What happens to me when I am old and I no longer have my looks to rely on?" Her dainty hands curled into fists, and she raised her head, mastering herself. "You were an easy target to take out my frustration on. I'm sorry."

Lady Alice spoke calmly, quietly, and clasped her hands together as if in prayer. But they twisted with repressed anger. In that one movement, she seemed nobler than Bronwyn had ever seen her look before. She felt sorry for Lady Alice, and at the same time, did not. She hadn't deserved Lady Alice's cruel treatment, and it was high time the noblewoman knew it.

"You hurt me. You do this so often. You get angry and then act like we are strangers, and you treat me poorly, then change your mind and act like we are friends again. I cannot, Lady Alice. I just can't."

"Bronwyn, please. We've been through so much. At Lincoln, and London…"

"Exactly. We barely escaped with our lives and depended on each other. So why do you have a change of heart and decide we are friends one day, and another day we are not, whenever it suits you? Why do you get to make that decision?" Bronwyn's words were biting, but she did not care.

For days, she had been hurt, and offended, and she could barely describe the depths of her emotions. Words barely sufficed. If only she could bake a cake or a pie and the eater could taste the levels of her sadness through cream and layers of sponge. But that would be a sad cake, indeed, and a rather silly notion, she realized.

Lady Alice said, "I'm sorry. I know I change my mind and act like some days we are friends and others not. I… have no excuse. I've always been flighty. I do not know how to have friends. You are the first one I've ever had. I never had friends growing up. My parents were adamant that I could not play with the other children, for they were all lower class. I had to sit and learn to read and write, or do needlepoint, or learn French."

Bronwyn lowered her eyes. How different they were. It was a far cry from her childhood, playing half-naked in the mud and rain, jumping through puddles in the city of Lincoln. Her days had been filled with laughter and joy. "That doesn't give you the right to treat people like that."

Lady Alice said, "You're right, to a point." She edged closer to Bronwyn and said in a voice so quiet, Bronwyn had to lean in to hear her. "Do you know what I have been taught? Ever since I was a girl?"

"No, but I expect you'll tell me," Bronwyn snapped.

That earned her a dark glance, but Lady Alice pursed her lips together. "I was taught that my purpose, my entire reason for existing, is to further the riches, reputation, and estate of my family. Namely, my father. I have noble blood and was born into a wealthy family. I cannot change that, and I make no excuse for being higher born than others or having the tendencies and attitudes of the people of my class."

Bronwyn raised an eyebrow. "No one asked you to."

Lady Alice continued. "We have acres of land and serfs to till it. But I was always taught that those people were there, not as friends or neighbors, but to serve me and my family, just as I am here to attract a man and marry well, to bring increased wealth and prosperity to my family. Boys are meant to continue the family bloodline; girls are to be traded off as breeding stock and secure alliances with other wealthy or noble families. We are like cows, but highly prized ones." She said this last bit with an air of disgust and looked Bronwyn in the eye. "Do you have any idea how insufferable that is?"

Bronwyn cocked her head. "What does 'insuf—'"

"It means 'annoying.' For years, I thought I was being instructed in learning and was given an education so that I might someday rule a chateau or a castle in my own right. Be like the chatelaine, but not a glorified housekeeper. To be wise, and to rule, to be in charge, and to have ownership of the families and lands beneath my keep. It wasn't until I reached my womanly courses that my father took notice and told me otherwise. He didn't want me to be uneducated, as some men want a wife with at least some learning. And I was pretty enough. So when the war started, he sent me to the empress's court to try to gain her favor."

Lady Alice idly traced her fingers across a wooden cross grave marker that stood at an awkward angle. "You've seen how well that's worked. I shuffle back and forth with the empress and now Matilda, hoping to be useful. And then there's you. Somehow, you manage to convince these people that you can solve crimes and murders, when no woman should. And even worse, you succeed. You sniff out these criminals like a dog with a bone. It's no wonder the nobles joke and call you Mistress Hound. You are deserving of the name."

Bronwyn flinched and breathed in through her nose. "I don't like that name." She was half-ready to leave.

"Wait, don't go. What I mean to say is that I grew jealous."

"Of me?" Bronwyn stared.

"Of course. Of your success. Do you have any idea how often I heard you mentioned every day? It's always, 'Bronwyn solved this crime, which is a wonder, considering her low birth.' Or, 'I have a fancy for some sweet bread rolls with honey. Shall we see if Bronwyn can make us some?'"

Lady Alice rolled her eyes. "Is it any wonder I got jealous? You're either like a champion saint or a cook. Either way, you could do no wrong, and there was nothing I could do about it but watch and see you rise in their estimation. And both sides too. Matilda values your opinion, and you're the empress's favorite investigator. You've risen above your low birth, and it's only a matter of time before you get rewarded for your trouble with lands and a title, or a high position at court. Frankly, it's…"

Here comes the insult, Bronwyn thought. *I might just punch her in the nose.*

"It's incredible," Lady Alice breathed. "And it's why I got so angry and frustrated. I could see you doing so well, and I was just another pretty face. I might as well just collect flowers all day, for all anyone cares. No one expects anything of me because I'm just a lady-in-waiting. I'm there to look nice, smile, wear pretty clothes, and serve the empress, or would-be queen in this case. No one tells me anything. Which is why, when Crispin came to me offering a chance to spy on Matilda in captivity, I said *yes*."

Bronwyn blinked. She'd found that out already, but it was a change for Lady Alice to admit it herself and reveal her reasons why.

They walked on through the graveyard, coming to where they'd found the body of Lady Muriel. Bronwyn was sure of it, for she vaguely remembered the path. There, she saw the indentation in the grass, and the muddy footsteps of the guards and the tracks of the wheels from the cart that had taken her corpse away.

Lady Alice said, "I began to meet him in secret. You've seen us argue before. But one thing led to another and… our meetings began to take on a different turn. An alternative reason for us to meet. After a time, I found myself looking forward to seeing him and going on rides together. People thought we were romancing, when in truth, we were exchanging information, until we weren't. And then the lie became the truth."

"So you fell for Crispin?"

Lady Alice's blush was answer enough for that.

"What about Rupert?"

Lady Alice's head snapped up. "What about him? Ever since

he went on that fool's errand to escort Matilda and her son to Devizes, he's had his brains addled. Maybe it was getting hurt in that fight. All I know is he's not cared a whit about me. He only seems interested in flirting with serving girls and scullery maids. It's sad. And they're all dead, anyway. That's a grim trail of broken hearts for a man to leave behind." She shuddered. "And even Lady Muriel, who is—*was* sweet, but not that smart. Honestly, he has no taste. All a young woman has to do is show him a little bit of kindness, act like she cares, and he's lost. He goes off giving her roses, when that's so silly. And of course, the young women fall for him and get their feelings hurt because that was bound to happen. He never really cares for any of them. He's only doing it to…" She pointed. "What is that?"

"What?"

"There. Something gold. In the grass."

Kneeling in the grass, Bronwyn pawed at the area, looking amongst the tall, leafy green grass for something, anything small that might've fallen from Lady Muriel's body. Then her fingers hit something solid. She dug and then, feeling in the grass, she found it and pulled it out to hold it in the sunlight. "Well, I'll be." It was a golden ring.

"Ha. I knew I spotted something. Always trust me, Bronwyn. I have good taste."

Bronwyn grinned. "Meaning you can spot something shiny from ages away."

"Yes."

"You know what else has that ability?"

"Royalty?"

"Crows and magpies."

Lady Alice pouted.

Bronwyn laughed. She slipped the ring on one of her fingers. Far too big and bulky. This was a man's ring. Some man had strangled Lady Muriel to death and lost his ring in the process, likely as she'd fought back.

Bronwyn pocketed the ring and looked around the tall grass

that moved with the wind in the graveyard. A lone crow perched on top of one of the stones, looking at her. It cawed, sending a chill through her. It was time to leave.

Lady Alice stopped and looked past Bronwyn, muttering a curse.

Bronwyn paused. "What?"

Lady Alice schooled her features into a pleasant smile. "Good morrow, Crispin."

"Hullo, love." Crispin approached and bowed. "I was looking for you. Thought you might fancy a stroll around the gardens. I never thought you'd be in the castle graveyard. Last night wasn't enough scares for you?"

Lady Alice gave a little laugh and sidled up to him, touching his arm. She smiled up at him. "You know Bronwyn; she always likes to do strange things. I couldn't dare let her go alone. What if a spirit had appeared?"

He trapped her hand with his. "Indeed."

Lady Alice fluttered her eyelashes at him. "But this tires me. I would much rather see the gardens than some horrid old graves."

"Allow me to accompany you. I'm sure no spirits will jump out at Mistress Hound in the daylight," he teased Bronwyn.

Lady Alice linked her arm in his, and together, they walked on.

Bronwyn let out a sigh. They hadn't gotten a chance to finish their conversation. But she rather suspected she knew what Lady Alice had been about to say. Namely that Rupert was romancing other women in an attempt to make her jealous. If that was true, then his kiss on Bronwyn's cheek last night, had it been meant as friendly and affectionate, or something more? She'd gone to sleep thinking about it, and it had been first on her mind that morning. But if what Lady Alice insinuated was true, then he didn't hold any romantic feelings for her at all. He just… was either trying to annoy the noblewoman he truly fancied or was being friendly. Either way, the kiss had meant nothing.

Despite her wishes to the contrary. She had made up with

Theobold, but now she questioned her feelings for Rupert. What Lady Alice had said was true; he did have a singular interest in flirting with servant girls. And his kiss earlier. It would be so easy to assume it had meant something more. But if she were being honest with herself, she knew that these flirtations were just his nature. Rupert could no more stop himself from flirting than he could breathing. She just had to accept that fact, and enjoy his friendship. Her feelings for Rupert sat inside her heart like a little nugget of gold, but she could already feel a shift in her thinking, and began to dismiss all ideas of her ever having a crush on him. It would only lead to her ruin, she knew.

Regardless, Bronwyn needed to think of her next move. She was fairly confident whom the gold ring belonged to, for she had seen it blink in the light at dinner before. The only question was: how to make the culprit confess? Would a missing gold ring be enough proof to reveal a murderer?

Chapter Twenty

A N HOUR LATER, Bronwyn found Lady Alice, thankfully free of her lover, and after conferring with her, requested a private audience with the chatelaine, which was granted. They were shown into a room that Lady Mabel used for her business, which was not like a throne room, as Bronwyn would normally have expected. The woman sat at a table covered with parchment, a goose-feather quill, ink, a bottle of wine, and a cup.

Bronwyn was shown in by two armed guards, who took up spots outside the room. She realized that she posed no threat to the chatelaine, who sipped her wine and surveyed her. "What do you want?"

"To tell you I've solved them. The crimes."

"*We* have solved them, Lady Mabel," Lady Alice said.

The chatelaine's mouth quirked in a smile. "You too? Have you really? How funny. And here I thought you were just an empty-headed young woman. Well, well. Go on. This should be good."

Lady Alice's eyes flashed, her upper lip twitching. Then she maintained a calm demeanor. The only sign of her displeasure was a slight gripping of her skirts.

Bronwyn disliked the older woman's air, as if seeing a jester or minstrel set up to play. This was not a diversion or amusement. This was serious.

"Well?" the chatelaine said.

A page knocked on the door and entered. "Some wine for you, Lady Mabel."

"Good. Bring it here." She motioned.

The page poured her a fresh cup of wine, bowed, and left. Everything seemed fine until Lady Mabel coughed and began choking.

"Lady Mabel?" Lady Alice said. "Are you all right?"

Bronwyn stopped and stared. The noblewoman was coughing, her face turning red. She pointed at her throat and coughed, gasping for breath. Lady Mabel pushed back from her chair and stood, leaning over the table.

"Oh, God, help her!" Lady Alice said. "Guards!"

Lady Mabel fell over the table, knocking the papers and pitcher. Red wine flowed over the parchment, soaking the paper and dripping over the sides of the table. She coughed as guards came into the room.

"Get the page who came in here. Find him!" Bronwyn said, hurrying to the chatelaine. "And get a surgeon here. Now."

Lady Alice fretted as Bronwyn said, "Bring us some fresh ale or wine. Do it."

Lady Alice disappeared. Bronwyn tried clapping the chatelaine on the back, and she brought up the wine, vomiting. Bronwyn held the woman's hair back as she purged her guts on the floor, as guards and Lady Alice came back in, a pitcher in her hands. "This was in the next room. Do you think it—oh."

Lady Mabel coughed and vomited. Once she'd finished, she looked up weakly and uttered, "I think I've been poisoned." And crashed into the floor.

Bronwyn and Lady Alice stood back as one of the guards carried the older noblewoman to her bed as the other guards searched for the page. Once Lady Mabel rested in bed, with a guard posted outside her room, Bronwyn and Lady Alice returned to the scene of the poisoning.

"Do you think it was poison?" Lady Alice asked.

"Bound to be. But who was the page? Have you ever seen

him before?" Bronwyn sniffed the wine that had spilled on the papers, and what remained in the pitcher the page had brought in. To her nose, it smelled earthy and slightly spiced, but also acrid, and like a wet dog. It was strange—and did not smell like something she would want to drink. "Smell this. Tell me what you think."

Wrinkling her nose, Lady Alice gingerly lifted her skirts and stepped around the puddle of vomit that littered the floor. She sniffed the wine. "That smells horrible. Not anything I'd drink, for certain."

"So it's not something you've smelled at dinner here before."

"Certainly not. They actually have decent wine and ale here."

Bronwyn nodded. The guards brought in a youth with sandy-blond hair, narrowed eyes, and a set jaw. He held himself stiffly, as if he half-expected to be clapped in irons at any moment. Bronwyn barely recognized him, but there were many pages at court and she had not been there long enough to get to know all the servants. "Did you prepare the wine?"

The youth stood and briefly glanced at her face and chest, ignoring her words entirely, until one of the guards poked his back with a spear. "Speak up."

The youth jerked and said, "No."

"How'd you get it? The kitchens?"

"No. A man came up and told me to bring it to the chatelaine. Gave me a coin, too."

"Who was it?"

The youth shrugged. "Dunno."

Bronwyn breathed in through her nose. "What did he look like?"

"He was tall. Head full of black, curly hair. Big. A warrior, I think."

"That could be anyone," Lady Alice said.

"But who does it remind you of?" Bronwyn said. "It makes me think of someone who recently lost a ring."

"So it does."

The youth was sent away.

With Lady Mabel sick and near death, there was no chance for Bronwyn to tell the noblewoman what she and Lady Alice had discovered. The cooks were all questioned, but no one knew where the poisoned wine had come from, as the man who normally looked after the ale and wine swore that his stock was pure and was offended at the notion he might have tried to poison the chatelaine. But with so many bottles and pitchers of ale and wine around the castle, it would have been easy for anyone to doctor such a bottle and have the page bring it.

With no sign as to where the poison had come from, Bronwyn felt stifled, and no closer to revealing the truth of the crimes committed. She wanted to prove Rupert's innocence, once and for all, and to see the culprit get the judgment they deserved. But it was unsteady ground she walked on at the moment. She didn't feel safe. Lady Alice stayed with the queen day and night, usually too afraid to go anywhere alone, unless she was with Bronwyn.

In the days that followed, the nobles there ate and drank, and Sir Bors held court with the others, laughing and joking around, toasting to Lady Mabel's hopeful recovery and drinking her wine, as Bronwyn watched and waited. His every word and phrase of good cheer rang false with her, and she wondered how it was no one else could find him dastardly. His every move spoke of treachery, she felt. Until the happy day when word came via messenger that Sir Robert had been freed and was now on his way to return to the empress. This was soon followed by the arrival of a few of Stephen's knights, including Sir Baldwin of Clare, Rupert's original master, among them. Rupert was soon freed, much to Bronwyn's relief and delight. She was happy to see him, but he was too relieved at being out of the jail cells to pay much attention to her, for he too was keeping a public face of open cheer. But he was also prone to staring into the fireplace at night, the shadows playing on his face, revealing the wariness that lay there.

The news of the hostage negotiations having finished sent

waves of chatter and gossip through the castle as people prepared for the inevitable journey. The queen, it seemed, may not have had her followers, but she did have enough honorable knights and men present that she was assured of an escort.

Lady Alice came to her and said, "Matilda has a request."

"What's that? More sweet honeyed bread rolls?" Bronwyn said, looking up from the soup she was stirring.

"No. She requests that you join her party. You are invited by Matilda to join her as one of the cooks on her journey to Winchester, and then London."

"Me?" Bronwyn stared. She had wondered what would become of her now that the hostage negotiations had ended and the exchanges were essentially complete. Master Gregory had offered her a chance to stay if she wanted, but she wasn't sure. She liked him well enough but didn't know if she could ever feel entirely comfortable or safe serving a chatelaine who would just as soon interrogate her in a dungeon as she would drink wine.

"Yes. Will you come?" Lady Alice asked.

Bronwyn licked her lips. This was a chance to tell the king and queen and reveal all that had happened. Let them decide what to do.

Lady Alice added quietly, "Sir Bors will be part of the party. I expect Rupert and Crispin will be too." At Bronwyn's expression, she added, "Crispin claims to support the empress, but I think he simply chooses which side will be to his advantage more by the day. I haven't heard anything about Theobold."

Bronwyn averted her gaze and focused on stirring the soup. It was a thick soup, rich with chicken, peas, and purple carrots. "I'll come."

The next few days were a flurry of activity. Lady Mabel was slowly on the mend but was not accepting visitors to her solar and only allowed her most trusted servants to bring her food and wine. If the rumors were true, she only ate and drank after having the servants try some first. It was an uneasy situation for all. But there were no more deaths or killings, and aside from the occasional wrestling match or fight amongst the men, nothing of consequence happened. Bronwyn would have been relieved, were it not for the presence of Sir Bors there, drinking happily and acting like nothing was amiss. She couldn't feel safe.

Lady Mabel at one point sent for her, and in the privacy of her solar, received Bronwyn. The chatelaine lay in bed, looking pale. She said, "So you are to leave tomorrow. We have unfinished business, you and I."

Bronwyn opened her mouth to speak, when Lady Mabel held up a finger to her lips and beckoned her forward, to her side.

Taking a breath, Bronwyn knelt by the chatelaine, who whispered, "The walls have ears here. I believe that whoever tried to poison me still has people watching, listening. I cannot trust anyone."

Bronwyn nodded. She knew the feeling well.

"But I have wondered, who was behind all of this? Tell me now."

Bronwyn whispered her suspicions, and the evidence she and Lady Alice had found.

The chatelaine laid her head back on pillows and nodded. "If that is so, then God's teeth, he has been living here, enjoying himself while I almost die in my bed. God be with you, Bronwyn. I do not think we shall meet again." She coughed, her stomach shuddered, and she reached for her dish and was sick. The strong woman was pale and pasty, and Bronwyn felt for her. Once the chatelaine was finished, Bronwyn wiped her brow with a linen cloth and removed the dish, replacing it with another as quick as she could.

ON A BRIGHT and chilly morning in November, Bronwyn joined the party of knights and armed men. The queen was taking no chances, and she and Eustace sat atop their horses, bundled up against the cold, their breaths pluming out like white streams in the air.

Bronwyn said goodbye to Master Gregory, but only him, for none of the other cooks had gotten to know her, nor she them. Alan ignored her entirely, which she rather thought was the best thing for all involved. Master Gregory touched her arm and said, "Whenever you return to Bristol, you can have a place here, if you want."

She smiled at him. "Thank you."

Then came the shout, and they were off. Bronwyn walked with the food, pulled by donkeys and packhorses, and began the slow trek back to Winchester.

There was no incident along the way, which was a relief. Bronwyn kept close to the other servants and made sure not to go anywhere alone if she could help it. She kept an eye on Sir Bors as much as she could, but with hours of walking the long roads, she quickly fell asleep at night under the stars, bone-tired and often too exhausted to think. She wondered if Sir Bors was truly allegiant to the king and queen, or if it was all a ruse. Why else would he kill women for no reason?

During the days, Crispin kept close to Lady Alice, who laughed and amused all with her lighthearted cheer. But in the evenings, she grew tired, listless, and dark hollows grew beneath her pretty, dark eyes.

When Bronwyn asked if she was unwell, Lady Alice always smiled sweetly at her, patted Crispin's hand beside her, and said it was simply the journey. It had been weeks since she had been in the saddle and she rather had gotten used to having little exercise. Her legs were sore, she said, as she tried rubbing feeling back into her sore muscles.

This time, the group avoided Devizes, and within a week, traveled safely to Winchester. Upon arrival, the queen and prince went directly to the king, whilst the other members of the party stood by and took refreshment.

Bronwyn reported to the castle kitchens and met some cooks

she had known before. She had been dreading seeing Master Christopher, the former head cook of Winchester Castle, and a bully, who despised her. Shortly before she had left for Devizes with the empress's party, there had been a change, and Sir William of Ypres, a loyal follower and Flemish military commander of Stephen's, had seen how poorly Bronwyn was treated and stood up for her, taking Christopher out of his post. He'd given the head cook position to another man.

Upon entering the kitchens, it was this man Bronwyn saw. Master Christopher was still there, though, working in a corner, and he shot her a glowering look.

She smiled and ignored him, then introduced herself to the head cook, a tall, tow-headed man. The man paused from his cooking, wiped his hands on an apron and held out a beefy hand, still dusted with flour. It was a test. Would she accept it and show she had no care for getting her hands dirty, or would she be like a proper lady and balk at the thought?

She almost laughed and shook his hand, feeling the brush of flour on her palm. "Bronwyn Blakenhale."

"Godwin Saunderson. Welcome." He cocked his head at her. "You've worked here before. I remember you. Last I recall, you had sauce dumped on your head and you had William of Ypres throw out old Christopher here." He grinned and shot a look over her shoulder. Christopher glowered. Godwin asked, "What brings you here?"

"I came with the queen's party. From Bristol. She bid me come," Bronwyn said.

"'Course she did." Christopher snickered.

Godwin shot him a dirty look and said, "Aye, well. Work hard and don't mess about and you can work here. You can start by plucking these birds for dinner." He nodded to the small group of capons and pigeons on a side table. She nodded and tied her hair back. That work would suit her just fine.

For a day, she was almost happy. She worked in the kitchens and did whatever task was asked of her. Then came the summons.

A page arrived. Master Godwin said, "What is it?"

"Mistress Bronwyn Blackhalle is called to the throne room," the youth said. "Right now."

"It's Blakenhale," Bronwyn said. "Blakenhale."

"Correct him later," said Godwin. "Best go see what they want."

Christopher the bully muttered something beneath his breath, which Bronwyn chose to ignore. No doubt it would be insulting.

She wiped her hands on her apron and followed the page to the throne room. They knocked and were admitted, and she swallowed. The room was full of nobles and unfamiliar faces. Many men and women present were dressed in finery, and they looked upon her with curiosity, others with downright disdain. She could well understand their thoughts. Who was this cook called into the king's presence? It was a curiosity, for sure. She bit the inside of her cheek. Where was Sir Bors? Had he managed to charm the king and queen into thinking he was innocent and loyal? She looked around but did not see the man anywhere amongst the nobles present. But the room was crowded, and there were many milling bodies about.

At the head of the room sat the king and queen in two large, wooden chairs, with Prince Eustace standing at the left hand of the queen. All looked at her with severity.

Bronwyn breathed in through her nose and did not speak. She swallowed and willed her hands to stop trembling. She would not be scared. She wouldn't. Instead, she curtsied low and slowly rose, gripping her thin skirts.

"Mistress Bronwyn Blakenhale," came the king's voice. The man looked to be in his middle age, with blond hair that shone lighter, as if strands of silver had crept in. His eyes were intelligent but kind, and even though he had a pleasant-looking demeanor, Bronwyn knew better than to trust it.

"Your Grace," she said.

"I gather there has been quite some excitement since my queen and son have left for Bristol. Mind you tell us here just what happened."

Bronwyn looked around at the nobles present, seeing Sir Baldwin of Clare, Rupert, Crispin, and Sir Bors. She swallowed. The man was here, standing with the other nobles like he belonged there. It made her skin crawl. Also present were Sir William of Ypres, and many other knights and men-at-arms. These men were not armed themselves, but all looked upon her. Her knees threatened to tremble beneath their gaze, but then she lifted her head, looked directly at the king, and began her story.

At some parts, the queen interjected, and Rupert added, particularly at the beginning, when they revealed that their party had been attacked in the woods by bandits, with Rupert being one of the sole survivors, along with the Lady Muriel.

Bronwyn said, "What is largely unknown, Your Grace, is that the queen and prince were stolen and kept captive, then ransomed to Maud."

"Why her? Surely, it is I who would wish to pay the ransom," the king said.

Watching Sir Bors's face, she said, "I cannot say, Your Grace. Only that she was closer, and so would have reason to want them."

"It is easy enough to assume why, Your Grace," Sir William of Ypres said. "Maud would want to weaken your position as king. She might have used them as pawns to end the war."

King Stephen listened, stroking his blond beard, which was now flecked with gray. "Continue, Mistress Blakenhale."

"Maud was not going to pay a ransom; she thought it was a trick. So some of her knights and squires devised a plan to capture the ransomers and rescue the captives. But there were incidents that night, and things did not go well."

"What incidents?" He leaned forward on his wooden throne.

"It was dark, there were drunken people about and fighting, and it all got very messy." Bronwyn did not want to seem like she was bragging, but she had no wish to hide the truth. "I spotted someone nearing the ransom bag, and I followed them. I fought this person and she said that if I wanted to see the queen and prince again alive, I would follow her. So I did."

"'She'? A woman?" King Stephen said.

Some of the nobles present murmured amongst themselves.

"Yes, Your Grace. A noblewoman. A lady-in-waiting of Maud, Lady Morwenna."

"That's a lie!" a woman shouted. "A filthy lie. I never did any such thing. She's making up tales, Your Grace."

Bronwyn stopped and stared. Lady Morwenna was here? Ye gods. The woman herself, here with Sir Bors. They were back together. What trouble would they cause now? Her hand darted to her throat.

Lady Morwenna, dressed in finery with her hair pinned back, pushed forward past noble people until she stood in front of the crowd and swept a grand curtsy to the king. "I would never. This foul commoner seeks to hide herself beneath a blanket of lies and abuse my character. I—"

"I saw you, Lady Morwenna," the queen interrupted. "I did not recognize you before, but now that I know who you are, I do. Did you think we would not remember the pretty face and voice of our captor?"

Chapter Twenty-One

VOICES HUSHED AS the queen rose from her wooden seat, her bright eyes sharp. Bronwyn held her tongue as Queen Matilda stood, a terrific sight, but did not step down from the dais.

At her raised height above the others, the queen gave off a sense of strength and purity, and her raised head and firm countenance gave the impression of a woman not to be trifled with.

Lady Morwenna knelt to the ground. "An innocent mistake, Your Grace. I would never dream of disagreeing—"

"But that is precisely what you are doing. Do you dare, nay, *presume* to tell me that yours was not the face and voice of the woman who kept my son and me in a foul pit, and threw us food scraps that not even wild dogs would eat?"

There were scandalized gasps as noblemen and women reacted. Their murmurs grew to an angry buzz, and people began openly talking over one another.

"Enough," Stephen said. "Let us hear from the kitchen maid."

Eyes fell on Bronwyn, who said, "The Lady Morwenna led me to a pit, where the queen and prince were. I saw them and with the help of Crispin Ashe, the squire, we fashioned a rope to help them up."

"Is this true, my dear?" Stephen asked his wife.

"It is. It was dark, but there was no mistaking our rescuers.

Or our captors." Queen Matilda shot a dark glance at Morwenna, who glared at Bronwyn.

"'Captors'? Continue," King Stephen said.

Bronwyn spoke. "Crispin and I knew that to bring the queen and prince back to the castle at Devizes would be to risk their lives, and they were too important for these hostage negotiations to fail. So we decided to split them up. He took the queen to a nunnery on the outskirts of the city and entrusted me with Prince Eustace."

Heads turned to the prince, who stood with his hands clasped behind his back, and shifted his feet. He gave a nod.

"Where was Lady Morwenna in this?" King Stephen asked.

"Gone. I do not know where she went. Only that when Crispin and I worked to help the prisoners out of the pit, she was nowhere to be found."

Lady Morwenna's eyes blazed as she rose to her feet. "Why, you little—"

"Lady Morwenna, hold your tongue," Stephen said. He nodded to Bronwyn.

"On the way back to the castle, I met with Rupert, the squire of Sir Baldwin of Clare." Ignoring the heads that turned to glance at them both standing nearby, Bronwyn said, "He had been part of the queen's entourage earlier and recognized the prince immediately. He offered his aid, and together, we decided the best way to hide the prince was to have him pretend he was one of us."

"What do you mean?" King Stephen asked.

"We told the head cook that he was a lost boy and got him a place to stay to work in the kitchens until his mother could be found."

Nobles stared, wide-eyed, at this. Some laughed out loud at the absurdity.

"You mean to say you had my son work in the kitchens, as a servant? Right under Maud's very nose?" King Stephen's eyes were wide.

"Yes, Your Grace. And very good he was at it too. Everyone liked him."

Prince Eustace grinned. The king laughed.

"But Lady Morwenna joined the court," Bronwyn said, "and she declared she had been coerced into helping with the attack and the ransom, on account of her lover."

Lady Morwenna lowered her gaze and stood quietly, her hands clasped. She almost looked demure but didn't quite achieve it.

"It wasn't until we learned that she planned to visit the nunnery where the queen was held that we knew we had to move. So we made plans and left the next day."

"But from what my men tell me, your timing was very convenient, for a maidservant died that morning," King Stephen said.

"Yes, Your Grace. Found with a rose. I was unable to view her body to tell if it was an accident or not."

He nodded at this. "What then?"

"We were joined by Lady Alice, and together, Crispin, Rupert, and I safely moved the queen and prince to the castle at Bristol."

"Tell me more of this ransom."

Bronwyn nodded. "We know that the queen and prince's entourage was attacked, and they were stolen away for ransom to the empress. Lady Muriel escaped and came here, and the Lady Morwenna and her lover kept them in captivity and held them for ransom."

"That has yet to be proven," Sir Bors said.

Lady Alice cleared her throat. "Actually, Lady Morwenna bragged about it to the empress. The squire Theobold told me."

"Lady Alice! How could you?" Lady Morwenna cried. She glanced at Sir Bors and bit her lip. To the king, she said, "What bold lies she tells. Honestly, Your Grace, these two women have made a pact to ruin my character before this court, and I know not why." Lady Morwenna's face almost squished into tears, but not quite.

Lady Alice snorted.

Bronwyn said, "Sir Robert of Gloucester's squire, Theobold, shared that Lady Morwenna tried to take credit for the entire plot, but no one believed her. She refused to say whose orders it came from until she was imprisoned. The empress sentenced her to death, but she escaped. No one knew where she'd gone, and the empress sent Sir Robert's squire to find her."

The king stroked his beard. "I find it hard to believe Lady Morwenna would lay claim to such a ploy. Since she joined us here not long ago, she has acted like a well-born lady should, with grace and decorum. To hear these accounts of her behavior seems wrong. But... I cannot ignore my wife's account of her time in captivity. I trust her word."

Bronwyn and Lady Alice exchanged a look.

"And who was behind the order?" the king asked, as the queen returned to her seat.

"I can tell you," Bronwyn said. She rounded on Lady Alice. "Lady Alice, is it not true that you were present at Bristol Castle and stayed close by the queen? You acted as her lady-in-waiting, did you not?"

"Yes, I did," Lady Alice said, curtseying to the queen.

"What are you getting at, Bronwyn?" asked the queen.

"Only this. That you recall your time knowing Lady Morwenna from before. What happened in London? Back in June?"

Lady Alice turned red. "I don't think this is the time—"

"Tell us, Lady Alice," the king said.

Shooting Bronwyn a look, Lady Alice said, "We were at Maud's attempted coronation. But the mob put a stop to that."

"And where was Lady Morwenna at the time?"

"Missing. She never made it to the coronation. I never saw her after, either. I'd heard that the empress sent Theobold after her to track her down."

"She was one of the empress's ladies, was she not?" Bronwyn asked.

"Yes. It was of a particular pain to the empress that Lady

Morwenna missed her grand occasion." She glanced at the nobles grinning and smirking amongst themselves, and said, "I did see her earlier, though. That day in June, shortly before the coronation."

"Oh?" Bronwyn said.

"She was missing," Lady Alice said. "Earlier that day, she had lured you down to the cells. I'd seen Lady Morwenna acting strangely and suspected something was wrong when she led you away. I followed and saw you being strangled with a garotte. Lady Morwenna fled, but if I hadn't hit the man over the head with a chair leg, you might have died."

"What man?" the king asked.

Lady Alice swallowed. "Lady Morwenna's lover."

"Who is?"

Lady Alice paused.

Lady Morwenna glanced quickly at Sir Bors, then away. She bit her nails.

"Tell us, Lady Alice," the queen said.

Lady Alice took a breath. "It was Lady Morwenna and Sir Bors, Your Grace."

"That's a lie!" Sir Bors said.

"Is it?" Bronwyn said.

Lady Alice shook her head. "It's true. I'll never forget it. You don't easily forget seeing someone almost die. I saw him facing Bronwyn in the jail cell back in June and she was unconscious. I knew something was seriously wrong, as they weren't friendly. Then she fell, and I realized she was hurt, so I hit him over the head. If I hadn't stunned him, Bronwyn might not be here today."

Sir Bors growled. "She's lying to you, Your Grace. This little harlot thinks she can worm her way into your good favor, but she's nothing but a snake. They all are." He glared at Lady Alice and Lady Morwenna.

"And yet, we have known you, Sir Bors. You are sometimes of this court, sometimes not. Are you denying a relationship with Lady Morwenna?" the queen asked.

"I…" He paused. "I may have known her in the past, but not now. Too common for the likes of me."

Lady Morwenna's jaw dropped. Of all the things to insult her with, he'd stung her pride, Bronwyn realized. She knew that pain well.

Lady Morwenna launched herself at Sir Bors, hands reaching for his throat. "You *dare*. You dare turn on me, when you said I was the best woman you'd ever known. You promised to marry me, you dolt!" Screeching, she flew at him with a tangle of clawed hands and wild hair.

He fell over, fending her off. "Get her off me! This bloody harpy'll claw my eyes out."

"You deserve it, you foul creature. You deserve it." Lady Morwenna fought back against the two knights who pulled her off of Sir Bors. The man himself clambered back on his butt, a bloody scratch down his cheek.

"Well. After that little performance, I'd like some answers. Are you or are you not working together?" the king asked.

Panting, and with a severe glare at Sir Bors, Lady Morwenna hung her head and uttered, "We are, Your Grace. We were. He led the attack on the royal party. He came here and pretended to pay court to you, but he is allied with Maud. He's been her man since the beginning. You shouldn't trust him."

Sir Bors roared, "That's a filthy lie. You witch. She's blinded by rage, Your Grace. It's all because of this kitchen maid. She's had it in for me from the start, since she and her pa tried to poison you both back at Lincoln a year ago."

People gasped and stared at Bronwyn, whose cheeks flamed at being the center of attention.

Sir Bors grinned nastily and said loudly, "She's at her old tricks again, I tell you. She's nothing but a piece of traitorous scum, and she deserves to be in prison. Let me take her there, Your Grace." He marched forward, large, beefy hands at the ready.

"Hold, Sir Bors." The king held up a hand. He turned to Lady

Morwenna. "That is a serious allegation. Why did he want to disturb the party traveling to Bristol and the hostage exchange? He has pledged himself to my service."

Lady Morwenna raised her head. "With respect, Your Grace, Sir Bors is all muscle and no brains."

That earned her a curse from the man.

Lady Morwenna continued. "He was following orders, same as me. Sir Miles Fitzwalter gave the order to disrupt the party."

Gasps rang out.

The king said, "Lady Morwenna. Are you certain of this? What proof have you?"

"Only my own knowledge, Your Grace. What I have seen and heard with my own eyes and ears. Men talk." She glanced at Sir Bors.

"Sir Miles is a close and loyal follower of Maud. What would he want with disrupting the hostage exchange?" the king asked.

"To create confusion. To have you both blaming the other, and so when the queen and her son were either ransomed or dead, he wins. Either way, he gains the upper hand, for he'll either have collected the ransom or they would have been dead, and both of you would have been weakened. The hostage exchange would fail, utterly, and he would move against the empress to take power. It was only when things went awry that ruined his plans. For now."

The king thought on this seriously, gripping his bony knees. "And what of these other deaths at Bristol?" the king asked. "A maid and a lady-in-waiting. What of them?"

Bronwyn took a deep breath. "My friend, the squire Rupert Bothwell, is a flirt. His biggest crime is he is too nice, too friendly, and he often gives young women the wrong idea. But this is the first time it really got him into trouble."

Lady Alice said, "He often chats with young women, Your Grace, be it maids, ladies-in-waiting, anyone with a pretty face." She scowled. "He either thanks them for their kindness, their generosity, or just having a nice smile. He's too kindhearted.

Why, back in Devizes, he escaped the attack on the entourage and was discovered in the woods wounded, and a maidservant nursed him back to health. What does he do? Walks around with her and gives her a rose."

"I call that kind," the king said.

"Some would call it *romantic*," said Lady Alice. "*He* certainly thought so. Right up till when she died. Killed mysteriously at Devizes."

Bronwyn continued. "We learned that Lady Morwenna was about to discover our plot to hide the queen and prince nearby and knew we had to move them. So we left the next day, around the same time a maidservant had been discovered dead—the same one Rupert had been flirting with. By all accounts, her body had been found with a rose."

The king raised an eyebrow. "So Rupert was supposedly killing even then."

Rupert gritted his teeth on the sidelines and squared his shoulders, as if readying himself for a fight.

"Someone was. But it wasn't Rupert," Bronwyn said. "We didn't know anything was amiss until we were leaving Devizes castle. We didn't even hear of the maid's death until well after we'd arrived there."

The king steepled his hands. "I know Rupert well. He is very loyal to his master and to us. It disturbs me to hear this account of him. A man can flirt all he likes, but killing? I cannot believe it. His actions make me think he is a lover, not a fighter. Certainly not a killer of women." He paused and thought. "Assuming he could have done such a thing, Rupert could have killed the girl in a rush that morning or the night before and used the opportunity to move the queen and prince as a chance to escape suspicion," the king said. "I do not like it, but you must admit, the timing is perfect."

"Yes, Your Grace, except that Rupert isn't a killer. Like you say, he is very loyal to you. He wouldn't have done this," Bronwyn continued. "On one of the first nights after we arrived at the prison, he got into a fight with Crispin. They both fancy Lady Alice."

"I heard about that," the queen said.

"Then perhaps you also remember hearing about Rupert's light romance with a kitchen maid, who tended his wounds. She had seen him before and they instantly began flirting with each other. Her name was Mary, and her biggest fault was that she fell in love too easily—and too quickly. She made plans with Rupert to walk out in the gardens that evening. But her other fault was that she had a bad habit of eavesdropping on private conversations."

Bronwyn had the court's full attention now. "Mary and Rupert walked out in the gardens together that evening. But Mary came on too strong and was expecting too much from Rupert, when all he'd planned was a bit of a kiss and tickle. He'd never planned on anything serious with her."

Lady Alice gave a firm nod.

"So they argued, as Mary didn't like it when he explained he wasn't serious about her. That his heart belonged to another. He left, and that was the last time he saw her alive."

"You make it sound so mysterious," the king said. "But my men say her body was found with a rose. Didn't you say yourself that he liked to give the women he flirted with roses? How do you know he didn't do it?"

"He was seen leaving Mary that evening, by the head cook," Bronwyn said.

"What was he doing outside that late at night?" the king asked.

Bronwyn bit her lip. Should she wish it, she could reveal what she knew about the head cook's romantic liaisons with Alan. But she respected the man too much, and even if his personal choices were considered forbidden in their society, she would not comment on another person's private affairs. She had no need to, so she didn't. "He was out for some night air and was taking a piss."

Some of the noblemen grinned. A few chuckled, the king among them. "I see. And he will confirm that he saw Rupert leave Mary alone?"

"Yes. He has no great liking for Rupert but will not lie to get him in trouble," Bronwyn said. "He also cared for Mary and did not think she was in danger. Otherwise, he would have gone himself to protect her and intervene."

"But what of the rose, found with her body?" the queen asked.

"She was killed that night, hit on the back of the head with a bottle of ale. But the rose we found in her hand, there was a thorn from it, lodged deep in her palm. Someone wanted her body to be found holding the rose so as to implicate Rupert, and so they stuck it there, so there would be no mistaking who must have done the crime."

"Your tone suggests something is amiss here," the king said.

"Indeed. When I examined her body, I found one of the rose's thorns stuck in her palm. But there was no blood from it. So if she had a large thorn stuck in her palm, why did she not bleed?"

"Why?" Lady Alice asked.

"Because Mary was already dead. Whoever killed her had put the rose and stuck the thorn in her hand as an afterthought, to frame Rupert for her death. But dead bodies don't bleed, which is why we know that he didn't do it."

"Now we're getting somewhere," the king said. He leaned back in his seat, the wooden back creaking. "Go on. You appear to have cleared Rupert of her murder, but you still don't know who killed her."

"I believe it was Sir Bors, Your Grace."

Sir Bors let out a foul tirade of cursing, until one of the guards prodded him with a spear, and he shut up.

Rupert let out a sigh of relief. A few noblemen murmured, and an older, middle-aged man clapped a hand on Rupert's shoulder. Rupert smiled and nodded, accepting thanks from the men standing around.

The king said, "So now a lady-in-waiting is dead."

"Yes. That brings us to Lady Muriel," Bronwyn said. "She had received a rose on her pillow. She thought it was from the killer. It wasn't intended to be. It was a mistake. It was meant to be a gift for Lady Alice."

The king smiled at the noblewoman. Lady Alice's cheeks turned pink and she glanced away.

"What I want to know is why were you were told by the empress to spy on me, Bronwyn? Lady Muriel said so," the queen said.

"I think it was an act by Maud to secure my loyalty and promise me rewards if I served her well. I had already disturbed her and was banished from her court. I think she wanted me to spy and if you knew, it would mean you had fewer people to rely on. I refused the offer. People didn't believe me, however. But it didn't matter. It just meant that while in captivity, you would have to rely more on Lady Muriel and Lady Alice."

"So were these killings meant to disturb the queen? As a way to bother her mind? Was it all a plot by Maud?" the king asked.

"It wouldn't surprise me. But I think all three deaths were a case of the killer protecting himself. Lady Muriel's death was most disturbing to him, I think. He had to act fast to prevent her from revealing his identity. She interrupted a church service and the guards took her. I thought she'd gone to her room, but when I searched for her, she wasn't there. She'd been taken down to the prison cells. When I found her, she declared she caused the scene at church because she realized something. You recall how she was one of the few survivors of the attack on the queen's entourage?"

Bronwyn continued. "She was at the church service and when the men were talking, saying the lord's prayers, she heard something. A voice. She remembered that voice, and how it belonged to one of the men involved in the attack. She ran immediately to warn the queen and was going to tell me, when I was attacked."

The queen's eyebrows rose. "You were?"

"It's true, Your Grace," Lady Alice said. "We found her locked in Lady Muriel's cell, bleeding from where someone had hit her and left her for dead. They obviously didn't want her nosing around."

"Clearly."

"But we did find something. A word scratched into the dirt, likely by Lady Muriel herself. A message, before she was taken away," Bronwyn said.

"What was it?" the queen asked.

"We think it was a name," Lady Alice said. "The name of a man here at court. The one Lady Muriel remembered and wanted to warn you about. But of course, Bronwyn can't read, so she wouldn't have known what it said. And to be honest, it was completely illegible, none of us could make it out."

Bronwyn blushed. She really did want to learn to read. "That night, we found Lady Muriel, dead in the castle graveyard. She had been strangled. But on her neck, with the bruises, was a strange imprint. It came from a ring, a large one, that had pressed into her neck as the man had been killing her, and it fell out of her hair when the guards took away her body."

"Ugh. This sounds disgusting," the king said. "You found the ring?"

"I have it here." Bronwyn fetched it out of her pocket and handed it to him.

The king examined the large, gold ring. "I know this ring. But who is its owner?"

"The man whose name Lady Muriel likely scratched into the dirt of her cell, who attacked me, and who led the attack on the queen's party. Sir Bors."

Sir Bors pushed away from his guards and pulled Bronwyn's head back, gripping her hair. She cried out in pain and staggered back. He said, "That's the last time you smear my name in the mud, little witch," he said. "Give me leave, Your Grace, and by and by, I'll gut her like a fish. She'll trouble you no more."

"Let her go!" came the cry, and Rupert dashed forward.

"You would defend her, boy? What's a pup like you going to do against me?" Sir Bors laughed and fished out a wicked-looking dagger from his sleeve.

"Release her at once, Sir Bors," the king ordered, rising from his seat. "Now."

Tears sprang to Bronwyn's eyes. The man's grip on her hair had been so painful, it had taken all of her grit not to yell. She breathed in through her nose and let out shallow, pained breaths.

Sir Bors leaned in close to her ear. "When next we meet, I'll do more than hit your head." He released his hold on her hair and gave a sharp kick to her backside, sending Bronwyn sprawling on her hands knees to the floor.

Sharp pain bloomed on her behind. A few people laughed and tittered, but she got to her feet, red-faced. Rupert stood by, helping her up.

"Well, this is a fine mess. We have women dead, and no one to blame for it but a man who serves two courts." The king hefted the gold ring.

Sir Bors eyed it. "I am loyal to you, Your Grace. And a ring does not make a murderer, Your Grace."

"No, but with testimony, it does," the queen said. She said, "Your story rings true, Mistress Blakenhale. The Lady Muriel did reach me that day. She called up through the tower before she was taken. 'Sir Bors, she told us. Sir Bors did it. He was behind it all.' But then she was dragged away, and I never saw or heard from her again. I decided not to speak of it to anyone, for I knew not who I could trust."

"Is this true?" The king looked to the prince.

"Yes, Father," Prince Eustace said solemnly.

"If you knew, why did you not speak a word of it till now, my love?" King Stephen asked.

"I wanted to see how he acted. Besides, we were guarded at all times. We were completely safe. And… I wished to see how he would conduct himself here. I rather suspected he would be found guilty."

The king patted his wife's hand. "You are a wonder, my dear."

Bronwyn said, "Your Grace, I accuse Sir Bors of murder. He attacked your queen's entourage and tried to hold her and the prince for ransom, and he killed the maidservants Philippa, Mary, and the Lady Muriel."

"You're wrong. I didn't do it," Sir Bors said. "I didn't kill all those women. I never even heard of the maids. Why would I kill some maids? I've got uses for maidservants and it's not lying in a ditch."

Bronwyn cocked her head. She didn't know his motive for him killing the maids, other than perhaps making Rupert look bad. And what would Sir Bors have had to gain from that? That would make sense, to have him be set free in order to further frame him, but something didn't sit right with her. Could she have been mistaken about Sir Bors's involvement? She knew for certain he had killed Lady Muriel, but the other two victims? Was she wrong?

"Let's not forget Lady Morwenna as his accomplice," Lady Alice said.

Lady Morwenna glared at her and shook her head. She prostrated herself on the floor. "I throw myself at your mercy, Your Grace. I was led astray by this man. I bear you no ill will; it was solely his doing."

"*You—*" Sir Bors cursed.

"Have a care, Sir Bors. There are ladies present," the king said.

"Not from where I'm standing." Sir Bors growled.

Guards pushed forward and in seconds surrounded Sir Bors, their spears tipped at his body.

He raised his hands, "Oi! I did nothing wrong. This is all lies. All of it. Who are you going to believe? Are you really going to take the word of a scullery wench over mine? Me, who has served you loyally all these years? Yes, I was in her court. But I was spying for you, Your Grace. I have always been a king's man.

Honest to God."

The king straightened and said, "I am ready to pass judgment."

The people in the room quieted. The king said, his voice loud and clear, "I am disturbed by these turn of events. I had thought my family relatively safe during these hostage exchanges, but events have proven otherwise. For his part in leading an attack on my men, on my queen and son, I accept the accusations against Sir Bors."

A hush fell over the room.

The king said, "These negotiations have been so carefully planned, to use my family like pawns in your game, for ransom. You would have gladly traded their lives for coin." He rose, the wooden armrests creaking beneath his weight. "That traitorous deceit, I cannot forgive."

His gaze fell on Lady Morwenna. "For your part, good lady, I am willing to show leniency."

"Oh, Your Grace." She crossed herself.

"You came here not long ago and have conducted yourself well, as a lady-in-waiting should. I accept your story, that you acted under duress, and out of love for a man, however misguided it was. No harm will come to you here."

She bowed her head, a slow smile crossing her lips.

Bronwyn gritted her teeth. The queen's eyes narrowed, her lips pursed with displeasure.

Bronwyn wanted to rub her backside, which ached from Sir Bors's kick, but instead rubbed the side of her right thigh. She was so sick of noblemen and women sticking up for each other when problems occurred. It truly was like one rule for all of them, and another set of rules to live by for commoners like herself. It wasn't fair. Why couldn't they see Lady Morwenna for who she really was? A lying, thieving, duplicitous traitor with a title.

"Whether it is true this man killed these people, I cannot be certain. But there are parts of the maid's story I find truthful and cannot ignore."

"But I didn't kill the damn maids! That was—" Sir Bors stopped as a guard jabbed him in the side with the butt of his spear.

The king said, "I do believe this matter can be solved." He waited for all eyes to fall upon him. "With a joust. We will have a joust to decide this. Sir Bors, versus…" He looked at Bronwyn. "My dear, you have no one to stand for you."

"I'll do it. I'll fight for her," Rupert said.

"Rupert, no," Lady Alice said, her eyes wide. "Don't you dare. You don't know what you're doing." She took his arm.

He shook her off. "I mean it. I will stand and fight for the maid."

The king glanced at Sir Bors. "It feels harsh to pit a seasoned knight against a mere squire." To the knight, he asked, "Have you a squire you would stake against him as your proxy?"

Sir Bors grinned, a slow smile that sent a chill through Bronwyn's heart. "I do. I call on Crispin Ashe to fight in my stead."

Crispin started, his mouth falling open. He frowned but nodded. "I would not defend a traitor, but I will accept if my king commands it."

"Done. We will hold a joust in two days' time," the king announced.

"No," Lady Alice hissed, falling to her knees. "No."

Chapter Twenty-Two

BRONWYN STOOD BY and put a hand on Lady Alice's shoulder, but the noblewoman shook it off. Lady Alice got to her feet and followed Rupert out of the hall as the people there were already disbursing and murmuring amongst themselves.

Once outside of the main hall, Lady Alice renewed her protests for Rupert to rethink this course of action, but he shook his head. "I'm doing it, Lady Alice. Don't try to stop me."

"But you don't need to do this. Don't need to be so pigheaded. You don't need to put your life in danger just to prove to me—"

He rounded on her. "Is that why you think I'm doing this? For you?"

Lady Alice balked. "Aren't you?"

Rupert let out a curse and ran a hand through his hair. "No. I'm not. I'm doing it for her." He nodded toward Bronwyn.

"But why? You don't even like her."

Bronwyn flinched. *What?*

"Don't be ridiculous. Of course I do. We're friends. And sometimes friends need help. That's why I'm doing this."

"So you're throwing your life away for a friend. Who didn't even ask you to do this." She turned. "Bronwyn, talk some sense into him."

"Stay out of this, Bronwyn," Rupert warned.

Bronwyn stood by, at a loss for words. She did not want

Rupert to fight for her. She didn't want anyone to. But at the same time, a joust was a good way to solve disputes, and it served as popular entertainment. But she didn't want Rupert to get hurt. "I don't want you to get hurt… fighting for me."

"See? She said it herself. Now stop this foolish charade, Rupert, and tell the king you've had a change of heart. I'll do it for you. He won't care." She moved toward the doors of the throne room.

"Stop." His voice was loud and cutting. A sharp command.

Lady Alice stopped.

Rupert came to her and put his hands on her arms. "Why are you so against my jousting? Are you afraid I'll get hurt?"

She scoffed. "You fool. No, I'm not afraid of a few broken bones. Although maybe that would knock some sense into that thick skull of yours. No, Rupert, I'm afraid you'll *die*." She practically spat out the words.

Rupert stood stiffly, his entire body still. "You believe that."

"I do." She looked him in the eye.

"What if I promise you that I won't?" he said jokingly. He gave her a warm smile.

"Don't jest at a time like this. It's not funny," Lady Alice said.

"Not all jousts end in death," he told her, rubbing his hands up and down her arms.

She shivered.

He spoke quietly then. "For too long, Bronwyn has been treated poorly, when she is more than a servant. She deserves to have a man fight in her honor. I owe her a debt for clearing my name. To fight for her would be my privilege."

Bronwyn felt something warm bloom in her heart. She wanted to thank Rupert, but now wasn't the time.

Lady Alice said, "That's it. If you are determined to be foolish, I won't stand by and do nothing." She slipped out of his grasp.

"Where are you going?" Rupert asked.

"To talk to Crispin. Maybe he'll see sense and put a stop to this foolish joust."

"And if he doesn't listen?"

"I'll ask to speak with Stephen and Matilda." Lady Alice lifted her head and walked away, her shoes echoing down the hall.

Bronwyn waited. Rupert came up to her and said, "She acts this way because she cares. If she didn't, I wouldn't love her so much."

Bronwyn swallowed. He loved her? That was the first time he'd said it out loud, at least to her. All of a sudden, whatever hopes she had, whatever half-formed romantic feelings she had for Rupert, crumbled like dust. "I don't want you to fight for me."

"Oh, not you too," he said. "Look, I know what I'm doing. Despite what you and Lady Alice seem to think, I actually do know how to fight." He grinned.

"Sure, but joust?"

"I can joust." He raised his belt and puffed out his chest importantly.

She smiled softly. "Why are you doing this?"

"Because I want to."

"But you could get hurt."

"That's not the point." He stepped closer to her and squeezed her left hand. "I mean what I said. You deserve someone to fight in your honor. Too often, people are overlooked and ignored when it's not right. And you know, I get to show off my skills. This is a chance for me too." He winked.

She leaned in and kissed him.

A light peck on the cheek, nothing more. But he jumped and dropped her hand, touching his cheek. His eyes were wide.

"Thank you."

There was a gasp. She turned.

There stood Theobold in the hallway, not fifty feet away. His face looked bloodless. He came over and said, "Bronwyn?"

"Theobold," she breathed.

He was so handsome, it hurt. She ached to run her fingers through his black hair. Even the shadows of the castle corridor and the flickering golden torchlight, his fair skin reminded her of the pale moonlight that drifted across gravestones, or freshly fallen snow.

Her heart rose at the sight of him, then faded at his expression.

His dark eyes, already shadowed from likely nights of sleeping in the woods, had a haunted look. She had betrayed him. It was written in his eyes.

She looked up at him. "It's not what you think. I mean, it's not what it looks like." Her words sounded false, even to her.

His dark eyes bored into hers. "On the contrary, I think it's exactly what it looks like. Or did my eyes deceive me and you didn't just kiss Rupert?" Theobold's mouth twisted.

"I did. But only to say *thank you*."

"You've got a funny way of thanking people. Words wouldn't have sufficed?"

She put her hands on her hips. "He is fighting a joust for me."

His eyes widened. "Why?"

She let out a small sigh and relayed what had happened in the throne room.

Theobold ran a hand along the side of his face and tugged at his black curls, almost as if to wake himself. "I've ridden hard for the better part of a week because I heard Morwenna had come here. Instead, I find *you*, with him." His voice was accusing.

Rupert started, "It's really not like that, mate. She was just—"

Theobold shoved Rupert. He fell back a few steps, and straightened, his face angry. "You want this? Fine, let's go."

"Stop it. Stop it right now." Bronwyn stood between them, her hands out. "I mean it."

"And what could you possibly have to thank him for?" Theobold's dark eyebrows narrowed. "So he offers to fight in your name. Like you're some sort of lady. We all know that's not true."

Bronwyn's mouth dropped open.

Theobold spoke, and his words were ugly. It was as if the darkness from his being, the sleepless nights, the agony of ever-waiting night, slipped out of his throat like a snake.

Bronwyn stared at him, her body stiff. "I thought you cared for me."

"I did. But that was before I saw you kissing other men."

"I'm telling you, Theobold, it's not like that," Rupert said, his voice heated.

"Unless you've got something worthwhile to say, I suggest you leave us," Theobold snapped. "Or better yet, I'll leave. I've got to find Lady Morwenna. Don't let me disturb your kisses." He stalked away.

Theobold made a rude sign with his fingers and kept walking. Bronwyn's shoulders slumped to see the back of him.

"Don't worry about him. He's clearly tired and isn't thinking straight. He'll be all right. Just give him some time."

"I'm not sure about that," Bronwyn said.

"It's all right. Even if he's too foolish to see it, I know you care for him." Rupert patted her on the shoulder. "And you've got me." He rolled his shoulders. "I'd better go see what Lady Alice is up to. You'll be okay?"

Bronwyn nodded. They parted ways and she reported to the kitchens, keen to lose herself in some honest work.

The next day passed quickly. Bronwyn stayed in the castle kitchens. She worked steadily from dawn until dusk, impressing even the new head cook with her doggedness to do any chore, no matter how low. She scrubbed dirty pots and pans with the scullery boys; washed, peeled, and chopped carrots and other vegetables; stirred soup and worked her fingers until they ached. And it wasn't enough. She wasn't tired enough.

It might never be enough. She wanted so badly to run to Theobold and again explain what had happened, to make him listen and convince him. It had just been a friendly kiss. A thank you, for putting his life on the line for her reputation and honor. But like Lady Alice had been days ago, he seemed fixed in his opinions and had decided she was no longer worth the trouble. No longer worth loving.

The next day, she rose with the other servants, yawned at the sight of the November darkness outside the castle walls, still in shades of purple and black from the approaching sunrise, and readied herself. This was the day when Rupert would fight for her. For her honor, to decide whether Sir Bors was truly at fault for his crimes and would be found guilty.

It was also the day Rupert might die.

Chapter Twenty-Three

B RONWYN RUBBED HER eyes. She had not been able to sleep for fear of what might happen to Rupert. In a matter of hours, she would see him spar with lances against Crispin. She wondered what Lady Alice had said to him the day before, or if she had heard about her and Rupert's kiss.

She paused. *That kiss.*

It had only been meant to be a friendly gesture of thanks, like he'd given her. A kiss for a kiss. A simple touch of affection between friends, nothing more.

But was it? She wondered now. Was she lying to herself? Had she meant for it to be something more?

She remembered how his eyes had widened. His surprise. His wonder. And the warm touch of his hand on her shoulder.

But the warm butterflies that began to scattering in her stomach fell flat. What about Theobold? The dark hurt in his eyes had replayed in her dreams. The stilted curtness of his tone, the stiffness of his body, as if afraid to move or risk striking out at something. So angry.

How could she betray him so? She felt like she'd been mistaken. She should never have touched Rupert. How could she have been so foolish? And yet… Theobold had been too quick to anger. Too fast to judge her. Their relationship was fragile, like butterfly wings. Had she ruined it before it had truly begun?

Her temper rose. Firm words sat on her tongue, ready to

strike out at him. And yet, she wanted them both. She admired Rupert and thought of him often, but she also felt a firm loyalty to Theobold. He was the stars and moon, while Rupert was the sun.

But they were just friends—he had made that clear. He adored Lady Alice, whether they were together or not, and Bronwyn would not get in the way of that. She cared for him, yes. But at times she also thought of him like she would an older brother, if she'd ever had one. He was friendly and playful. He didn't stare into her like Theobold, or make her heart race. Not anymore.

Bronwyn yawned at the world with bleary eyes and made her way down to the kitchens. That day, they worked hard for hours, making sweet cakes, savory bites, and small buns and meat-filled pies, so small that a person could hold them in their hand. They would taste best when hot but would still be delicious chilled. All these and more, for when people attended a joust, they grew hungry.

The weather was not the best for it. Rain pelted down that morning against the castle windows, as if to decree all was not right in the world. Bronwyn frowned and hoped the joust might be delayed. What if it was rained out?

But her wishes were not granted. The rain cleared and within an hour, the sun came out, shining. The king and queen's men had arranged a large area on the outskirts of the city, in a series of fields, that would serve as the jousting grounds.

As Bronwyn went about her morning chores in the kitchen, helping load dozens of pies, buns, breads, and sweet and savory treats into baskets and boxes, there came a polite cough at her shoulder. She turned.

"Rupert," she said, a little breathlessly. "Good morrow."

"And a good morning to you too." He smiled, but his smile was faint, and shadows hung beneath his eyes. He hadn't slept well, either, she supposed.

She passed him a meat-filled pie and he bit into it, chewing fast. He burped and wiped his mouth with his sleeve. "I came for your favor."

"Sorry?"

"Your favor." He grinned and blinked from tiredness. "When a knight jousts, sometimes his lady will grant him her favor. Especially if it's in the lady's honor. It might be a silk, or a bit of fine cloth, maybe with some gold thread."

She smiled briefly and glanced at her feet. "I don't have anything like that." She shifted her weight on her feet and felt shy.

"Sure, you do." He reached out and tugged at the old kerchief that held back her blonde hair. "This will do."

She unknotted the kerchief. It was faded, a dark color that might have been purple once, but now was so old and covered with flour, its original color was indeterminable. "You want this?"

He nodded, taking it from her. "Yes. If you'll grant me the honor."

"What fine words."

He laughed and wound the kerchief around his wrist like a pretty bracelet. "This is serious business. It's not every day I get to fight in a lady's honor."

"She's no lady," a bitter voice called.

Bronwyn blushed. Trust the old head cook, Christopher, to try to once again make her life a misery. Good timing too.

Rupert cursed the man who had spoken and turned back to her. "Wish me luck."

"Good luck."

He held her gaze a moment, as if waiting for some other signal or thought to pass between them, then nodded. "I'll see you out there. You'll be watching?"

"I wouldn't miss it."

"Good." He took his leave.

The next hour passed, and in no time at all, the head cook stood at her elbow. "Bronwyn," the man said, "if you're going to come with us to the jousting, now's the time."

"All right." She helped bring boxes and baskets onto carts,

then followed the trail of cooks and servants who brought victuals. They would give them out free to the royal family, but any others would have to pay.

The day was bright and sunny as Bronwyn trudged along. With each step out of the castle, into the city and out through the streets, to the fields for jousting, she felt regret and worry dog her steps.

She saw the tall, wooden stands, like a round, oval fence. It would no doubt keep the men fenced in during the fight. Above it on one side stood a large, raised, wooden platform, where she imagined the royal family would sit.

"Come on, Bronwyn, don't dally," a voice said behind her.

She kept on with the other servants and helped set up a long table that would serve as a sort of grand market stall. There were already other tables and stalls popping up around the area, as word had spread of the fight to come.

"All this to see two squires fight?" she said aloud.

One man near her said, "It's not just that. Some fight over a lady. Some lady's honor's at stake."

"A lady, you say?"

"Aye. But you know these grand noblemen. Always jumping at any excuse for a fight." The market trader winked at her and she smiled back.

The sun shone on her face and she briefly closed her eyes. For a moment, it was like being back at home in Lincoln, running her family's market stall of breads. There was a sense of good cheer amongst those present, almost a festive air, and she realized that it was infectious.

People weren't cheering about the fact that a man might get hurt or die; that was the risk the fighters took. They were keen to have something to be cheerful about, and to celebrate.

Prices were agreed with the other cooks and she began calling out their wares, offering pies—meat and vegetable filled—sweet cakes, honey cakes, oat cakes, small bread rolls, and sticky buns. The castle cooks' stall became quite busy and soon people were buying the food almost as fast as the cooks could sell them. Long queues began and Bronwyn kept order, keeping things moving as she counted money and passed it to the head cook whilst she sold more.

For a time, it was a delight. She laughed and cheekily teased and chatted with the local people, and actually started to enjoy herself, when loud trumpets sounded. Horns called, their ringing sounds echoing over the crowds.

"What's that?" Bronwyn asked.

"Joust's about to start," the head cook said. "Better hurry up and finish selling these. Our men are making more back at the kitchen, but we'll be sold out soon." He looked at her. "You should be there. It's for you, after all."

Bronwyn bit her lip. "Yes, thanks." She sold one more bun, passed the coins to him, and slipped away into the crowds. The stands were already lined with people and more men and women were heading toward the stalls. She'd be lucky to see anything, she realized.

Bronwyn looked around the makeshift arena. She hoped to find Rupert's stand and wish him good luck. She slipped by and entered the tent, where a young man was bent over on a chair, putting on pieces of armor.

"Hello—" she paused.

Crispin looked over his shoulder. "Come to wish me luck?" He grinned. "Or death?"

She swallowed.

He snorted and went back to tying on the armor. A liveried servant was helping him. "Go, I'll call if I need you," he said.

The servant disappeared, leaving them alone in the small tent. The flaps closed, shutting out the noise from the people in the arena.

"What do you want?" he asked.

"Did Lady Alice talk to you?"

"We talked. She begged me not to fight. At first, I thought she was worried for me, but then I discovered she was only worried for her pet squire."

Bronwyn swallowed. She hadn't seen Lady Alice around anywhere today. Was she all right?

"And before you start getting any wild ideas, she's a lady. I would not harm a hair on her head." Crispin fastened on a leg brace as he spoke. "I simply told her what I plan to do to her precious Rupert." His smile was nasty. "But you must be pleased. You solved the mystery. Sir Bors definitely did it, but I think he and Rupert are still too friendly. They knew each other from before—you should have heard Sir Bors at dinner back in Bristol, telling everyone how wonderful Rupert was as a squire, and how he'd stolen him right under Sir Baldwin's nose. Right proud of himself, he was. I still think they were working together. Sir Bors does one murder, and Rupert the others. It'd have been easy for him."

Except she knew Rupert, and he was no killer of young women. "Well, that's one theory, even if it's wrong."

Crispin's upper lip twitched. "Ah, yes, I forgot. You still fancy him. Theobold must be tearing his hair out."

"We're just friends, Rupert and I."

"I'll believe that when I see it." Crispin smirked. "Anyway, even if Sir Bors did it, he was still close to Rupert, and that's highly suspicious. Who would've known he'd had a thing for killing maids?"

Bronwyn smiled. "I know. And all his attempts to frame Rupert for it. I'm impressed he was able to get roses each time."

Crispin tied on his other shin guard, fastening the straps around his right leg. "Ah, but he was sloppy, wasn't he? Left his gold ring with Lady Muriel and he didn't even bother getting a rose for her. He only stuffed some grass in her mouth. Nothing to be impressed about there."

Bronwyn's answering smile was tight as she froze. No one knew that a rose hadn't been found with Lady Muriel. Only she, Lady Alice, Gregory, and the killer.

Bronwyn looked at him. Her blood began to pound in her

veins. Her voice, riddled with fear, came out high and squeaky. "Well, I'm sure you're right. I'll just be going—"

She turned to go when a knife flew at her head, tearing at her sleeve. She fell and got to her knees.

Crispin towered over her. "You're not going anywhere."

Bronwyn gasped and clapped a hand to her upper arm. There was a sliver of pain, and the bright metallic tang of her blood stained the sleeve. "And Lady Alice knew. She figured out you did it. You murdered Philippa, Rupert's nurse, back at Devizes Castle, and you murdered Mary the kitchen maid. You're the one who hit me when I was talking to Lady Muriel in the prison, weren't you?"

He snorted. "Sounds like you have it all figured out."

"I know how you did it. But I don't know why. Why did you kill all those women? And why work with Sir Bors?"

Crispin frowned at Bronwyn. "You really want to know?"

"Yes." If she could keep him talking, she might be able to escape.

He stood with his hands on his hips. "I realized after a short while that the empress was volatile. A powerful woman, but I could not trust my lot with her. She would see me killed as a pawn in her war and sleep well that same night. Sir Bors found me in a tavern. Heard me talking with some others. He took me aside and told me there was another man who would see me honored for my efforts, and rewarded. Introduced me to Sir Miles Fitzwalter, who told me what I could to help. It was a damn sight better than going around bowing and scraping to a woman who might order my death or throw a plate at me."

"So you offered your services to him and Sir Miles Fitzwalter."

He sneered at her. "I am not the first, nor the last to seek my fortune. Don't judge me. You don't have the right. I'll not be judged by a mere kitchen maid."

She nodded. "The scullery maid at Devizes castle. Rupert's nurse. That was you, wasn't it?"

"She had a bad habit of listening at doors. Caught her listening as I'd offered my services to Sir Miles, and told her she'd keep quiet if she knew what was good for her. She nodded like a regular churchgoer, but I know the type. He told me to get rid of her. Otherwise, he wouldn't think me serious about my future with him. So I did." His face was drawn, and he pulled on another piece of armor.

"And the rose?"

"I didn't plant it there. She already had it in her hands. A gift from Rupert."

"But you also put one in Mary's hands when you killed her."

He gave her a sidelong look. "You're smarter than you look. You should've taken up my offer to spy on the queen."

She shrugged. "Why frame Rupert?"

"It was so easy. I'd seen them walking around the courtyard and the gardens and knew he liked to give ladies flowers. She was already by the rosebush when I found her. I did us all a favor by getting rid of her."

"But why kill Mary at all? She was innocent."

"She wasn't. She'd overheard you and I talking about spying and threatened to go to the queen if I didn't pay her."

"Blackmail? She wanted money?"

"For her silence, yes. But I know her type. They never stop. She was going to tell the queen and Lady Mabel that neither of us could be trusted, for we were both spies for the empress. She's known Lady Mabel for years. If she told that one of the empress's men was spying on the queen and in turn spying on her, maybe to get her in trouble for something, that would be a problem. The chatelaine is a smart woman. She would have believed it. Likely had both of us strung up in that dungeon of hers."

Bronwyn repressed a shudder. "So you killed Mary."

"I did what I had to do."

"Would Lady Mabel really have reacted so strongly to learn that you were reporting on her to the empress?"

He snorted. "You still don't understand how this works.

Everyone spies on each other, yes. But the empress was mad about the hostage exchange. It was agreed to behind her back, and she blames Lady Mabel for getting involved when it wasn't her place. Rumor has it the chatelaine struck a deal behind the empress's back with the queen to exchange hostages, and so the empress had to take the credit for it. But Maud was furious. She doesn't like people acting against her. All she'd need would be some good information about Lady Mabel acting in the wrong, and she'd be replaced."

Bronwyn's mouth fell open a little. "And the queen? She was told I was a spy, anyway. She didn't trust me. Is that why you asked Lady Alice to spy on her?"

"That was just to put the queen on her toes. To know that someone was always watching, listening, and reporting on her. Why should she have life easy? She's a prisoner. Or was. Lady Alice needed no convincing. She came to me of her own accord. Was jealous of all the attention you were getting and wanted the chance to earn some recognition of her own."

Bronwyn nodded.

"But now, Mistress Hound, it's time for you to clear off." He rose menacingly, a small blade in his hands.

Bronwyn backed away, slipping on the wet grass. She scrambled back on her hands and knees. "Don't come any closer. I'll call for help."

Crispin laughed. "No one will hear you. And no one's going to care. Everyone's at the joust." He passed the blade from hand to hand and stepped on the hem of her skirt.

She was stuck.

He raised his arm and launched the blade at her, just as Theobold lunged into the tent and flung himself over Bronwyn.

"Theobold!" she said.

He grunted, having fallen on top of her. His body felt tough with muscle, but she could feel him stiffen in pain.

"Theobold," she hissed.

He rolled off her with an easy grace and turned his back to

her, protecting her. The blade fell from his jerkin and hit the ground. "I should have known you were behind this. I heard everything. I ought to challenge you to a duel."

"Wait your turn, mate. Once I'm done slicing Rupert in two, I'll happily oblige," Crispin said.

Bronwyn could see a small patch of red on the back of Theobold's right shoulder, which bled through his olive-green jerkin. She fretted with worry for him, her hands darting to her mouth.

They were joined by a servant and a guard. "What's happened? I heard a commotion."

"This man just tried to kill this girl," Theobold said. "The king must be told."

"But he's about to enter the joust," the guard said, eyeing Bronwyn. "And this girl is nobody. The royal family is already seated. This will have to wait until afterward."

It was obvious to all that Crispin was suiting up for the joust. He fastened an arm brace on and grunted. "We'll sort this afterward, mate. I've got another squire to deal with first."

"I'll be waiting." Theobold stood back as the guard stood at attention at the tent flap, while the servant helped tie on the rest of Crispin's armor.

Theobold backed away and put a hand on Bronwyn's shoulder, steering her out of the tent and into the crowd. Once they were some distance away, he put his hands on her shoulders. "Are you all right?"

"Yes. I'm fine. But you're hurt. You're bleeding."

"It's nothing. I've had worse hunting," Theobold said.

"Nonsense. I've got to see to it. Turn around," Bronwyn said, reaching for him.

He took her hands in his, grasping her by the wrists.

She slowly looked up at him.

"I'm a fool. I should never have doubted you. Will you forgive me?" he asked.

"Yes. It was just a friendly kiss. But..." She paused. Rupert had made his feelings clear. She might have cared for him, but he would never love her back. Not in that way. "I do care for Rupert. I did love him once. But now, I care for him as a friend. It was just to say *thank you*, truly. For putting his life in danger for me."

He frowned and gripped her wrists tighter, pulling her hands to his chest. He covered her hands with his left hand. "You have my heart, Bronwyn. Wholly and completely. I am sorry I doubted you and for my actions with Mistress Agatha, and that I treated you like you were less than you are."

Her answering smile was tight. "I'm sorry I gave you cause to doubt me."

"Did Rupert know of your feelings for him?"

A slight gasp came from behind her. Bronwyn looked over her shoulder.

Lady Alice stood there, her face bloodless. "You care for Rupert? As a lover might?"

Bronwyn felt a wave of head come over her face. It was the time for honesty. "Yes, I did. I'm sorry."

Lady Alice scoffed. She strode over and struck Bronwyn in the face. Her cheeks instantly stung.

Lady Alice said hotly, "How could you? After all we've been through? After all the times we've been together and thought we might die, and now this. Was I ever right to trust you?"

Bronwyn turned away from Theobold. "Yes, of course. I am your friend." Her words sounded hollow.

"Bah. I have no friends. Only servants and enemies. I never thought you would be so traitorous as to stab me in the back."

Bronwyn's mouth dropped open. "Lady Alice, we are only friends. I never meant to—"

"You expect me to believe that?" Fresh tears sparked in her eyes. "I can see now I was wrong. You only pretended to be loyal to get closer and weasel your way into Rupert's affections." She leaned in close and hissed, "If Rupert dies from this, I will never forgive you."

Bronwyn said quietly, "If that happens, I will never forgive myself." Her words were soft but true and for a split second, the two women shared a moment of understanding. Both loved Rupert in their way. Both would cry their eyes out if he died. But Bronwyn wondered if they both would continue loving him, even after he was gone.

Lady Alice's expression softened, just for a moment. "This is too much for any woman to bear." Louder, she said, "Good luck with her, Theobold. I hope you two are very happy together. Although why you would want to waste your time with a woman who loves another man is beyond me." Her black hair snapping over her shoulder, she stalked away.

Bronwyn looked at the ground. "I deserved that."

"She refuses to listen to reason. She never gave you a chance to explain. But she's always been harsh with you. I could never understand why you two were friends in the first place," Theobold said.

Bronwyn swallowed. "Will you let me tend your back?"

He shook his head. "I'll find a surgeon. They're easily spotted 'round here." He kissed her hand. "Whatever your past feelings for Rupert, I shall prove to you that I am the right choice." He left her then.

The horns blared again, and people moved toward the stands.

Bronwyn let out a breath and followed the crowds. A slight gasping fear filled her, making her chest tight and her lungs breathless for a moment. She remembered feeling lost and overwhelmed in the crowds at the battle of Lincoln, and how she and Lady Alice had survived, largely due to luck.

The people had moved like water, and she'd gotten separated from her father. That was the last time she'd seen him. A pang of homesickness filled her, and she swallowed it down, blinking away a tear that had come to her eyes.

She moved with the crowd that soon dispersed, and she managed to find a space amongst some other people, but still far back from the front. The sun shone overhead, and she squinted in the bright light.

Then she saw it. Two men, mounted on horses, came out on either side of the arena. A light-gray steed, with green trappings, and a knight in pieces of mismatched armor. His armor fit, but one could tell it was not a set of armor made for him. It looked borrowed. The rider sat his horse well, and even though he wore a visor, she knew it was Rupert.

Across the arena sat a rider on a dark stallion, its coat so brown, it looked dipped in mud. It had black mane, braided tightly, with dark-blue trappings on its body. Its rider sat straight up in the saddle, yet his posture was stiff, almost arrogant, and confident. This was clearly Crispin, Bronwyn thought.

The trumpets blew again as well-dressed people climbed onto the raised viewing platform. Applause rippled through the crowd, and the king and queen took seats on two grand chairs, with Lady Alice sat nearby with Lady Morwenna, whose face was grave. Also nearby was Sir Bors, under armed guard.

The king raised his arms and he said some words, but it was so loud, Bronwyn couldn't hear what he was saying. Then he sat down, and drummers began drumming, a slow, steady beat that picked up speed, getting louder and louder until it reached a frantic pace, then stopped.

Bronwyn's breath stuck in her throat. Her heart thumped loudly in her chest. She watched as a herald walked to the middle of the arena, a flag in hand, waiting for silence.

Then the man lowered the flag with a mighty wave, and the joust began.

✦

Chapter Twenty-Four

T HE SQUIRES RAISED their lances and began to ride. Their horses charged forward, the drumming of their hooves striking the ground.

Time seemed to slow as Crispin raised his lance. Rupert raised his lance slightly slower, and he did not tilt so well. Crispin was practiced; Rupert was slow. Clumsy, even.

Crispin's lance scored against Rupert's chest, and he was flung back, almost half off his saddle. He hung on, but almost dropped his lance.

The crowd gasped, and Bronwyn gasped with them. "Rupert," she said, her hands gripping her skirts.

"A point," a few members shouted, and a white flag was raised on Crispin's side of the arena.

The squires rode around to their corners, lances raised. They wheeled around and at the drop of the herald's flag, charged again. This time, Crispin's lance broke on Rupert's shield, and Rupert launched backward but kept a hold of his lance again. He rode around to his side of the list again, shrugging off the blow.

Being a squire, Rupert had no squires of his own. But to Bronwyn's surprise, a familiar figure strode out to help bring his horse back to his side.

"Theobold," she breathed.

Sure enough, Theobold stood by and exchanged a few words with Rupert, holding the horse's reins at the ready.

Across the arena, Crispin barely waited for the herald's flag to lower before he was off, his horse's hooves thundering across the field.

Her heart leaped in her throat as Rupert charged, almost not giving Theobold time enough to step away.

Rupert leaned forward in his saddle, riding in sync with his steed. His eyes were forward, and this time, his lance broke on Crispin's shoulder, shattering into pieces.

A hit. The crowd roared.

The next time the herald dropped his flag, Crispin wasn't playing around. He rode hard and fast in the saddle, his lance out in what looked like straight and, even to Bronwyn's untrained eye, perfect form.

Rupert leaned in and lowered his lance. Both lances struck. But this time, Crispin launched back in his saddle, for Rupert's lance had broken on his helmet, smashing the metal visor into his head.

Fresh blood trickled out from beneath Crispin's visor, dripping onto his neck. Rupert had won two points. "Surely, the match is over?" she said to no one in particular.

"One more lance left," a man told her.

Bronwyn watched as both men replenished their lances.

At the drop of the herald's flag, both squires rode forth, caring for no one but their opponent. The steady drum beat of the horses' hooves striking the ground was like the staccato rhythm of Bronwyn's pulse. She watched as Crispin and Rupert both struck at once, and Crispin fell off his horse, tumbling from the saddle while Rupert rode on. He raised his lance in delight.

"He's won. The lad's won!" a voice said, and the crowd applauded wildly. Rupert tossed his lance to the ground and climbed down from his horse, waving. Bronwyn jumped up and down. People cheered and whooped as he walked and held an arm up in triumph.

He didn't see Crispin lunge for him until it was too late.

Crispin held something small in his hand, and it was with that he attacked Rupert. "No!" Bronwyn cried.

Rupert fell to his knees, then turned at the sight of Crispin standing over him. He rolled and came to his feet, stepping back.

"What's this?" one person asked.

"Oi, that fighter's attacking him. He didn't see him coming."

A few members of the crowd booed as two swords were thrown into the arena. There was a collective gasp and a hush as both squires picked up their swords.

Rupert pulled something out of the left side of his back. It was small, jagged, and bloody, and he tossed it to the ground. He rotated the sword in his right hand experimentally and took a fighting stance, at the ready.

But this was no practice bout, and Crispin was not waiting for someone to referee. He simply lunged at Rupert, his blade swinging in the air. The blades struck each other with a loud clang, and the match was on.

Rupert blocked and parried each of Crispin's thrusts with his blade, stepping back as the taller squire took ground, again and again. Their blades clashed as Rupert was done parrying and went on the attack. He advanced, his knees bent, in a classic fencing stance, as Crispin parried his thrust easily and struck him, slicing his right arm.

"A hit!" someone in the crowd yelled, and people cheered and clapped.

Bronwyn realized that these people around her, these spectators, did not care about the reason for this joust and fight, nor did they know the men fighting. These peasants cheered and clapped, simply for whoever was winning. And at that moment in time, it was Crispin.

Rupert may have done better with the lance, but Crispin was more skillful with the sword, and it showed. Crispin raised his sword in an overhead arc and sliced it toward Rupert's head.

A woman in the crowd screamed, and Rupert lost his step. He faltered and slipped backward, narrowly escaping Crispin's slice at his body. Crispin went on the attack, sweeping his sword in large arcs, meant to slice.

But to meet his great movements, Rupert rolled to his feet and, taking the pommel of the sword in both hands, used it to block, parry, and attack, with more rudimentary motions, but they worked.

Crispin was forced back, and he changed his stance and movements, this time coming in to use the pommel and hit Rupert in the face. Bronwyn didn't hear the crack of his nose breaking, but she could see the instant it happened, for Rupert stumbled back, blood rushing down from his nose.

He swiped at his nose with a sleeve and kept on, shifting his feet in the dirt, turning as Crispin circled him. Then Crispin came at him and slipped, his foot going out from under him. He fell to his knees, when Rupert crashed into him. The crowd roared.

But Crispin shuddered and dropped his sword. Rupert rolled off Crispin and kicked the sword away. He held the tip of his own sword at Crispin's throat. "Do you yield?" he shouted thickly.

Crispin coughed and gurgled, and his hand raised and fell.

Rupert repeated the demand, but Crispin did not respond. Rupert leaned forward, when Crispin kicked his legs out from under him, sending Rupert tumbling to the ground. His sword went flying, and Rupert held something up as Crispin pounced on him, crushing him beneath his weight.

Then everything stopped. Bronwyn stared. Rupert shoved Crispin off him, rolled to his knees, and stood, standing over him. He said something, then said, "He's dead."

A lone cry could be heard from the stands. Heralds and servants ran out into the arena. Rupert stood off to the side as people went to check on Crispin. But then it was clear. A herald stood, walked over to Rupert, and raised his arm in the sky. "Here's the winner," he shouted.

The crowd roared.

Bronwyn breathed a sigh of relief.

The matter was done. Crispin, the killer of women, was dead. She let out a breathy sigh. Bronwyn's attention was drawn to the king and queen, who stood at the head of the raised platform, surrounded by members of the nobility.

The king announced, "In respect of this grave matter, I pronounce judgment. That Sir Bors has lost, and his guilt is proven in trial by combat, through the valiant fighting and death of the squire, Crispin Ashe. Sir Bors, do you accept this judgment?"

"No," Lady Morwenna cried out. "No. It is unjust."

Bronwyn rolled her eyes. The man had basically broken off all contact with the noblewoman and yet Lady Morwenna was *still* loyal to him. Bronwyn dimly heard an echo of Lady Alice's voice in her mind. No accounting for taste, she supposed.

But the noblewoman's protests went unheeded, as Sir Bors, surrounded by four armed guards, bowed his head in acquiescence.

"Then it is decided. Take him away."

The guards removed Sir Bors, with Lady Morwenna screeching and following them through the crowd.

Once the noise had died down, the king motioned for Rupert to come forward. "Let us congratulate you, good squire, for winning an excellent joust with the lance and the sword. It was not meant to be to the death, but you conducted yourself very well." The king paused. "In light of Squire Bothwell's win, and his role in saving the queen and prince, I am proud to declare that he has proven himself worthy of knighthood—and shall be made a knight."

Rupert's head lifted. "I am?" he said thickly.

People clapped and shouted their approval, pounding their fists on the wooden makeshift barriers. Rupert stood almost shyly, then squared his shoulders and lifted his chin, but he stiffened. Something pained him.

Bronwyn cheered with the spectators present and grinned as Rupert bowed to the king and queen in thanks.

"You will be knighted during Yuletide. We need more good men like you, Squire Bothwell." The king nodded and the crowd and nobles present clapped with him.

It seemed as though people were beginning to disperse, and Bronwyn turned to join the crowds when a voice called out, "Wait."

People turned. The queen stood at the front and said, "There is another matter before us. Mistress Bronwyn Blakenhale, come forward."

Bronwyn swallowed. She moved ahead through the crowd and stood by, facing the raised platform. The queen descended and said loudly, "There is an honor we must bestow. For your grace, your quick thinking, loyalty, and service, I grant you this ring, as a token of our gratitude, for saving our lives, more than once." She held up a gold ring for all to see.

Bronwyn's eyes widened. She couldn't believe it.

"With this ring, I do pledge that Mistress Blakenhale is now a member of our court, and my royal household. She will hold the position of Mistress of Whispers and serve me in a special role of my choosing. As she has no living family, she is under my protection, and should anyone dare lay a hand against her person, they do so as if hurting myself. Let no one dare raise a hand against her, or suffer the consequences."

Bronwyn blinked. What was this?

She looked over at Rupert, whose eyes were wide. But he caught her looking at him and offered her a slow smile. Theobold, not too far away, bowed his head. His handsome black eyebrows knit together as he frowned, and his shoulders slumped, as if he'd lost a battle. Lady Alice's mouth twisted and her eyes narrowed, her pretty face a picture of elegant distaste.

Bronwyn was motioned forward by the queen, and curtsied low, accepting the gold ring with a blue jewel that was presented to her. She slipped it on and held her hand aloft, looking into the queen's eyes. "Thank you, Your Grace."

"Thank *you*, Mistress Blakenhale." The queen turned, and the joust was ended.

People clapped and began to turn away, when Lady Alice came up to Bronwyn, her dark eyes assessing. "Well. I hope you realize your good fortune."

"Lady Alice?"

"You don't understand, do you? She's marked you. You're hers now." Lady Alice practically seethed.

"What do you mean?"

Lady Alice scoffed and patted her silken-black hair. "You recall how the nobles at the empress's court teased and called you 'Mistress Hound'? The queen heard of it and thought it a good idea, so she decided to give you the honor before the empress could. You're too valuable, so now she's bought you. You're hers now, to sniff out and catch any secrets or clues. You're her personal Mistress of Whispers."

"But what does that mean?" Bronwyn asked, confused. She looked at the shining, gold ring on her finger. She'd never seen anything so pretty in her life. It felt heavy on her hand.

"Ha. You still don't know. Don't you understand, Bronwyn? You're her servant. She's decided that if you're going to sniff out any intrigues, it will be for her. You're bound to her service now, Mistress of Whispers. Now and forever."

Epilogue

As it turned out, Lady Alice was right. Bronwyn's fortunes had changed, and while she was permitted to continue working in the kitchens at her desire, she also was now a part of the queen's household, and that meant a change in her status.

She was no longer just a scullery maid, working in the kitchens, cleaning and cooking. She was someone else. Someone higher, with social standing. When she entered a room, people stopped talking and watched, as if she were someone to guard their tongues around.

They were right to do so.

Bronwyn was given a room of her very own to share with the other maids of the queen's close attendants, and even a bit of coin. While she was still getting used to the idea of having a change in circumstances, she didn't mind. It was the best of both worlds, it seemed, for she was able to look into curious matters for the queen and return to her baking when she pleased. And yet... she pondered her change in status. She had not chosen a side in this war, but one had been selected for her. Bronwyn was now under the queen's protection and was elevated to a sort of useful position, but that also meant she was bound to the queen. Lady Alice's words rang in her mind more than once. *"Now and forever."*

How far she had come from wheeling up a cart of bread rolls with her father to serve the king and queen almost a year ago.

She had been so hungry for adventure, for a change in her life. If she was given the chance, she would give it all up, just to spend more time with her family. Their loss was like a gaping hole in her heart, and not knowing if they lived or died plagued her at times. But she also relished her new role and what it might entail. No longer dismissed as a busybody, nosy kitchen maid, she was given license to inquire into matters for the queen. That was something to look forward to.

When Bronwyn inquired and went to view Crispin's body, she found the reason for his death. A shattered wooden shard from a lance, that looked deadly as a spike. She rather suspected it was what Crispin had attacked Rupert with following his fall from his horse, and what he later was stabbed with through the armpit, killing him instantly. She shed no tears for the turncoat, but rather suspected Lady Alice would, in private. She had found Lady Alice and taken her aside, revealing Crispin's treachery. As her suspicions had confirmed, Lady Alice had figured it out too, but Crispin hadn't left her side, and so she had never gotten a moment alone. Together, they decided it didn't matter reporting it anymore, for the man was dead.

She later learned that Theobold, following a trip to the nearest surgeon, had whisked Lady Morwenna away, under the queen's watchful eye, and with permission from his master, escorted the treacherous noblewoman from Winchester, presumably back to her home. Bronwyn wondered if she would ever see Theobold again.

She hoped she would, for his dark smile haunted her dreams. It hurt her that he hadn't come to say goodbye. She had rather thought he would. The look on his face when she had been declared Mistress of Whispers… It was as though a dagger had struck him. He had not spoken a word to her since then. She almost wondered if he was avoiding her. She hoped not. Meanwhile, Rupert was enjoying his newfound status as an expectant knight and was throwing himself into training, with support from his master.

When the news came that Bishop Henry of Blois declared himself again for the queen and king, and called for their official coronation to take place in London that December, Bronwyn rose and prepared to pack her things, for she knew she would be called upon again, and soon.

She looked at the window at the first whisper of November's crisp, autumn wind and the barest breath of approaching snow. As the queen's royal Mistress of Whispers, she would be ready.

About the Author

E. L. Johnson writes historical mysteries. A Boston native, she gave up clam chowder and lobster rolls for tea and scones when she moved across the pond to London, where she studied medieval magic at UCL and medieval remedies at Birkbeck College. Now based in Hertfordshire, she is a member of the Hertford Writers' Circle and the founder of the London Seasonal Book Club.

When not writing, Erin spends her days working as a press officer for a royal charity and her evenings as the lead singer of the gothic progressive metal band, Orpheum. She is also an avid Jane Austen fan and has a growing collection of period drama films.

Connect with her on Twitter at twitter.com/EJJohnson888 or on Instagram at instagram.com/ejgoth.

www.ingramcontent.com/pod-product-compliance
Lightning Source LLC
Chambersburg PA
CBHW051306300726
48976CB00002B/283